For Frank

DARK DAY, DARK NIGHT

A Marijuana Murder Mystery

a Bartender

JONAH RASKIN

Alfred Pyce in These Probably

Sean appears pages. no connection to You!

McCaa Books • Santa Rosa, CA

In Gratitude Jonah 22 July 21 19

McCaa Books
1604 Deer Run
Santa Rosa, CA 95405-7535

ISBN 978-1-7337770-0-1
Library of Congress Control Number 2019935695

First published in 2019 by McCaa Books,
an imprint of McCaa Publications.

Printed in the United States of America
Set in Adobe Garamond Pro

Cover design by James Retherford, Hot Digital Dog Design, Austin, TX. Front cover photos: Volodymyr Tverdokhlib (top) and Aleksey Tugolukov (bottom). Back cover photo: Jizell Albright.
Digital editing: James Retherford.

www.mccaabooks.com

Dedicated

To

Waights Taylor Jr.

The Characters

Aden – sommelier at the Mar Monte Hotel

George Ambrose – chief of police

Phyllis Ambrose – George's wife

Mitzi Ambrose – their daughter

Dorothy (Dot) Baynes – femme fatale

Mrs. Edna Baynes – Dorothy's mother

Billy Bones – pig farmer

Maggie Brazil – owner of Mexican restaurant

Matt Chehab – ex-Lebanese banker

Clark – deputy police officer

Bobby Cohen – Sacramento lawyer & lobbyist

Tomás Contreras – Tioga Vignetta's ex-husband

Sean Dyce – bartender at the Underground

Jonny Field – the executive chef at the Mar Monte

Flor – homeless Mexican woman & mother of two boys

Katrina Hawley – worker in the marijuana industry

Aaron Holmes – African-American concierge at the Mar Monte

Roxanne Jacobs – alias of Dutch woman living in California

Jeremiah Langley – editor of *The Gazette*

Lawrence – boy who lives part-time at the Mar Monte

Paul Lipski – (aka "Lip") maître d' at the Mar Monte

Terry McCoy – owner of the Mar Monte

Gina McCoy – Terry's wife and shop owner

Louis Marchetti – grape grower & wine maker

Isabel Marchetti – Louis's wife

Maya – woman in hiding

No Name – Yaqui

Pablo – No Name's Brother

Buddy Moscosco – Mar Monte's house detective

Camilla Sanchez – Tioga's apprentice

4

The Characters (continued)

Victoria Sanchez – Camilla's mother & cook at El Buen Comer
Randy Scheck – criminal defense lawyer
Dr. Silver – marijuana doctor
Storm – torch singer at the Mar Monte
Travis Syrah – repair man, mechanic
Tioga Vignetta – private investigator or "op" as she calls herself
Philippe Vignetta – Tioga's father & an artist in San Francisco
Reginald Wentworth (aka Hawk) – friend of Terry McCoy

"Well, sir, here's to plain speaking
and clear understanding."

—Casper Gutman to Sam Spade, *The Maltese Falcon*

Part I
The Raid

A Woman in Braids

Two helicopters, salvaged Black Hawks, came out of the sky, hovered over the field and landed together, the wind from the propellers bending but not breaking the bright green marijuana plants. A woman in braids raised a machete and ran toward the man in the mask who struck her with the butt of his rifle, stripped her of her weapon and kicked her in the stomach with his boot. "Bitch," he shouted. "Die, bitch." At the far end of the field, two men in sneakers and shorts leapt over the barbed wire fence and disappeared in the woods.

Men in camouflage attacked the field, tied the marijuana together and laid them inside gigantic nets. Then the copters carried the decimated crop into the sky. A flatbed truck sputtered and coughed and took the masked harvesters from the field to the road. The blood from the woman on the ground covered a stray marijuana plant that lay under her body. Everything was suddenly still. A vulture peered down. A skunk crossed the dirt path, and flies swarmed around the mouth and the nostrils of the dying woman with the braids.

Part II
The Set Up

Dorothy Baynes's Body

She woke from a dream, opened her eyes one at a time, rubbed the sleepers with her knuckles and sniffed the flannel sheets that smelled of sex and blood. Something didn't feel right. She tossed aside the down comforter, spread her long legs and noticed a red splotch with a black dot on the inside of her right thigh.

"Damn spider bite," she said aloud. She scratched it until it bled, slipped into a kaftan, shuffled across the floor, put a kettle up to boil and added a tablespoon of Russian Caravan to a white teapot. To an orange mug that read "CALIFORNIA," she added cream and filled it to the rim with the steaming tea. On her cell, she punched in the number for the pharmacy, followed the commands and added twelve digits, 1758896-03081.

She sighed and called a second number. "Hey, Doctor Doom, Tioga Vignetta here. Have my Bupropion refilled before I flip." Then with mug in hand, she stared into the mirror. "Who the fuck are you?" She brushed her teeth, combed her hair and put on a pair of white jockey underpants and an underwire bra, though she quickly removed the bra and tossed it into the wastebasket. "Goodbye. I never liked you."

She added gray slacks, a leather belt, a white shirt and a black tie, along with polka dot socks and a pair of flats. Into a blue valise, she threw enough clothes for a week, zipped it closed and placed it near the door.

To the sleeper in bed, she wrote: "Dear Storm, had a panic attack. Gotta get away. It's not about you. It's about me. Love you, Ti."

She sat down on the edge of the bed and rolled a joint. "Come on, baby, get me stoned." She lit the joint and inhaled. "Oh, you taste so good. I like you. I wonder where you've come from?" After the third toke, she placed the roach in the ashtray, then sucked on a mint and with backpack and purse walked to the end of the hall.

The elevator door opened. She stepped inside and watched it close. On the third floor, a small boy joined her. He wore a Boston Red Sox baseball cap and a T-shirt with an image of a lollypop and the words, "Suck On It."

"Having a nice day?" she asked. On the ground floor, the boy rushed from the elevator and darted into the dining room.

At the coffee cart, Tioga asked for a macchiato and a brioche from Aaron, the hotel's one and only barista, who wore leather trousers and an apron. At the newspaper rack, she snagged a copy of *The Gazette* with the headline, "Wolves ravage Valley Ranch. Vintner Louis Marchetti offers big reward." She shook her head and turned to the letters to the editor where Mrs. Baynes denounced Tioga Vignetta as a "bogus private eye who has aided and abetted known criminals who roam our streets freely. One of them waylaid my daughter." That felt like a knife in her back.

Tioga tucked the paper under her arm, crossed the plaza, took the elevator to the top floor, unlocked the lock, nodded to Camilla Sanchez, who stared at her computer screen, and entered her own office. The coffee and the brioche went on top of the desk and the newspaper clippings on the wall. She sat down and opened the file that read, "Vignetta: Divorce," turned the pages and read, "No Contest" and "Irreconcilable differences." There was a letter from a Tomás Contreras—K-93465, PBFP Building, 68-F-113, P.O. Box 6009-8990, Crescent City, California, 95532— who wrote, "Tell me, Tioga, how do you sleep at night with the devil in your bed laying right by your side." Now he was just another number and there was nothing she could do for him. Not that she wanted to do anything for Tomás.

The door to the hallway opened and then closed. "Chief Ambrose here to see you, Tioga." Camilla entered the inner office. Ambrose followed her. He removed his porkpie hat and revealed a shiny head that had been a kind of landmark in Tioga's life ever since girlhood when his daughter, Mitzi, had a humongous crush on her. George Ambrose placed an attaché case on the edge of the desk and noticed Mrs. Baynes's letter to the editor that Tioga had tacked to the wall. "You got a bum rap." Then he tried to like a large framed painting titled "Leda and the Swan." "A bit risqué, no? Some people might get the wrong idea."

Ambrose cleared his throat and opened his attaché case. He removed a stack of black-and-white photos and arranged them on Tioga's desk. "These pix were taken on the west side of the highway, opposite Metafor Winery, Friday. A county road crew found the body. There were no tire tracks."

Tioga used her cell to photograph the images. "Something unusual about the body?"

Ambrose rubbed his chin. "There were two bullets from a .357 and two bullets from a .38. It looks like an execution-style murder. The bullets from the .357 entered through the buttocks and traveled toward the stomach; the bullets from the .38 traveled from the top of the head and then down toward the esophagus. Two bullets fired from opposite directions, collided and caused massive internal bleeding."

Ambrose put one hand on his own buttocks and the other on the top of his head. "Weird."

Tioga nodded her head. "Sick. Really sick, but go on."

Ambrose wanted to touch Tioga. She sensed it and moved closer to him as if to dare him.

"The woman didn't jump from a moving vehicle and she couldn't have been pushed," he said. "She didn't have those kinds of bruises. A motorist didn't strike her either. That's what the coroner thinks."

Tioga nibbled on the last of the brioche and swallowed the last drop of the macchiato. "You're afraid something like this might happen to …"

Ambrose cut her off before she could finish the sentence. "I'm worried because the Baynes girl disappeared and turned up dead and now Mitzi's gone."

Tioga moved back and forth, and then back and forth again as if to say that she didn't know what to make of the pix. "Her eyes might have been brown. Her hair could have been blond and maybe she once had a set of front teeth."

Ambrose came around to Tioga's side of the desk. "You recognize her, don't you? Go on, take a closer look."

He pointed to the cut and swollen upper lip and the broken nose.

Tioga lifted the photo and examined it with the magnifying glass that lived on the top of her desk. "I can't say that I do recognize her and can't say that I don't," she murmured. "Who is she, George? Someone I knew or ought to have known?"

With the tip of his tongue, Ambrose wet his dry, cracked lips. "I was hoping you would recognize her. I'm sorry you don't."

Tioga sat down again and waited for Ambrose to speak. He took his time. "Dorothy Baynes is her name. Her mother, Edna, reported her missing middle of July. I thought that she might have asked you to find her daughter. You have a reputation as a missing persons expert. I understand. A case of a missing person can be more intriguing than a murder."

Tioga perused the creased, tattered copy of *The Gazette* that she had discarded and then retrieved twice already from the recycle bin.

"There's zero here about anyone named Baynes. You'd think a murder would be news."

Ambrose shook his head and shifted his weight from one foot to the other. "A story about Baynes ... well ... the editor didn't think the timing was right, especially with no suspect in custody and the fear that a story about a murder would panic readers. Whenever a corpse shows up, there's a hue and cry for me to make an arrest. I don't like to move unless I have something definite."

Tioga folded the newspaper neatly and held it in her hands.

"Poor George. But I agree. Speed ought not to be paramount. A lot of mothers think I can solve their problems; I tell them 'I'm not a fairy godmother.'"

She paused and studied the only photo that offered an enlargement of Dorothy Baynes's round, battered, bruised and nearly unrecognizable face.

"From the abrasions it looks like she might have was been strangled," Tioga said and handed the photo to Ambrose who borrowed the magnifying glass.

"You could be right. You have good instincts and, unlike my wife, you're not squeamish. Phyllis refused to look at these photos. I wanted her to see the world as I see it."

Tioga reached for two tumblers on the shelf behind her desk.

"That was probably not the wisest thing to do with Phyllis's nerves on edge," she said and filled the tumblers with fizzy water from a bottle of chilled Pellegrino. "I'm bone dry. What about you?"

Ambrose placed his glasses in the pocket of his jacket. "Dry as the Mojave." He smacked his lips. "I wish Phyllis were as courageous as you. I don't like people who bury their heads in the sand."

Tioga handed one tumbler to Ambrose and sipped from the other, the fizzy water tickling her throat. "Oh, that feels so good going down. I think I'm the opposite of an ostrich. I gotta see."

Ambrose set the tumbler on the desk, rubbed his jaw and grunted. "I feel a bit better already."

Tioga dropped the tumblers into the sink. "I know you're worried sick about Mitzi, but don't let it kill your soul, George. Remember when Franklin Olivera was shot and killed, and Mabel put you though the ringer?"

Ambrose wobbled on his feet; blood rushed to his face. "You know too much. There are things you ought to forget and yet …"

He started to say something else and hesitated. "I, err … um … well," he began and then stopped abruptly.

Tioga tapped the tip of her right shoe on the floor. "Out with it, George."

Ambrose cleared his throat. "Dorothy Baynes has no direct connection to the Oliveras, not that I know of, but her body reminded me of Mabel Olivera's body. Dorothy was sexually assaulted, probably by two different men, and she tested positive for heroin. The coroner thinks she was still alive when she was dumped along the side of the road and then covered with dried leaves and thistles. They tried to remove a solid gold ring on her wedding finger. Look here!"

Ambrose pointed to a close-up of Dorothy's right hand with the fingers spread out on the ground. "When the ring didn't come off easily they tried to hack it off with a knife. You see?"

Tioga scanned the photo, felt sick to her stomach and beat back the impulse to throw up. "Yes! They must have panicked. Someone saw them and they had to scram."

Ambrose went to the window and looked down at the plaza.

"The coroner figures the body showed up on the highway three or four days ago about 5:30 a.m. Maybe an early morning commuter saw something."

Tioga looked at the calendar on the wall. "What day is it? Oh, yes, Friday already."

She took more pictures of the photos on her desk and then sent them to her email address, shewolf@gmail.com.

Ambrose watched her work. "Make sure you get these," he said and pointed to Baynes's feet, one of them with and the other without a shoe. "She must have taken a four or a five, like my wife."

Tioga brought the photo closer to her eyes. "There are scratches around the ankle without the shoe. I wonder if we might find the other one?"

Ambrose collected the photos, placed them in the envelope he had brought with him and tucked the envelope under his arm. "Could be the killer has it, or maybe he tossed it."

Tioga placed her cell phone on top of the files. "Did you notice the label in the shoe? That would be helpful."

Ambrose exhaled slowly and then filled his lungs again. "Red leather flat. Made in Italy, probably by Chinese. That's how they do it these days."

He backed away from Tioga's desk, reached into his pocket and came out with a small plastic bag with a key inside. "Then there's this. Collected during the autopsy. This one is a copy. The coroner thinks it's a kind of key that's not manufactured anymore. Dorothy must have swallowed it intentionally. You can have it. It might get you in or out of someplace."

He handed the bag to Tioga who turned it around and read the capital letters "GSW" on one side and the name "Lobos" on the other.

Ambrose wiped his brow with his white handkerchief. "Lobos was the name of the hardware store on the plaza. Mescans ran it. Then the son murdered the father and went to prison."

Tioga inched toward Ambrose and placed her right hand on his left shoulder. "It's not Mescans," she said. "It's Mexicans."

Ambrose waved his hand as if to dismiss her. "Whatever," he said and went on. "The Mescan widow sold it. It was reopened as a juice and smoothie bar. I don't know what to make of GSW."

Tioga held her phone in her hand, clicked on her contacts and with her index finger scrolled down the list of names. "I don't have anything for Mitzi. If you do, send it and I'll contact her."

Ambrose placed the envelope with the photos in his attaché case and walked toward the door that led to the outer office. "Sure. I'll text it as soon as I have it. Phyllis knows it by heart. I don't."

Ambrose stepped into Camilla's office. Tioga followed him. "See if you can find something online about Dorothy Baynes," he said.

Ambrose smiled at Camilla. "You can always work for me. We need a bright one like you."

15

Camilla's fingers flew across the keyboard. "Thanks, chief. I might do that, if Tioga doesn't stop pushing me around. She's tough."

Tioga opened the door to the hallway. "Camilla's pulling your leg, George. She wants to become a PI like me, only not like me, if you know what I mean. She certainly doesn't want to become a cop like you."

Camilla clicked her mouse and then clicked it again. Tioga walked into the hallway and stood outside the door to her office while Ambrose adjusted the porkpie hat on his head. "You'll crack this case," she purred and then followed the chief to the far end of the hall where he punched the down button for the elevator. The green light came on.

"I hate to see young women end up in a ditch and not just young women, but all kinds of women: old women, fat women, thin women, rich women, white women, black women, poor women, missing women, women, women, women." He seemed to enjoy his litany.

Tioga stared at the door to the elevator. "I understand: mothers, sisters, daughters. I'll find out what's up with Mitzi, and I'll let you know as soon as I know something."

Ambrose looked down at the black-and-white tiles on the long dark hallway. "Did I leave my glasses in your office? I feel like I've lost something."

Tioga held the elevator door when it opened. "I don't believe you have. Your glasses are in the pocket of your jacket."

Ambrose laughed. "Two heads are better than one. I wish you would poke around in Dorothy's past and see what you can dig up."

Tioga went on holding the elevator door so that it would not close. "I can't poke around now. Sorry. I'm all booked up for the next few months." With her index finger she drew an imaginary line across the top of her head.

Ambrose stepped into the elevator. "One more thing: Dorothy's murder is drug related. I know it and not just because the coroner found heroin in her blood."

Tioga moved away from the elevator and leaned against the wall. "You think everything is drug related."

Ambrose pressed down on the button that said, "Open." "In the Valley it is all drug related. You should know that better than anyone."

Tioga took a step forward and looked up at the battered ceiling of the elevator. "I don't know it."

The elevator bounced up and down as if attached to a giant elastic spring. "No hurry getting on board the Baynes case," Ambrose said. Then he looked right at Tioga and added, "Some people around here disapprove of your methods. It's probably best if nobody knows I've been here. I assume Camilla won't blab."

He tipped his porkpie hat and removed his thumb from the "open" button.

The elevator door closed and the motor made what sounded like an elephant galumphing in a jungle. "Oh, George," she said to herself. "You are so transparent."

In the outer office again, Tioga sat down on the edge of Camilla's desk and swung her right leg back and forth. "George showed me a dozen or so photos of Dorothy Baynes's body that was found on the side of the road. I told him I didn't recognize her. She certainly doesn't look the same as in the photos that her mother showed us."

Camilla glanced at the calendar on the wall. "Dorothy Baynes's murder is already on Facebook and Twitter. I found your notes on the case in my computer. They're dated last December, the day before Christmas. Mrs. Baynes would not say who recommended you. Apparently you didn't entirely trust her."

The printer spit out half-a-dozen pages that Tioga collated, stapled and scanned. "Parts of this I remember and other parts I don't. I do remember the part about the boyfriend that Mrs. Baynes didn't like, but I don't recall the stuff about Dorothy's drug problem." She cleared her throat. "George doesn't need to know what we know."

Camilla nodded her head. "But we ought to know what he knows. He's slippery as a greased pig."

Tioga gathered her cell, backpack and her purse. "It's time to pay a call on Mrs. Baynes. I want you to come with me."

In her office, she removed the compact from her purse, applied lipgloss, grabbed a red silk scarf that was draped on the back of the chair and then returned to the outer office where she tossed her key ring in the air, caught it in the palm of her right hand and placed it in the pocket of her jacket.

Then she wrapped the scarf around her neck. Camilla put her computer to sleep, grabbed her purse, exchanged the purple beret for an orange beret and tilted it at a rakish angle. "I have the Baynes's address in here," she said and waved her phone in the air. "I can drive, if you want."

Raised by Wolves

In the hallway Tioga locked the door to the office. "Yeah, I want you to drive." She tossed Camilla the keys to her car. "It's parked in front."

She followed Camilla down the stairway. On the sidewalk, she stopped and stared at the marquee that now read,

OUT OF THE PAST

Dynamite Duo!

Robert Mitchum Jane Greer

"I saw it with my ex and loved it," she said wistfully. "I do have one or maybe two good memories of my marriage." She turned away from the marquee and added, "I hope you'll join Storm and me."

Camilla walked around Tioga's Mini Cooper, stopped and glanced at the bumper sticker that said, "I was raised by wolves" which made her laugh.

She unlocked the car, turned her head and looked up at the marquee. "I've never heard of Mitchum or Greer or *Out of the Past*. But anything rather than stay at home and play Scrabble with my mother. She beats me every time. That's because she insists we play in Spanish."

Camilla opened the door and peered behind the front seat. Then she sat down and turned the key in the ignition.

Tioga wiggled in her seat until she was comfortable. "I've noticed you do that. I mean, check the seat behind you. You did it the last time we drove to El Buen Comer for tacos."

Camilla looked over her shoulder. "Like this?" she said, turned her head and peered behind her seat. "I don't want to be strangled by a killer hiding back there. That's why I do it. It's not superstition."

Tioga fastened her seat belt. "You're crazy!" she said, then punched the "On" button and dialed the radio to 107.7 KWLF. Camilla raised the volume and snapped the fingers on her right hand while she held the steering wheel with her left. "That's Taylor Swift on the vocals 'Out of the Woods.' Listen to the way she bends the notes. The video is cool, too. I hear something different every time I watch and I watch lots."

Tioga lowered the visor and looked at her face in the mirror as if she might see her own future. Then she opened the glove compartment and removed a pair of sunglasses which she placed on the dashboard. Camilla honked the horn twice, backed out of the parking space, circled the plaza and headed north on the highway. Tioga kept her eyes directly ahead on the flatbed truck carrying boxes marked "Organic Kale."

"Stop at CVS," she said. "I have to pick up my meds."

Camilla pulled into a parking space reserved for the handicapped and shifted into neutral. "What?" she asked incredulously when Tioga gave her a disapproving look. "I'm not gonna get a ticket. Don't sweat the small stuff."

Inside the pharmacy, Tioga raced down an aisle that offered earplugs, toothpicks and laxatives. At the back of the store, she waited on line and read the sign on the wall that said "Ask your friendly pharmacist about Oxycontin." When it was her turn at the counter, she provided the answers before the clerk asked the questions. "Prescription for Vignetta. D.O.B. nine one eight three, address, Sebastiani Building, nine five four seven six."

Well, yes, she practically lived in her office, even slept there when she pulled all-nighters. Maybe that was the problem: those all-nighters!

On the way out of CVS, she stopped for a moment, swallowed two Bupropion and felt them make their way down her throat. "Go to work, girls. Make me good again."

In the passenger seat she checked the side view mirror and barked orders. "Take Arnold Drive, not the highway. It's faster."

Camilla shifted into reverse, honked twice, backed out of the parking space, pressed down on the accelerator and then went forward. "Your meds make you manic. I've noticed."

Tioga glared. "I haven't." She held the strap above the window and swayed in her seat when Camilla took the "s" curves without slowing down. "You might stop speeding."

Camilla put her foot on the brake. "Make up your mind. Do you want me to go fast or go slow?"

Tioga ignored the question. "Get this," she said in a burst of energy. "Dorothy Baynes was raped and murdered and dumped on the side of the road. She had a ring on her wedding finger that the killer couldn't remove, so he tried to cut it off. Also she wore size-four shoes. One of them was missing when they found her body across from Metafor Winery. Right before she died, she swallowed a key with the letters GSW and the word Lobos, which must be the name of the hardware store that made the key. It's long gone; the key came out the other end when Bubba did the autopsy. That's the skinny. Oh, and she was shot with a .38 and a .357. Two bullets fired from each gun. They messed up her insides something ugly."

Tioga peered into the side view mirror, while Camilla nodded her head and stared at the blue Mazda in front of her. "You're always checking the mirrors. Must be something your father taught you when you were first learning to drive."

Tioga tapped her fingers on the dashboard. "Keep your eyes on the road, please and slow down. It's a gauntlet through here"

A pedestrian with a pipe in his mouth and a cane in his hand shouted at a boy whose bicycle nearly hit him. On the straightaway, where the road narrowed, a tractor inched along a vineyard. Tioga raised her voice. "Your reflexes aren't as good as you think they are. Nobody's are, except for linebackers in the NFL and Mafia hit men."

Camilla laughed.

Tioga added, "It's nothing personal. But if you want to be a PI, you have to follow the rules."

Camilla gripped the steering wheel. "You mean your rules."

The traffic stopped and started, crawled ahead, sped up and slowed down. When the cars ahead finally began to move again, Camilla accelerated until she hit the posted speed limit—fifty-five miles an hour—and learned back in her seat.

Mailboxes raced along the side of the road. Overhead the branches and the leaves on the eucalyptus trees formed a canopy that blocked out the sky. "The Baynes place is off Aqua Caliente. One one zero seven Mazatlan. Keep your eyes peeled."

"I know," Camilla moaned. "You don't have to tell me."

Tioga lowered the volume on the radio that played Ry Cooder's "Dark was the Night (Cold was the Ground)." Then she went on as if she had not heard a word Camilla had said. "Take a left here," she growled and pointed to a sign that read "Sunset Mobile Home Village." "Park in front of the mailboxes. We'll hoof the last leg."

Camilla lifted her foot from the accelerator. The Mini Cooper slowed down and came to a complete stop. Atascadero Creek trickled. The wind scattered the leaves that had fallen from a Valley oak, and a squirrel leapt from branch to branch.

Camilla rolled down the window, inhaled and gasped. "Smells like a dead animal out there. A squirrel or possum."

She removed the key from the ignition and leaned back in her seat. "Who the hell would rape and murder Dorothy? When Mrs. Bayes came to the office, she made her daughter sound like the all-time, best-ever Girl Scout."

Tioga released her seatbelt, climbed out of the car and slammed the door. "Girl Scouts have enemies. I know. Boy Scouts can be mean."

Camilla locked the car. "I'm sorry," she said, and didn't sound facetious.

She followed Tioga, who walked down the middle of a street that boasted well-kept mobile homes on both sides and not a single inhabitant in sight. Tioga counted out loud, "eleven hundred and three, eleven hundred and eleven, eleven hundred and one." There was no pattern to the numbers. They jumped around, but it didn't bother her. "I like random," she said.

Camilla merely nodded.

At number one thousand and seven, Tioga stopped, turned to the right, and squeezed between a brick wall covered with grape vines and a blue Mazda sedan that had seen better days. She climbed the steps, walked across a shaded patio and aimed for a sliding glass door that was flanked by a purple bougainvillea in bloom.

On the "Welcome" mat she wiped her shoes and rapped on the door with her knuckles. "If only we could persuade Mrs. Baynes to talk," she said and then turned to Camilla and added, "Give her your best smile, dear."

Camilla leaned against the door. "Yes, boss," she said and smirked. "Anything else?"

Tioga rapped once again. "Yeah, stand up straight, don't lean on the door and don't smirk."

She heard the yapping of a dog and a series of muffled footsteps. For a moment, silence enveloped the visitors at eleven hundred and seven Mazatlan. The bougainvillea looked like it might collapse under its own weight.

One lock turned and then another. The door opened wide enough for Tioga to recognize the face of Mrs. Baynes, longer and whiter than she remembered it. But she had taken the time to put her hair in curlers.

A terrier with an oversized collar began to yap incessantly. "Back, Rudy, down boy," Mrs. Baynes said and the dog obeyed instantly. "Good boy, Rudy." The dog wagged its tail.

Tioga felt a tad safer. "Mrs. Bayes," she began. "I don't know if you remember me. I'm the PI you came to see not long ago about Dorothy."

Mrs. Baynes looked down at the "Welcome" mat in front of her, as if unwilling to make eye contact with her visitors.

Tioga went on undeterred. "This is my assistant, Camilla Sanchez. Her mother, Victoria, lives nearby. We're here to offer our condolences and, uh, ask a few questions."

Camilla smiled reluctantly. Tioga took a step forward and noticed the deep lines around Mrs. Baynes's eyes. Then she waited.

"I have nothing for you," Mrs. Baynes said as if she had rehearsed the line. "Now excuse me. I have to get on with my life ... my daughter's ... you see ... I ..."

She seemed incapable of speaking a complete sentence. Tioga offered a tentative smile. "Perhaps we can help," she said and felt that she was clutching at the air itself.

Now Mrs. Baynes's eyes darted from Tioga to Camilla and back to Tioga until they came to rest again on the "Welcome" mat. "I went to you and asked for help, and you stuck a knife in my back."

Tioga winced. "I didn't mean to be hurtful. If you remember I explained that I couldn't start looking right then and there, especially since the police couldn't find a trace of Dorothy. I'm not turning my back on you now. I am right here. I understand how you must feel. I know how it is to lose a loved one. I lost my own mother."

Tioga took a step forward. Mrs. Baynes began to slide the door closed, but she stopped and raised her right hand that boasted a wedding ring. "I want the ring Dorothy was wearing. It's the twin of this one and it belonged to my husband. Dorothy took it without my permission. Meanwhile, save your tears for someone more gullible than I. You are wasting my time and yours unless you can produce the ring."

Tioga withdrew her right foot just as Mrs. Baynes closed the door with a whoosh. She stood still for a few moments before she touched the tip of her nose. "No blood! I could have sworn that she nicked my nose when she slammed the door in my face." Then she added, "We struck out, didn't we?"

Camilla took Tioga by the arm and tried to lead her to the car, but she broke away and walked ahead on her own. Then she stopped, turned and looked back with a weary expression on her face. "I don't know what we could have done differently. Maybe called ahead of time, sent a condolence card or asked someone to act as an intermediary."

Camilla unlocked the car and nodded her head. "Mothers blame themselves when they lose their daughters. But don't beat yourself up. We'll try again."

Tioga climbed inside the Mini Cooper. "You're too nice." She fastened her seatbelt and turned on the radio in time to hear Junior Walker sing "Snatch It Back and Hold It," which seemed to stir something deep inside.

"It all reminds me ..." she said and then paused before she added, as if lost in thought, "Oh, I don't know ... It's useless. I don't know why I thought I could persuade Mrs. Baynes to talk after I had turned her down."

Camilla started the car, backed up and then went forward slowly while the sign for the Sunset Mobile Home Village grew smaller and smaller in the rearview mirror. "It reminds you of what, Tioga?" she shouted and turned up the volume on the radio in time to catch the last of the traffic report.

"Accident on 12 at Boyes," the announcer said. "CHP advises drivers to avoid the highway and use Arnold instead."

Tioga took a deep breath, held it and then exhaled slowly. "What do you think it reminds me of?"

Camilla turned right on Railroad, right again on Aqua Caliente and aimed for the roundabout on Arnold. "I haven't a fuckin' clue. I'm not a mind reader. That's why I asked you what came to mind."

Tioga put on her sunglasses and looked into the mirror. "Well don't get pissy," she said and watched the trees that lined the road. Around the bend, she surveyed the bright green golf course and the golfers in plaid trousers and orange caps. "Let's not lollygag," she said as if lollygagging was a sin. "Go to Metafor Winery and park along the opposite side of the road. We'll have a look-see."

At the roundabout, Camilla went clockwise and continued on Arnold until she reached Manzanita where she took a right. "Come on. You start to say something, you hook me and then you drop it. It's not fair."

Tioga kept an eye on the vineyards as they unfolded, one after the other, with clumps of men here and there pruning the tops of the vegetation with red-handled clippers. "Nothing's fair," she said. "Not in any life that I know of."

Camilla reached out, and brushed Tioga's left cheek with the fingertips of her right hand. "I'm sorry you had a crummy marriage. You'll have better luck next time."

Tioga made a fist with her right hand. "Bad guess. I wasn't thinking of my crummy marriage, but my crummy childhood."

Camilla sighed. "Why do you insist on punishing yourself? I grew up with a single mom and had a lovely childhood."

"Bully for you!"

Blood Along Cooper's Creek

The sun went behind the clouds: Tioga removed her sunglasses and twirled them around and around. "You know, there are millions of sad stories in this world of ours. And then there are really, really sad, sad stories like Dorothy and her mother."

Camilla shook her head. "You're wrong. You'll see. There's always a silver lining."

Tioga rolled down the window and let the wind blow through her hair. "The mile marker we want is 'Son 26.' It's a bit after the county sign for 'Cooper's Creek' that has a fish, a butterfly and a flower. I suppose that's a silver lining of sorts, though I doubt there are fish in the creek. It's been polluted for as long as I can remember."

Camilla accelerated on the curve. Tioga leaned to the right, then reached out and grabbed hold of the dashboard to steady herself. "Slow down. See the marker over there by that tree?"

She pointed to an oak with low-hanging branches that couldn't support themselves. The ground itself propped them up.

"Pull in and park. And don't slam on the brakes."

Tioga placed the sunglasses in the pocket of her jacket and listened to the traffic that zoomed in both directions. Then she got out of the car and squinted at the rays of the sun that poked through the leaves of the oak. A county sign on the east side of the road read, "Danger! No Parking. Violators will be towed and prosecuted."

On the west side, a large red and white sign screamed,

METAFOR WINERY
Open 10 to 5 daily.
Wine & Weed Weekends
Saturdays and Sundays
Reservations at Metafor.com

A red Corvette raced toward town. The driver sounded the horn and Tioga enjoyed the Doppler effect.

"You can't park here. If you do we'll get a ticket and the car will be towed."

Camilla put on a pair of gloves and glanced at the sign on the opposite side of the highway. "Wine and Weed Weekends! It's about time. Let's get tickets."

Then she looked up at the No Parking sign in front of her. "Who's going to write a ticket this time of day?"

Tioga mimicked Camilla's cheerful tone of voice. "What the hell. We won't be long."

She raised her chin and pointed it toward the west. "Go for the creek. Take note of everything you see, and everything you don't see. Got it?" It felt like hard work to give instructions and teach her apprentice to be a PI. She didn't like it.

Across the highway, beyond the sign for Metafor Winery, a man in a cowboy hat sat on a tractor that kicked up dust as it inched along. On the shoulder of the road, a dozen Spandex-clad bicycle riders peddled madly and scattered the leaves. It was just another sunny day in paradise.

Tioga walked into the chaparral. A cool breeze shook the branches of an acacia tree. White clouds drifted across the blue sky. Beyond the fence, the man on the tractor turned a corner and went down another row in the vineyard.

Tioga lifted the collar of her jacket and leaned forward. "Whistle when you see something. Meanwhile, I'll go this way for a bit and then look on the other side of the highway."

Camilla removed her gloves, put her index fingers in her mouth and whistled. "Like that?"

Once again, Tioga studied the no parking sign and then stared at Camilla.

"Yes, whistle like that!" she said and turned and walked away from the sign and the car, away from Cooper's Creek and "Brie Bridge."

Tioga glanced over her shoulder and watched Camilla as she pivoted on her heels and walked toward the steep incline that led down to the creek, the wind blowing her forward faster than she wanted to go.

The ground was littered with bottle caps, crushed beer cans, cigarette butts, plastic wrappers, plastic straws, spent chewing gum and large turds that had to be dog shit. Apparently the road crew hadn't done its job. Maybe Dorothy's body had been a distraction. Further ahead, Tioga read the outline of Dorothy's body where it had pressed into the wet earth. With her cell, she took photos and then looked back in time to catch Camilla as she went down toward Cooper's Creek.

Tioga looked at the sign for Metafor Winery, watched the traffic and, when it was safe, crossed to the other side where there was no debris and no dog shit. Along the fence, red roses were in bloom; calla lilies still showed signs of life. Grape vines raced toward a Victorian with gables that rose toward the sky. The tractor she had seen was now a small dot in the distance, the roar of the engine swallowed by earth and sky. She had forgotten how big the Valley could be.

Tioga heard Camilla's whistle. She looked both ways, then crossed the road again and aimed for Brie Bridge. Nailed to a tree was another sign. This one read, "No hunting and No Trespassing. Violators will be prosecuted."

Moments later, she stood near the edge of the creek. Camilla's back was bent. Her eyes were cast down toward the tangle of blackberry bushes. In her right hand, she clutched something. Then she stood up straight and arched her back.

"I saw somebody down here," Camilla said. "She had short hair and wore jeans. She was looking for something in the underbrush. Must have heard me because she fled. I didn't see which way she went."

Tioga stared at the thing in Camilla's hand. "She? Are you sure the somebody you saw was female?"

Camilla nodded. "Or else a cross dresser," she said and laughed. Then she opened her palm and revealed a pair of pink panties. "I found these stuck to a blackberry bush; lotta gnarly thorns that must have cut Dorothy's ankles. There's not much else, except signs of foot traffic in the mud along the creek."

Tioga read the faded label on the panties. "It's a small and it's from Louise's Lingerie Plus on the plaza. I know it well. And this looks like blood."

She pointed to a stain in the crotch.

"Maybe she had her period," Camilla suggested.

The wind whipped the branches overhead. A crow cawed and a turkey vulture swooped.

"Anything else catch your eye?" Tioga asked.

Camilla squinted her eyes. "Yes, one shoe: a Ferragamo."

She handed it to Tioga and added, "The person I saw wore men's clothes, but walked like a woman."

Tioga arched her eyebrows. "Maybe the person was a cross-dresser," she said. Then she asked, "Where did you first see this individual?"

Camilla pointed to a sickly tree that had lost its leaves and that hugged the ground near the top of the embankment on the far side of the creek. Under the limbs of the tree, the blackberry bushes looked like a machete had attacked them.

"Over there. I know it's a plum tree because my mother has one in her backyard. This one must have gone wild. They do that on their own."

Tioga scanned the thicket where a red-winged blackbird perched in a clump of cattails. Then she handed Camilla the undies.

"Check out Louise's Lingerie. Ask about someone who buys a size small and then take the undies to the lab. After that, go to Pandora's on the plaza and inquire about a woman who wears red Ferragamo flats. She must have dough. They're beyond my budget."

From her purse, Camilla removed two plastic bags. In one she placed the shoe; in the other the undies. "Oh, yes, I remember. There's a drop of blood on the ground, over there." She pointed toward a muddy patch along the edge of the creek. Then she added, "There's also blood on the incline on the other side, like a body had been dragged along the ground."

Camilla sliced through the blackberry bushes. Tioga circled around the edge. "You have a vivid imagination," she said dismissively.

Camilla emerged from the thicket, shrugged her shoulders and stared at the moist ground. "So what if I do?" she said. "It's not a crime to imagine." She pointed to a rock along the path that Tioga had followed. Then she added, "Look at that! It's a spot of blood."

Tioga stopped, squatted on her haunches and then lifted the rock that had a red speck, added it to yet another plastic bag and placed the bag inside Camilla's purse. "We'll have it analyzed."

She walked along the bed of the creek, her body low to the ground, her eyes peeled for more signs of blood, but she didn't see a single drop.

"What happened here?" she asked aloud, and then, against her better judgment, began to imagine a killer who might have been male or female and who had dragged Dorothy Baynes's body through the thicket.

The imagination could be a friend or an enemy, she told herself. She better not dismiss it, though it sometimes gave her fits.

Using the rocks in the stream as steppingstones, she crossed to the other side and followed the trail up the incline. "No blood here."

A moment later, Tioga stepped into a grove of willow trees at the top of the ridge. An open field extended in front of her. In the distance, she saw a row of eucalyptus trees that had been topped and, further away, a fence and a shed. In the foreground, she noticed several scattered bales of hay that had been bleached by the sun.

Camilla walked toward the John Deere that sat in the field. It had rusted in the rain and baked in the sun and looked like it might never again plough another field.

Tioga wandered toward the telephone wires that stretched from pole to pole until they disappeared in a clump of redwoods. A white cloud passed in front of the sun. A red-tailed hawk perched on a branch. Tioga watched the bird while it watched the field. "Everyone's hunting for something today."

Camilla stopped at the edge of the field, out of breath again. "The sign says 'St. Mary's Lane,' and there's another at Brie Bridge that reads, 'Cooper's Creek.' I went to grade school with a girl named Angelina Cooper."

Tioga sneezed and then covered her mouth with her right hand and sneezed again. "Allergies," she said. Then she added, "There's no blood here and nothing else for us either, I'm sorry to say. Look at this field, Camilla. Somebody musta come through here with a tractor and cut down all the hay, though it wasn't with that John Deere. It looks like it died ages ago."

Camilla took a handkerchief from her back pocket, bent down and wiped away the mud from her shoes. "Somebody carried Dorothy's body down the slope on this side. He or she pulled it across the stream, dragged it up the embankment and then dumped it in the culvert, where it was certain to be found. From the footprints in the mud it looks like there were two people down here, but perhaps not two big people and not at the same time. The prints don't go very deep."

Tioga shielded her eyes from the rays of the sun and peered toward St. Mary's Lane and a row of mailboxes.

"That is possible," she said, though she sounded skeptical. "But why would he or she have gone to all that trouble?"

Camilla looked up at the hawk and then down at the ground. "He or she or they wanted the police to think the body had been tossed from a moving vehicle on the highway. Didn't want them to imagine that it came from this side."

Tioga walked toward St. Mary's Lane. "Let's go back this way. It's easier than tramping through the mud and the blackberries."

A red pick-up truck passed on the left. Then a young girl on a bicycle emerged from a long narrow driveway and aimed for the mailboxes. She removed a handful of letters, a magazine and several mailers, and placed them in the wicker basket behind the seat.

"Anybody weird live around here?" Tioga asked and felt once again that she was grasping at straws.

The girl climbed on her bike, and then, as if the question itself had unsettled her, peddled madly toward a white farmhouse at the end of the long driveway.

"It's too quiet here," Tioga said. When the girl disappeared, she turned to Camilla, who was admiring a wild iris and said, "Actually, Mrs. Baynes reminds me of my mother who would lock herself in her room and drink Manhattans all day and sometimes all night. My father lived in his studio at the opposite end of the house and painted all day and sometimes all night. Occasionally, they'd meet in the kitchen."

At the end of St Mary's Lane, Tioga looked at the stop sign that had been punctured by bullets. "Idiots. I know them too well."

Camilla had picked the iris, which she now wore behind her ear. "So you're an adult child of an alcoholic! I'm not surprised."

Tioga turned away from the sign and watched the endless flow of traffic on the highway. "Psychobabble. Spare me please."

Camilla pursed her lips and made a sound that a rude preteen might make. "Touchy, aren't we? Adult Child of an Alcoholic. ACA. I learned that in my psych class at the junior college."

Tioga shrugged her shoulders. It was her job, she thought, to give her assistant a hard time, much as her mentor had given her a hard time in his office in North Beach and turned the wilderness girl into an op.

"Passed the class, did you?" Tioga said scornfully. "I never found that psych shit helpful."

Her Mini Cooper lurked in the shadow of the oak tree that had basked in sunlight just a short while ago. She raced toward it at breakneck speed.

"There you go again," Camilla shouted. "Moving the way a man moves."

Tioga slowed down, laughed and then waited until Camilla caught up with her. "About my mother, I'm touchy. Now you know. You can use it against me, the way my ex did, or not."

Camilla brushed aside a lock of her hair that had fallen across her forehead. "I would never do that to you, not ever, and just so you know, in my opinion, your ex was and probably still is an asshole."

Tioga stared at the driveway for the vineyard where the tractor driver climbed down from his perch and sauntered toward a row of mailboxes. She waved and waited for him to acknowledge her presence, but he grabbed the mail without a glance her way. "My ex was a sex addict, my mother an alcoholic, my dad's a workaholic. I'm just a pathetic druggie with no way out."

She removed her sunglasses and placed them in the pocket of her jacket. "When I was married to Tomás, I was terrified of being alone. There! Now you know. That's why I didn't leave him."

A red light swirled around and around on the roof of a white sedan with the words "Valley Police Department," and below it "Your Safety Is Our Business" and a 707 area code phone number.

"Oh, shit. Stop! Please! Don't write that ticket."

A tall, lanky cop with short red hair stood at the rear of the Mini Cooper and stared at the license plate for the vehicle. Then he reached for the pen in the pocket of his shirt and began to fill in the blank spaces on the citation form in his black book.

Camilla cupped her hands around her mouth and shouted, "Wait … we're just leaving." The officer looked toward Camilla, who didn't seem to realize that she had veered off at an angle and came close to the traffic on the highway.

"You, watch out," the officer shouted and then lunged forward, grabbed Camilla by the arm and pulled her toward him. "You gotta be more careful where you're going. It's not safe around here."

Camilla looked at the bike lane and at the traffic. "Yes, I mean, no, I didn't realize how close I'd come to the highway. Thanks."

The officer returned to his black book. "There's no parking here. Can't you read?"

Camilla covered her mouth for a moment and laughed. "I remember you now from my sophomore year. You were ahead of me."

The officer stared at Camilla, leaned forward and said, "Little Camilla Sanchez, yes, I remember now. You wouldn't dance with me at the prom."

He gave Tioga the once-over and said, "You're the PI, aren't you? I remember you from the Kiko Martinez case. People like you make it harder to keep the Valley safe for citizens."

Camilla rested her still-muddy right shoe on the rear bumper of the police car. "This is my boss, Tioga Vignetta." Then she glanced at Tioga and explained, "This is 'Clark the Narc.' In high school, he wanted to be a cop. Gordon Clark is his full name. He was a terrible dancer. He always stepped on my shoes."

Tioga extended her right hand. "Please to meet you, Mr. Clark. But you must be confusing me with someone else if you think I had a hand in Martinez's escape."

Clark shook Tioga's hand reluctantly. "Maybe. And maybe I won't write you a ticket. We're not as cold-blooded as you like to think we are."

Camilla put on her high school cheerleader smile. "Thanks. We appreciate it."

Clark looked at Camilla's muddy shoes. "You wanna remove those from the vehicle! You ought not to wander along the creek. Ladies can get taken advantage of down there."

Clark rested the palms of his big hands on his big hips. "It's private property along here and posted, too. Didn't you see the 'Keep Out' sign?" He looked at the license plate and the sticker in the upper right hand corner of Tioga's vehicle. "Your registration is about to expire. You better renew."

Tioga put on her sunglasses and looked up at the bright blue sky. "I always follow all the regs."

Clark took out his car keys. "Drive carefully," he said and then paused a moment and asked, "Just why were you down at the creek?"

Tioga peered at Clark's badge and name tag. "Checking water levels and stream flow for Save Our Rivers and Streams. Somebody has been stealing water. It's an environmental crime. Maybe you saw the report from Fish and Wildlife."

Camilla turned toward the sun and squinted her eyes. "Oh dear. That's not good for the poor fish." Then she fired a question at the cop: "What happens to women along this creek?"

Clark clenched his jaw. "Bad things."

Tioga moved her eyes from Clark's badge to his revolver and then to his handcuffs. "Like what kind of bad things? We ought to know because we'll be back to monitor water levels. We're cool, Clark." In a mournful tone of voice, she added, "I know you don't normally investigate when there's a report of a sexual assault, but you ought to."

Clark frowned. "Nobody's reported any assaults."

Tioga put her hand inside her jacket and felt the snub nose. "Not reported? Or swept under the carpet?"

Clark turned his body from side to side. "I would know whether it was swept under the carpet or not. That's my job, to look out for unprofessional conduct."

He climbed behind the wheel of his cruiser, turned off the flashing red light, turned on the directional, waited for a gap in the traffic and then sped off.

Tioga tugged at Camilla's elbow. "Let's get out of here."

She opened the door to the Mini Cooper, sat down in the passenger seat, straightened the seat belt that had become tangled and snapped the buckle. Camilla put the key in the ignition and started the engine. Tioga watched the bumper-to-bumper traffic along the highway headed east.

Before they could make a move, the police cruiser made a U-turn, pulled off the highway and then came to a screeching stop. Clark's car and Tioga's were now practically kissing. Clark rolled down his window and extended his arm. "Here, take this," he said and handed Camilla a ticket. Then he sped off again.

Camilla placed the citation in the glove compartment and gauged the traffic on the highway. "He didn't have to do that. Or maybe he did. He doesn't like us. We're too uppity for him."

She pressed her right foot down on the accelerator and joined the commuters going to work, coming from work, headed to the mall, or from the mall, all of them exceeding the posted speed limit, except when traffic stalled and they went nowhere at all.

"Why the fuck did you bring up the subject of sexual assault along the creek?" Camilla asked. "You don't know that for a fact."

Tioga leaned back and stretched her legs. "It stands to reason. You found a pair of bloody undies in the thicket.

Dorothy Baynes was raped and murdered someplace near here. Then her body was dragged through the underbrush. I wanted to push Clark's buttons and get him out of his own fucking comfort zone."

Tioga pulled down the visor, looked at her face in the mirror and pursed her lips. "For a change, I'd like to stop something bad before it starts."

She took out her cell and sent a text to Phyllis Ambrose, George's wife, that read: "Pls send Mitzi's #." When Phyllis's response arrived moments later, Tioga sent Mitzi a text that read: "We have to talk. Love you, Ti." Then to Camilla she explained, "I bet Mitzi never gets back to me." She looked in the rearview mirror. "There's a maniac on your tail."

Camilla adjusted the mirror and watched a white stretch limo swerve from the highway to the bike lane and then back to the highway. She pulled off the road and let the limo pass. "You are one hell of a Ms. Negative today, Tioga. Mitzi loves you. She will call."

Then she asked, "Who the fuck do you think is stealing water?"

Tioga leaned back and relaxed. "People are stealing water."

Camilla took the "s" turns slowly. "I know people are stealing water. But the big-time thieves have to be ag."

Tioga opened her purse and looked at the rock with the spot of blood. "It's people watering lawns and washing cars. There are no more good guys or gals in the Valley. Maybe there never were any, except the Miwok."

Camilla changed the dial on the radio from 90.5 to 102.7, raised the volume a couple of notches and listened to Wolf Girl, the DJ who explained that for the next thirty minutes she was going to play hits from 1968.

"Fuck '68." Tioga snapped the fingers on her left hand and sang: "I go to pieces every time I see my baby." Then she stopped in the middle of the next line and yelled, "Dumb lyrics."

She killed the radio, took out her cell and ran through the photos of Dorothy that she took in the office. "Ugly, ugly. I hope she didn't suffer."

Camilla accelerated and switched lanes. "If you wanna know more about Clark, he tried to date me in high school. He was way too white bread. He fumed and got into trouble: drinking and driving. His parents sent him away. He came back and went to the police academy. Now he's married, has three kids, works his ass off and drinks at El Buen Comer. My mother sees him there all the time."

Tioga removed the snub nose from the holster and held it in the palm of her hand. "Just wanted you to know I'm packing heat today, and that I don't like it. It makes me feel like I'm not in control. But what am I gonna do? I gotta have it."

With her eyes on the road she added, "Bye ... Bye," and put the snub nose to bed. The Mini Cooper bounced in and out of potholes. Tioga gripped the strap above her head but banged her head against the window.

"Ouch," she said and rubbed the bruise. Then she yawned and added, "I'm tired. Hardly slept last night and ..."

Camilla turned up the volume on the radio again, in time to hear Imelda May belt out, "It's Your Voodoo Workin'."

Tioga yawned. "I know the lyrics by heart. 'My hands feel sticky and head's ice cold.'"

Traffic built up again. Cars in both lanes slowed down. A raccoon stood on its hind legs along the side of the road and waited to cross safely to the other side. "Poor coon," Tioga said. Then to Camilla she added, "Don't worry. I'm not going to pull any weird voodoo shit on you."

Camilla rubbed the back of her neck with her left hand. "I don't like it when you go on about voodoo. I've seen chickens slaughtered in the kitchen, their blood mixed with all kinds of shit by my uncle Roberto, who went to prison at La Tuna, Texas."

Tioga closed her eyes and leaned back. Then her phone rang. "Yes. Oh, Mitzi, I thought you'd never reply ... I'm great. What about you?"

Mitzi didn't bother with small talk. "My father put you up to this, didn't he?" Tioga put the phone on speaker. "You don't have to shout." Mitzi interrupted with, "Yes, I do." Tioga came back with "No, your father did not put me up to this. I'm not his stalking horse."

"Whatever," Mitzi said. Silence oozed from the phone and from the radio, too. Then Wolf Girl announced the single she had cued up: "Richard Berry's hit, 'Louie, Louie.'" Tioga turned down the volume, and Mitzi's voice came over the speakerphone again. "I want nothing to do with my father or my mother! I hope you haven't forgotten what he and Mabel did after Franklin Olivera's murder."

Tioga let out a long slow sigh. "I have not forgotten. I am extra careful what I say or don't say in front of George and in front of your mother. But I didn't call you to talk about them. I was wondering, do you remember Dorothy Baynes from high school?"

Now Mitzi encouraged Tioga to go on: "Yes. Yes." And then yet another "Yes."

Tioga banged her forehead on the dashboard. "Stop yessing me."

"Yes," Mitzi replied and fell silent again. Tioga wiggled in her seat. "The police found Baynes's body along 12. Raped and murdered. She swallowed a key before she died. One shoe was missing and a finger was bloody where the killer tried to remove a ring. Pretty picture, eh?"

Mitzi exhaled, inhaled quickly and her heart pounded.

"Mitzi, are you there? Mitzi?"

"I'm right here. I didn't go away. I'm thinking. I need more time than you to know what I want to say. You just blurt things out."

Tioga eyed Camilla, who puckered her lips as if she was a sassy female detective in a noir motion picture.

"In the beginning, when we met, you always talked first and me second," Tioga said. "I thought you'd remember Dorothy Baynes."

Mitzi made a hissing sound with her tongue and her front teeth. "I don't recall a lot, but I do remember that Dorothy ran with the fast crowd. She had sex before anyone else had sex and she did dope before anyone else."

Tioga clenched the fist on her right hand. "Can you give me a name please? Someone who knew Dorothy."

There was another long pause. "I'm thinking," Mitzi said and then after an even longer pause she added, "When I was fourteen, Dorothy ran away with a man who trained horses. Two years later, she came back with another man and with a baby she gave up for adoption. A year later, she wanted her baby back, but by then a couple had adopted her and had become the legal guardians. As far as welfare was concerned, Dorothy did not exist."

Mitzi paused once again. "I'm not surprised that she was found dead along the side of the road."

Tioga bit her lower lip. "I don't like the way that sounds. It's mean."

Mitzi reared back and fired. "I don't care what it sounds like, and I don't care if I never see my stupid parents again. When you find the man who murdered Dorothy, don't let my father get anywhere near him. Bullets in the street are faster than trials in the courtroom. That's what he always told me when I was growing up and at home. Now do you understand why I moved out."

The call ended. Tioga stowed her phone in her pocket and spaced out. Camilla pulled up to the curb at the front of the Mar Monte. "I thought wc could both usc a drink. Cool our jets." She looked into the mirror. "Do I look okay?"

Tioga bared her white teeth. "Smashing," she said and removed a blackberry thorn that had stuck to Camilla's beret. "Souvenir of the creek."

A beautiful woman with braids, dark skin and dark eyes crouched near the entrance to the Mar Monte. A boy sat at her side. The sign he held said, "Hungre. Will work for foud."

Aaron opened the door to the Mini Cooper and waited while Camilla stepped out. Then he darted to the other side of the vehicle and opened the door for Tioga. Meanwhile, Camilla applied eyeliner and lipstick. "You go ahead. I'll catch up."

Tioga walked toward the beautiful woman with the sign, opened her purse, took out a twenty and gave it to the boy who wore a T-shirt that said "The Rolling Stones," with the band's icon: a big red tongue. "*Por favor, señora*, would you please keep an eye on the street? I could use your eyes and ears. It's important. You see something you call me." The woman took the $20 from the boy and shook her head. "Bad here. Push me away."

Tioga looked at the boy. "I need eyes and ears in the *calle*; you understand? *Cómo te llamas?* I protect you."

The beautiful woman wore a sullen expression. "Flor. That my name. Give me your cell phone. I put in *mi número*."

Tioga smiled. When her cell came back, she saw the name, FLOR, in capital letters and then a long number that began with 50, continued with 647 and then seven more numbers.

"*Ciudad Juarez?*"

Flor placed the twenty-dollar bill in the pocket of a red-and-white checked apron. "I see everyone. I see night, day. Yes, I live Juarez."

Tioga felt a hand on her shoulder. She turned around slowly and saw Aaron's big white teeth and big red lips. "This woman bothering you? I chased her away earlier, but she came back."

Tioga shook her head. Aaron said, "You better go inside and keep an eye on Camilla. She's too hot to be un-chaperoned." He mounted the steps. Just as quickly, Tioga followed him. "That woman is too beautiful for you to persecute."

"I'm doing her a favor," Aaron snarled. "If she gets into the hotel, they'll drag her out face down and claim she fell down a flight of stairs. She's a royal pain in the ass. I told her to get a job."

At the entrance to the Mar Monte—the door handles in the shape of fire-breathing dragons—Aaron smiled. "The hotel staff just put the finishing touches to the papier-mâché elephants and the palm trees made with silk and bamboo. They're so fake they look real."

He took a deep breath, grabbed hold of one of the gold handles on the front door and waited until Tioga reached the top step.

"Terry wanted real elephants, not papier-mâché," he continued. "He found a nut with a private zoo who wanted to sell him a couple of bulls. Terry was eager to seal the deal, but when he went to check them out they attacked him and he called it off."

Aaron paused for a moment before he let go and laughed so hard that his Santa Claus-size belly shook vigorously. "Imagine, real live bulls with more testosterone than Terry."

Tioga adjusted the collar on Aaron's brocade jacket. "Be nice to women and children. Be kind. What goes around comes around."

She plunged into the hotel, only to pause at the edge of the atrium, unsure whether to laugh or to cry at the scene that unfolded and made her think of a comic book for kids, with lurid colors, exotic females and grotesque villains. But there was no Superman, no Wonder Woman or Spider-Man. Just as well. She would be her own action hero and rescue herself, if need be.

Two men in blackface, pointy slippers and white turbans moved like robots around the room, counterclockwise carrying silver trays with fluted glasses filled with bubbly. "Talk about over the top," Tioga said to herself. "This beats all."

Two slender women with push-up bras, mounds of make-up and matching yellow and red saris, served pakoras and samosas. They couldn't serve them fast enough. The crowd seemed to be starved, and not just for food, but also for drinks, drugs, sex and cheap thrills that would last a moment or two, like crack cocaine, and then puff, vanish. A blissed-out musician with tiger-eyes sat cross-legged in an alcove and plucked the strings of a sitar. At his feet the boy Tioga had seen in the elevator—and who now looked older than his years—watched the performer in adoration.

A tall incense burner with what smelled like pinyon pine stood next to a raj-size hookah. There were a dozen stems and just as many pious smokers—including Storm, who wore silk pajamas and who inhaled waves of smoke and choked, coughed, sipped champagne, laughed, giggled and wiggled her toes and her nose as if she'd finally discovered the lost childhood she had never had. The Mar Monte had turned into a playpen for adults.

Tioga waved to Storm, but she was too preoccupied to wave back. Two men in guayaberas, seated around the hookah looking nearly identical, competed for Storm's attention and received nothing except a look of disdain. One couple, of ambiguous gender, stood up and drifted toward the back of the hotel, arm-in-arm.

One wave of smokers abandoned the hookah, and a new wave took their place A cloud of smoke rose toward the blue silk canopy that stretched from one side of the room to the other. Camilla, who stood at the edge of the spectacle, sniffed the air and then winked at Tioga, who inhaled and coughed.

Matthew Chehab—in a paisley shirt, a seersucker jacket, blue pants, loafers and an ascot—sliced through the tightly packed crowd. His big, awkward body didn't make it easy. Still he managed to move across the room like a crab that moved sideways. When he saw Tioga, he paused and rolled his big dark eyes as if to say, "Isn't this insane?" or maybe it was "Isn't this heavenly?" It could have been either one or both.

Chehab didn't seem to be stoned or intoxicated, but he appeared to be was high on something. Maybe, Tioga said to herself, it was a deal he had sealed, or the woman in the bodice whom he seemed to be undressing with his eyes as if she was Valley real estate.

"What the fuck is Chehab thinking?" Tioga asked herself. But perhaps at that moment and under the influence of the woman in the bodice he wasn't capable of thought. He stood next to Camilla and whispered in her ear, though it was clear from the roar in the room, that Camilla couldn't hear him. She inched closer to his lips, though that didn't appear to help matters either. The crowd didn't care whether she could hear Chehab or not. All anyone wanted to do was to drink bubbly, smoke the hookah, devour canapés and rub their bodies against one another as if they all belonged to one big inebriated exercise class bent on breaking boundaries.

Finally Chehab gave up on the idea of having a conversation with Camilla. He sidled up to Tioga, showed her an image on his phone and said something, though she could not hear him. "Speak up, please."

Chehab cleared his throat and raised his voice. "Come closer."

Tioga leaned against him, felt the warmth of his body and the scent of something that made her think of a harem, though she had had no actual experience in a harem.

"We canceled the hotel's no-smoking policy, and after we greased a few wheels, the health department gave us a pass on the new rules about events with weed and wine," Chehab said. "A guest from out of state complained about the noise and the smoke, but there isn't a single empty room in the hotel. We must be doing something right, even if it's not legal, strictly speaking."

Chehab looked from face to face as if in a trance. "I've never seen so many stoned people in public in my whole life. Have you?"

Tioga looked around the room hoping to recognize the face of a friend or at least an acquaintance. She nearly gave up until finally she saw Terry McCoy, who stood in front of a tall, thin man who wore a fedora, or maybe a Borsalino. From a distance she couldn't tell the difference.

Tioga could not see the man's face, nor could she hear his voice, but she noticed his long arms that he waved in the air as if trying to conduct an orchestra that had run amuck. The tall, thin, hatted man nearly struck McCoy, whether by accident or on purpose it wasn't clear. McCoy gestured ambiguously with his right hand. Then the tall man dashed from the room.

Chehab scarfed a canapé. "He's an old friend of Terry's. They were in transportation together. Now they don't see eye-to-eye."

Chehab changed his tone of voice and added, "I'm sorry about your extended stay in the Mar Monte." When Tioga looked at him with a blank expression on her face, he grimaced. "I guess you haven't heard. Tsk tsk."

Tioga kept her eyes on McCoy as he put his arm round a young woman who had cozied up to him and offered him a blunt. Then she watched with a sense of apprehension as they disappeared down the dark corridor that led to the Underground, which had to be more suitable for canoodling than the blue silk canopy. "Haven't heard what, Matt? Tell me!" Tioga asked.

Chehab extended his frog-like tongue, scored a canapé, swallowed it whole and then licked his fingers. "I'm really sorry," he said and sounded genuine, which was a part of his job. Then Chehab added, "We just couldn't go on letting you and Storm live rent-free in the penthouse. In our wildest dreams, neither Terry nor I ever imagined that the arrangement was permanent. I'm afraid you and Storm will have to *vamanos*. But the two of you always land on your feet, no matter what, so I imagine you'll do the same now."

Chehab had apparently convinced himself, though not Tioga, that the "eviction," to use a word he didn't deign to use, was a win-win for everyone. Nobody ever lost at the Mar Monte. That's how it promoted itself.

Tioga swallowed so hard she could feel her Adam's apple. "This feels awfully sudden. I hope we have time to find another place."

Chehab's face turned red. "We're not giving you the bum's rush. By the end of the month will be soon enough."

Tioga knew that she looked alarmed though she didn't sound alarmed. "Oh, that's great. Now if you'll excuse me, Matt, I need a real drink."

At the Underground, Tioga perched on the last stool at the very end of the zinc bar. She studied the lines on her face in the mirror and then looked at the back of the room, where Terry McCoy and Storm sat side-by-side in the last leather booth, their noses practically touching. In an instant, Tioga knew that she was both suspicious and jealous. Still she smiled brightly and waved at Sean Dyce who was mixing a cocktail. "Hi, Sean, baby."

Dyce waved back and then smiled a cherubic smile that accentuated his dimples. Camilla sat down on the stool next to Tioga and studied the list of drinks on the beverage menu which boasted an image of a woman wearing a beret and holding, between her front teeth, a long, slender cigarette holder. The smoke curled above her head and formed the shape of an animal, a wolf or a fox, or perhaps a wolf-fox. Tioga looked at the chalkboard with the list of the day's special cocktails: a Pimm's cup, a New York sour, a cranberry daiquiri and a mojito described as "Cuban style."

From the loudspeakers above the bar came a Jackson Browne tune that she didn't care to hear. It reminded her of her ex, who played the guitar and wanted to be Jackson Browne. While he had talent, he pissed it away. Tioga tried and then gave up trying to rescue him.

Sean Dyce shook a cocktail so vigorously that he looked like he might hurt himself. Still his black bow tie held firmly in place. He poured the frothy mixture into two cocktail glasses. A waitress in black leggings, a black blouse and a white apron placed the drinks on a tray, sashayed to the back of the room and served them to McCoy who held an unlit cigar in his right hand, and to Storm, who had changed from pajamas to a silky tank top. She looked at Terry reverentially; he seemed to bask in her adoration.

Tioga watched the cocktail waitress bend her body so that her ample cleavage was visible. Then she thrust her hips back and forth, lifted her rear and shook it as vigorously as Dyce shook the mixed drinks behind the bar. Now he paused and watched the performance. "Cindy did that nightly in Vegas. Terry saw her at Caesar's and hired her on the spot."

Tioga peered into the mirror and recognized a look of mild amusement on her face. "Yeah, I saw twerking in New Orleans. Juicy Badazz is the original bad ass. This woman is a lousy imitation."

McCoy gave the waitress a pat on her rear and inserted a bill between her breasts. "Nice cleavage," someone at the bar said. Sean Dyce had not turned away from the performance that took place at the back of room, not for a moment. "Now I need a drink," he roared. He wiped the smile from his face and added, "How about I make you a manhattan, Tioga? They're all the rage today."

Tioga placed her cell on the bar, checked her messages and then put the machine to sleep. "No thanks, Manhattans don't suit me," she said, scanning the list of cocktails on the chalkboard once more. She added, "I want the thing you make with gin and orange bitters and crème de menthe."

Dyce reached for a bottle with a yellow label that read Hollandse Graanjenever. "You mean a green dragon. With or without the cannabis tincture? I have a new strain that's killer diller."

In the mirror, Tioga stared at her face and decided that she looked bored. "Oh, I don't know," she said and sounded like she had a serious case of ennui. "Leave out the tincture. I got a contact high coming through the hotel lobby just now. It's foggy out there. I'll be stoned for the rest of the day."

She looked at McCoy and at Storm who were still sitting side-by-side, albeit restlessly. "I don't see why folks want to get stoned in a crowd with dozens and dozens of people, probably strangers. It ain't my thing. I'd rather get high by myself and listen to Miles and try to decide if the figure hidden in the wallpaper is a satyr or a nymph or a plain, ordinary bogeyman."

When she looked at McCoy and Storm again, she thought they might suddenly burst into flames. Something or someone had sparked a fire that smoldered beneath the surface. Then she turned back to Dyce and said, "Wait a sec, I changed my mind. Add the cannabis tincture. I need it. I'm having a hard day today."

Dyce rubbed his hands together. "If you're jealous or envious, don't be. Storm just likes to jerk him off, meta-phorically speaking, of course, and Terry laps it up."

Still with his hands together, Dyce waited patiently to hear if Tioga would say something, anything. She said nothing and only looked bored once again. "Green Dragon with cannabis coming up right away," he warbled as if he meant to liberate her from her ennui. He might have mixed the drink blindfolded. He was that sure of himself. He didn't spill a drop. He finished the cocktail with a green tincture that he poured from a small vial that sat next to Jose Cuervo on the shelf along with a dozen other tequilas. Finally he poured the mixture into a cocktail glass with a long thin stem. "Terry and Storm have been at it for half-an-hour. I can't imagine what they've had to discuss all this time."

Tioga lifted the thin-stemmed glass, held it up to the light and admired the colors. "They go back a long way. Maybe I've told you this before, Sean, or maybe you've known it all along. In any case, I'll remind you. Storm's parents adopted Terry when he was in high school. Since they didn't have a son, they groomed him to take over the estate. Franklin Olivera wanted him to become a judge, but by the time Terry graduated from the junior college he was on the other side of the law. And now, look at him, he's getting his ego stroked."

Tioga listened to the second cut on the Ry Cooder album. This time it didn't remind her of her ex or anyone else. "Terry turned out just as you'd imagine he might turn out." She sipped the drink and added, "This green dragon better kick the blues that have bugged me all day. If it doesn't, I don't know what I'll do." After a long pause, she murmured, "Storm and Terry have secrets they don't even share with me."

Camilla was too stoned to pay attention to the conversation between Tioga and Sean. She went on studying the list of wines and beers on the beverage menu as if about to make a momentous decision that would affect the rest of her life. Tioga kept a close eye on her. Finally she'd had enough. "Come on, make up your fucking mind already. It's not like you're going to get married to the drink."

Camilla looked up from the beverage menu. "I'll have the Sorelle Bronca Prosecco. Make sure it's really chilled or I won't drink it." Every so often Camilla surprised Tioga with her sophistication. She had better not typecast her.

Dyce opened the bottle and filled Camilla's glass. "If it's not to your liking I'll open another bottle."

Camilla lifted the glass, brought it to her lips without spilling a drop, and then finally sipped. "Yes, it's perfect. There's nothing like chilled bubbly on a hot day."

Tioga sipped her cocktail. The beautiful bubbles rose slowly to the surface and dazzled her eyes. Yes, she was stoned again and now she knew it.

Dyce winked at Tioga and then winked at Camilla, who also seemed to be stoned, but didn't know it.

Dyce nodded his head. "I didn't realize you were so fussy," he said and then opened a large bottle of Pellegrino, added ice cubes to a mug and filled it. "This is what I'm drinking today."

He stared at the entrance to the room as if he could see the sky overhead and Mayacamas Mountains in the distance.

Tioga thought he seemed out of sorts. "Weird weather we're having. I swear it's worse than last summer when I was ready to buy a ticket to the Arctic."

Dyce returned the prosecco to the refrigerator that sat behind the bar. Then he dried his hands on his white apron. "It was so hot that an old lady waltzed into the bar stark naked with a pit bull which curled up in the corner and didn't move. A snake slithered up to check out the scene and you, Tioga, my dear, you were a mess. I had to work overtime to put you back together after you broke into pieces."

Tioga raised her glass to the light. "You're exaggerating again, Sean. I wasn't that bad off, and snakes didn't come up from below. You're forgetting that last summer we had crazy weather that was both hot and cold."

Tioga looked at her reflection in the mirror and fussed with her hair until it finally fell into place. Dyce reached into the cash register, took out a stack of bills and separated them into twenties, hundreds, singles and fives.

"But, of course, you are right," Tioga said, sounding flip. "This weather does make people crazy. That's for sure. And the heat is worse than the cold!" She reached inside her jacket, touched her snub nose and smiled. "I'm okay, now." Then she placed her hands on the bar and turned them palm-side up. "I woke this morning with a spider bite and told myself 'You're not going to make it through the day.' But George Ambrose showed up and made me an offer I couldn't refuse. It's strictly hush-hush."

Tioga clinked her glass with Camilla's and sipped her cocktail. She lifted the coaster—with the iconic image of the woman in the beret with the cigarette holder—and tapped it on the zinc bar to get Dyce's attention, which had drifted again toward the booth at the back of the room. "Yo, Sean, me, over here."

Finally he turned and brought his eyes to rest on Tioga's placid face. "Yeah? What now?"

Tioga looked at him imploringly. "Did you know a woman named Dorothy Baynes?" Dyce reached for a white towel and began to remove a lipstick stain from a wine glass. "Are you talking past tense? Is she not around anymore?"

Tioga peered into the mirror and nodded. "The EMT boys took her to the morgue. I thought maybe when she was still perpendicular she came in for a drink. I know a lotta people wash through here."

For the first time all afternoon, Dyce looked like he was lost in thought. "I'm trying to remember. It's Baynes with a 'y' not an 'i,' isn't it? Yes, of course. I met Mrs. Baynes once. She came in with a shopping bag and sat down at the bar. I thought she wanted a drink, but she told me that her daughter had vanished and asked me to help find her. I said, 'I'm not running a missing person's agency.'"

He paused and held the immaculate wine glass up to the light. The lipstick stain was gone. "Mrs. Baynes showed me a photo of her daughter's confirmation at St. Francis. She asked me to call when I saw her. I remember she said when and not if. I never did see Mrs. Baynes again."

Tioga reached into her pocket, produced her cell and showed Dyce a photo she had taken of Dorothy from George Ambrose's collection.

Dyce winced. "Ouch. That hurts. Do you know who did that to her?"

Tioga shook her head. "Whoever murdered Dorothy made it look like she was dumped along the side of road. That's what Ambrose thinks. There was very little blood where the cops found the body, but there was blood in the thicket that runs along the creek. Ambrose doesn't seem to know anything about that, or if he does, he's not letting on."

Dyce reached for another wine glass, this one with a larger smudge on the rim. Then he went to work as if he was a man obsessed with perfection. "You've never seen eye-to-eye with Ambrose, have you? Ambrose doesn't know when to quit."

Camilla adjusted her beret. "The way I figure it Dorothy was dragged through the underbrush along the creek. The blackberry thorns cut her pretty bad. We found a pair of undies and a shoe, too, a Ferragamo. When we got back to Tioga's car an asshole cop I know from Valley High wrote us a ticket for parking in a no parking zone. That sucked."

Dyce nodded his head and then poured himself another Pellegrino. "Lucky you didn't have your car towed. Valley cops are dickheads, especially that kid Clark. A month ago, he pulled me over and wanted to ticket me for driving while intoxicated. I told him I hadn't had a drop of alcohol all week. He looked at me funny and said, 'Aren't you the bartender at the Underground.' I said 'So! That doesn't make me a lush.' He told me to prove I was sober."

Dyce placed his index finger on the tip of his nose. Then he walked in a perfectly straight line from one end of the bar to the other. "That's what I did. Just like that, but dickhead tells me my tires are bald, says I have thirty days to buy new ones, show up at the department and have him sign off on the order. It was total bullshit. My tires had great treads."

Just then Tioga heard what she assumed was the snap of a whip. When she turned away from the bar and looked toward the leather booth at the back of the room, she saw McCoy standing in Jodhpurs and leather boots. He moved swiftly toward her with a whip that he held in his right hand. First he coiled the whip and then he uncoiled it and stroked it as if it was a living, breathing thing.

Tiny beads of perspiration appeared on his brow. Was McCoy anxious or terrified or drunk or stoned? Storm, who walked in step with him, seemed goofy, perhaps because she was high. After all, the air in the Underground was now infused with smoke and smelled like weed. At the bar, Storm air-kissed Tioga on both cheeks and then plopped down as if her legs couldn't keep her up.

"I'm freaked about Dorothy Baynes. Terry told me. Of course, it brings up all my old shit. On top of that, we have to move. But what the hell. It's all good."

Tioga nodded. News had traveled fast. If Storm knew about Dorothy, she told herself, then nearly all the Valley musicians had to know. The jazzmen and the blues women must have known, as did the hipsters, the drunks, the dancers and all the lonely Eleanor Rigbys of the Valley who came to hear Storm spill her angst on stage and in public.

Tioga nodded her head once again, only more slowly this time. "About the move. It's no biggie. We were cool before we lived here and we'll be cool when we live in some other town that's a tourist trap."

She put her arm around Storm's slender waist. "Yeah, I can imagine that Dorothy's murder has activated your shit. It has activated mine."

She reached for McCoy's coiled whip, held it in her right hand and felt the heft of it. Then she uncoiled it slowly and cracked it with a fury that startled everyone: Dyce, Storm, Camilla and McCoy, too. "It's not a crop is it? It's a proper whip. You'll need it, Terry, to beat back the stoned mob out there, but maybe they're too stoned to heed a whip."

Terry gave Sean the high sign.

"Stout coming right up," Sean bellowed. He knew his master's preferences whether they were alcoholic or not. A moment later, McCoy held a snifter in his right hand and admired the frothy head on a rich dark beer that smelled of hops and barley; better than the aroma of the harem that lingered about Chehab.

"It's beautiful, isn't it?" McCoy asked. "I don't just mean the head on the beer. I mean everything today. I've been planning this for a year, along with Matt and with Jonny Field, who has outdone himself in the kitchen. The Mar Monte is champs! Nobody's gonna catch us now."

Tioga coiled the whip and handed it to Terry, who grabbed hold of it and arranged it, on the zinc bar, so that the head touched the tail. Then he lifted the snifter and sipped slowly. "We have the best weed, the best wine and the best food. We have the best-looking women and the best-looking guys. Don't underestimate the guys."

Tioga beat back the urge to puncture McCoy's balloon. "Amazing that you have the permits. The Cannabis Czar in Sacto announced a moratorium on permits until the market stabilizes."

Terry laughed. "That's very funny," he said and didn't look amused. "I'll tell you this, Tioga, we don't have a single permit and we didn't need one. We're exempt. As for the cannabis market it isn't going to stabilize until …"

Before he could finish his sentence, Camilla interrupted him. Dyce gave her a look that said, "You have balls, interrupting the boss."

Camilla stamped her foot. "Matt Chehab just explained that…"

Now it was her turn to be interrupted.

"Yeah, yeah," McCoy said. "You probably think the earth is flat and that human beings are descended from dinosaurs."

Camilla poked McCoy with her index finger. "But you didn't let me finish. I was going to say…" Once again, Terry wouldn't let her finish. "I know what you were going to say. I can read your mind. You're so transparent." After he paused he glared at Storm and at Tioga and added, "I have far too much respect for all of you, Dyce included, to hand you malarkey."

He went on glaring, this time just at Camilla. "In case you need a translation, miss, malarkey means nonsense. You're probably too young to know the word or to appreciate its nuances. Your grandparents, who must have been kind, loving people, didn't come from County Cork, did they? No, indeed, they didn't. I wonder, how did they get here?"

He extended his hand in Camilla's direction and smiled a real smile, or at least what passed for one in the gloomy atmosphere of the Underground. Tioga thought Terry meant, for once, to be magnanimous, or rather to appear to be magnanimous. After all, he was the king; he owned the Mar Monte, pulled the strings and collected nearly all the news and the gossip in the Valley.

"I don't believe that we have ever been formally introduced, though to the best of my recollection I've seen you here once or twice or maybe even three times with Randall Scheck who had the good sense to return to Brooklyn. He was much too … what shall I say … cocky. I don't know how you could stand to work for him."

Camilla's face turned white. McCoy's turned red. Loyal to Randy, whether he deserved it or not, Camilla looked like she was ready to smack McCoy. He looked like he was ready crack his whip and give her a few strokes.

Tioga put her body between Camilla, who held her drink in one hand, and McCoy, who held his whip and seemed, in that frozen split second, to wonder, "Yes, crack it." "No, don't crack it."

Tioga wasn't sure what he would decide. "Excuse me," she said. "I should have introduced the two of you. Terry McCoy, Camilla Sanchez, Camilla Sanchez, Terry McCoy."

For a few moments, none of them moved. "I hired Camilla when Randy left the Valley. She's a slow learner but slow is good."

McCoy finally shook Camilla's hand. "Oh Jesus, not another one! How many distaff dicks can we have in the Valley? The two of you snoop twenty-four seven; no one will have any privacy anymore. Is that what you want? The end of privacy?"

Tioga kept her eyes riveted on Terry who finally relaxed his grip on Camilla's hand. "Distaff detectives, I thought that was pretty funny. Have you all lost your sense of humor?"

Then he guffawed, coiled the whip and draped it around his shoulder. "I hate crime and I hate mystery which make me anxious and anxious is something I won't do."

McCoy didn't mean to be funny, but Tioga laughed and so did Camilla and Dyce, too, who leaned forward, making him seem more imposing than when he stood behind the bar.

Two men wearing long hair, beards, beads, boots and jeans stared at the chalkboard as if trying to decipher hieroglyphics. Tioga pegged them for gay guys and growers, too, who had strayed from the pot party to the watering hole at the Underwood and who felt out of their comfort zone.

"Enjoying your selves?" Neither gave any indication they had heard her. She tried again. "Great pot party, eh guys!"

They both turned and looked her up and down. Then the one with the ponytail asked, "What are you doing tonight? I have green crack. We could get it on."

Maybe they weren't gay after all. Green crack—she knew what it was, but she didn't like the sound of it. Why would anyone want to use cannabis that was like crack?

Tioga extended the tip of her tongue, provocatively. "I'm on call and all tied up. Sorry, boys, I can't join your party. Another time."

Storm took a step forward and looked at the two long-haired guys. "Keep your distance, assholes. Don't you know there's zero tolerance for sexual harassment in the Mar Monte! Isn't that right, Terry?"

McCoy drained the last of the beer in the snifter. "Yes, we're the first hotel in the Valley to have zero tolerance for sexual harassment. We're leading the charge."

The two longhairs both shook their heads. Then they turned back to the bar and signaled for Sean Dyce. McCoy grabbed his whip and shouted to Dyce, "Hand me one of my Cohibas. No, make that two. I want to give one to Jonny for the fab job he's done."

Dyce served two Coronas to the two longhairs and then presented McCoy with two cigars with labels that read COHIBA, HABANA, CUBA.

Terry put one cigar in the front pocket of his jacket, lit the other, puffed and puffed and blew the smoke above his head. Now the space smelled like tobacco and weed. "That's a genuine Cohiba. We might learn a thing or two from the Cubanos."

Storm borrowed McCoy's cigar, put it between her lips and drew the smoke into her lungs. Not surprisingly, she coughed and coughed and couldn't stop until Tioga handed her Dyce's Pellegrino which she sipped slowly.

Terry retrieved his Cohiba. Tioga leaned against the bar and then Storm leaned against her.

"Terry invited the governor. He texted back, 'I can't make it this time, but when I retire, I'll be there. Hope you don't have backlash.'"

Terry puffed on his cigar and looked like he was in a Nirvana of his own making. "Yeah, the gov gave us his seal of approval, though he's also wondering if he did the right thing and that makes me anxious. Bye-bye, kiddies. Daddy has to go back to work, make money to buy stuff, and then make more money, and buy even more stuff. Hey, I love you all!"

Storm looked like she was ready to leave with him, but something held her back. "It's a tough life," she said, sardonically.

Camilla offered McCoy a curtsy. "A pleasure meeting you, sir," she said and sounded sincere.

McCoy beamed. "Likewise, Miss Sanchez. I'm sure our paths will cross again."

With cigar in one hand and whip in the other, he walked toward the sign that read exit. Then he disappeared behind the black curtain that separated the bar from the long corridor that ran all the way to the lobby and the front desk.

Tioga turned away from the exit sign, looked at the CD on the shelf above the tequilas, then cocked her ear and caught the end of Jackson Browne singing "Tender is the Night."

"I try not to think of my ex when I hear this song. Tomás was at his best when he performed at Romeo's in the city. Then he went downhill fast. I wonder where he'll land."

Sean Dyce looked up at the speakers behind him. "It's a great tune. Jackson just nails it on that track." Then after a pause, he cracked his knuckles and in a serious tone of voice he added, "You know of course that the hotel has been running in the red for months. This crazy pot party is Terry's last-ditch effort to avoid bankruptcy. He's needed a goose with a golden egg. Who would have thought that it would be weed."

Camilla adjusted the beret on her head. Tioga took out her phone, checked her messages, and then went online. Jonny Field slipped into the room and sat all by himself at the far end of the bar, held his cell in his right hand and seemed to be communing with it. He had a cigar in his mouth. Dyce reached for a bottle of Pirate Rum with the skull and cross bones on the label. Then he mixed a daiquiri with enough rum for at least three drinks, placed a wedge of pineapple on the rim of the glass and set it down on a coaster in front of Jonny who slouched over.

Tioga put her arms around Storm and hugged her. "Imagine, Jonny Field, trying to be invisible in the Underground. Who's he kidding? No one could ever fail to notice the great Jonny Field!"

Dyce with his big broad shoulders occupied the space in front of the Mar Monte's chef. "No smoking," he said politely and pointed to the sign above the cash register.

Tioga cozied up to Jonny. "Do you have your American Spirits on you? I need a smoke. I mean tobacco, not weed."

Once again, Dyce pointed to the sign. "No smoking for little boys and no smoking for little girls like you either. So forget about feeding you nicotine habit."

Tioga removed a cigarette from the pack of American Spirits. "I feel better when I have a smoke between my fingers. Between my lips would be better."

Jonny's cell rang. He accepted the call, pressed the phone against his right ear and held his left hand against his left ear to block the noise in the room. Tioga tried to read his lips and didn't get far. When Jonny ended the call, he shook his head so violently that his hat flew from his head and landed upside down on the floor.

"Fuck, fuck!" he said and kicked the bar stool with his boot. "Fuck me. McCoy wants wild boar for Gina's dinner party. Now where the fuck can I get wild boar? I won't use frozen, and I don't have time to go hunting in the hills. Fuck, the son-of-a-bitch. If he thinks I have wild boar just lying around, he has his head up his ass."

Tioga played with the cigarette that she held between her fingers. "I bet my office mate can help you, Jonny," she said and turned to Camilla. "You can, can't you?"

Camilla wore a bemused expression on her face. "No, I can't help you. I don't deal in wild boar, but my mother does. She cooks at El Buen Comer. They have wild boar tacos, though I haven't tried them. I tend to be a vegetarian, but I'm not a purist."

Jonny looked at Camilla with disdain. "I hope you're not a full-time vegetarian!" he yelled. "If you are, you don't know what you're missing. I know that you haven't really sunk your teeth in my cooking."

Camilla borrowed a Sharpie from Sean and smirked. "Just pulling your leg, Jonny, about being a vegetarian. I'm not even part-time. Don't get so worked up, man." On a coaster for the Underground she wrote, "Victoria Sanchez, El Buen Comer, 707. 332. 8000." Then she handed it to Jonny.

"Thanks much," he said as he reached for his cell and punched in the number. "*Hola Hola* … Jonny Field *aqui* … From the hotel on the plaza … Yes, yes *si, si* … Friend of your daughter … I have to have wild boar … all you've got

… Okay … I'll be right there … Yes … *por favor* … No, leave it whole … Yes, of course, I'll bring cash … *Gracias*."

Jonny killed his phone, stood up and dashed for the same exit that had swallowed McCoy.

Tioga turned to Dyce and said, "Play something old, something your father would like."

Dyce reached for a CD on the shelf, popped it into the machine, turned up the volume and folded his arms across his chest.

Tioga listened to the opening bars and snapped her fingers. "Sinatra at Caesars in Vegas. My dad played it in the evening when he had a nightcap and smoked his pipe."

Dyce pumped his fist, as if to say he was juiced on the music.

"It's Sinatra, but this recording isn't from Caesars, as everyone thinks. It's from the Golden Nugget."

Tioga nodded her head, then reached for her phone and punched in the number that Flor had given her while they stood together near the front of the hotel. There was no answer. Maybe Flor had ripped her off, she thought. It wasn't impossible. She wasn't as innocent as she seemed.

Dyce wiped the zinc bar clean with a damp white linen towel. "I remember last summer. The heat swept across the Valley like a tidal wave and drove folks insane."

Storm had been listening to Sinatra with dreamy eyes. Now suddenly she snapped to attention, "Better a heat wave than a killer on the loose," she said to Dyce, and then to Tioga she added, "I wonder who's gonna show up dead next?"

On her way out of the hotel, Tioga saw the small boy with the cap and the T-shirt who had been in the elevator with her earlier in the day. This time he had a slingshot in one hand and three or four marbles in the other. He loaded his weapon, pulled back the rubber and fired away.

A schnauzer yelped; the boy laughed and retrieved his marble. Tioga followed him as he wandered about the lobby, then stopped and leaned against one of the pillars where he surveyed his battlefield. "That's not very nice, hitting the dog with your slingshot. You ought to stop before someone gets hurt."

The boy stuck out his tongue. "Make me."

She shot back, "Where's your mother?"

The boy had already vanished.

Robert Mitchum Busted for Possession of Pot

The line for the movie began in front of the box office at the Sebastiani and snaked along the sidewalk all the way to Tecumseh Alley, a block away. The marquee read the same as it had read that morning: "Rbt Mitchum & J. Greer Out of Past" and then in small letters "Midnight Show."

Storm arrived in tight jeans, heels, a rhinestone sweater and bright red lipstick. A dozen or so couples waited in line ahead of her, though she had already removed a credit card from her wallet and clutched it in her right hand. When she spotted Tioga crossing the street in front of the theater, she raised her left hand and waved.

"Over here," she shouted, and, when their eyes met, she added, "The lady just went into the box office. She's awfully pokey."

Tioga squeezed in front of a pale, fat man and a pale, thin woman, both of whom wore sweaters that were the same color as their pasty faces. They stood behind Tioga and took turns scowling. She scowled back. "We live here! We're not tourists."

Tioga and Storm both had sour expressions on their faces. "This is my girlfriend!" Tioga exclaimed, then put her arm around Storm and squeezed. "It's our big night out."

She turned her back on the couple and kissed Storm on her lips.

Camilla arrived out of breath in a purple beret that Tioga had not seen before. "I drove here right from the lab. Dropped off the blood sample and didn't have time to change. I feel grubby."

The line inched ahead. Storm chewed on her fingernails. Tioga looked toward the round face of the elderly cashier who sat in the box office, took money and credit cards hand-over-fist and issued tickets.

Camilla removed her beret, showed Tioga the label that read "Equity" and put it back on her head. "I just bought it at Louise's. She has splendid hats as well as lovely lingerie. But listen to this: Dorothy Baynes bought undies, bras and camisoles there. She didn't use a credit card, but paid in cash—twenties and hundreds—so Louise didn't have an address for her. Sounds like drug money to me. She recognized Dorothy from the photo I showed her. 'When we were girls,' Louise told me, 'Dot and I went to mass together at Saint Francis. Confession wasn't her thing. Neither was staying at home with mother.'"

Camilla took a deep breath and then went on buoyantly, as if delighted to be telling Tioga a story. "Louise explained that a horse trainer at the fairground didn't have to twist Dorothy's arm to persuade her to run away with him when the racetrack shut down for the season. Dorothy came back with a baby. Louise said that the father of the child was insanely jealous whenever she looked at another man. She saw him explode at Esperanza, Esperanza! He decked a guy twice his size."

Tioga trailed behind Camilla and Storm who now stood at the front of the line.

"Three adults," Storm said to the cashier, then handed over her credit card, took the tickets and gave one to Tioga and the other to Camilla.

"This is gonna be great," Tioga said. "I can feel it in my bones."

In the foyer, she studied the vintage black-and-white posters for *Pickup On South Street*, *Kiss Me Deadly* and *Out of the Past*. "I've never seen so many people show up for an old movie," she said. "It feels oddly validating, if you know what I mean."

At the counter, Storm bought a large box of popcorn. "No butter. Thanks." Turning to Camilla she said, "Cute hat," before she sprinkled salt, pepper and wheat germ on the popcorn. Tioga picked out a row near the front of the theater, selected seats in the middle, then waited until Storm and Camilla caught up with her, before she sat down with Camilla on her left and Storm on her right.

Storm placed the box with the popcorn in Tioga's lap. "I hated coming here with my sister when we were little, but now I love it," Storm said. She squeezed Tioga's hand and then leaned forward and explained to Camilla: "*Out of the Past* directed by Jacques Tourneur. Check out the lighting. Kirk Douglas was Mr. Nobody. Robert Mitchum was arrested after the film came out, along with Lila Leeds, and charged with possession of pot and went to prison. Isn't that crazy!"

Camilla scooped up a handful of popcorn. "Thanks for the lecture," she said sarcastically. Then she tapped Tioga on the shoulder. "I need to clear up one thing."

Tioga placed a handful of popcorn in her lap and nibbled one piece at a time. "What's that?"

Camilla squirmed in her seat. "Jonny and Gina are having an affair, right?" she asked.

Tioga shrugged her shoulders. "It's none of my business."

Camilla nodded her head and then turned toward the screen. "Maybe it's not your business now. But I bet it will be. You make everything your business." Tioga shrugged her shoulders again.

Storm leaned forward in her seat and turned toward Camilla. "No talking during the movie."

Not long after the opening credits—just when Mitchum lets down his guard and reveals his dark past to his goody-goody girlfriend—Storm explained, "This is a flashback."

Camilla looked at the screen and murmured, "Oh really, I thought it was the future."

When Jane Greer shows up in a white dress in a café in Mexico, and Mitchum swoons, Camilla whistled. "She's hot."

Storm blew on her hand as if she had burned it. "Hella hot." Then she scooped up another handful of popcorn. "Beautiful and deadly. That's the way we like 'em."

Finally Storm and Camilla both settled down and watched without comment, while Tioga wandered in and out of the picture and wondered about Dorothy Baynes and her mother.

In fact, she didn't pay much attention to the movie until Jane Greer kills Robert Mitchum's partner and Mitchum goes berserk. "It's like *The Maltese Falcon*, except that Bogie doesn't die in the end," she said. Then, under her breath, she added, "I love sweet Dickie Moore as the deaf and dumb kid, but I don't like the miserable ending."

When the screen turned black, she sat quietly with her hands in her lap. So did Camilla and Storm, while everyone else in the row stood up and filed out of the theater. Camilla picked up the popcorn box and held it in her hands. "Don't you see, the movie had to finish that way. To tell you the truth, I hate happy endings."

Storm blinked her eyes when the lights came on. "Not me. I have to have a kiss at the end, or I can't go to sleep at night. Mitchum and Greer could have run away to Acapulco."

Tioga shook her head and then nudged Storm with her shoulder. "Impossible! Don't you see? They're doomed from the start like all crazy lovers."

Camilla stood up, made her way down the aisle and tossed the empty popcorn box into the trash at the back of the theater. Storm and Tioga followed her into the lobby and then across the plaza and toward City Hall, its white walls illuminated by bright lights. Storm, who had taken the lead, stopped abruptly and turned around to face both Camilla and Tioga who walked side by side and at a leisurely pace. "Looks like we're headed back to the hotel."

Tioga lowered her head and trudged forward. "Force of habit. Wild horses couldn't keep me away. The Mar Monte is an addiction."

A crowd of potheads—she could smell them—milled about on the sidewalk in front of the hotel. Gridlock engulfed the plaza. Horns honked. Motorists shouted. Aaron stood in the middle of the street and tried to direct traffic, but that was a feat more challenging than he or anyone else could handle, except perhaps, Tioga mused, Superman or Wonder Woman. "Outta the way, boy," someone shouted.

Tioga watched as Aaron's face turned blue-black. "Who said boy?"

Aaron shook his head. "I don't know, but the numb chucks all share the thought," he said as if neither sticks nor stones nor words could break his bones or tarnish his soul.

With an industrial-size flashlight, he went back to directing the traffic that finally began to move foot-by-foot and car-by-car.

Tioga hoped she might see Flor and the boy with the Rolling Stones T-shirt that he wore as if it protected him from all evil. When she didn't see them, she dashed up the carpeted stairs, pulled the door toward her and held it open for Storm and Camilla who had walked lazily behind her. At the front desk, not a single clerk was on duty, though a phone rang and rang, and a guest with luggage clamored for "service."

The hookah was gone, though the lobby still reeked of marijuana. The tent had been dismantled, the papier-mâché palm trees had been disassembled and the faux elephants—with their trunks and tusks—pushed into a far corner of the lobby, which now took on the appearance of an ersatz elephant graveyard.

Someone had scrawled graffiti on the wall that said, "Free Weed For All!" and "Thank you, Terry for a Great Pot Party!" A man in overalls had just started to remove the slogans. The two bearded fellows that Tioga had seen in the bar now reclined, obscenely, she thought, on the carpet, naked from the waist up, their tattoos visible to one and all. The waitress who had performed her act in the Underground for McCoy and Storm lay sprawled between them in a pair of red thong underwear. Beer and wine bottles littered the lobby, along with pipes, roaches and rigs for dabbing. Candles had burned out and wax had dripped on the floor and the carpet. The previous evening was now only a memory.

Storm seemed to be lost in her head. Camilla surveyed the damage in the lobby. Tioga tried and failed to tune out the muzak that sounded like, but wasn't, the Beatles. Matt Chehab raced toward the three women, then pulled up short, and at the proverbial last second avoided a collision with Tioga who yelled, "Hey, watch where you're going."

Bug-eyed and blue in the face, Chehab grabbed his throat with his left hand and squeezed as if to force his words into the open. "Bit of a cold," he squeaked. Then in a raspy voice he added, "Every room is taken and we're booked solid for the month. That means we're out of the red! Hallelujah!"

Storm scowled. Camilla frowned. Tioga smiled reluctantly. "I guess that's good news. Lucky for Storm and me, we have the penthouse for another month."

Chehab walked bowlegged toward the front desk, stopped and glanced over his right shoulder. "Enjoy it while it lasts," he said wickedly. Camilla wandered across the lobby and then darted down the hallway that led to A Chez Nous, the Mar Monte's three-star restaurant where a hostess in a short skirt and a blue gauze blouse greeted her and her companions.

"Table for three," Camilla said and helped herself to menus and the wine list. One-by-one, they followed the hostess to a table at the back of the room that was covered with a white linen tablecloth.

Camilla plopped down in the leather booth. Tioga sat on one side of her and Storm on the other. "We have you trapped," Storm teased.

Camilla opened the menu and then looked up at the hostess who towered above her, pad and pencil in hand. "Is Jonny cooking tonight?" Camilla asked. "I hope so."

The hostess wore a weary expression on her face. "Jonny prepared everything on the menu and then had to leave with Mrs. McCoy," she said, then turned and surveyed the dining room. "As you can see, the place has emptied out, though earlier we had a full house. It's our policy to stay open as long as someone wants to eat."

Camilla examined the entrées with much the same intensity she had examined the list of drinks at the Underground. "Pappardelle with wild boar ragu! Sounds out of this world."

The hostess played with her pigtails. "Unfortunately, we've run out. It was a sensation."

Camilla folded the menu and tossed it on the table. "Oh shit. That's the story of my life. I'm always too late, or too early for everything."

Tioga stood up and excused herself from the table. "Order for me. I want something with protein." She looked at the time on her cell and walked to the ladies room at the back of the restaurant. Standing in front of the mirror above the sink, she studied her own reflection.

"Who the fuck are you?" she asked, and, after a pause, added "You still don't have a clue, do you?" The door opened and closed and heels clattered on the tile floor. A woman stood at the adjacent mirror and applied lipstick.

"It's okay, dear," she said. "I do it, too. I mean, talk to myself in the ladies." Tioga peered at the reflection of the woman with blond hair, blue eyes and the palest complexion.

"What's that?" Tioga asked. "I was distracted and didn't hear you."

The woman puckered her lips. "Talk to myself. I do it all the time. My husband can't carry on a conversation. I have to talk to myself."

Tioga turned away from the mirror, looked directly at the woman and decided that she preferred the reflection; it made her features seem less harsh.

"Do you know who you are?" Tioga asked. "I certainly don't know who I am."

The woman shuttered her blue eyes for a moment and then returned the lipstick to her purse. "Oh, there's no real me, not anymore. Not after this marriage. I'm just a shadow of a self. Maybe it's the same for you."

Tioga stared into the mirror and mimicked the woman's tone of voice. "There is no real me," she said and sounded like the woman with a face but no self who stood next to her. Then she repeated the same words, this time with emphasis on the word real: "There is no real me either."

The woman washed her hands—the whitest hands Tioga had ever seen—and then dried them with the machine that blew hot air. "Now you've got the hang of it," the woman said. "If you'll excuse me I'm going back to the orgy in my suite." She paused for a moment and added, "Or should I say, the party."

The door closed with a bang. Tioga looked at her cell. How much time had lapsed while she gabbed in the ladies? She didn't remember what time it was when she stood up from the table and excused herself, though she had consulted her cell. Had an hour disappeared? She had lost track of time, again. She could blame the weed.

When she returned to the table, Camilla and Storm were sipping margaritas. Sean Dyce had joined them; he was AWOL from his post at the Underground and looked as if a liberated man. In his right hand he held a stein with a frothy head. For once he was drinking and not serving drinks. Storm eyed the bus boy who carried a stack of dirty plates. "Dyce was telling us about a guy who deals weed right here in the Mar Monte. He swears the hotel gets a cut."

Dyce banged his stein on the table. "I did not swear that anyone in this hotel gets a cut or that anyone besides me knows the dealer. What I said was ..."

Camilla cut him off before he could finish. "Yeah, yeah. Always covering for Terry McCoy. Don't want anything to come back and bite your butt, do you?"

Tioga laughed harder than she had laughed all day. There had not been much to laugh about and certainly not with Mrs. Baynes in her curlers and her impossible request for the gold ring on her daughter's finger.

The weed had not only made her lose track of time. It had also made her feel frisky; she reached for Sean's mug, lifted it and drained the last of the beer. "I think you're being excessively harsh about Sean, Camilla. He's looking out for himself, not Terry."

She rested her head on Dyce's shoulder. Just then the waitress arrived with the entrées: a Cobb salad for Storm; a grilled pork chop with mashed potatoes for Camilla and duck confit for Tioga, who took one look at the plate and recoiled. "I absolutely won't eat duck," she said to Storm. "How could you not remember?" Storm lifted Tioga's plate and replaced it with her Cobb salad.

"Okay," Tioga said and began to remove the bits of bacon.

Camilla unfolded her napkin and placed it in her lap. "I was teasing Sean about covering for Terry. I'm in a teasing mood tonight." She put her arm around him and pulled him toward her in a lovey-dovey manner that seemed to have become contagious in the Mar Monte. "Come to me, big boy," she said, looking more fetching, or so it seemed, than she had looked all evening.

Tioga reached for Storm's margarita. Camilla looked alarmed. "It's a bad idea to mix drinks, especially when you had the cannabis concentrate in the green dragon."

She paused, then stared at Tioga and asked, "Are you still stoned." Tioga drained the last of Storm's margarita.

"Yeah," she said to Camilla. "The dope kicked in about half way through the movie. Jane Greer never looked more ravishing."

Tioga turned to Dyce and said, "I'd like to meet the guy who's dealing dope in the hotel." Sean lifted his head and raised the empty stein. "I would also like to meet him," he said slowly and deliberately as if he didn't want anyone to misconstrue his words. "I'm told he gives away free samples the first time. After that, the price is pretty steep. But he's elusive. I've only actually caught him dealing twice; he takes the money in one hand and gives out the weed in the other and then he splits."

Tioga looked at the empty glasses on the table and frowned. "Is it illegal to deal in the Mar Monte?" she asked. "Would he have to have a permit?"

Dyce stood up and backed away from the table a step at a time. "Terry's not going to let a rogue dealer operate here." Then with the grace of a courtier, he added, "Excuse me, ladies. I gotta go back to work and get folks juiced. Each to her own poison." To Tioga he whispered, "I'll try to hook you up with the guy, but don't count on it. He only takes cash, no checks, no credit cards and he won't make change either; he's a born hustler.

Tioga looked at the Cobb salad and didn't know where to begin to attack. Storm cut the duck leg into small pieces and then ate them one-by-one, along with the bite-sized potatoes roasted in duck fat.

Camilla admired the pork chop on her plate and then signaled for the waitress. "Mustard, please." When it arrived she slathered Grey Poupon on the chop and sliced the meat from the bone. "In the bar, I thought Terry was going to whip one of us," Camilla observed. "I wasn't sure which one." Storm put down her knife and fork. "When he was at the JC, I took him to The Rubicon, the S & M place, in the city. A teenage girl whipped him good. Then he grabbed the whip and lashed her. That's his MO—bait and switch."

Tioga eyed the empty tables in the room. Her body, she noticed, felt oddly detached from her head and that wasn't the work of the weed. It came from someplace deeper. "We ought to blackmail Terry," she quipped. Then she added mournfully, "I'm joking, of course. Blackmail Terry and he'll blackmail you. I'm sure he has a ton of dirt on me. After all I haven't been an angel."

Camilla looked distressed. "You're paranoid," she said and could barely keep her eyes open.

Tioga didn't like Camilla's accusation. Indeed, her comment went beyond insinuation. "You better hope Terry doesn't have shit on you!" She pushed her plate toward the edge of the table, and glanced at the food she hadn't eaten. "Lunch for tomorrow." She signaled for the waitress who boxed the leftovers and then handed out dessert menus. Tioga refused to peek at the list of pies, tarts, flans and more. "No thanks," she said stubbornly. "Dope never makes me crave sweets—quite the opposite. I like savory when I'm stoned."

Storm added, "Ditto" and Camilla echoed her, albeit in Spanish, "*Lo mismo*." The waitress placed the check on the table, and Storm signed her initials. "The food and drink are on me," she said and then asked the waitress, "Did you happen to have a joint on you?"

The waitress looked flummoxed. "Excuse me?" she asked, as if she hadn't heard the question.

Tioga wasn't amused. "Don't play dumb!" she shouted. "We know you're a stoner." She reached into her wallet and placed two crisp twenty-dollar bills on the table. The waitress pocketed the cash and then made herself very small, indeed.

Tioga patted Camilla's hand. "You can spend the night on the couch in the penthouse. It's pretty comfy. You'll have hot water and a lovely view of the plaza. In the morning I'll howl and show you I can sound like a she-wolf."

Camilla stood up and grabbed hold of the table to steady her knees, which had buckled. "Tasoray," she said and slurred her speech. She had had way too much to drink. Then she gathered her wits about her, forced herself to enunciate slowly and clearly and added, "Yeah, I can sleep on the cot in the office and be early to work, for a change."

"Whatever! Whenever!" Tioga said to herself. In the lobby, she kissed Camilla on both cheeks and then hugged her tenderly. "Are you sure you can make it to the office by yourself?"

Camilla arched her back. "I'm fine," she asserted, though she did not look fine. Then she added, "See you in the morning."

Tioga looked for Storm and didn't see her. She walked up the stairs and counted from one to one hundred twenty-five as she climbed higher and higher. On the top floor, she pushed the half-opened door with her foot, then stepped inside the penthouse and silently nudged the door closed. Storm lay sprawled naked across the bed, her hands cupping her breasts. Jeans, blouse, bra and socks were scattered across the bedroom floor. Her earrings sat on the table next to the alarm clock. From the speakers came two voices harmonizing. The CD read, "Tony Bennett and k.d. lang: What a Wonderful World."

"I'm be right with you," Tioga said. "Gotta wash off the grime and the crime."

Storm sat up, fluffed her pillow and leaned back. "No rush. I'm not going anywhere. It's too comfy here. I'm lovin' it."

Tioga removed the clothes she had worn all day until there was a second pile on the floor.

Storm watched her undress. "No bra, I see, but you're wearing a man's underpants again. A kind of chastity belt."

Tioga picked up the underpants, hurled them at Storm and hit her on her nose, though no harm was done.

"I bought these on the plaza," she said. "Fortunately they had my size. And the color is right." She blew Storm a kiss, went into the bathroom, left the door ajar, sat down on the toilet and peed. Then she showered, brushed her teeth and wrapped herself in a bath towel. In the bedroom, she collapsed next to Storm who looked up at the ceiling that was decorated with blue stars against a black sky and that made Tioga think of heaven.

"Terry told me I ought to take a break from my nightly performances," Storm said. "The crowds aren't what they once were." Then she added mournfully, "Terry has been flirting with me again. He must be bored with Gina." Tioga kissed Storm on the lips; they were little kisses, fleeting kisses, but they tasted no less sweet to her than kisses that might have lingered longer. "Flirting never hurt anyone," she said slowly. "If I were you, I wouldn't sue for sexual harassment, not yet anyway."

Storm removed the bath towel that Tioga had wrapped around her body. Then she fluffed Tioga's pillow and placed it against the wall.

"Taking a break sounds good to me," Tioga said. "It would give you time to come up with new material."

Storm moved her eyes down from the stars on the ceiling to her own toenails that were painted chartreuse. Then she turned and rested her head on the pillow. "Yes, I could take a break. I could work up a new act, reinvent myself and surprise a bunch of people, myself included." With her outstretched arms, she reached up for Tioga. "But come here, come to me," she said and stretched her legs all the way to the end of the bed, placed her hands behind her head and opened her round mouth as far as it would go. "I'm ready to leave this place before it gets overripe and feels rotten. The pot party was too much. I don't like Terry bringing weed into the Mar Monte."

Tioga stretched out on top of Storm. "I see. You're a purist."

She pressed her lips against Storm's lips. This time her kisses lingered. She kissed Storm's eyes and her mouth ferociously, moved slowly from her lips to her throat, then to her breasts, her belly and her firm, white thighs. Tioga rolled onto her back, looked up at the ceiling with the blue stars that twinkled brightly and heaved a sigh. Storm massaged Tioga's neck. "Oh, oh, oh," Tioga cried. "Don't stop." But Storm stopped. Then she began to kiss Tioga again. She started at her ankles, turned her over and inched her way up to her mouth, with a long interlude at her mons and then at the delta of her Venus. Tioga's mind, which had run roughshod over her ever since she woke that morning, now went blank; she could not think. For the first time that day, she did not wonder who or what she was. It didn't matter. Nothing mattered now. Nothing except her body and Storm's body, their legs entwined, mouths wide open, legs spread apart, two lovers moving slowly, taking short breaths, the stars above looking down at them as they heaved, and then found the rhythm that carried them into the darkness in which they were as one and indivisible.

Part III
The Deal

Enter Hawk

Tioga slept in, though she woke before Storm and wasted no time in the shower or before the mirror where she admired her girlie outfit with its frills and lace. Then she wrote a note: "Love you, Ti," and left it on the bed table. By 9 a.m. she was already running late; she grabbed her phone, her purse and her backpack. Downstairs, the lobby had already been scrubbed and vacuumed, dusted and waxed. No graffiti remained. There wasn't a trace of the marijuana madness. The air smelled like lavender, though Tioga didn't see any lavender. The aroma seemed to be piped in through the ducts for heat and for air conditioning. "Where's the lavender coming from?" she asked Aaron, who looked as if he had slept on a rock.

"Don't know," he said in a grumpy tone of voice and with both hands tried to remove the wrinkles from his face. "The A's clinched in extra innings on a walk-off home run by Semien. I won back the money I lost the previous day when I bet on the Giants. That was dumb of me. Giants aren't going anywhere, except down to the cellar and not coming back this season."

He had Tioga's undivided attention and went with it. "Around midnight I hooked up with my cousin, Niasha, from Richmond. She drove us to Esperanza Esperanza in her BMW. Right away a sleaze bag from New Jersey with speed hit on her. I bugalooed to James Brown. Got a ride home from Jonny Field, who had stopped for a nightcap."

Tioga straightened Aaron's polka dot tie and adjusted the blue Mar Monte cap that he must have tossed on the top of his head without looking in the mirror to adjust it properly. "We can't have you looking unprofessional," she said as she checked the time on her cell, which made her all the more anxious. It was nearly ten and she had already lost precious minutes. Then she added, "Last night I heard from Sean about a guy selling weed in the hotel."

Aaron smiled sweetly, and his big round cheeks puffed out. "Aside from me, I don't know anyone else in the Mar Monte who's really dealing, though there's a sleazebag who thinks he's hot shit. You know, I don't advertise. Those who want weed find weed or weed finds them. Tourists think folks like me smokes pot, so they hits on me."

Tioga nodded and pointed to the croissants under the glass. "I'll take two of those and two cappuccinos. Camilla slept in the office last night and probably didn't get much rest. She'll want her fix."

She nibbled on the crispy end of a nicely browned croissant and sipped on one of the cappuccinos. Then she handed Aaron a twenty. "When you have something really kick-ass let me know. I heard there's a glut and that the price is way down."

Aaron counted the change. "Yeah, the big boys have flooded the market to put little guys like me out of the biz. Before long, it's gonna be Walmart weed."

Aaron offered Tioga a handful of coins, but she pushed his hand aside. "Keep the change." Then she knit her brow and added, "I've heard it's down to five hundred a pound, and not that long ago, when my ex was dealing, it was four thousand. It's fucked up."

On the sidewalk outside the Sebastiani, she looked up at the marquee that now read, Bogart & Astor, on the top line, and below it, in all caps, THE MALTESE FALCON. Tioga took the elevator to the top floor and listened to the comforting echo of her shoes on the tiles. She stopped in front of the door to her office and read her own name in big black letters on the opaque glass: "Tioga Vignetta, Op," and added "That's who you are now. That's all you need to be."

The door was closed, but not locked. Tioga turned the knob. Camilla's fingers flew across the keyboard. She removed the headphones, looked up and saw Tioga standing before her in a girlie dress and bangles on her wrists. "I slept okay," Camilla said lazily. "It's surprisingly quiet here at night."

She grabbed one of the coffee containers that Tioga held in her outstretched hand. Then she reached for one of the croissants that she ripped apart and devoured. "You have a visitor," she said and raised her eyebrows. "A man wearing a fedora and a pendant around his neck. Calls himself 'Hawk.' Looks like one, too."

Tioga peered at the opaque window on the door that separated the inner from the outer office, as if she might see the visitor, or at least his silhouette, but it was no go.

"I tried to keep him out here, but he insisted on going in," Camilla said. "Claimed he had to make a call and had to have privacy. Before I could stop him, he opened the door and went in. I heard him on the phone. I'm sorry. I tried."

Tioga sipped her coffee. "I'm sure I won't enjoy meeting him. I'm sure I won't want to work for him either, not after he's been in there poking around."

Camilla swallowed the last of the croissant and washed it down with the last few drops of the now cold coffee. "Oh, man, I needed that. Now I can think straight."

Tioga opened the door to her office, took in the clutter on her desk and stared at the back of the man who examined the framed "Leda and the Swan" on the wall. "It's for sale," she said. "We're asking $25,000, though that's negotiable. My father's the artist. I don't get a commission."

The man turned 180 degrees and looked as if that was a real achievement. "Leda seems to be a young boy, not a young girl or a young woman. The short hair does it, though your hair is also quite short now that I get a closer look." He studied the background of the painting while he rubbed his chin. "Very interesting. The landscape, with redwoods, pines and eucalyptus trees, must be the Valley."

Once more he admired Leda. "The figure does have some feminine features, but the breasts are rather small."

Tioga stared at the hat—a Borsalino, not a fedora as Camilla thought—that sat precariously on the man's large head as if he dared it to fall. His gestures, his stance and his facial expressions made Tioga think of someone she had seen in a movie, but she couldn't remember which one. "Yes, Leda has small breasts," she said as if to test the waters between her and the man in the Borsalino. "Almost pre-teen breasts."

His cell buzzed. He answered the call immediately and turned to face the window that looked out at the plaza. "That's brilliant. I'm so glad you told me. Yes, I'll take all of it. Yes, right away. I'll be over."

He ended the call and turned to face Tioga once again and with an apologetic expression on his face. "Excuse me, but that was unavoidable," he said and extended his right hand, which oddly enough, he had not yet done. He glanced at the opaque window behind Tioga. "It's noisier in the front office than in here."

Tioga took his hand and noticed that his skin felt smooth as silk. She looked at the pendant and then at the hat, which he removed and held in his hands.

"Funny office," he said. "I can hear the movie downstairs. It must be the early show."

Tioga cocked her right ear. "Ah, yes, *The Maltese Falcon*. It just started a few minutes ago. They test the print to make sure there are no glitches. That's Brigid O'Shaughnessy now. She wants Sam Spade to find her sister."

The man twirled his Borsalino. "Oh, don't reveal the plot and ruin it," he said in a voice that reminded her again of a man in a movie, the name of which she couldn't recall, though it was on the tip of her tongue. Then he added, "I was hoping you'd find a woman, not my sister, but a friend who has disappeared. I've heard that you're a missing persons expert." He smiled and revealed teeth that looked pearly white. "Excuse me, I neglected to introduce myself. Bad of me. Call me Hawk. Not my real name, but that's how I'm known, even at the Mar Monte. I saw you the other day at the shindig. Maybe you didn't see me. I was dressed as a Thuggee, since the theme was South Asia. I decided not to play the Raj."

He handed Tioga a business card with the name Hawk, a phone number in area code 415, and in the upper left-hand corner the image of a raptor with a large beak. "You notice the resemblance, don't you," he said and turned his head to the side so that Tioga could appreciate his hawk-like nose.

Tioga took a cigarette from the pack on her desk, offered one to Hawk and then allowed him to light hers before he lit his own. She might have been Jane Greer. He might have been Robert Mitchum. Perhaps they, too, were doomed. She inhaled once and then again quickly, flicking the ash into the coffee cup that sat on her desk. "That's not a fedora you're wearing, is it? I believe it's a Borsalino."

Hawk nodded. Now he looked perfectly happy. "Most people don't know the difference. Yes, it's a Borsalino made in Milano, Italy. The pendant I'm wearing, which has the yin and yang symbols, was made in China. It's very old and very valuable, at least to me, though I don't know the monetary value."

Perhaps, Tioga thought, Hawk with his hat and his pendant was a spiritual pilgrim who had washed ashore in the Valley.

He twirled the pendant until yin turned into yang and yang into yin. Then he added slowly, as if he had to find the right words, "It's a gift from the woman I want you to find. Her name is Roxanne Jacobs and, no, she's not my sister." He reached into his gray jacket that matched his trousers, retrieved a black-and-white photo and handed it to Tioga, though he seemed reluctant to let go of it. "That's her. It's the only photo I have. Roxanne never liked to have her picture taken. Vanity I suppose."

Tioga studied the photo, and, while the face of the woman struck her as familiar, she couldn't remember where or when she might have seen her. She turned it over, then righted it quickly and noticed how cautious she felt in Hawk's presence. "She's striking, isn't she? Looks Nordic, and while she seems familiar, I can't place her. It's been that kind of week."

Hawk paced back and forth. "Roxanne was spotted at La Bamba, the taco truck that's parked in Boyes Hot Spring across from Cervantes Hardware. Maybe you could start there. I'm eager for you to make contact."

Tioga circled her desk and then stood behind it and looked down at the stack of files. "Do you know a woman named Dorothy Baynes?"

Hawk turned his head to the side and, with his fingers, rubbed his nose, perhaps hoping he might make it look less like a beak. "No, I don't know a Dorothy Baynes. Am I supposed to?"

The door opened and Camilla poked her head into Tioga's office. "I'm going to the morgue at *The Gazette*. I'll have my cell."

At the copy machine behind her desk, Tioga made a facsimile of the photo of Roxanne and handed it to Camilla. "See if anyone at La Bamba and in Boyes Hot Springs recognizes her."

Camilla stared at the photo as if committing it to memory. Then she opened the door, stepped across the threshold and closed it behind her.

The outer office went dark. Camilla's shoes echoed in the corridor. Hawk leaned forward. "Your secretary strikes me as unfriendly. Before I opened my mouth, she made up her mind not to like me."

Tioga lowered the Venetian blinds that helped to keep out the rays of the sun. Oh, dear, poor Mr. Hawk. Somehow, Tioga couldn't feel sorry for him, though he seemed to want her sympathy.

"Camilla's new, and she's not my secretary. She's my apprentice and, yes, she can be impulsive, but impulses can be helpful in our line of work. I wouldn't judge her harshly if I were you."

Hawk raised his arms as if he might take wing and fly. Then he lowered them slowly until they came to rest. "Camilla could use manners." Then he paused a moment and added, "Roxanne Jacobs is thirty-seven, stands out in a crowd, disappeared from a house at number forty-nine Avenida del Virgen, where she was visiting friends. The girls out there haven't seen her for sometime. But if she was spotted at La Bamba, she hasn't gone far."

Tioga paced in front of her desk, all the while keeping her eyes on Hawk. "I see you've been playing detective," she said in a dismissive tone of voice. Then she peered down at Hawk and asked, as if the idea had just popped into her head, "Why not go to the police?"

Hawk turned his Borsalino round and round. "The cops here are notoriously sloppy. Besides I need someone who won't make waves."

Tioga nodded. "You want someone to move surreptitiously."

Hawk looked up from his beloved hat. "Discreetly," he replied. Then with real force in his voice he added, "My biggest fear is that Roxanne is being held somewhere against her will."

Tioga examined the black-and-white photo and once again tried to place the face. "Hmmm. I think I understand what you mean about the police, and if Roxanne is jumpy, you wouldn't want to scare her off."

Hawk recoiled for a moment and then composed himself. "I'm sure she's alive, though in dangerous waters," he snapped. Then he added, "By the way, Miss Vignetta, you come highly recommended."

Tioga smiled reluctantly. "I do have a reputation," she said and tried not to sound boastful. Then she couldn't help adding, "I handled a case not long ago that made the tabloids. I found a woman who had left her husband, moved a block away, changed her appearance and her name, got a new job and remarried, though she never got a divorce. Husband number one wanted her back. Go figure. Then she was hit by a car on the street in front of her house and died instantly. Both husbands attended the funeral. So did I."

Tioga laughed at her own story. "But who touted me?"

Hawk smiled a real smile, though it didn't last long. "Oh, the person who recommend you was Gina McCoy. She says you're great."

Then after a moment that seemed to drag on, he added, "Of course, I'd heard about you previously. On the big island, I met your ex. We're both surfers. He mentioned casually that he'd been married to a woman who worked as a PI."

Tioga looked down at the file that read "Divorce" and turned it over. "And what kind of work do you do now, Hawk?"

He walked to the window and peered down at the leafy green trees. "Great view of the plaza," he said enthusiastically. Then he turned around and said, "I'm in sales. It's the only thing I know how to do, though I've also grown grapes and made wine. Who doesn't around here?"

Tioga stared at the yin and yang pendant. "You're a spiritual fellow?" she asked.

Hawk smirked, then lifted the pendant and twirled it. "I wear this for good luck. I'm superstitious and for good reason. As long as I wear it, I know Roxanne will turn up alive." Then he paused for just a moment and added, "I'm not like the spiritual sluts in this Valley who migrate from one religion to another. I wouldn't be surprised if people around here worship their own ancestors."

Hawk stepped forward, took a deep breath and held it. He seemed to suck all the air out of the room. Indeed, he occupied far too much space for his own good, Tioga thought. He was too big, too tall, and too loud. He exhaled and went on. "Two girls, Katrina and Maya, live in the house at forty-nine Avenida de la Virgen in Boyes Hot Springs, not far from the highway," he said. "They don't think well of me, but then again they don't think well of men. I'm sure you'll have better luck than I."

Tioga added the names Katrina and Maya to her cell, along with the address on Avenida de la Virgen. "And Roxanne, is she partial to men or to women?"

Hawk reached into the rear pocket of his slacks and removed a bulging leather wallet. "Roxanne has gone both ways for as long as I've known her. Apparently, it works."

Tioga nodded, then glanced at the calendar on the wall and calculated in her head. "I charge by the tenth-of-the-hour, plus expenses, though I'd accept a retainer if you want to go that route. I carry a gun. I've been a licensed PI for twelve years. I've found a lot of missing persons, mostly alive, but not always. It's odd, but people come to the Valley to disappear. There's something about the place. They say that geography is destiny."

Hawk removed a thick wad of bills from his wallet. "This ought to cover you for awhile," he said, and handed the cash to Tioga, who took one look and said, "You've given me far too much."

Hawk twirled the yin and yang medallion. "Oh, no. I know you're worth every penny."

Tioga took a white envelope from the top drawer of her desk. "Since you put it that way, I'll take it."

She wrote "Hawk" and "$10,000" on the outside of the envelope and dropped it on top of the file labeled "Divorce." "Why don't I call you tomorrow, and I'll let you know what progress, if any, I've made. I assume I can reach you at the number on your card."

The Borsalino man covered his mouth with the back of his left hand and laughed nervously. "If you call the front desk at the Mar Monte and ask to speak to Hawk they'll connect you to my room. Maybe you'll join me later for a drink or maybe you'll burn one with me."

Tioga glanced at the envelope on her desk, as if it might suddenly take flight and vanish. "What about Maya and Katrina? Do you have last names to go with the first names?"

Hawk rose from his chair and smiled. "I guess everything is right as rain."

Tioga smiled and waited for an answer to her question, but it never came. In fact, Hawk looked as if he had not heard her. He placed the Borsalino on the top of his head, adjusted the brim and saluted Tioga. "I learned that in the military. I have that in common with your ex, that and surfing and a few other things." He reached inside his jacket, removed a small, shiny cylinder and tossed it to Tioga. "It's *pakalolo* from your ex. He grows good shit."

Tioga tossed the cylinder back to Hawk. "That's kind of you, but cannabis would be wasted on me. I don't indulge. Find someone who'd appreciate it."

Hawk looked displeased. "Oh well, your ex led me to believe that you were a stoner."

Tioga smirked. "I was a teenager once and a surfer, too. But we all grow up, don't we? Pot doesn't agree with me, and I don't agree with it."

She followed Hawk from the inner to the outer office. Then she walked with him along the hallway with its black-and-white tiles and stopped under the chandelier halfway to the elevator.

"What I've been meaning to ask," she began and then repeated herself a second time, "What I've been meaning to ask is, if and when I find Roxanne, then what? I have to know that you don't mean to harm her. Because if you think there's even the remotest possibility of that, I can't help you. If you want your money back, I'll give it to you. We can make a clean break. There's still time."

She meant what she said, and yet at the same time she knew instinctively that she didn't want to return the money. After all it was now hers.

Hawk removed the Borsalino, held it in his right hand, and focused his eyes on the floor as if trying to read the pattern in the black-and-white tiles. "You've got me all wrong if you think I could or would harm Roxanne. I love her too much. I just have to see her and know that she's alright."

Tioga peered into Hawk's dark brown eyes as if she might see the inside of his big head. "I trust you only so far," she said.

Hawk rocked back and forth on the balls of his feet. Then he took Tioga's right hand in his, bent down and kissed it before she knew what he'd had in mind.

"If you leave the Mar Monte let me know," she said, sounding flummoxed. "And if you hear anything new about Roxanne call me immediately."

She turned and walked back to her office, while Hawk raced for the elevator, just as the door opened and Camilla stepped into the hallway.

"I'm coming," Hawk shouted. He darted into the elevator. The door closed and then the motor made the sound of a galumphing elephant.

Tioga stared at the black-and-white tiles. "A man who can't miss an elevator going down is a man in an awful rush," she sneered.

Inside the office, Camilla removed her beret and placed a manila envelope on her desk. "The other day, I saw that fellow in a booth at the Underground, groping a woman. She kicked him and fled."

Tioga sighed. "He just forked over ten thousand dollars in cash. We don't have to accept it. I could call him and tell him the deal is off."

Camilla sat down at her desk and booted up her computer. "That kind of money will buy a lot of very pretty things."

Tioga sat down on the edge of Camilla's desk. "It will," she said and sounded agreeable. Then she looked at the screen on Camilla's computer and asked, "Did you find anything juicy at *The Gazette*?"

Camilla handed Tioga the envelope that she had carried into the office. "Yes, a black-and-white picture of Dorothy Baynes. I made a copy and there's a news story to go with it. When she was eighteen, she worked at the county fair. At the end of the season, she ran off with a man twice her age. Her mother reported her as missing. Dorothy made a habit of that—running off, I mean. There's nothing about the man in the story, except that he trained racehorses. Then a year or so later, there was a second story about Dorothy with the headline, 'Hometown girl returns.' I also copied it. Mona, at the front desk, told me that Mrs. Baynes sued Terry McCoy, Jeremiah Langley and *The Gazette* for invasion of privacy and libel, too. Her lawyer argued the story cast mother and daughter in false light. McCoy's lawyer offered a First Amendment defense. The judge didn't buy it, though rumor had it that McCoy tried to pay him off. It backfired."

Camilla arched her back and stretch her arms. "Mrs. Baynes won an out-of-court settlement. There's nothing about that in the paper, but I ran into Sean Dyce outside the Mar Monte and he said that McCoy hired Randy Scheck and that Scheck worked out a deal with Baynes. That was before I went to work for him."

She stopped short, looked up at the ceiling and then down again, as if she'd found a lost thought. "Oh, and get this, Mona said that Randy told her that Dorothy Baynes fucked a lot of guys at the race track, though she didn't use the 'f' word. 'Dated' was what she said. We all know what that means."

Tioga picked up the envelope with Hawk's cash and handed it to Camilla. "Go ahead, crunch the numbers," she said and waited while Camilla counted to ten thousand. She added, "Deposit it in my business account and enter the amount in the ledger. With Mr. Borsalino, we'd better keep the books straight." Tioga lifted the file marked "Divorce." "Hawk mentioned some weird shit about me as a stoner that he claimed he heard from my ex. I didn't like what he said. I didn't like it one bit. It made me angry at my ex all over again."

Camilla looked like a little lost girl—if not exactly like a little lost girl then like a woman who was over her head and in danger of losing it. Still Tioga could see that she refused to let herself go under.

"I know what you mean about Hawk," Camilla said. "I'm beginning to wonder because for one thing, at La Bamba, I couldn't find anyone who recognized Roxanne from the photo. But I didn't believe them either. At La Bamba they're all related and they're covering for one another, the father, the two sons, and an aunt they call Wonder Woman. I talked to her in Spanish and she talked to me in English. The father, who does most of the cooking, told me, 'I have papers; we all have papers.'"

Camilla threw her hands in the air and then smiled knowingly at Tioga. "Then the father made me a pork *torta* with enough *jalapeños* to choke a horse. 'Have a nice day,' he said and wouldn't take my money. As I was leaving, he shouted, "Come back, with your friends!"

What she made of Camilla's story, she didn't say. She didn't seem to be sure what to make of it. She opened her purse, removed her compact, and applied lip gloss. Then she studied the photo of Roxanne that Hawk had given her, turned it over and noticed on the back what she had not previously read in small letters, in pencil and faded: "Fourth of July, Mar Monte." "Maybe that's where I saw Roxanne," Tioga said. "She looked mighty familiar in an eerie kind of way. Like I was looking at a ghost. So what I think is this, Camilla: After you go to the bank, hit the Hall of Records and find out who owns the house at forty-nine. Maybe Hawk owns it. Maybe they owe him rent or something. You might go there and case it. Also, if you have time, dig around about a horse trainer at the county fair. As for me, I'm going to the hotel to talk to Gina McCoy and it's not just for girl talk. She'll know about Hawk and my ex. You and I can meet up later and compare notes."

Camilla looked as if she was pleased that Tioga trusted her with so much to do. "Don't worry. I'll lock up before I go." Then in a way that seemed to come naturally to her, she added, "This means a lot to me."

Tioga took the envelope from Camilla and held it in her outstretched hands as if weighing it on a scale. "I think I know what I'm doing. It feels like a test of nerves, and I don't know if I'm up to it."

Camilla laughed. "A test of wills. It's your will and my will against the will of the world. Pretty cool!"

Tioga paced back and forth like a big cat in a small cage. "You make it sound like a comic book with good battling evil." Then, once again, she lifted the thick white envelope, brought it to her nose and sniffed as if she expected to smell a kind of swamp where rank things grew wild, where everything was always wet and never saw the sun.

She shook her head and laughed at herself. "It's just the intoxicating smell of newly minted bills." Then she heard herself say what she could not remember herself saying before: "Money! It's all about whether you let it to push you around, or not," she told herself. Still she didn't look or sound convincing. "This could be a royal fuck-up," she added and tossed the fat white envelope to Camilla, who caught it with one hand and squeezed it.

At her desk, Tioga opened the file marked "Divorce" and thumbed through the documents. "Hawk must have found this. He could have learned heaps."

Camilla put the envelope in her purse. "Well, I don't mind telling you that Hawk is a creep. That's why you should take his money: to fuck him over for being a pig. Besides you have to pay the rent, we both have to eat and if you're in the PI biz you can't expect to work for saints." She paused for a moment, closed her purse and quipped, "Us girls gotta stick together."

Tioga grabbed her cell and her backpack. She dashed along the hallway, scampered down the stairs, cut across the plaza and aimed for the hotel.

At the top of the flight of stairs, Aaron winked at her and she winked at him. "You're looking cool. Maybe it's the red tie." Aaron held the door. "I think it's the haircut," he said and did a complete turn.

Tioga admired the trim. "Yes, I can see, it's the hair. I like it." Then she asked, "Have you seen Mrs. McCoy?"

Aaron put his lips together and whistled a few bars of a melody. "Recognize the tune?"

Tioga thought for a moment, and though she was in no mood to play a guessing game she guessed anyway. "*Tea for the Tillerman*! You must mean that Mrs. McCoy is having tea on the patio."

Aaron smiled, then wet his lips and sang, "Red wine for the women who make the rain."

Tioga yanked his tie. "Not exactly the lyrics that Cat Stevens wrote, but close enough. Google and you'll see."

Aaron looked offended. "I know, I know. I was being creative."

Tioga turned and looked back at a leafy oak and the red-winged black bird perched on a lower branch. Then she turned around and studied Aaron's face which was cast half in light and half in darkness. "What about a man who wears a Borsalino and has a nose like a hawk? Drives a Prius." She would play with Aaron. Indeed, she watched him as he studied the cars in the circular driveway in front of the hotel: Mercedes-Benzes, BMWs, Lexuses and one white Cadillac Escalade. Aaron wanted to own them all. He certainly loved them all.

"A Prius! Are you kidding me?" Aaron snarled. "Hawk drives a Tesla S model … lets me park it. Nifty car, cool guy. His name definitely goes with his face if you can call it that. I haven't made up my mind if he's beautiful ugly or just plain ugly. Some faces are like that."

Tioga plunged into the hotel, crossed the lobby and raced along the corridor that led to the kitchen, the walk-in larder and the cubbyhole where Buddy Moscosco lived for much of his waking, as well as his napping, hours.

She leaned against the wall. Moscosco dozed in a big chair that took up much of the space in his office. On top of the desk, there was a bottle of Bulleit Bourbon, nearly empty, a tumbler, a pair of eyeglasses and a copy of a paperback novel by Michael Connelly opened about midway and with the cover facing up. Tioga moved the paperback, sat down on the edge of the desk and pressed the toe of her right shoe against Buddy's argyle socks until he woke with a grunt and a sleepy expression on his face. "I must have dozed off for a second."

Tioga slipped out of her backpack and tossed it on the desk. "Hey, Buddy, wake up and act like a respectable house dick."

Moscosco wiped his runny nose, poured himself a two-finger shot of bourbon and sipped slowly. "This stuff is too valuable to share with people like you, who don't appreciate it," he said and sounded like he had a frog in his throat. "It's been hell. Last night, I tackled the sous chef after he threw a carving knife at the dishwasher. I wanted to call the cops, but Jonny said no, not unless I was willing to lend a hand in the kitchen. You know what I said to that!"

He paused for a moment, removed a pocket square handkerchief and dabbed his lips. Then he went on at top speed. "There was the fellow in a bathrobe and flip-flops who accosted a woman in the lobby. I gave him a tongue-lashing, though he deserved more than that. People like him think they can get away with stealing hotel towels and ashtrays and anything not bolted down. Has a face like a bird ... actually like a hawk. In the old days hotel dicks called the shots. Now we're told the customer is always right, even when he, she and it are assholes."

Tioga swallowed Moscosco's information in one long gulp the way he swallowed his whiskey. Then she reached for the crossword puzzle and looked at the clues and the spaces already filled in. "You've made a big dent, Buddy. Want help?"

Moscosco grabbed the puzzle. "Just remembered a word." He added the word "ague" in the upper left-hand corner. "If I want help, I'll ask. More to the point, can I be of assistance to you, Ms. Vignetta?"

He was not so old that he didn't remember to offer his help. Tioga lifted the bottle of Bulleit and shook her head. "Please don't drink yourself to death, Buddy," she moaned. Then she shifted her weight and came down slowly from Moscosco's desk, took two small steps forward and closed the door.

"So how about it, Buddy? Tell me what you know about Hawk?"

Moscosco wiggled in his seat, rubbed the back of his neck with his left hand and then poured another shot.

"What I can tell you and what I know aren't exactly the same."

Tioga scrunched her nose. "I don't like the sound of that, Buddy. I thought we didn't hold back with one another."

Moscosco looked hot under the collar. "I can tell you this: He was a chum of Terry's. Hawk showed up out of the blue and demanded a room. Cheeky bastard. Funny thing, Terry gave it to him on the house. But the other day at the blowout they were ready to fight. You could tell that Terry wanted him dead.

Tioga took a deep breath and then leaned her body against the door. "Maybe Terry's a generous soul and likes to help old chums," she said. "Have you considered that possibility?"

Moscosco laughed. "Yeah, yeah, lady," he said and sounded as if he might have been one of the cops in the dog-eared Michael Connelly novel that lay on his desk. "Try telling Terry about his own generosity."

Then he zipped his lips closed as if to say that he'd said too much already. He grabbed his stubby number two pencil, and shook his head at the puzzle that now seemed to stymie him, though only two blank spaces remained. After a few moments, he glanced at Tioga. "You ask too many questions," he said and sounded hurt. He grabbed his hat, held it in his hands, got to his feet, wobbled a bit, opened the door and stepped into the hallway, with its framed color photograph that depicted a vineyard cascading down a hillside.

With a placid expression on his face, he turned away from the photo and stared at Tioga. "I hope you don't think I'm prying," he began. He paused and whispered, "I realize this might sound like it comes out of left field, but I was wondering, do you take marijuana?"

Tioga leaned back and eyed Moscosco from the pointy shoes on his feet to the bald spot on the top of his head. "Gee, Buddy, why would you think I had anything to do with marijuana?"

Tioga looked at another large color photo on the same wall with the matching photo of the vineyard. This one depicted a man in a hat on a Kubota tractor nestled between rows of grapevines. "I know pot is big around here," Moscosco said. "There's a man who sells pre-rolled marijuana cigarettes here. I'm not sure if I should bust him or not."

Tioga leaned against the wall to make room for Jonny Field—in white hat, white apron and white coat as he dashed toward the walk-in larder with its boxes and jars and ladders and began to search the items on the upper shelves. "'Cuse me. I need arrowroot."

Tioga stepped into the corridor again. "People don't take marijuana, Buddy. They smoke it, eat it, use it as a tincture or apply it as a salve. You could add it to the whiskey you drink."

She peered again into the depths of the larder that had swallowed Jonny Field. Then she listened to what she thought of as Moscosco's constant refrain, though this time he sounded wearier than ever before. "Everyone's in a rush. Why can't people just slow down? They'll live longer. I mean, look at me. I'm eighty, and I can still get up and come to work and be here eight hours a day six days a week. I'm not complaining. Terry McCoy takes good care of me. He remembers me from the time I helped Mrs. Olivera find that wild stepdaughter who had run away. Turns out she was living with an uncle, attending school in Ojai and didn't want to come back to Sonoma."

Jonny Field popped out of the larder like a cork released from a bottle of Dom Pérignon and then dashed for the kitchen; Moscosco made room for him to pass. "You see what I mean by rushing? In the old days, I took my sweet time even when I snapped photos of husbands in hotel bedrooms with the kinds of lovers in the cop story I'm reading. I would hand the photos over to the wives and girlfriends who might want to cash out. I sold some porn, strictly soft stuff, no hard core to *Reveille* for fifty bucks a pop, and made enough dough to have a booth at the Barbary Coast Grill where I ate myself silly and drank myself under the table."

The kitchen doors swung back and forth. Moscosco and Tioga stared at one another from opposite sides of the hallway. "I don't mean to scold you, Buddy," Tioga said. "About your photographing lovers in hotel bedrooms … that doesn't feel right!"

Moscosco shook his head, put on his porkpie hat, locked the door and pocketed the key. "I'm going out. Fresh air will do me a world of good."

Tioga walked with him toward the patio. "What does the man who sells marijuana cigarettes look like?" she asked.

Moscosco pulled down on the brim of the hat that sat awkwardly on the top of his head. "Thin as a string bean. Curly hair. Hyperactive. Makes me nervous just to look at him." He removed his hat and scratched his head. "Sorry but I don't have a name. He doesn't seem to give it out, but I'm gonna bust him away, with or without a name."

Tioga closed her eyes and asked, "And what about Gina McCoy? Have you seen her?"

Moscosco drew Tioga toward him, as if he wanted her to be his dance partner. He had rarely if ever been so affectionate. Tioga moved toward him as he moved toward her and hummed a Tony Bennett tune. Then he stopped, looked at Tioga and asked, "Why so interested in Marie Antoinette? What's up with her majesty?"

Tioga wasn't sure how much how or how little to confide in Buddy. "Oh, girl talk," she said.

Buddy removed his arm from Tioga's waist and looked as if he was in over his head. "Girl talk? That sounds dangerous." In a puzzling tone of voice he added, "You'll find Gina on the patio. She's alone, except for Fritz, who has been suffering from indigestion and won't take his medicine. I had a man-to-man with him, but he won't listen to reason. He's a bad boy."

The kitchen doors swayed back and forth. Buddy went one way and Tioga the other.

"Right, oh, Buddy, you're the best."

In an instant, Moscosco smiled like a Cheshire cat that had been stroked and now purred loudly.

Tea Time

If someone had asked her about Gina, Tioga would have said that, with her schoolgirl complexion, she looked a decade or so younger than McCoy. In the bar, she had noticed he didn't care an iota about his expanding waistline or the protruding hairs from his nostrils and ears, which made Tioga think of Fritz's ears and snout. Suave Terry had become slob McCoy.

The toy poodle sprawled across Gina's lap and looked like he had been spoiled rotten from the earliest days of his puppydom. The wait staff at the Mar Monte spoiled him too, as Tioga duly noted, with fresh drinking water and treats from the table. Gina lifted her teacup from a matching saucer. She was as neat about drinking tea as Moscosco was about drinking bourbon.

Tioga looked up at the white clouds that drifted across the big blue sky. Gina placed her right hand atop her hat to prevent it from blowing away in the breeze. "Won't you join me? We haven't seen much of one another recently, but perhaps we can catch up." Then she added. "I'm really not the princess I've been made out to be. I'm more of an Irish peasant girl."

Oh, yeah, she was an Irish peasant girl in much the same way that Marie Antoinette was a French dairymaid. Tioga's long thin body cast a slender shadow across the patio which was paved with large flat stones that had been excavated from the Valley floor, as nearly every schoolgirl and boy learned in seventh grade geography class.

"I'd love to join you. It's been ages, I know. I've wondered where you've been and what you've been doing."

She sat down next to Gina who signaled for the waitress—a young woman wearing black trousers, a black blouse and a dainty white apron—who promptly made herself available. Before Tioga knew what had happened, a cup and saucer that matched Gina's materialized in front of her, along with a teapot beneath a plaid cozy.

Gina scratched the space behind Fritz's floppy ears. "You might not see me all that often, but I'm here everyday behind the scenes," Gina said in an accent that Tioga had heard before and assumed was Irish, given the way that Gina bent her vowels and consonants. Then she added flirtatiously, "I know you're in the penthouse with Storm, but I think of you in your office above the theater, across the way, and I wonder: does her heart belong with us or against us?"

Tioga lifted her teacup and sipped. "Umm, that's good. Tea always suits me." She returned the cup to the saucer. "I'm impressed that you still have an Irish accent. It's quite remarkable."

Gina looked the opposite of nonplussed. "I hope you haven't fallen for the stories that circulate about me. I can assure you that ninety-nine point nine percent of them are false. Galway was my home for the first twenty years of my life. My parents happened to be passing though Bayonne, New Jersey, when I was born. The whole Garden State is a blip on my screen."

Tioga followed the white clouds that moved swiftly across the blue sky, as if they might inspire her. "I've always thought of the Mar Monte as my home. I know I divide my time between the hotel, here, and my office, there, but I don't think of this side or that side. There are no sides, if you know what I mean."

Gina added a cube of sugar and stirred, then added a second cube and stirred again while Tioga watched her hand move around and around. "Well, yes," Gina said. "We're all in this together."

Tioga cleared her throat before she spoke. "That's not what I meant. We're not all in the same boat. That's poppy-cock, but to think in terms of us vs. them isn't helpful."

She lifted an éclair, took a bite and then licked the whipped cream from her fingers.

Gina looked chagrined. "Are you and Storm ..." she began and paused as if she didn't know what was proper to say and how to finish her thought.

Tioga pulled the dog's right ear. "Are we getting along, are we in love, are we still an item? Is that what you'd like to know?"

Then before Gina had a chance to answer, Tioga frowned and asked, with as little provocation as she could manage, "How's life with Terry?"

Gina looked startled. "Sorry, what did you say? I was distracted by Fritz and didn't hear."

Tioga lifted the teapot and poured another cup. "Never mind. It wasn't important."

Gina smiled benevolently. "Terrible news about the young woman found face down along the side of the road. I'm told she was assaulted."

A curious word, Tioga thought. What exactly did Gina mean by assaulted and where had she heard the news?

"Oh, yes," Gina said as if anticipating a question from Tioga. "Clark, one of George's wet-behind-the-ears deputies, told me. He's awfully sweet and he's local, too. He wants everyone to like him. I'm sure he has a crush on me. He said the murder was drug related, though I find that hard to believe. After all, this is the Valley."

Once again, Gina motioned for the young woman in the apron.

When she arrived, she looked at the depleted assortment of pastries on the platter. "Bring the freshest ones from the kitchen! These are already old."

Tioga looked at Gina's diamond ring. It now struck her as far too big and far too showy for the Valley. "Dorothy Baynes was shot and raped. Actually raped first and shot second. I will spare you the details. No suspects yet, but Ambrose will get his man or men. He always does. I'm running interference for him. That's the way he likes it, and I don't mind."

She paused, listened to the ticking of a clock she couldn't see but could hear distinctly, and then went on: "But to get back to Storm and me. We have our ups and our downs, though we've hit it off recently. Two weeks ago, we went to MOMA in the city to see the Klee exhibit and to City Lights to buy all of Lucia Berlin's book—don't you just love them—and then to El Farolito for margaritas and tacos. I guess you could say we're still very much in love." Now she sounded like her own press agent. "Thanks for asking."

The waitress placed a platter with pastries on the table. Gina served herself a *mille-feuille* and then admired it as if it was a work of art. "Jonny works miracles," she said and took a tiny bite before she went on. "Life must be so much easier when one lives with another woman and not with a man. Though I don't have experience in that department, other than a crush on a girl when I was at boarding school in Galway."

That was as far as Gina was prepared to go into her own past. Then a curtain came down and separated her from the world. "You'll have to excuse me. I was always told it was bad manners to talk about one's self."

Tioga looked at one of the newly delivered éclairs. With her fork she removed the top layer of chocolate, devoured it and then licked the prongs clean. Gina shook her head disapprovingly.

"Silly," she said and laughed. "You have to eat the whole thing." Then she leaned back in her chair and gathered Fritz in her arms. "I'm curious what you're working on now. I suppose that's confidential."

Tioga nodded her head and wondered whether the reason for Gina's invitation to tea was to find out where she was snooping. "You didn't happen to recommend me to a friend of yours, did you?"

Gina offered Fritz a taste of her Napoleon. "I suppose I shouldn't spoil him. But I have to spoil someone. My husband won't allow it." She looked directly at Tioga and added, "It's not that I wouldn't recommend you, but I haven't recommended you. I don't know anyone in need of a private investigator, or op as you call yourself, though I imagine you're quite good. You seem to fit in everywhere, like a chameleon, and to be able to draw everyone out. I mean that in a complimentary way."

Tioga looked toward the roof of the hotel. The flag of California with its Grizzly bear and red star fluttered in the warm breeze. "Everyone needs an op sometime or other. Even you might need me one day. "

Gina retrieved her linen napkin and returned it to her lap. "My husband might require your services, but I steer clear of anything the least bit unsavory. I don't want to see my name and my picture splashed across the front page of *The Gazette*. I know what the paper did to Storm when you investigated the death of her mother."

Tioga lifted the teapot and filled Gina's cup. "Then you don't know anyone named Hawk? He's a large fellow, wears a Borsalino and a yin and yang pendant. His nose looks distinctly beak-like. I guess that's why he has his nickname."

Gina chortled. Tioga's description of Hawk seemed to amuse her. "Heavens, no. Never heard of anyone named Hawk with or without a Borsalino and a pendant with the yin and the yang. I never can remember which one is yin and which one is yang."

Tioga lifted her teacup and sipped. "Google them," she said, then reached out and pulled the dog's tail. "You learn more about yin and yang than you want to know."

Gina signaled for the waitress. When she arrived with the bill, she signed her initials, "G.M," with a flourish. Then she lifted Fritz in the air, kissed him on the lips and placed him on the patio, where he wagged his tail, lifted his left rear leg and peed on the peonies. Gina watched as if Fritz was her one and only child. "That's a very good boy."

Tioga looked down at Fritz and asked, "Do you know the name of the weaselly fellow who sells marijuana in the hotel?"

Gina adjusted her pink hat and then put on her white gloves. "Haven't a clue. I've never tried it, though I couldn't help but smell it at the fête the other day. I believe I had what's called a contact high."

Suddenly she looked as if a bright idea had come to her out of the blue. "I've heard you can eat it! Which means Jonny could add it to the éclairs!"

She put on her best Marie Antoinette smile and added, "I'm sorry I can't help you with Hawk or the fellow who sells weed in the hotel, but Mr. Moscosco should be able to assist you. He gathers gossip and squirrels it away; Terry says he could make a mint as a blackmailer."

Gina turned away from Tioga and admired the potted plants that ran along the edge of the patio. "I do adore flowers, especially hydrangeas this time of year," she said. "Don't you?"

Now for the first time, Tioga noticed the flowers in bloom. "Yes, they're lovely," she said and looked as if she truly admired them. A few moments later, when she took her eyes away from the hydrangeas, and searched for Gina and Fritz, she saw that they were gone and so were the cups, saucers and pastries. She had spaced out again. "Try to be aware," she told herself, "and don't make yourself anxious."

On the patio, where Fritz had made a mess, the waitress, on hands and knees, scrubbed the pavers clean.

Tioga sat down, found her father's number and called. "Hello. I've been thinking of you ... trying to sell your paintings."

Philippe Vignetta was caught off guard. "Who is this? I didn't catch what you just said."

Tioga switched her phone from her left to her right side. "It's your daughter. I was hoping that you had a phone number for my ex. I don't. It's urgent."

Philippe Vignetta cleared his throat. "Your divorce is final, isn't it? Don't give me a heart attack."

"Yes," Tioga said. "Something has come up, but don't worry I can handle it."

There was a long pause from Philippe's end of the conversation. "Just a minute. His number is in my computer. I have to boot it up." There was another long pause. "Here it is. Do you have pencil and paper?"

"Yes, Dad," she said and sounded like the dutiful daughter her mother wanted her to be. "Eight zero eight four six nine seven three four two. I hope it works. Let me know. Love you, Ti. And come down to the city and see my new work. We'll go to Gavin's for drinks."

Tioga didn't waste a moment. No sooner did she end the call to her father than she punched in the number for

Tomás and drummed her fingers on the table. "Come on, pick up, you bastard."

Tomás answered after the fourth ring. "Aloha."

"Tomás, sorry to bother you. I wouldn't call unless I had to."

When Tomás didn't respond, Tioga plunged ahead. "I met a fellow who calls himself Hawk, claims he met you and that you talked about me. I hope that's not true."

Tomás took a deep breath. "Is what not true?"

Tioga was distracted. She saw a skeletal fellow remove a fat marijuana cigarette from his shirt pocket, hand it discretely to a man in a short sleeve shirt, a bathing suit and flip flops. The man pulled out a handful of bills, peeled off a twenty and a ten and forked them over. He put the joint in the pocket of his shirt. The runt vanished.

"Tomás, are you still there?"

"Are you still there?"

Tioga swallowed hard. "Did you talk to Hawk about me smoking dope, yes or no?" Tioga asked. "Tell me, Tomás, you didn't tell him I was a fucked-up stoner, did you?"

Tomás sounded like he was smoking weed right then and there. "I can't remember what I say from one day to the next. I talk to a lot of people. They all want surfing lessons. Besides what business is it of yours who I talk to and what I say? You wanted the divorce, Tioga! I didn't!"

There was nothing more to say, except to get into an argument about drugs and their divorce. There was no point in carrying on the conversation. But she was curious about one thing.

"Where are you now?" she asked. "Tell me that."

Tomás fired back, "I don't have to tell you diddly-squat, you fuckin' cheat."

Tioga extended the middle finger of her right hand. It felt good, though Tomás couldn't see her. But maybe he could hear her rage.

"Asshole," she shouted and attracted the attention of a waitress who glared. Then she ended the call, looked for the runt who sold dope, and when she didn't see him, she found the man who had made the purchase. "Where did the runt go? He was just here!"

The man scratched his head. "There's been no one here but me. You wanna join me for a drink?"

Pot Doc & Dispensary

In an alcove of the lobby, Tioga collapsed in an armchair. The Mar Monte had reverted to its banal existence as a three-star hotel that catered to the leisured classes and not a playground for potheads. Perhaps it had a split personality, Tioga thought. She stretched her legs, kicked off her shoes, took out her cell, did a Google search for "pot doc" and found "Dr. Wayne Silver."

She recognized the name from *The Gazette*, which ran ads that pandered to the cannabis trade. Dr. Silver, Tioga remembered, had written too many recommendations for cannabis and had run afoul of the California Medical Alliance. He had promised to be a good boy and he was reinstated to the profession. *The Gazette* had rallied behind him.

Tioga added Silver's name to her list of contacts, along with his phone number and street address. The website for "Holistic Silver" provided no email. According to Google Maps, Dr. Silver maintained an office in Boyes Hot Springs, a short distance away, provided there was no traffic. Tioga called Silver's office and made an appointment for that afternoon.

Then she walked barefoot across the lobby and wandered into the dining room where she saw the dealer whom she had observed on the patio. With her cell she took his photo and emailed it to herself. But when she tried to find him, she couldn't. He wasn't in the kitchen, in the larder or around the pool. He seemed to have a built-in system to avoid detection.

She had an hour to kill. Near the front desk, and against a wall painted hot pink, she snagged a copy of *Vanity Fair* that beckoned from the magazine rack.

In the same armchair, where she had collapsed only a short while ago, she glanced at the glossy ads for shoes and accessories and scanned an article about Prince William and his brother Harry, disappointed that there was no new gossip about them. But she sank her teeth into a long piece about a scandal at Amazon that had rocked the company. "Serves them right," she said aloud.

Then it was time for her appointment with Silver. She slipped into her shoes and ambled across the lobby. Aaron wasn't at his post at the top of the flight of stairs. That was disappointing, but then she saw him under an oak tree in the plaza engaged in an argument—it was too heated to be a conversation or a discussion—with the skeletal dealer.

With her camera, she took more pictures, then looked at the time and realized that she was running late again. She scampered across the plaza, dashed down the cobblestone alley between Henry's Gastro Pub and Louise's Lingerie Plus and found her car where she had left it in the lot behind the Sebastiani. She drove north until she reached Boyes Hot Springs. Dr. Silver's office occupied a stucco building that was wedged between Golden Springs Chinese—"Szechuan Cuisine" the neon sign read—and El Jalisco, a *carniceria* with a large handwritten sign in the window that advertised "*cabrito*, $14.95 a kilo."

Tioga parked her car in the lot near the back of the stucco building, walked to the front and saw Flor, the woman she had first observed on the sidewalk near the entrance to the Mar Monte. Now she wore a shiny black sweater, black stretch pants and red shoes. She had suddenly come up in the world and held a new, improved sign that said, in capital letters, "HELP PLEASE. WE ARE HUNGRY."

Flor had learned to spell or else someone had spelled the word hungry for her and added "PLEASE." Flor's boy, who wore the same Rolling Stones T-shirt, slipped away as if he didn't want to be seen anywhere near the tall, skinny *guera* who asked funny questions. Tioga thought they were funny.

Flor leapt to her feet, walked quickly toward Tioga and smiled in a way that made her look, not just pretty or merely attractive, but beautiful. Tioga smiled. She knew that she had been seduced by Flor's beauty. Now she would rescue her.

Whatever timidity Flor had shown outside the Mar Monte, she had lost.

"I tried calling you and you didn't answer," Tioga said. "*¿Qué pasa?*"

Flor reached into her apron, pulled out two singles and handed them to the boy, who had crept back and who now wore an expression of curiosity on his face. "Go and buy Coca-Cola at the market. Don't drink all at once and bring the change." Then she turned to Tioga and explained, "I try to make him learn English, but he lazy."

Tioga watched the boy cross the parking lot and dash toward Broadway Market with its display of mangoes, papayas, plantains and bananas. Flor smiled seductively. "I'm sorry. My cell was stolen and I don't have money for another."

Tioga felt like scolding Flor, and then decided that would get her nowhere. Flor might prove useful. And twenty-dollars a pop wouldn't break Tioga's bank account now that it had jumped by ten thousand dollars.

"Have you seen anything strange or unusual?" she asked, though she didn't expect Flor to say anything that would surprise her.

Flor's face blossomed. "I saw my husband. I mean I saw someone who looks like my husband only he's not the same Mack. I race after him, but he disappear at the market where they sell vegetables."

Tioga was genuinely surprised. "I'll buy you a new cell at Verizon after I finish at the doctor's. It won't be long." Then with her index finger she pointed to the ground. "Wait for me right here. I don't want to lose you again." In just a short while she had come to think of herself as Flor's guardian. Tioga studied the cars in the parking lot as if they were beasts from another world and spoke a language she didn't understand.

Flor admired the fruits that were displayed outside the market where her boy stood alone. "Why go to the doctor? *Enfermo*?"

When Tioga shook her head, Flor added, "I will stay here until you come back," and sounded like she might wait forever.

Tioga backed away slowly and then stopped. "What does your husband look like?" she asked and watched Flor's boy cross the parking lot with a Coca-Cola and potato chips. "Tell me later."

Inside Dr. Silver's musty, dusty office—which felt like a hothouse for contagious diseases—she stood at the front desk and scanned the color photos on the wall that depicted turtles on a tropical island. "I have an appointment."

The dark-haired, round-faced receptionist looked up and smiled. "You must be Ms. Vignetta. You're punctual."

She handed Tioga a clipboard. "Fill out this form and sign it and date it," she said and pointed to a line with the letter "x." "I'll need to see some ID."

Tioga surrendered her driver's license. The receptionist copied it on the machine that sat against the wall and then placed it in a file marked "Vignetta," along with Tioga's application form. "Do you want my fingerprints?"

The receptionist didn't appreciate the sarcasm. "No, that won't be necessary. How did you want to pay?"

Tioga took out her wallet. "Ah, yes, money."

She removed her MasterCard, handed it over the counter and waited while the computer connected to her bank and made more money vanish magically. Moments later she returned the card to her wallet and pocketed the receipt that indicated she had paid $75 for a "consultation" with Dr. Silver.

She sat down in an armchair opposite two longhaired, middle-aged, white-skinned men who looked poor and might have been called "poor white trash," though that wasn't politically correct Tioga reminded herself.

They also looked infirm. That would be in their favor, at least with Dr. Silver. Tioga sneezed, then sneezed again and turned up her nose at the magazines on the table that looked as if they'd been recycled, perhaps from the Mar Monte.

She waited impatiently until the receptionist called her name, and then pointed toward the hallway where the two longhaired men had vanished ages ago, or so it seemed. "Over there, miss. First door on the right."

Tioga grabbed her purse. "Down the rabbit hole again. I'm making a habit of this."

What surprised her most of all about the room was that, except for a chair, a table and a TV monitor, it was empty; no sunlight penetrated the Venetian blinds. She sat down, stared at the monitor and peered into the face of a man who wore glasses, a beard and a shirt open at the collar. "I'm Dr. Wayne Silver. I'm pleased to meet you, Ms. Vignetta." Then he added, "Sounds like vignette."

Dr. Silver looked nearly as pale as his longhaired patients. Perhaps, Tioga thought with more than a touch of meanness, Dr. Silver lived in the monitor and never saw the light of day.

"What can I do for you?" he asked as if he cared immensely.

Tioga had not thought what she might tell Dr. Silver about her condition. Now all she could say was, "I'd like a recommendation for marijuana, I mean cannabis."

Dr. Silver wrinkled and then unwrinkled his brow. "Let's start at the beginning. What prompted you to come to see me? What are you suffering from?"

As far as she knew, she wasn't suffering from anything, at least not severely, except for depression and the chills and the burning sensation as a result of the spider bite. Except, too, for the lingering feeling that she didn't know who or what she was. But that couldn't be cured, she thought, at least not with cannabis, opioids, steroids, dieting, or sex.

"I have severe back ache, insomnia, anxiety and depression," she said, sounding as if she could go on and on and never reach the end of her infirmities. She turned away from the monitor and murmured, "Sometimes I wonder who I am," as if her uncertainty about her self might spread like a contagious disease.

Dr. Silver smiled smugly. "Is that all? I hope you're not leaving anything out." He paused for a few seconds and then added, "It looks like you're holding a lot of tension in your shoulders and in your neck. The right side of your face doesn't seem to be exactly aligned with the left side. A layperson might not detect those differences, but it's my job to notice things like that. Did something happen to you?"

Dr. Silver's tone of voice irked Tioga. "Yeah, I was born! I came into the world imperfect." Then she looked away from the monitor and added, "I get terrible menstrual cramps every month."

That was a white lie. In fact, Tioga could not remember when she had last suffered from cramps. Still, if Dr. Silver wanted her to describe all her ailments and infirmities, she was only too happy to oblige. She returned to the monitor and peered at the face in the box. "You can see the tension by looking and not touching?"

She could hear doubt in her own voice.

Doctor Silver put his hands together and rubbed them as if trying to warm them. "You have a tendency to be manic. You store tension in your shoulders and probably have, ever since childhood. Over the years it has built up."

Tioga swallowed hard. "That's bullshit. You have no idea what you're talking about." Then she asked herself, "Was the man in the box a psychic, a quack, or a scoundrel out to make a quick buck on the back of the gullible, the mindless and the psychotic?"

Dr. Silver leaned back, relaxed and added, "I'm happy to write a recommendation for you for cannabis. I'm sure it will help with anger management, anxiety, tension and sleep disorders. You can pick up your card at the front desk. There's a dispensary on the other side of the parking lot where you can find the medicine you'll need."

Tioga felt oddly inebriated. She had been redeemed, resurrected and reborn. She had a green light to get stoned for her health and her well-being, not just or only to fuck with her own head, which she did for the first time when she met Tomás at Bolinas and accepted a joint he offered her. She had taken off her wet suit and stood naked on the shore. What was it he called her? Oh, yes, "Venus on the Half Shell." What a line! What a sucker she had been!

What would her ex think about Dr. Silver? He would swear that he would never stoop so low as to request a medical marijuana card for a real or an imaginary disorder. Now with form in hand, Tioga moved like a rocket toward the neon sign that depicted a large green cross against a white background and the words "HOLISTIC AMERICAN HEALTH."

The stars and stripes flew on the roof of the building. At the entrance to the dispensary, Tioga moved between two muscle-bound security guards in uniform. Then she showed the receptionist her driver's license and her marijuana card. "Wait a sec, miss, I have to log you into the system."

It didn't take long. Tioga returned her license to her wallet and the wallet to her purse. A buzzer sounded. Tioga pushed the glass door, stepped into a large room with white noise in the background and display cases along three walls. "Am I still stoned?" she asked. "Is the tincture from the green dragon still breathing fire?"

Tioga saw an array of products labeled "cannabis" that she could eat, smoke or apply as a topical. There were concentrates as well as dried flowers sold by the gram at prices far too extravagant for a product commonly known as "weed," though that word didn't appear anywhere in Holistic American Health, nor did the words marijuana, pot, dope, *ganja* and grass, all of which she had used interchangeably since she was a teenager. It was cannabis, cannabis, cannabis—the mantra for the marketplace.

"What can I show you?" a plump saleswoman behind the counter asked. She wore jeans and a T-shirt with Bob Marley's image. In her right hand she held a blunt the size of a cigar fit for Che Guevara; the smoke curled around her dreadlocks.

"We have a special on concentrates," she added, then looked at Tioga in much the same way, she thought, that Dr. Silver had looked at her from inside his box, as someone who was sick and needed medicine ASAP. "I haven't seen you here before. Is this your first time?"

Tioga didn't like the insinuation. "No," she barked. Then she added, "I'm not a fucking virgin. I'm a stoner!"

The saleswoman appealed to a tall muscle-bound security guard—a green giant in green hat, green shirt, green pants, and even green shoes—who didn't look one bit like a jolly green giant. "I'm sorry, but we don't allow that kind of language here. It impacts negatively the mood we're trying to create. I'm sure you understand."

Tioga made a monkey-like face. "I'm having withdrawal symptoms. As soon as I take my meds I'll be fine. I know. It's happened before. Let's get this over and be done with."

The security guard backed off.

On an impulse, Tioga bought a small round jar labeled "Nirvana." "It will calm you down," the saleswoman said, though the idea of nirvana seemed to agitate Tioga. Her heart raced, skipped a beat, and then another. She took a deep breath, held it, then exhaled and pointed to two jars with dried marijuana flowers: one called "Silver Bullet," the other "Pussy."

Tioga put her right hand over her breast. "Excuse me, but what happens if you mix "Silver Bullet" and "Pussy?"

The woman wore a look of alarm. "Oh, that's a recipe for disaster. Don't do it."

Tioga chuckled and then reached for her wallet. "I'll buy two of each. Good idea to stock up. And throw in a BIC lighter while you're at it."

At the last moment, she picked out a pomegranate-flavored ice cream. The label read "Nepalese" and "20:1, CBD THC."

The saleswoman took Tioga's credit card, poured over Tioga's driver's license and studied her face. She processed the purchase and added the items to a plastic bag with the single word, "HOLISTIC."

Tioga peeled the wrapper from the ice cream bar and, with the tip of her tongue, began to lick it. Suddenly she heard the booming voice from the green man who commanded: "Put that down. There's no consumption of product inside the building or within three-hundred feet of the front door."

Tioga stared at the green man. Then she took a big bite of the ice cream bar, let it melt in her mouth and sauntered toward the exit.

"Fuck you," she said to no one in particular. Cannabis was supposed to calm her down, or so Dr. Silver said, but it now made her oddly aggressive. Maybe I can write myself up for *The New England Journal of Medicine*, she said to herself. Outside she searched for Flor and her boy and found them sprawled on a cardboard box in an alcove near the entrance to Golden Springs. Tioga had avoided the restaurant ever since *The Gazette* ran a story about a dishwasher named Wang Wang who died of a heroin overdose while scrubbing pots and pans in the kitchen.

Flor and her son were sharing the remains of something that might have been moo shu pork and seemed to have been modified to look like a taco.

Tioga opened the dispensary bag, removed the jar with a bright green leaf that was labeled "Pussy" and showed it to Flor, who shook her head. "I no use *mota*. Make me *loco*."

Tioga watched the boy who was eating the moo shu pork with his hands, as was Flor. "Let's go and buy your mother a phone."

The boy did not have to be encouraged and neither did Flor.

At Verizon, Tioga did the talking, while Flor listened and while the boy wandered from aisle to aisle with envy in his eyes and put his hands on every device,

The salesman tried to persuade Tioga to purchase the most expensive phone; she bought the least expensive, along with the most economical plan. On the sidewalk in front of the store, Tioga entered her name, her number, her email and the address for her office. She offered the phone to Flor, who admired it and then handed it to the boy who clutched it.

"You never told me what your husband looks like," Tioga said. "Or his name. Where you married here or in Mexico?"

Flor touched the boy's head and messed with his light brown hair. "Mack *muy importante*. He gamble, make money. We go Zihuatanejo."

While she spoke, Flor kept her hands on the boy who tugged and tugged, as if eager to break away and explore on his own.

"Not marry. How do you say?" With both hands she shaped a round belly.

"Pregnant?" Tioga asked. The word caught in her mouth. "Did you say Mack?" She thought of Mack the Knife in *The Threepenny Opera* which she watched on the big screen at the Roxie in SF with Randy Scheck, who had his own version of the lyrics: "The shark has teeth that everyone sees, but Mack has a knife that he conceals." Tioga whistled the tune. Flor nodded her head. "Mack plant *semillas*. You say *semillas*, no?"

Tioga nodded her head. "*Si*. In English, seeds."

Flor took the word in her mouth and rolled it around as if making friends with it. "Seeds."

Tioga fired back, "Do you mean, Mack or McCoy? Which is it?"

She bore down on Flor. "They sound similar, don't they? Maybe your English wasn't that good in Acapulco, and maybe he didn't want you to know his real name."

Flor tried to smile but she only looked forlorn.

Tioga watched a vintage Volvo as it circled the paved wasteland, the driver searching for a space to pull in and park. "Mack forced you into his bed? Do you have a photo?"

Flor's sadness made her look more beautiful, or so it seemed to Tioga. "Mack *gabacho*. I make baby. Mack come back. Make more baby. Mack take first, send money."

The vintage Volvo pulled into a space for the handicapped. A man on crutches aimed for Verizon and a woman on a bicycle sold flavored ices. Flor kissed her boy and gave him another dollar. "Go!" To Tioga she said, "Mack *guero* Sayulita friend give car keys. *La migra* find *cocaína*. I say *nada*. They hit hard. *Mamacita* take boy *casa*: lawyer come; he pay money. Mack *guero* friend bring here."

Tioga watched the white clouds that made her think of cocaine, now that Flor had dropped the word *cocaín*. The clouds galloped across the blue sky like jacked-up race-horses. Tioga reached inside her jacket and touched the cold, hard snub nose. "What did Mack's *guero* friend look like?"

Flor looked like she had flipped back in time. "He tall, drive truck. I not like he touch me. Call me *sucio* Flor. Then I not Betzy."

Tioga's lips curled at the corners of her mouth. "I bet you didn't like the surfer! He set you up."

The woman with the ices stopped her cart along the curb. The boy gave her a dollar. The woman handed him a green snow cone.

Tioga folded her arms. "This business with Mack started, what, five, six years ago?"

Flor did the math on the fingers of both hands. "Too long. Baby now boy. He not remember." She put her hands on the shoulders of the boy with the green snow cone. "This one need brother."

Tioga's mind turned kaleidoscopic. In a flash, she saw red panties, a Borsalino and a beret. The pictures came and went, whether she wanted them or not. Then she leaned back and howled. Flor laughed. It was funny, howling on the edge of a parking lot that sizzled under the sun.

"My boy understand English. *Pero no mucho*. He not know *cocaína*. Better if stay TJ."

Tioga rubbed her forehead and sighed. "Did you smuggle just that one time?"

Flor put her arm around her boy. "*Gracias por el telefono*. I will look and I call when I see something."

She marched the boy across the parking lot, the heat rising from the pavement, wave after wave.

A Game of Chicken

Men in tuxedos and women in evening gowns floated down the stairs as if on air. Aaron's blue uniform sparkled in the bright light that seemed to come down from the sky itself like a giant torch that left nothing in darkness.

Tioga fingered the topmost button on his brocade jacket. "Very snazzy and very you. A bit Sgt. Peppery." She stepped back so that she could take in the entire effect. "So what's new?"

Aaron brushed away a ladybug that landed on the lapel of his jacket. "Fly away my beauty. Fly away home. Your house is on fire. And your children all gone."

Tioga turned around and glanced at the plaza. "I saw you with the runt who deals weed. What was the ruckus about?"

Aaron's eyes sparkled. "Nothin'."

"Nothing?"

Aaron swayed from side to side like a ship listing at sea. "Nothin', 'ceptin' he agreed to stay off my turf."

Tioga moved her eyes away from the ribbon of grass at the edge of the plaza to a woman in an evening gown and a bouffant hairdo. "Nothing is something. Too bad the runt isn't here now. I thought he might know something about Dorothy Baynes's murder."

Aaron repressed a smile that finally broke out, albeit briefly. "Bones," he said as if he didn't want to utter the name. "William Bones, though everyone in the Valley calls him Billy. When he's not dealing weed he's raising pigs in Kenwood and hustling someone. He tried to con McCoy, and when McCoy went to the D.A., he weaseled his way out of an arrest."

Tioga rubbed the bridge of her nose. "Apparently a horse trainer ran off with Dorothy Baynes and knocked her up."

Aaron's eyelids drooped and his jaw dropped. He was weary. "An urban legend. I've heard it so many times I'm sick of it." He reached into the blue jacket that matched his blue trousers, pulled out a blue envelope and handed it to Tioga. "Mr. Hawk asked me to give this to you. I almost forgot."

Tioga glanced at the front and then the back of the envelope. "There's no writing on either side." She brought it to her nose and sniffed. "Lilac. Once you smell it you never forget it." She removed a single sheet of paper from the envelope, along with five one-hundred-dollar bills and handed one of them to Aaron. "For your troubles."

Aaron folded the bill in half. "No trouble at all. Is there a string attached? There always is."

Tioga unfolded Hawk's letter and read aloud: "A pleasure meeting you, Ms. Vignetta. I have never met a lovelier woman dick. Your ex underestimates you. This letter ends whatever agreement we have."

It was signed "Hawk" in big loopy letters that spread across the bottom of the page. She handed the letter to Aaron, who paused for a moment to watch another ladybug, or perhaps the same one, that had landed on his lapel earlier. This time he didn't brush her away, or urge her to fly, but watched her explore the nooks and crannies of his brocade jacket. "Live and let live," he said and then read the letter to himself, chuckled and returned it to Tioga. "Mr. Hawk took off in his Tesla. Had a woman with him in the passenger seat. She was wearing wrap-around dark glasses and a floppy hat. I could not see her eyes, though I noticed the shoulder-length hair. It looked like a wig."

Tioga folded the envelope and placed it in her purse. "What about the Mexican woman with the small boy? They were here not long ago."

Aaron wore a guilty look. "I didn't mean to come on like a gangsta, but I musta scared her off. I have not seen her since."

Tioga frowned. "Yeah, yeah. You don't know how frightening you can be."

She plunged into the hotel and crossed the lobby that smelled of lavender. The props for the pot party—the elephants, the palm trees and the hookah—were all gone. In their place, she took note of an exhibit of framed watercolors that depicted the Valley as surreal, as grotesque and as exotic, all of them for sale, none of them as naughty as anything that her father had ever done. She took the elevator, unlocked the door to her apartment, and read the note Storm had left on the table next to the bed: "Ti, Gone to the Boom Boom Room in SF. See you at the movie, Love, S."

Tioga showered and shampooed, put on a camisole, a green T-shirt, a very short skirt and flats. At the mirror, she combed her hair and applied lipstick and eyeliner. She grabbed her purse and her cell and took the elevator to the lobby. Along the way, she hummed a tune from *The Little Mermaid* which had never entirely disappeared from the soundtrack of her life. "I just want to be a part of your world." It was a long way from Mack the Knife.

At the far end of the bar, Tioga picked out a stool, sat down and watched Sean Dyce who was doing exactly the same thing he had been doing the last time she saw him. With a dishtowel in hand, he removed a lipstick stain from a fluted champagne glass.

"You caught me at my least favorite task," he said, his cheeks puffed out like a chipmunk who had stored a week's supply of nuts in the pouches on either side of his mouth. "Onerous but necessary work."

Tioga lifted the glass he had just cleaned and held it up to the light. "Did you ever hear Terry McCoy called Mack?"

Dyce tossed the towel into the stainless steel sink. "I have heard him called Mac Coy, the Real McCoy and Terrence, but I can't recall anyone addressing him as 'Mack.' If they did, he would not have liked it. Macks are good ole boys and that's not our Terry McCoy."

Dyce examined the glass he had been polishing. "If I didn't remove stains religiously, Chehab would have my ass in a sling. He's on my case. 'No more drinks on the house,' he told me. I told him, 'It pays to give stuff away occasionally and at the discretion of the bartender.'"

Dyce opened a Pellegrino and poured the bubbly into a tall glass. Then he placed the glass on a coaster that said "Underground" with the Mar Monte's iconic sultry woman in a beret, holding a long cigarette holder. The cigarette smoke formed a halo around her head, though she looked more like a sex fiend than an angel.

Dyce selected yet another champagne glass with yet another stain, this one darker than the previous one. "Lipstick will be the death of me."

Tioga squeezed a slice of lime into the bubbly water and then lifted the glass and sipped slowly. "You'd outlaw a lot of stuff."

Dyce laughed. Then he placed his big hands on the bar and leaned forward. "Well, I sure as hell wouldn't outlaw Storm. She was hella hot last time I heard her, though the yahoos around here don't appreciate her. I include McCoy. He's a killjoy. The bottom line is everything and fun be damned!"

Tioga covered her mouth with the back of her left hand and yawned. "I missed the performance. Got in too late and the next morning I felt like shit. I mean, I didn't know who the fuck I was. Howling didn't help, though I revived when Ambrose told me about a dead body on the side of the highway. There's nothing like a murder to lift my spirits."

Dyce selected a Bonnie Raitt CD, *Luck of the Draw*, and popped it into the boom box behind the bar. "I know who you are, even when you think you're going out of your mind."

Tioga heard footsteps behind her. It was Mr. Matt Chehab, who sported a paisley ascot and a silk shirt. His head was bandaged and he walked with the aid of a cane that had a carved handle. Over his left shoulder, he carried a Winchester. He sat down gingerly at the far end of the bar and pointed to the beers on tap. "A pint, Seanie," he said smugly.

Dyce reached for a mug, filled it with the Stella on tap and admired the head he'd so expertly crafted. "You see what I mean. He won't even call me by my right name. I mean no one calls me Seanie and gets away with it. Not even my homie, Aaron Holmes."

Tioga stirred the Pellegrino with the swivel stick and cast her eyes in Chehab's direction, though she didn't make direct eye contact with him. Chehab placed the Winchester on the bar, sipped his beer, turned toward Tioga and offered her an expression as if to say he wanted her shoulder to cry on. "Matt," she began, and then added, ironically, "you're a sight for sore eyes," though her irony was lost on Chehab. She stood up, walked toward him, sat down on the stool next to his. Up close he looked even more sorry for himself. "I was bulldozed by a wild hog. Four hundred pounds. Blindsided me—a sow with piglets. But, *kaboom*, Terry bagged her with one shot. She keeled over and the piglets scurried for cover."

Tioga looked at the Winchester and scowled. "Nifty toy. It won the West, or lost the West, depending on how you look at it." She turned to Chehab and asked, in as innocent a tone of voice as she could muster, "Is it loaded, Matt?"

Chehab shrugged his big round shoulders. "How in the hell should I know!" he barked. "I don't know anything about guns or ammo, though this stupid thing is registered in my name. Terry usually keeps it under the desk in his office in case of an invasion. You know home invasions could become a way of life around here. They are out in Sebastopol; that place is pot central. I wouldn't be surprised if the cartel guys hit the Mar Monte, but we're ready. Buddy Moscosco has taken his guns out of mothballs. Anyone gets inside is not going to leave alive."

Tioga lifted the Winchester, placed the stock against her right shoulder, released the safety, put her finger on the trigger and aimed for the framed black-and-white-photo of General Mariano Guadalupe Vallejo that hung on the wall, his eyes watching everyone who went in and out of the bar, as if the territory still belonged to him. "Cover your ears! Just in case." She paused, put down the gun and added, "Let's see what happens. An experiment in firepower."

She placed the stock against her shoulder once again, aimed at the general, pulled the trigger, felt the kick of the rifle as it recoiled, heard the *kaboom*, and the sound of breaking glass.

"What the fuck!" Chehab screeched. "You're out of your mind."

Tioga shot her eyes across the room and saw that the bullet had punctured the General's ox-like neck. "I never liked the guy. He jumped ship and joined up with that maniacal killer, William Tecumseh Sherman."

Dyce looked at Vallejo and clapped his hands. "I've been sick and tired of looking at his puss."

Chehab took the Winchester away from Tioga as if taking a toy away from a delinquent and placed it behind the bar where it was out-of-sight. "You enjoyed that, didn't you," he said smugly. "Cheap thrills!"

Tioga opened her jacket and revealed the snub nose in its holster. "I live with this baby everyday, but it feels good to take target practice with a real weapon."

Chehab looked as if he had regained his composure. "The photo of the general is easily replaced. I can order another on the Internet, but, as for now, there'll be no more firing of any weapons in the Mar Monte. Anyone who violates that rule will answer to me."

Tioga heard Terry McCoy's voice at the back on the room, though she couldn't make out anything that he said. His words were all scrambled in one long undecipherable sentence that reminded her that when her father was drunk he read William Faulkner aloud. The story never made sense to Tioga when she was a pre-teen and already posing in the nude, though she remembered that she liked the character who was named Joe Christmas.

"Gee, thanks, Dad," she'd said when he reached the last sentence in the last paragraph of *Light in August*. "Not exactly a story for kids."

Tioga glanced over her shoulder hoping she might actually see Joe Christmas, but that was not meant to be. Terry McCoy was wearing a plaid hunter's cap and a tweed vest. He stopped just short of Chehab and put his arm around his shoulder.

"Ouch," Chehab said and winced. "Be careful. It hurts."

McCoy turned to Tioga and gave her a look of disapproval. "From where you're standing and where the bullet pierced Vallejo's neck, it must have been you who fired the Winchester. I thought you hated guns, but maybe you've had a change of heart. Maybe you'd like to kill a few wolves.

Matt and I saw a she-wolf in the hills above Cazadero. You'd fit right in, Tioga, along with the bobcats, the coyotes and the wolf pack that lives above Bielawski's biodynamic farm. Hey, I have a new source, but don't repeat that."

McCoy removed the pocket watch from his vest, held it in the palm of his right hand, checked the time and then bore down on poor Chehab. "I should have known not to take my Beirut buddy on a hunting expedition into the wilderness. But he's had his baptism of fire."

McCoy paused for a few seconds and then smiled benevolently at Chehab, Dyce and Tioga. " Now we have an unlimited supply of wild boar. I bagged two. We had help transporting the big carcass from a guerrilla grower who calls himself 'Lone Wolf,' and who said he hadn't seen a fellow human for a month. I don't think he even knows what human is anymore." McCoy turned to Chehab as if asking for confirmation of his report.

"'The fellow didn't look human," Chehab said. "He wasn't communicative, except with sign language. He excelled at that. His pot farm is strictly, hum, what shall I say … under the radar."

McCoy scanned the bottles of booze on the ledge behind the bar. "Don't know what I want," he said indifferently. "What do you think, Sean? This is your area of expertise."

Dyce didn't bother to see what was available on the shelf. "We have a 2017 Calamonaci cab that just came in. I've tried it. I like it. It's rich and fruity and it has a great finish."

McCoy removed his vest and plaid cap and placed them on the hook under the bar. Then he squeezed an invisible trigger. "*Kaboom*. Yes, I'll have the Calamonaci. I've heard it's the best rocket juice around."

Tioga stared at McCoy and he stared at her. Neither blinked, nor backed down. It was a stand off. McCoy puffed out his chest. Tioga set her glass down on the bar and rolled up her sleeves. Then she sipped her Pellegrino, though the fizz had gone and the slice of lime looked as if it had been squeezed to death.

"You know, Tioga, I worry about you," McCoy said and shook his head. "I thought you had spunk. When Storm first introduced you to me, I had high hopes."

Tioga felt as if McCoy could see right through her. His look was piercing.

"You've turned out to be more conventional than the most conventional of the couples who roll into town in their Porsches, go to a tasting room or two, eat Jonny Field's food, spend a night in one of our suites and pretend they're still madly in love. They act like they have to pack it all in before the world ends."

Tioga turned away from McCoy. "You mean it's not the end of the world?" she asked facetiously.

McCoy laughed one of his signature laughs. "Of course not. The Valley isn't going away and neither is the plaza or the Mar Monte. Forget about doom and gloom. Party!"

Tioga took out her cell and held it her hands. "I'd like to take your picture, Terry, if you don't mind."

McCoy's head jerked back. "Oh, but I do mind. How 'bout I put my hand up your skirt and find out what's really there."

Dyce uncorked the cab and poured just enough for McCoy to taste and decide whether he wanted it or not. McCoy tilted the glass and inserted his nose as far as it would go. Then he sipped. "Not bad. Not bad at all."

Dyce filled McCoy's glass about halfway.

Tioga aimed her cell at McCoy. "Smile. I'll take your photo and we'll negotiate the rest." She took one photo and then another and yet another after that one, until McCoy raised his hand and held it in front of his face. "That's quite enough. I don't like to have my photo taken."

Tioga waited for the next salvo. She knew it was coming.

"You call yourself a dyke, Tioga, but there's nothing really queer about you. My Beirut banker buddy, Chehab, is more of a misfit than you. Hell, he doesn't know if he's Christian, Muslim, or Jew, whether he's supposed to make a pilgrimage to Mecca or Jerusalem, and if he ought to celebrate Ramadan, Christmas or some other frickin' holiday. Talk about fucked up, if you'll pardon the expression. Matthew Chehab is one fucked-up human being."

McCoy lifted his wine glass and stared at Chehab. He seemed to enjoy the verbal drubbing he gave his hunting buddy. "I don't mean to hurt your feelings, Matt. But sometimes you've got to hear the naked truth."

He turned his whole body around and glared at Tioga. "That applies to you too, Ms. Vignetta," he said, sounding like a priest. "Life outside the walls of the Mar Monte will do you and Storm a world of good. You have had it far too plush in the penthouse."

Tioga sat motionless and stone-faced and waited patiently until McCoy ran out of steam. She knew him well enough to know that he wouldn't keep going. In fact, he was already beginning to tire. "How well do you know Acapulco? I'm curious."

McCoy glanced at Tioga's ankle and then worked his way up to her knee. "Planning a vacation?"

Tioga spread her legs and lifted her skirt. "Sort of. I heard you know the scene down there." She looked at the spider bite. The swelling had gone down and the redness had faded. No wonder she was beginning to feel her old self again, though she wasn't certain who or what her old self had been. It seemed like such a long time ago that she knew. "Is there anything else you'd like to say to me, Terry? You might as well get it off your chest."

Tioga knew, or thought she knew, that McCoy wanted to grope her, fondle her and molest her, though for the moment he merely let his eyeballs do the heavy lifting.

He peered at the neon sign that said, "Exit," and turned his head quickly—his neck bones snapped—without moving the rest of his body.

Slowly and rather methodically, he walked his eyeballs all over Tioga's thighs, which glimmered in the soft light. McCoy leaned back. For the moment, he seemed to be satiated.

Tioga scratched the spider bite. "I hope you've enjoyed yourself. 'Cause I've enjoyed watching you make a fool of yourself."

She crossed and uncrossed her legs, pulled her skirt a tad higher and watched as McCoy's eyes bulged. She had pulled his trigger. "I heard that you once went by the name Mack and scattered your seed freely."

McCoy stood up and leaned into the long shadow that fell across the floor. "Your ex must have told you a lot of fairy tales."

Tioga swirled the last of the ice in her glass. "You and your buddy, Hawk, must have a lot of dirty laundry between the two of you."

McCoy's nostrils flared. "Fuck you, Tioga. I'm not sorry you're moving out; the sooner the better as far as I'm concerned. Now if you'll excuse me I have to find my dear wife."

He started for the exit and then stopped and looked back. "You haven't seen Gina, have you?" he asked and sounded like yet another desperate husband. "I haven't seen her anywhere today."

Tioga glanced at Dyce and Dyce in turn glanced at McCoy. "Relax, man," Tioga said.

Sean poured himself another sparkling water and added, "I haven't seen Gina either."

Tioga took Hawk's money from her purse and arranged the bills on the bar. "Anyone want to take another shot at the general? I'll wager a hundred no one can hit the whites of his eyes."

McCoy looked distressed. "I gotta find my wife," he said and walked to the back of the Underground, drew the black curtain aside and vanished in the darkness.

Dyce gathered McCoy's wine glass and placed it in the dishwasher. "What was all that about McCoy and Acapulco?"

Tioga grabbed her purse and tucked it under her arm. "Playing chicken."

The house phone rang. Dyce took his time getting to it.

"Yes," he said and held the receiver away from his ear. "Yes, I understand ... Wait a sec ... are you alright? ... Yes, she's here now ... Should I put her on? ... Okay ... Wait till I have paper and pen." He put down the phone and fumbled for the pencil and the pad that lived next to the cash register. "It's Camilla," he said to Tioga. "She sounds freaked."

Tioga unrolled her shirtsleeves. "Why is she calling the Underground and not my cell?"

Dyce picked up the phone. "I'm here. I'm ready ... Yes ... try to stay calm ... I understand ... Yes, Camilla, she knows. You can tell her when you see her ... I got it. I got it. I'll give it to her right now. Bye, baby."

He hung up the phone and tugged at Tioga's elbow. "Camilla wants you go and get her. She's at 565 Avenida de la Virgen, two blocks from Juarez. A nifty Mexican dive called El Buen Comer which made it into the Michelin Guide."

Tioga took the note that Dyce handed her and looked at the address he had written down. "Oh, yeah, I know the place. Camilla's mother works there."

An Inside Job

Behind the counter at 565 Avenida de la Virgen—the nifty Mexican dive with three Michelin stars—the pug-nosed cashier smiled and revealed two gold-plated front teeth.

"I love your mouth," Tioga exclaimed. "The gold looks great on you."

The cashier smiled again—she couldn't help it—and tossed back her shoulder-length hair. "Thank you. They're real gold. My boyfriend thinks they make me look like I'm in a *telenovela*."

Tioga turned away from the gold teeth and looked at the menu, the *agua fresca* and the tables that were packed tightly together in a large room with windows on three sides and a door that led to a gravel parking lot, which also served the clientele at *Mantequilla dulce*, the tattoo parlor.

Camilla's mother, Victoria, who ruled the roost at El Buen Comer, wore a white apron and a white hat. She might have noticed Tioga had she paid attention to everyone who entered the restaurant through the front door. But she was in the midst of an animated conversation with a man who sat opposite her and who swung his arms wildly as if to underline and italicize his words, oblivious of the waiters who took detours around him, lest he hit a plate with *chile rellenos*, cream, pomegranate seeds, black beans and avocado slices. He didn't seem capable of talking without putting everything in caps with exclamation marks and in bold.

Tioga did not recognize him, though she stared at the back of his head—he had short brown hair and a thick neck. His clothes—he wore a black leather jacket, dark slacks and pointy black shoes—didn't provide her with a clue as to who he was either.

"I'm supposed to meet Victoria's daughter here," Tioga said to the cashier who was adding up the bill for a white-haired customer who had cut to the front of the line and handed over his credit card, all while he fidgeted with his cell.

"Just a minute, sir," the cashier said. She turned away from the white-haired gentleman and from the line of tourists—they were all tourists—that extended from the front door to the sidewalk that wrapped around the building.

The gold-toothed cashier whispered in Spanish to the dapper dishwasher who stood at the stainless steel sink, his hands submerged in soapy water.

To Tioga the words sounded like "*Si, maricón.*"

"*Si, maricón,*" she echoed.

There was hardly room to turn around and no proper lane to the tables. Customers had to move sideways. Tioga peeked into the kitchen, which was as cramped as the dining room, but where two men and two women, all of them in white aprons, performed a ballet with gigantic spoons and huge knives and didn't collide with one another.

"I don't see Camilla, but I see her mother," Tioga said to anyone who might be listening but to no one in particular. "Her mother is with a man I don't know, at least not from the back of his head."

The cashier smiled again and blinked her eyelids. "He's a cop, and he's here all the time. He makes everyone nervous."

Tioga nodded her head. "Yeah. Cops make me nervous too. I never know if they're going to cuff me or kiss me."

The cashier handed the customer—who talked on his cell throughout the transaction—his credit card, which he examined as if looking for a reason to complain.

"Sign," she said and sounded belligerent. Then to Tioga she added, "Camilla's in the way back, at the very last table, trying to look invisible, but I'm sure she'll be relieved to see you. She's freaked about something."

A large photograph on the dining room wall depicted the Mexican actor and comedian, Cantinflas, who wore a funny hat and the oddest—and most abbreviated—mustache ever. It was signed, "For Maggie, from your secret admirer, Cantinflas." Another photo seemed to be missing. Tioga noticed a vacant space on the wall about the same size as the autographed photo. At the far end of the dining room, she sat down opposite Camilla and stared at a round black dot the size of a thumbprint on her forehead. It had not been there when she left the office earlier that day. "You're a marked woman. How fitting!"

Camilla wore dark glasses. Tioga couldn't see her eyes, though she saw instantly that she was out of sorts. "Are you eating or drinking?"

Camilla ventured a smile. "I'm starving but I'm afraid if I eat, I won't be able to keep it down."

Tioga tried to read the writing inside Camilla's head—a hopeless task—though she kept at it. "Thanks for the medical report."

A waiter with a black moustache and slicked-back black hair—who wore high-waisted, pegged trousers—placed a frosty Dos Equis on the table and then disappeared. Camilla reached for the bottle, brought it to her lips and sipped. Then she rolled it across her forehead, closed her eyes and leaned back. "Oh, that feels so good."

Tioga hopped, visually speaking, from table to table, hoping to recognize at least one or maybe even two locals and turned away disappointed. She didn't know a single person, save for Victoria, who still sat with the cop who punctuated the air with italics and exclamation marks.

Camilla pressed her thumbs against the temples of her forehead. "These people are too dumb to know they're eating gourmet food. They're doing what they were urged to do by some foodie magazine."

Tioga looked at two men in overalls splattered with paint. "Those guys are for real. They've done a day's work." Then she turned to a group of young women—girls really—who sat around a large table, munched on corn chips, giggled and drank Coca-Cola. When their food arrived, they picked at it.

Tioga crossed her legs. "Would you like ice cubes? Would that help?"

Camilla moaned. "Oh, yes, please." She looked like a voyager who had been blown off course and who was now back home, but who seemed more lost than ever. "It feels like a man with a sledgehammer is inside my head banging away."

Tioga pushed her chair away from the table, stood up, filled a bucket with ice from the ice chest, and borrowed a towel from the mustached waiter who hovered nearby, ready to serve. She sat down again, opened the towel, added ice cubes, folded it in half and placed it on Camilla's forehead. "Shall I drive you to the ER at Mercy? Are you in critical condition? Or shall I kiss it and make it better? I can play fairy godmother, if you'd like."

Camilla removed the compress and laid it on the table. "That's funny: you as a fairy godmother. I like it. There's nothing Julie Andrews about you, is there, unless you're hiding it?"

She lowered her head and held it between her hands. "No, I don't need the ER at Mercy. Maggie gave me something herbal. I took a ton of it. It's kicking in now. I can feel it clearing my head."

The waiter with the moustache and the slicked-back black hair hovered above Tioga. If Hawk dressed like a Zen gangster, the waiter dressed like an Aztec gangbanger. "Would you like to see a menu?" he asked, then bowed ever so slightly and fired off another question: "May I tell you the specials?"

Tioga looked at the list of appetizers and entrées that were written in chalk on the blackboard next to the photo of Cantinflas. "I'll have an IPA and the fish tacos with black beans. Hold the rice."

Camilla rubbed her belly. "Same for me, but hold the black beans."

Tioga took out her cell and placed it on the table. "So what's going on with you?"

Camilla removed her hands from her belly and put her palms on the table. "You go first. Tell me what's going on with you."

Tioga sipped the IPA. "Okay here goes. Hawk gave me the old heave-ho, but he coughed up even more money. It feels like he's trying to buy me off."

The waiter served a basket of chips and a bowl with guacamole. "Compliments of Señora Maggie."

Camilla dipped a chip in the guacamole. "I don't like Hawk one bit. He's a pervert"

Tioga scooped the guacamole with a chip. "That sounds extreme. Of course, you're not your normal self. You could be suffering from PTSD."

Camilla added salt to the chip in her hand, placed it on her tongue, then chewed, waiting to speak until she had swallowed. "You'll probably think I'm hallucinating, but Clark is sitting with my mother in the far corner of the room."

Tioga turned her head and looked behind her, though she still couldn't see Clark's face. "How do you know it's Clark? He's turned away from you."

Camilla made a funny face. "I sat behind him in school.".

Just then the zoot-suit waiter served the entrées, though he mistakenly served Camilla the plate with the beans and Tioga the plate with the rice. Tioga switched them, lifted her fork and attacked the black beans. Camilla stared at the rice in front of her. Then she raised her eyes and looked into the distance. "I knew it," she said. "Clark is coming toward us."

Tioga resisted the urge to turn her head.

Camilla cut her fish taco into pieces, speared one of them and swallowed it slowly to make sure it would go down and stay down.

Clark towered above Tioga. He smiled and dropped a plastic container on the table. "I hope you're enjoying the food," he said. "I did. I always do."

Tioga looked at his pointy black shoes, size twelve, she thought, and his rayon shirt, extra large.

"Have a seat, Clark," she said. "Come down to our level and drop the capital letters."

Clark sat down and folded his hands in his lap. "What capital letters? I was just talking to Mrs. Sanchez about the robbery that took place here. She's very cooperative. We have a few leads."

Tioga scooped the black beans on the end of her fork. "Capital letters … it's a figure of speech."

Clark seemed no better off with the explanation than without it. He gaped at Camilla's forehead. "Wait a minute, what's with the black dot? It's not Ash Wednesday."

Camilla shrugged her shoulders. "What dot?" she asked. When Clark pointed to her forehead, she took out her compact and stared at her face. "Oh, that. Not to worry. I'll make it go away." She soaked a napkin in water and rubbed her forehead. "Better now?"

Clark indulged her with a smile. "Not really. It looks weirder."

Tioga chewed a taco. Then she raised her eyebrows and turned to Clark. "You're not working on the Dorothy Baynes case now, are you?"

Clark cleared his throat. "No, not now, ma'am. Ambrose took over the investigation. He's taking a real personal interest."

Tioga held her fork in one hand and her knife in the other. "Listen, Clark, I was hoping you could do Mrs. Baynes a huge favor. It would mean a lot to her."

Clark leaned forward and gave Tioga his undivided attention. "Yeah, what favor is that?" he asked and followed it with the word, "shoot."

Tioga looked at Camilla, who wore an expression of disbelief on her face, and then at Clark, who tilted his chair back until it stood on its hind legs. "I know this is highly irregular. But give Mrs. Baynes the ring. Dorothy took it without her mother's permission. Now Mrs. Baynes doesn't have much longer to live. It's a kindness you won't regret."

Clark no longer wore a smile. In fact, he looked dumbfounded. "I understand where you're coming from, miss. But you're pushing it." He paused and looked at Camilla as if he felt sorry for her and embarrassed for himself. "I can't respond. Good day, ladies."

He stood up, turned his back on Tioga and Camilla and walked toward the gravel parking lot at the back of the restaurant. Tioga watched him swing his big body into the cruiser as if he was Tarzan of the Apes in the jungle.

Then she drummed her spoon on the tabletop." Why were you unable to drive? I mean I came all this way thinking you were desperate, and now you're just spacey."

Camilla wrapped the cold compress around her forehead. "I'm getting there. If I seem spacey, it's because I smoked a ton of wicked hash. It's not easy to think."

She glanced at the photo of Cantinflas as if he might jog her memory. "I don't understand, Tioga, why you asked Clark to return the wedding ring to Mrs. Baynes. It makes no sense. There's nothing in it for him."

She pointed to the photo of Cantiflas who wore a three-cornered-hat, an impish smile and a bandana around his neck. "Do you know who that is?"

Tioga squinted her eyes. "Yeah! That's Cantinflas! He made movies. Do I win a teddy bear?" She beamed like a schoolgirl. "I asked Clark about the ring because I wanted to see how far I could push him. Now I know. But the main thing is we know he's not working on the Baynes case. I bet Ambrose never showed him the photos he showed me. He wants Clark as far away from this case as possible."

She stood up, moved closer to the photo and read the handwritten message that read: "To Señorita Brazil, *con mucho armor,* Cantinflas, D. F., April 1, 1993."

Now Maggie Brazil—tall, thin, blond and Nordic-looking, despite her Latino surname—sauntered toward Camilla and Tioga and sat down in the chair that Clark had just vacated. Maggie placed a folder on the table and smiled, Tioga thought, the way her own mother smiled at cocktail parties when she wore a little black dress and sipped a martini. Tioga felt intimidated in Maggie's presence. Intimidation seemed to be built into her DNA. It came in handy; she didn't beat anyone over the head with a lead pipe or add rat poison in the enchiladas she served those she didn't like. So she used her face and her body.

"Clark has been zero help on the robbery!" Maggie said as if complaining about a dishwasher in the kitchen. "Next time I won't bother calling him."

Tioga put her knife and her fork across her plate, the way she'd been taught at the Badminton School. "A polite, well-mannered girl," the headmistresses had explained, "would not be a depraved girl."

Tioga gave Maggie a sisterly gaze. "Come to us next time," she said. "That is, if there is a next time." She turned to Camilla. "Right, Miss Sanchez?"

The music pulsed from the loudspeakers. The room shimmied and shook, and the zoot-suit waiter snapped his fingers and danced down the aisle. Tioga sang, "Boys say, 'When is he gonna give us some room'/Girls say, 'God I hope he comes back soon.'"

Camilla beat a rhythm on the top of the table. "I swear I'd recognize that man if I saw him."

Maggie glanced from table to table, all of them filled. Then she looked toward the kitchen, which echoed with the bang and clang of pots and pans.

Camilla lifted the Dos Equis and wrapped her lips around the bottle. "It's starting to come back; I know I'll remember more if we go up Avenida de la Virgen."

Maggie raised her hand and waved it above her head. "*Dos mas cervezas, por favor,*" she shouted at the mustached waiter. She looked down at the formica tabletop. "I think you've heard the news already. Someone—or some ones—broke in and stole one hundred thousand. I know … I know …"

She raised her hands as if surrendering her naiveté. "We did well two weeks in a row, and I didn't have a chance to get to the bank. After we made the Michelin Guide, this place went crazy. Look at it now."

She paused, surveyed the room and stared at the wall. "The thieves stole the other photo of Cantinflas and me in Xochimilco when I was nineteen."

147

Camilla didn't seem to be impressed. "Bully for you and for Cantinflas. The robbery has to be an inside job."

Maggie sneered. "Go ahead, make fun of me."

Camilla locked eyes with her. "I wasn't making fun."

Maggie opened the folder that she had placed on the table and removed the photos. There were four of them. The men looked like brothers or perhaps cousins and had more or less the same features: dark skin, matted black hair and scars on their cheeks. "These are the suspects. I showed the photos to Clark, who swore he recognized them from The Springs. Ne'er-do-wells."

She looked at Tioga imploringly. "Clark said that the sheriff arrested them, handed them over to ICE and that they were shipped to the border. But when I called Randy Scheck, he said that the sheriff doesn't cooperate with ICE and that the suspects have to be at-large."

Tioga scrutinized the photos and turned them over one by one. "Seems everybody around here has photos to share."

Brazil looked at her quizzically. "Excuse me. I don't get the reference."

Camilla reached for the photos and then turned up her nose. "Private joke. George Ambrose showed Tioga photos of Dorothy Baynes, who was raped and murdered, her body apparently dumped on the side of the road."

Maggie flinched. "I heard. It's terrible. The Valley needs a rain to wash away its sins."

Tioga raised her Dos Equis. "So Maggie, it seems like you found these photos on the internet and printed them."

Maggie nodded and then gathered the photos and returned them to the folder. "Clark says there's nothing he can do. There are no witnesses, no fingerprints and no DNA. A dozen or so people knew the money was here."

Tioga looked toward the parking lot and saw Clark sitting behind the wheel of his cruiser. "I'm sorry. It must hurt to lose all that money. If you're serious about Camilla and me investigating, we'll give it serious consideration. A case we were working on just folded like a house of cards."

Camilla rolled her big brown eyes. "You're a big target, Mrs. Brazil. Everyone in The Springs knows you're ... how shall I put it? ... you're damned rich."

Maggie shook her head. "I'm not Mrs. Brazil. I'm Maggie. And no one makes better Mexican food than we do."

Camilla pounded both fists on the table. "My mother makes the food authentic. The recipes come from her and my grandmother."

Maggie kicked her right leg back and forth. "Yes, I know. That's why we have your mother's and your grandmother's names on the menu: 'Victoria's red mole chicken tamales in banana leaf.' Can't you read? Those recipes would be lost without me."

Then she stormed off. The waiter cleared the table. Camilla seemed distracted. Tioga glanced at her cell and then at the parking lot where Maggie now sat in the passenger seat of Clark's cruiser. The preteens at the adjacent table gathered their backpacks and filed out the back door. Tioga wanted to join them. They would be loads of fun, more so than her classmates had been.

Camilla looked like she was ready to explode. "I wouldn't be surprised if Maggie took the money and has a scheme to cover it up with Clark."

She smiled at her mother, who stood under the photo of Cantinflas. "*¿Qué hay de nuevo, mamá?*"

Victoria Sanchez wore a cute expression that the preteens might have appreciated. "*Nada excepto el estúpido policía que piensa que él y yo somos viejos amigos. Me cuesta mucho deshacerse de él.*"

Tioga saw the likeness between mother and daughter: soft dark eyes, light brown hair and round faces. "Can you

149

translate, please? I got the part about the stupid police, but I missed the rest of it."

Camilla wrapped her arms around her mother. "Victoria said the stupid policeman acts like he's an old friend and it's very hard to get rid of him. *Gracias, mamá*. You better go back to the kitchen before all hell breaks loose. Ms. Vignetta and I have to hunt for my car on the hill. I don't remember where I parked it."

Victoria picked up the check and tore it in little pieces. "You never pay. Not as long as I'm here."

She disappeared in the kitchen, which suddenly went silent.

Camilla reached into the basket on the table, grabbed a handful of corn chips and filled her pockets. Tioga looked at her cell and shook her head. "We're late. We're always late."

She took a last look at Cantinflas, who had gotten under her skin, and blew him a kiss that might have made him swoon. "*Adiós, mi amor. Mas tarde.*" She linked arms with Camilla, though Camilla pushed her away and walked alone. Tioga led the way uphill. Before long, she stopped and admired the raggedy street that boasted small, brightly painted houses packed closely together, two-stories high, with cement steps that led to front porches. "Talk," Tioga roared. "Tell me what the fuck happened to you!"

Camilla munched on a corn chip. "Okay, okay. I was stoned and couldn't drive. I called you and you came and found me. That's what happened."

Tioga's cell buzzed. "I gotta take this. Don't run off." She held the phone to her ear and nodded. "Are you sure … Okay, I'll meet you at the market. Wait for me." To Camilla she said, "Sorry. Go on with your story, please."

Camilla looked down hill toward El Buen Comer, then turned and looked uphill where Avenida de La Virgen dead-ended at Zacatecas where the sign read "One Way," though cars were going every which way. "Well, I'll tell you, I park outside 49 Avenida de la Virgen and don't see in because the curtains are drawn. Then a car pulls up and two men get out."

Tioga looked down hill at a slender figure in shorts, a boy or man, she wasn't sure, who kicked a soccer ball into a wall again and again and again. "Okay, I get the picture, Camilla, but do you have to use the present tense?"

Camilla put a corn chip in her mouth and chewed slowly. "What, you don't like the present tense! You're awfully picky."

Tioga looked back at the figure with the ball: a small man with short legs. He went on kicking the ball against the wall. "Go on with your story, in whatever tense you want."

Camilla offered Tioga a chip. "Take one. It won't ruin your figure." Tioga took one, and, though Camilla gave her an encouraging look, wouldn't take a second.

"I see the curtain move," Camilla continued. "A woman's face appears, the blue front door opens and one of the men comes out of the house, walks up to me, sitting in the car, and squats down so he's eye-level. He says, 'Señorita, why don't you come inside and see for yourself? It will be on the market very soon. You can be the first to make an offer.'"

Camilla stopped and adjusted the beret that had slipped from her head. "You got the story so far? I'm trying to sim-plify for you."

Tioga took a cigarette from the pack, which lived in her purse, fired it up and inhaled. "I'm glad you're going chronologically."

Camilla took the cigarette from Tioga, put it between her lips, inhaled slowly and blew the smoke above her head. "I'm always chronological. Except when I'm not. I go both ways. I mean, I do was and is, and did and does, and loved and loves. Got it?"

She handed the cigarette to Tioga and looked at the house with green awnings and a purple door, just down from forty-nine. "I didn't have a choice. I had to go inside."

With the heel of her shoe, Tioga extinguished the cigarette on the pavement. A car low to the ground cruised uphill slowly. The sun beat down, and the wind kicked up.

"The two guys had guns," Camilla continued. "They were smoking hash in a pipe. I wanted to blend in, so I smoked and got stoned. That's when they put the dot on my forehead and told me not to wash it away or it would bring bad luck. I started to hallucinate and then one of the guys hands me his gun, tells me it's an AR-15, and explains that he and his brother are Yaquis, only his brother won't admit it. There were two women. One had dark hair and dark skin; the other was an Asian. She made an altar with candles, incense and black-and-white snapshots of people and animals: bears, foxes, wolves and such."

Tioga walked to the sidewalk. Camilla followed her and looked at the door of the house where she had been stoned out of her mind. "They had a ceremony, and then they ate rice, tofu and beans. I wandered upstairs, went into the bedroom, which was stripped bare. Then I went down the backstairs to the kitchen, and, from there, to a basement that would astound you."

Tioga nodded her head and walked further uphill. "I'm sure I would and it will," she said and sounded enthusiastic. "I like basements." She stopped and examined the black dot once again. "Then what happened?"

Camilla adjusted her beret again. It had to be a certain way. "The storage bins in the basement were piled high," she said. "I tried to open one and couldn't. Then I passed out. Next thing I knew one of the Yaquis carried me upstairs.

The front door opened. I didn't want to go into the street. I felt safe in the house. 'Bye bye,' the Asian woman said and the other added, 'Watch out, dearie, so the big bad wolf won't get you.' Ha, ha, ha. I didn't think that was funny, but they did."

Tioga had reached the top of the hill. She stopped and looked back at the street below and saw neither a boy nor a man with a ball, but a woman who carried two sacks, one in each hand, which swayed back and forth as she walked. "I like it better when you use the past tense. Like was, not is; said, not says; knew, not knows; went, not goes, and stopped, not stops."

Then she turned to Camilla and asked, "Did you see a man kicking a ball at the bottom of the hill?"

"No, I didn't. Maybe you're stoned and are seeing things."

A moment later, Tioga heard Camilla's cry from around the corner. When she turned the same corner, she saw Camilla's Subaru lodged between a white pickup truck glistening in the sun and a Honda Civic caked with dust. The Subaru was now barely recognizable. The windshield was shattered, the side-view mirrors torn from the body and broken into pieces that were scattered on the pavement. No repo man would bother with it.

"Oh, fuck!" Camilla shouted. "Oh, fuck! Oh, fuck!"

Tioga circled the wreck and shook her head. "There's nothing salvageable here. Call a tow truck." She picked up the twisted antenna from the pavement and added, "I'm sorry." Then she read the graffiti that had been spray-painted in black Gothic letters on the side of the vehicle: *vete a la puta perra*. The words didn't make sense. But "Go to the bitch" probably wasn't meant to make sense.

In the background, Tioga heard the sound of drums, and, when she looked ahead, she saw two loudspeakers perched on the ledge at an open window. Then she looked sadly at Camilla's car. "This isn't the work of the Yaquis. I've known Yaquis. Even dirtbag Yaquis wouldn't do this. Somebody else wrote this shit. Somebody mean."

Camilla followed Tioga as she circled the Subaru. "Fuck, fuck, fuck!" she shouted, her voice getting louder and louder each time she said "fuck." With the final expletive, she pounded her fist so hard on the hood of the vehicle that she broke the skin, and blood began to flow, not a lot but enough to frightened her. "Oh, shit," she said and looked mournfully at her bloody hand. "I can't believe somebody did this to me. I swear I'll kill him or her or them."

Tioga removed her shirt, tore it into two strips and wrapped one of them around Camilla's bloody hand. "Keep your arm above your head. It'll slow the bleeding."

Camilla raised her arm toward the sky and moved her neck from side to side until her bones cracked. "You're nearly naked, Tioga. You'd better cover up before someone call the cops and complains."

Tioga walked toward the steps that led to the front door at number 57 Avenida de La Virgen where the sound of the drums originated.

Camilla took out her phone, and with the fingers on her left hand began to hit numbers on the keypad. "*Sí, mamá, es horrible,*" she wailed while she held the phone in her left hand and kept her right extended above her head.

Bike Man

Tioga watched the rear wheel of an upside-down bicycle as it spun around and around so fast that the spokes were invisible. A muscular man with a beard and a baseball cap tilted to one side pushed the pedal that propelled the wheel. On an oily cloth there were a few tools: a pair of pliers, a wrench, a screwdriver and a hammer that struck her as menacing.

Tioga zeroed in on the beard. "Hey, you, Mr. Bike Man," she yelled.

The fellow removed the rear tire from the bicycle and then tried to bounce it on the pavement, but it had no air, and so it just collapsed on the pavement. "Yeah," the fellow said, not bothering to look at Tioga. "Whazzup?" Then he did look and added aggressively, "You sunbathing or somethin'?"

Tioga shrugged her shoulders and watched the guy as he began to patch the flat. "Nice bike," she said. Then she added, "Do you think I could borrow something so I can cover up. I had to use my shirt to make a tourniquet for my friend over there holding her hand above her head. She's hurt." Tioga looked at Camilla, who was now using her cell to take photos of the wreck, and then she asked Bike Man, "Did you see what happened?"

He smiled rather idiotically. "See what happened?" he asked in a defensive tone of voice. He turned his big head slowly and glanced in the direction of the wreck without really seeing it, or so it appeared to Tioga, who was trying to read his body language, which made her think of a pimp on his knees at confession with a Bible in one hand and a gun in the other.

"Oh that," Bike Man said as if he had not previously noticed the car. With a pair of pliers he removed a lug nut from the bike. "No, I didn't see nothin'. I was inside. I was listenin' to Ndugu. Can't get enough of him. You know what I mean? Ndugu—he's the dope."

Tioga moved toward Bike Man and the bike under repair. "What about the neighbors at forty-nine? Have you seen them?"

Bike Man put the pliers away and wiped his hands on a black rag he removed from his back pocket. "Yes, as a matter of fact, I did see 'em. But you're too late to catch 'em. They moved out lock, stock and barrel, and they're not comin' back."

He sauntered toward the front steps leading to the porch and the front door swinging back and forth on its hinges. After a minute or so, he emerged with a flannel shirt, which he had rolled into a ball and held in his left hand. "Cover up," he said.

He tossed the shirt to Tioga, who grabbed it midair. She turned her back to Bike Man, put on the shirt, rolled up the sleeves and buttoned the buttons. She opened her purse, removed the photo of Roxanne that Hawk had given her and dangled it in front of Bike Man's big round eyes. "Have you seen this gorgeous woman?"

Bike Man shook his head. "No, I haven't seen that gorgeous woman. I would remember if I had."

Tioga returned the photo to her purse. "Do you know who she is?"

Bike Man returned to the bicycle, turned it right side up and squeezed the hand brakes. "What do you mean by know?" he asked, wearing a cherubic smile.

Tioga shook her head. He was impossible! She opened her wallet, removed one of her business cards and offered it to Bike Man, who studied it as if it was an artifact from another civilization.

"Tioga Vignetta, op," he said out loud while he flicked the card across the stubble on his chin. "Sebastiani Building, Sonoma Plaza. I know it. My great-great grandfather had an office there ... sold insurance. It was pretty nifty. Had a view of the plaza."

He reached for a can, squirted oil on the bicycle chain and then rotated the pedal with his right hand. The wheel spun around and around. "Op? That rhymes with cop and whop and bop, if you know what I mean." He laughed. Tioga eyed him as he eyed her, though not in the lascivious way that McCoy had looked her up and down at the Underground. He added, mischievously, "You don't look like a cop, sound like a cop or dress like a cop. Cops don't parade half-naked in the street."

Tioga heard Camilla's heels clatter on the pavement. She turned and looked downhill.

"Hey, I know you," Bike Man said to Camilla and sounded pleased with himself. "You live on the next street over. I seen you walkin' with a lady who looks a lot like you, only older."

Camilla extended her left hand. "I'm Camilla Sanchez. I work with this lady. I live on Playa del Carmen, though there's no *playa* there."

The fellow laughed again. "Hey, that's pretty funny. No *playa* on Playa del Carmen. And there are no virgins on Avenida de la Virgen either." He extended his right hand and noticed the bloodstained cloth that Tioga wrapped around Camilla's hand. "Ouch," he murmured as he stepped forward and gently squeezed the fingertips on Camilla's unbloodied hand. "I'm Travis Syrah," he said as if he might have been King of The Springs. He shook Tioga's right hand and asked, "What's an op if not a cop?" When Tioga and Camilla both ignored his question, he looked again at the bloody rag. "You wanna come inside? I'm right over here. I can fix you up."

He pointed to a two-story house, which had been painted green a long time ago, or so it seemed, and which now needed a new coat. The number 57 was scrawled on the curb in front of the building.

Tioga stared once again at the bike and then at the tools on the pavement. "You're just going to leave everything out here?"

Travis reached down and covered his tools with an oily rag. "Everybody knows not to mess with me!"

Camilla followed Travis, and Tioga followed her. They climbed the steps that brought them to the front porch and into a large room with a high ceiling. The drumming was less loud inside than outside.

Tioga picked up the CD from the table and read the title, "Leon 'Ndugu' Chancler Funky Bootleg Tapes with Miles Davis." She tapped Travis on the shoulder and shouted, "Oh, yeah, this is very funky music. I dig it."

The floors shook and the walls vibrated. A hot wind carried the melody from the open door at the front of the house down the long hallway to the open door at the back of the house. In the bathroom, Travis washed his hands at the sink and dried them on a white towel. Camilla stood at his side and held her bloody hand above her head. Travis flicked the light switch, opened the medicine cabinet, and from the top shelf removed gauze tape and a tube of Neosporin.

He removed Tioga's makeshift bandage and with a clean, wet towel carefully wiped away the dried blood on Camilla's hand. Well, well, he cared, after all. "Sit down."

It sounded like an order, but Camilla did what she was told to do.

Tioga sat down next to her on the cusp of the tub, stretched her legs and looked at the faded wallpaper with yellow ducks in a green pond. "Did you know a woman named Dorothy Baynes? Used to hang out with a horse trainer at the fairgrounds." She would ask everyone she met about Dorothy.

Travis tossed the bloody rag into the wastebasket under the sink. "Yeah, I knew Dot Baynes. I had a crush on her in high school, but so did everyone else. She was the class slut slash homecoming queen."

Tioga found Travis amusing. She wanted to mess with his head. "You mean she was the virgin and the whore!"

Travis squeezed Neosporin on Camilla's cut. "This won't hurt a bit," he said, though Camilla yelped anyway. He bent down, kissed her bloody hand, wrapped gauze around it and taped it closed. "You will heal I promise you, Camilla from Playa del Carmen."

He returned the Neosporin, gauze and tape to the medicine cabinet, shut the door, looked at the stubble on his chin in the mirror, opened his mouth wide and revealed his white teeth. "All of us wanted and needed Dot, the gals as well as the guys," he said, still staring at himself in the mirror. "She ran away, came back with a baby and looked like shit."

Tioga stared at her cell and then fired back at Travis, "Do you know where she is now?"

Travis washed and dried his hands again. "Probably on the way to Cemetery Hill. I heard they found her body along the highway." Then he added sarcastically, "Big Surprise!"

Tioga stood up, peeked outside the bathroom window and ran her eyes along the alley packed with old appliances:

refrigerators, washers, dryers and vacuum cleaners; another sort of graveyard. "News travels fast, don't it?" she said.

With a rag, Travis wiped away the drops of Camilla's blood, which had fallen on the floor and made a curious pattern that looked to Tioga like the head of dog. "In the Valley, news is money," Travis said. "It never stops, never rests and never gives up. That's what Dot never understood, and that's why she's dead now."

Tioga sat down again on the edge of the bathtub, put her arm around Camilla's shoulders and pulled her close. "When you were taking photos of your car, I showed Travis the picture of Roxanne. He said he hadn't seen her and that everyone at forty-nine had cleared out and won't be coming back."

If Travis heard her, he didn't show it. He turned Camilla's hand one way and then another, admiring his work. "You'll be good as new. But go easy for a day or six or ten." Then he laughed. He had a screwy way with numbers.

Camilla stood up and touched her bruised right hand with the fingertips on her left hand. "It still hurts," she said in a whiney tone of voice that elicited no sympathy from either Tioga or Travis, who looked at one another as if to say, "Hey, it's just a bruise, honey, not life threatening."

Tioga stood up and gazed again at the alley that ran from the front to the back of Travis's house. How could he not know anything about his neighbors? Was he hiding behind the music that he played?

Tioga arched her back. Camilla rolled her shoulders and glared at Travis. "You don't know who wrecked my car? How could that be? You live here. You know the neighborhood."

Travis bared his white teeth. "I wish I did know who messed with your car. I heard somethin', but I didn't see nothin'. By the time I came outside, whoever had done the deed was gone. But maybe there are fingerprints. Maybe the cops can find the creeps who fucked up your vehicle royally."

Travis reminded Tioga of her ex-husband before he went rogue, though that didn't mean that she trusted him any more than she had trusted Tomás. She had wanted Tomás to trust her, and now she wanted the same from Travis, if only so he would tell her what he knew about Dorothy Baynes, the virgin and the whore. Tell her, also, what he knew about life inside number forty-nine. "Do you smoke dope?" she asked.

Travis closed the window that overlooked the alley and ran his finger along the sill. "My crop isn't ready to be harvested," he said. "I have at least two more months to go, so I don't have anything on hand right now." He squeezed his throat as if he knew he'd revealed more than he wanted to reveal. Now it was too late to take back his words.

Tioga leaned against the bathroom wall. "Thanks," she said. "About my business card and the word op. It's shorter than private investigator."

Travis chortled. "But not shorter than PI," he said and looked proud of himself. He did have a mind, after all, and knew how to use it.

Prohibitions

Camilla gave Travis a warm smile, despite his inability, or unwillingness, to identify the person or persons who had assaulted her vehicle and left it a wreck. "I was in your neighbor's house earlier today, got stoned, wandered into the basement and passed out. I lost my purse. I'd like to retrieve it. Can you help me?"

Tioga liked the distressed expression that Camilla wore on her face. How could Travis not agree to her request? He rubbed the stubble on his chin and walked from the bathroom to the living room where he turned up the sound of Ndugu's drumming. He was lost in the music, but not so lost that he couldn't stop himself from adoring Camilla. Then he darted off. "Let's go," he shouted. Tioga followed him toward the front door where a blast of hot air messed with the already unruly hair on the top of his big head. He stepped outside, stood for a moment on the porch and then waited on the sidewalk until Camilla and Tioga joined him. "That reminds me," he said and smoothed his hair.

Camilla picked up a bottle cap from the street and tossed it in the air. Travis went to the curb and opened the recycling bin. "I bet $100 you can't sink it."

Camilla held the cap between her fingers. "You're on," she said, then stood up straight, tossing the cap into the air.

Tioga followed it as it traveled up and then traveled down in a long, slow arc and landed squarely inside the bin. "Wow, you owe Camilla big! And what the hell were you thinking when you said a moment ago, 'That reminds me?' Or have you already forgotten?"

Travis removed his wallet and gave Camilla two fifties as if it was no biggie. "What I remembered is that I have to check next door about the broken-down appliance. I tried to fix it and couldn't. It's a washer-dryer combo. The Dulox boys from downtown were supposed to haul it away and leave me cash." For a moment, he seemed lost in thought again, perhaps thinking about the money waiting for him. Then he came back to Tioga. "I have a key. We can go inside, gals, and you can look for your purse, miss."

Tioga recoiled "Gals? You think of Ms. Sanchez and me as gals?"

A hurt expression came over Travis's long face. "Gals, girls, women, ladies, whatever," he said and shrugged his shoulders. Then he selected a key from the large ring that was clasped to his leather belt. At forty-nine, he climbed the steps and paused. "There were hella parties here. Everybody came for the music. The margaritas were to die for. El Buen Comer catered; it was killer food. Once, when we were all totally fucked up, one of the gals, I mean ladies, or should I say a female, stepped naked from a seashell. She had great tits. We went wild."

Tioga laughed. "Ah, another Venus on the half-shell," she said and wondered if Travis, like her ex, made stuff up. "I'm sorry I missed the performance." She followed her comment with a question. "It wasn't Dorothy on the half-shell, was it?"

Travis didn't reply instantly; he was too busy unlocking the lock on the front door. Apparently, he could only do one thing at a time. "Are you ADD?" Tioga asked.

Travis nodded his head. "Yup. Born that way. My mom was a pillhead." He inserted the key, turned it gently, and looked back at the street as if he was a thief and entering illegally. "Come to think of it, it was Dot on the half-shell. There were two guys who couldn't take their eyes off her, like they'd never seen tits like hers before. One of them tried to kiss her but she kicked him where it hurts. His hat went flyin' and he took a spill. His buddy scraped him off the floor."

Travis Syrah, aka Bike Man, aka King of the Hill, waited courteously on the front porch while Tioga and Camilla went ahead. He did have a modicum of manners, and a decent memory, too. It just took time for both to kick in. Travis stepped inside the long, narrow front room that was identical to the front room in his own house. He closed the door behind him and opened the burlap curtains a tad. Enough light penetrated for Tioga to see that the space was bare, except for a fireplace, a mirror on the wall and a rectangular-shaped rug that seemed far too small for so big a room.

Camilla wandered about as if trying to remember, Tioga supposed, what she had seen, heard and smelled in forty-nine before the hash had turned her head to ashes. Alone in the front room, Tioga sniffed the air until her nostrils burned from the ammonia that seemed to have been poured everywhere. The place was spotless. The occupants had removed everything. She bent down, rolled back the carpet and saw a stain that someone had tried to remove. A faint outline remained. "Looks like blood," she whispered, though no one was listening.

With her Swiss Army Knife, she scraped off a piece of the floor, placed it inside a paper towel and then folded the towel and added it to her already bulging purse. She took out her cell, photographed the stain and sent the image to her email address. Then she unrolled the carpet so it covered the stain again.

When she stood up, she heard Camilla and Travis in the distance. She followed the sounds of their voices and walked down the flight of stairs that began in the hallway.

A narrow stream of light helped her navigate the darkness. In the basement, she opened a door and entered a cold, damp room large enough, she thought, to park a fleet of delivery trucks. Ahead of her, Travis and Camilla faded into the shadows.

"What gives?" Tioga asked.

Travis pulled the string for the light bulb that dangled from the ceiling. Tioga could see the smooth cement floor, the whitewashed stonewalls, the beams overhead and the large door that led to the outside and was big enough to allow a truck to enter and exit the space. "This place was for bootleggers," Travis said. "My Uncle Jake stored booze for speakeasies down here. He took a hail of bullets and breathed his last, right where I'm standing. My Aunt Molly carried on after he died as best she could and then she couldn't."

The whitewashed stonewalls looked like they had been recently painted; the cement floor seemed to be immaculately clean.

"Is that a fact?" Tioga asked. "Your Uncle Jake died down here in a hail of bullets?"

Travis grinned mischievously. "Well, don't quote me. He died somewhere in this house. That was before my time." Then he disappeared in the darkness. In a few moments, he came back with cash in one hand and a wine bottle in another. "The Dulox guys took the washer-dryer combo and left me big bucks. That's one more thing off my to-do list, and now I can buy a shitload of bike parts."

With his shirtsleeve, he wiped the dust from the wine bottle and held it above his head as if it was a trophy he'd just won. "This is one of the original bottles that my grandfather produced and stashed here. Made mostly from Zinfandel grapes. He hauled cases down to the officers' club at the Presidio. This bottle is nearly ninety years old." He offered it to Camilla and added, "There's no label because he didn't want it traced back to him."

Camilla wiped away the dust that Travis had missed. "Thanks. I'll try it." She held the bottle under her arm. "Your last name is Syrah? How did you get it?"

Travis' face turned cherubic. He had obviously been waiting for Tioga or Camilla to ask. "It was Dureza over in Europe, but somehow or other it got changed to Syrah when my great-great grandfather came to California. I can show you the family Bible if you want to see."

Tioga took out her cell. "Thanks. But we already have a lot on our plate." She took the bottle from Camilla. "I'm willing to try it too, and how about you give me the number for the Dulox guys?"

When he did, she added the information to her phone. Meanwhile Camilla had aimed for a dark corner at the far end of the bootlegger's basement. "There were containers all along this wall," she said, reaching into the darkness with both hands. "I left my purse here, but I don't see it anywhere."

Tioga sniffed the air and then aimed the light on her cell into the shadows. "Your neighbors, the gals, must have done some bootlegging of their own, so to speak," she said to Travis, who stood with his back to the wall. Then she added, "It smells like weed down here."

Travis took a step backward and vanished in the shadows. "Yeah, they were modern bootleggers. They had good hash and great extracts. I spent a lot of time here, but it's all blurry now. I wish the gals were back. They were great!"

Tioga thought that Travis sounded sorry for himself. "You do have your house, your music and your bicycle, and Camilla is just two blocks away. You're practically neighbors."

She knew that she was matchmaking, and she wasn't sorry. Travis pulled the string on the light bulb and the room went black. Tioga couldn't see him or Camilla, though she could hear them. She followed the sound of Camilla's shoes on the cement floor and on the steps that led upstairs.

"I don't do well in the dark," Camilla murmured, stopping and looking back at Tioga. "It's like a morgue down there." She paused a moment and added in a loud voice that carried into the darkness, "I didn't see my purse anywhere."

Tioga climbed slowly. "Too bad," she said, hearing her words echo in the darkness. Suddenly the door to the basement opened and light poured in. Tioga blinked. "You didn't hear a gunshot at number forty-nine, did you?" she asked.

Travis stepped back as if the question had hit him like a bullet. "I heard something, but I don't know for sure what it was."

Tioga followed him. "That's a miracle. You heard something. Bravo. But I wouldn't put you on a witness stand. The DA would make chopped liver out of you."

Now they were in the street again, under the bright light of the sun. The bicycle was still there and so were Travis's tools. A yellow tow truck had arrived; the driver had hooked up Camilla's car. He raised the front end and locked it in place. Then he handed Camilla a clipboard with a form and said, "Sign here please."

Camilla signed. Tioga watched the tow truck and the battered car descend the hill slowly. Travis seemed to enjoy the spectacle.

Tioga glanced at the loudspeakers that sat on the windowsill. "You have selective hearing. One day you might lose it all if you go on playing the music this loud." Tioga felt a pinched nerve in her right hip. She shifted her weight from one leg to the other and then back again. That helped. Oh, for some of Dr. Silver's medicine right now, she thought to herself. "Keep an eye on things, Travis, and call me when you see or hear something out of the ordinary. You know what out of the ordinary means, don't you?"

Travis did not have a chance to reply. George Ambrose climbed out of the squad car and looked around as if he was a spaceman who had arrived on a distant planet and was looking for signs of life, intelligent or otherwise. In a moment his deputy joined him on the pavement. Clark approached Camilla, while Ambrose made a beeline for Tioga.

"I have to keep an eye on you," he roared. Then he shook his head and added, "I saw the tow truck with that nasty vehicle going downhill." He cast his eyes on Camilla's bloody hand and snarled, "And you're a mess, too, miss."

Tioga fired up yet another cigarette and inhaled. "We can't hide anything from you, George. You might as well know. We're investigating."

Clark threw his head back and snorted, but not Ambrose, who listened with an implacable expression on his face. "You must mean the robbery at the taco joint downhill," he said as he ran his fingers through the hair on the top of his head—or what was left of it. "You won't get anywhere on that case. It's a dead end. Clark poked around and came up empty-handed. Just a bunch of Mezcans who were picked up by ICE and sent to the border. They're not coming back, not in a zillion years."

Ambrose turned to his deputy for confirmation of the information he had just dispensed. What good was a deputy unless he provided backup in every sense of the word? "That's the long and the short of it, isn't it, Clark!" Ambrose wasn't asking a question, but rather making what he seemed to think was an assertion of fact.

Clark grinned, nodded his head and watched Camilla, who looked like she was still in pain and in shock, too. "I saw the graffiti painted on your car," Clark said, sounding like the proverbial fair-haired boy. "Somebody around here has a potty mouth." Then he came back to Ambrose's comment about the taco joint downhill. "Yeah, the thieves who robbed El Buen Comer are long gone and the money pissed away, if you'll pardon the expression, on whores and heroin. I'm as sure of that as I'm sure that we're standing here on Avenida de La Virgen and that your car, lady, is a total wreck."

Ambrose walked uphill huffing and puffing until he stopped and stood in front of Travis and the upside down bicycle. He smiled a smile that went from ear to ear. He turned around, placed his hands on his hips and surveyed the Valley below, where a ribbon of oaks, redwoods and eucalyptus ran along Cooper's Creek. "His grandmother inherited every square inch around here as far as the eye can see from her no good husband who spent a fortune on booze and poker," Ambrose said and pointed his thumb at Travis. "After that this neighborhood went to pot, if you'll excuse the expression, and became home to scum. We've cleaned up these streets nicely, if I do say so myself."

He took out a pad of paper and with a pencil scribbled a list of words that Tioga tried to read upside down and couldn't. "It was a mistake to park here, miss," Ambrose said to Camilla. "They don't like outsiders around here, though I understand that you live only a few blocks over. I know where everyone lives, works, eats and sleeps. You were just asking for trouble, miss."

Camilla snickered. "I thought you said you'd cleaned up the neighborhood. I'd say you have a long ways to go when you can't even park a car here safely."

"Now," Ambrose laughed, "don't quibble with me." He looked down at Tioga, who was listening to the conversation between poor little Camilla Sanchez and George Ambrose, the know-it-all chief of police. Ambrose added, "Take it from me, you won't get anywhere with that robbery, but if by luck or accident you come up with a lead, let me know."

Tioga flicked the ash from her cigarette, the second or the third of the day. She had lost count. "Unfortunately we don't have any leads. Believe me, George, we're not as swift as you and Clark."

Clark smiled; Ambrose scowled. "Just two dumb broads," he growled. His words had a way of dating him, though he didn't seem to realize it. "I don't believe what you've told me, not for one second." He climbed into the passenger side of the squad car, wiped the perspiration from his brow and waved goodbye. "Something's going on here that doesn't add up," he shouted. "But I can see that neither of you is going to fess up. Too bad for you."

Tioga looked at Ambrose and smiled sweetly. "I'll tell you this, George, I talked to Mrs. Baynes. She would like the ring that the killer tried to remove from Dorothy's finger. Do you think you could swing that? It wouldn't cost you a cent."

Ambrose folded his handkerchief and stuffed it in his back pocket. Then he looked at Clark, who clutched the steering wheel of the cruiser and revved the engine. "Still carrying that guilt, after all this time. I understand. It would have been different if you had found Dorothy Baynes alive. I can't give Mrs. Baynes that ring. You know as well as I do that my hands are tied." He gazed at Travis's bike and added, "You're always pushing the envelope, Tioga. Why don't you give it a rest?"

Ambrose and his deputy drove off. Travis reached into his pocket, fished out a key and handed it to Tioga. "You might want to go back one day and look again for Camilla's purse. Don't worry. I have a spare."

Tioga stood in the middle of Avenida de la Virgen, punched in the number for Dulox and got nowhere about Dorothy Baynes, though the woman who answered the phone explained that two men had, indeed, picked up a broken-down washer-dryer on Avenida de la Virgen and left two hundred dollars. "I think that's very generous," she said. "We're here to serve."

Tioga watched the smoke drifting across the sky; it seemed to have come out of nowhere and was going everywhere. She sniffed the air. "Smells like a wildfire. I'd know it anywhere. The wind is blowing from the north."

Indeed the wind had kicked up something fierce and the sun had disappeared behind the clouds. Tioga walked downhill with her hand over nose and mouth to keep out the smell of the smoke. Camilla followed slowly, as if lost in thought.

Tioga opened the trunk of her Mini Cooper—which she had parked in the shade of a lone poplar—and placed the wine bottle from Travis next to the spare tire. Behind the wheel, she turned the key in the ignition and ramped up the air conditioning, which helped her and Camilla breathe the air in the car without coughing or choking. Outside the smoke was now so thick that she might have cut it into wafers with her Swiss Army Knife. Tioga put the car in reverse, backed up slowly and drove downhill. At the intersection, she waited for a gap in the traffic and took a left.

She tuned the radio to The Wolf and listened to Billy Joel: "You may be right/I may be crazy." "This is the only decent song he ever recorded," Tioga said. "The rest is pure crap."

When the song ended, she turned up the volume to hear the news: "Wildfires have broken out in Lake County. Town of New Harmony is gone. Thousands have evacuated. Smoke has drifted south and blanketed the San Francisco Bay area. Stay tuned."

"At least we're not alone," Tioga said. She peered into the side-view mirror and then relaxed her grip on the steering wheel. The car purred. Along the highway, vineyards cascaded down the hillsides, sheep grazed and a field of tomatoes begged to be harvested. "I saw a blood stain under the carpet," she said, handing Camilla her cell. "Take a look."

Camilla examined the photos and shook her head. "I didn't see any blood when I was there. If I had, I would have freaked even more."

Tioga sighed. "I'm telling you there's a crime wave. It's either here now or it's coming, like the smoke in the sky."

Camilla checked her messages. "Everybody in the Valley makes shit up, though I have the feeling that Travis wasn't lying when he talked about Dot Baynes. But the stuff about his grandfather dying in a hail of bullets, I dunno. Ditto for the wine he claims is from Prohibition." Camilla rolled down her window, sniffed the air and promptly closed it again. "You don't have to fix me up with Travis, or anyone else. I capable of running my own affairs."

Tioga placed her sunglasses in the glove compartment. "The glass for that wine bottle is really old. They don't make it like that anymore, asymmetrically."

Camilla reached under the seat with her right hand and came up with a black leather purse. "It's been here all this time. I figured we needed an excuse to get inside forty-nine."

Now there was traffic on the road. Tioga pressed down on the brake and eased up on the accelerator. "You have Travis wrapped around your little finger. Might as well work it, girl."

Traffic began to move again, sluggishly, and Tioga urged the car forward. "Flor called. It sounds like she has something. But first I want get out of Travis's shirt and pick up something to wear over my chemise."

Outside Louise's Lingerie Plus, she double parked, left the motor running and the air conditioner on full blast. "Move the car if you absolutely have to," she said, then opened the door and felt the hot, smoky air hit her face.

In no time all, Tioga emerged from the shop, carrying a shopping bag with the image of a woman in a strapless bra. She wore a blue kaftan that covered her knees. "It's the best I could do, spur of the moment. Louise asked if we had made headway with Dorothy. I told her we'd made giant strides." A minute later, Tioga signaled with her directional and turned left before the sign that read Broadway Market. She parked in front of the building housing the food slash liquor store whose walls looked like they'd soon come tumbling down. She turned off the air conditioner and braced herself for the open-air sauna. She locked the car, pocketed the key and surveyed the "a la venta" signs for the *jalapeños*, *nopales* and *maize* that were on display.

Inside the market, she and Camilla breezed past the frumpy woman who stood alone at the checkout counter. They darted around the fruits—mangos, papayas, bananas, apples, pineapples and carambolas—piled high and in the shape of a pyramid that smelled both ripe and rank. Flor was not at the back of the store, nor was she at the table where tamales and enchiladas were wrapped in foil, and, as the sign indicated, sold singly or by the dozen.

Tioga and Camilla found Flor sitting outside in the shade on a milk carton near a dumpster overflowing with trash. Her hair was shorter. She wore a T-shirt that hugged her body, a pair of faded designer jeans and sneakers that looked like they'd been recycled from the dumpster. Her boy was not at her side.

Flor opened her mouth wide—she wore bright red lipstick—said "Hello" and sounded as if she had been practicing her English. But she looked so sad that Tioga couldn't help but want to lift her spirits. "*Hola,*" she said energetically. Then with more fervor she asked, "*¿Todo es bueno?*" and "*¿Dónde están tu chico?*"

Flor rose to her feet. She smiled warmly, embraced both Tioga and Camilla, who emerged from the shade at the back of the market. "My boy library. *Tacos y* books. He like *mucho. Señora* Lisa *bueno.*"

She went slowly and carefully from word to word as if crossing a border where she might be detained and tossed back the way she had come. Camilla grabbed two plastic crates from a tall stack of crates, offered one to Tioga and took the other for herself.

"This is Camilla; we work together and don't have secrets. She's from Zacatecas, about the same age as you and a Saggitarian."

Flor gave Camilla the once over and nodded indifferently. "I twenty-four."

Camilla moved her seat closer to Flor so she could hear her above the growling garbage truck that had pulled into the tight space behind the store and lifted the dumpster. A family of fat rats moved like sloths. "I'm twenty-six," Camilla said, keeping her eyes on the slow progress of the rats. "Just starting to feel at home here, though there's really no place I want to go, and no one I really want to see, not yet anyway."

The garbage truck flipped the dumpster upside down and emptied it. "You know what I mean? You must. You don't exactly belong here either, do you?"

Tioga showed Flor the photos that she had taken of the house at forty-nine. "Have you been here? It's in The Springs on Avenida de La Virgen."

Flor shook her head. "Never."

Tioga leaned back against the stucco wall. "You look so sad. Sadder than when I saw you in the plaza." Flor peeled a blood orange that sat in her lap and tossed the rind toward the family of rats. "I not see Mack ever," she said, offering a section of the blood orange to Tioga and another to Camilla.

Tioga retrieved her phone, scrolled through the photos, found the picture she had taken of Terry McCoy and showed it to Flor. "Is this the man?"

Flor looked puzzled. "Could be. But Mack no beard. Mack no fat."

Tioga retrieved her phone and sighed. "Not sure. Is that right?"

Flor nodded her head and then reached for the phone and studied the face again. "You show me this man. I know when I see."

Tioga chewed a slice of the orange and asked, "Did you call me because of trouble?"

Flor looked down at the bare ground. "I not trouble. *Pero* I see lady you want."

Tioga drew back. "Where was this? Do you remember?" She was patronizing, and she knew it. Some things couldn't be helped.

Flor looked at the rats. "I see the lady in plaza where boy plays. She wear hat, walk with man long way. Man go inside. She walk hotel, sit in sun. Face same as in photo."

Flor seemed to have learned how to tell a story that Tioga wanted to hear. "What did the woman do next?"

Flor opened the Coke that sat at her side and sipped a little at a time, as if it was as precious as water and maybe as good as anything else in her life. "Your friend tell me go away."

In the tight space at the back of the market, Tioga paced one way and then another. A man with large floppy ears and oily hair emerged from the store just in time to see the garbage truck pull into the street. Tioga sidled up to him. "We're going to buy the mangos on sale."

The man shoved his hands into his pockets, turned away and waddled inside the store. Tioga gave Flor an oversized smile. "This is good news about Roxanne. It makes me happy. We're getting somewhere." She opened her purse, lifted a twenty-dollar bill, offered it to Flor and asked, "Can you show me where Roxanne and the man went?"

Flor folded the twenty and stuffed it into the front pocket of her jeans. "Yes, I show you where she go with the man."

When Flor disappeared in the store, Tioga tugged at Camilla's elbow. "Terry's the father of Flor's boy. He was a smuggler along with my ex. Flor worked in the hotel where Tomás stayed. He fucked her, and then he fucked her over."

Smoke drifted across the sky. A rat scurried under the dumpster. A hawk screeched, and a squirrel leapt into a coyote bush that had lost its leaves. Tioga glanced down at her shoes. "Flor is unsure about Terry. I'm not. I have to figure out what I'm going to do about it. If I confront McCoy, he'll be very testy."

Camilla kicked the milk crates with her right foot and watched them tumble to the ground. "He's testy about everything. He'll deny it, deny it and deny it until he's blue in the face and swear that Flor is a hooker trying to rip him off."

Inside the store, Tioga used a paper towel to wipe away the grime, first from her hands and then from her shoes. She washed her hands at the sink, selected a dozen mangoes that were neither under nor over ripe and set them down in a shopping basket. "Do we walk or drive?" she asked Flor, who jammed the Coke bottle into her jeans. "Drive. Too hot and smoke."

Tioga peeled a mango and bit into it. "Okay, I'll drive." At the checkout counter, the clerk weighted the mangoes and placed them one by one in a brown paper bag. Tioga handed her a twenty-dollar bill, pocketed the change and led the way across the steamy pavement.

Flor took the back seat, while Camilla sat up front. Tioga turned up the volume on the radio. It was the top of the hour and time for the weather report, sports and headline news. In a city far away, a suicide bomber had blown up a mosque. In the White House, the president fumed about an army of immigrants that had invaded the country and seized a border town. Closer to home, a wildfire raged in the hills above Yorkville in Mendocino County. The heat wave would go on and on, with no relief in sight. At AT&T Park, the Giants had lost their tenth straight game and had tumbled to the cellar in the National League West.

"Oh, great, more smoke and more heat," Tioga groaned. "You know, studies show that in the Valley more crimes are committed in summer than in winter." She put the car in reverse, backed up slowly and then pulled into the line of traffic. "Flor, tell me where to go. I can't mind read. I need directions."

Flor leaned forward in her seat. "*¿Qué dijo ella?*"

Camilla turned her head. "*Quiere que le des instrucciones.*"

Flor did not ordinarily give instructions to anyone except her boy. She grabbed hold of the straps on both sides of the back seat, bounced up and down as the car went in and out of the potholes and watched the side streets race by. "Go plaza, left, left, park, walk."

Flor led them to an alley where one sign read, "Dead End," and another, "No Parking." Tioga scrawled a note: "Making delivery, please do not ticket, Tioga Vignetta, PI." She placed the note under the left blade of the windshield wiper. Flor ventured down an alley flanked by two red brick buildings. Another red brick building faced them where the alley dead-ended. Windows looked down from the second floor. Tioga craned her neck. "These bricks are so imperfectly perfect, if you know what I mean."

She and Camilla followed Flor until she stopped in front of a door with several keyholes and a steel plate that extended from top to bottom and left to right. Flor touched the red brick wall. "Walk here. Man go inside. He kiss her, door close, she go back hotel. I follow."

Tioga looked up at the windows on the second floor of the red brick building, saw the image of a John Deere in an open field and the words "Valley Gazette" and "Subscribe Today" with a 707 area code, a phone number and a website. "Was the man tall?" Tioga asked Flor. "Big shoulders and long hair?"

Flor rolled her eyes. "*Si*. He tall, she whiter than you, *investigador*."

Camilla stared at the window with the image of the tractor and the words "Valley Gazette." "Why would they have gone in the back way?"

A stack of newspapers had faded in the sun and the rain. A car came part of the way down the alley and stopped. Tioga turned to Flor. "I want you to keep watching Roxanne. Okay? I'll pay you the same. You call me right away."

Camilla tried once again to budge the door, but it refused. Flor looked lost. "I can go now? You don't need me more today?"

She sounded, Tioga thought, as if she wanted to be needed. "I always need you. I can't pay you more today. But I can give you a ride."

Flor's face looked more beautiful than ever before. "*Por favor* drive me library, find my boy. He waiting." She looked up at the second story window. Then she lowered her eyes and brought them to rest on Tioga's face. "Why you want me watch *Señora penal*?"

Tioga didn't know what to say or how to say it. She looked at Camilla for help, but Camilla had walked away and left Tioga to come up with something on her own. "Maybe she's a criminal. But it's too soon for me to say for sure. There's something weird going on, but I'm not sure what."

Tioga gave Flor a piercing look. "You know what I mean?"

Flor moved into the shadow along the wall that crowded the alley. She nodded her head. "*Maldad pura*. That Mack *guero* friend."

Tioga took out her cell and held it in her hand. "Can I take your photo, please? I want to."

Flor smiled cautiously. "Why you want? I don't like."

Tioga offered Flor her phone. "Take a selfie."

Flor shook her head. "No, you."

Tioga took several shots from several angles and then showed them to Flor. "Okay?"

"*Si*," Flor said. "*Mucho gusto. Por favor* send me. I show."

The steel door at the back of the red brick buildings opened and an elderly woman stepped out, along with a large poodle on a leash. She looked at Tioga and took a step backward before she stopped and her face suddenly turned white. "I have no money. I can't help you."

Tioga shook her head. "No worry. We're not beggars or thieves." She removed the car keys from her pocket, tossed them in the air and caught them in her outstretched palm. "Let's hit the library, girls," she said and handed the keys to Camilla. "You drive!"

Tioga took the back seat, rolled down both windows and felt the breeze on her face. The smoke had lifted, and the heat wave had started to break. In the front seat, Flor hadn't bothered to fasten her seatbelt; Camilla fastened it for her. "We have to keep you safe. You're valuable cargo."

Camilla circled the plaza once, slowed down outside the Sebastiani and glanced up at the marquee that read, in big letters: *The Maltese Falcon*. "Sounds cool. If I don't fall asleep after supper, I'll go."

She took East Nile Road and aimed toward the American flag that flew from the roof of the library. Flor's boy stood on the sidewalk and held a string attached to a red and a yellow balloon. When he saw his mother, he raced toward her and put his arms around her. Flor led him across the street toward the sign that read, "*Helado* Mexico."

Tioga waved. Camilla shouted, "*Mas tarde*," then gunned the car and aimed for the plaza. Tioga's phone chirped. A text arrived from Gina McCoy: "Come to my shop for tea."

Tioga replied, "Am on my way." Then she opened her purse, removed the Ziplock bag with her treasures: the blood-stained rock from the creek bed; and the blood-stained sliver that she had scraped from the wood floor at forty-nine. She placed the bag on the seat that Flor had just vacated. "Take these to Analytics and have them tested for DNA and everything else. Tell Lydia I'll pay whatever if she does it ASAP. After that, find out who has the title to the house at forty nine."

Camilla slammed on the brakes and honked the horn at a woman in braids and dark glasses who had stepped blindly, it seemed, from the curb into the street. Camilla honked the horn again.

Tioga rubbed her eyes. "I feel like I've been drugged," she said.

The car lurched forward. Camilla took the turns fast. "No wonder," she said. "You've been smoking weed all day. I'm amazed you can function." She cut a path through the crowd that ebbed and flowed from one side of the pavement to the other. "Stupid people. Just asking for trouble."

Tioga lifted her kaftan, poked the black dot at the center of the red splotch and scratched. The bite had come back again. That was its nature: to come and go. "Drop me at Gina McCoy's and give the mangos to your mom before they explode."

The crowd thinned. Camilla kept the speedometer at twenty-five miles an hour—the posted legal speed limit. "Why Gina's?"

Tioga didn't know for sure why she had accepted Gina's invitation. "We're sorta twins. Grew up with the same parents, more or less," she said, improvising as she went along. "Both sent away to the same kind of schools where we were the same kinds of truants. Her first marriage ended in divorce. So did mine. She remarried. That's where we've parted company." Tioga paused and added, "She's a bitch and I'm not." Then she laughed.

Camilla reached inside the shopping bag and pulled out a mango. "Would you peel this for me please, honey. There are paper napkins in my purse."

Tioga unfolded and spread two napkins and then peeled a mango. With her pocketknife, she sliced it into pieces, licked the juice and the pulp from her fingers and when Camilla opened her mouth fed her. "Oh, and one other thing," Tioga said. "My ex had an affair with Gina."

Camilla swallowed the mango, wiped her face with a napkin and licked the corners of her mouth. "How do you know about that? Aren't affairs supposed to be secret?" Before Tioga could answer, Camilla fired another question: "Is that why you became a detective, to spy on your husband?"

Tioga put her lips together and then opened them slowly. "No." She selected another mango, peeled it, sliced it, fed Camilla again, saving the last piece for herself. "Tomás lied for a year. When I asked him if he was sleeping with Gina, he stared right at me and said, 'I would never do that. It would hurt you too much.' That was right before he went down to Mexico and started to smuggle everything he could get his hands on."

Tioga turned up the volume on "Lullaby of Birdland." "Perfect accompaniment," she murmured and then picked up the thread she had dropped, the same way more or less that George Shearing picked up the melody he played with. "Sean told me that Gina told him, probably hoping he would tell me, that she was having an affair with Tomás. Gina and I have never said a word about it."

Camilla held the steering wheel with both hands and navigated the one-way streets around the plaza: first a left, then a right, then a left again. "We are a secretive lot here in the Valley, aren't we?" When Tioga didn't reply she added, "But maybe no more or no less than anywhere else." At the corner of Portugal Street and Marietta Road she parked opposite Gina's shop. "It's been a wacky day. I don't want more surprises."

Tioga watched Camilla as she took her eyes away from the windshield and puckered her lips. As first kisses go, it wasn't bad. Tioga turned away from Camilla and stared at the red, green and white awning and the black letters that read, "Gina's: Luxury Goods from Provence."

Camilla sighed. "I have to tell you. I'm not good at secrets. I have a crush on you."

Tioga shot back, "Thanks for saying so" and unlocked the door. "I'll talk to you later. Oh, and call Mrs. Baynes and tell her I tried to get the ring back but Ambrose said no way, José."

Camilla sighed again. "Is that all you're going to say?"

Tioga leaned toward Camilla and kissed her on her lips. "That's all that I'm going to say for now."

Queen Victoria's Pot Doc

It was cool inside Gina's shop and crammed with way too much stuff. Tioga turned over a teacup, looked at the price and then turned it right side up. Stephanie, the lanky shop girl who had waited on Tioga more than once, recognized her and turned her frown to a smile. "Oh, goodie, you're here," she said in a girlie tone of voice. "Gina told me to tell you when you arrived to go right back to her office. I hope you can cheer her up. She's been low down for a couple of days, even with big sales."

Tioga made her way around the display tables groaning with Spanish ceramics, Irish linen napkins, French butter dishes and Italian breadbaskets. She didn't stop to touch anything, but she took it all in—most of it anyway—and then turned and smiled at Stephanie who murmured, "You know, none of this stuff is bourgeois. Gina selects it all herself."

Tioga found Marie Antoinette, as Buddy called her, behind her desk in her office, apparently preoccupied with sums. From Tioga's point of view, it made no sense to keep records in a ledger that looked at least one hundred years old and was four times the size of her own modest account book. There wasn't much about Gina that made a whole lot of sense, including her devotion to her husband, who had probably fathered two children with a Mexican beauty called Flor and who had his finger in more Valley pies, legal, illegal and semi-legal, than anyone else that Tioga knew. Gina wore antique spectacles, a white lace dress with a stiff collar that accentuated her long, thin neck. She would have felt at home, Tioga decided, in a made-for-TV Victorian soap opera with an upstairs and a downstairs. In fact, her office at the back of the shop looked mid-nineteenth century, say, about 1851, Tioga thought. At the Badminton School for Girls, the headmistress had impressed on her and on all her schoolmates the virtues of Queen Victoria and her consort, Prince Albert. Well, maybe not exactly 1851, Tioga decided, but in any case, well before the advent of women's suffrage, mustard gas and Mr. Stravinsky's *Rites of Spring*, which was a favorite of the conductor of the Valley symphony, though not with Terry and Gina McCoy, who suffered through it. From the loge, Tioga watched them with her binoculars and read McCoy's lips and then Gina's. No doubt about it, they were uncomfortable with Stravinsky's noise.

Now in Gina's office, Tioga took the extra-large green chair with cushions and armrests that would have fit nicely in a London men's club circa 1851. Then she leaned back until the chair swallowed her up. "I wish I could stay and drink tea and chat all afternoon," she said as she crossed and uncrossed her legs. "Fact is, I've been putting Storm off all day; if I'm late for our date I'm afraid she'll never speak to me again. You know how cross she can be."

She slipped into Gina talk as if it came to her naturally, though Gina didn't seem to notice. "That is so like Storm to sweat the small stuff and take things personally. I won't make trouble for the two of you, and I won't beat around the bush either. I've been upset ever since we had tea on the patio. To be absolutely frank, I've never been able to tell a lie, not even a white lie, ever since I was a girl." She paused a moment and when she seemed satisfied that Tioga had followed her every step of the way she went on blithely, first one-way and then another. "I know Terry has told you and Storm that you have to pack up and leave the hotel. I urged him to reconsider. I'll raise the issue again, if you'd like me to. Just say the word."

Tioga tried not to wear a pained expression, though having to evacuate the hotel and become a refugee from the Mar Monte felt painful. Still she sensed that she was making a big deal about a little move. "Oh no, I couldn't put you in that position. I would never do anything like that." The room quieted. The clock ticked more slowly now, and the ledger seemed to grow dustier. "Am I stoned?" Tioga asked herself. "Perhaps so. Maybe I'll never come down. Maybe they'll have to drain my old blood and give me new blood."

For a moment or two or maybe three, she faded out. Then Gina's voice brought her in again. "But I didn't invite you here to talk about lodgings. I invited you here to explain that I've known Hawk for ages, though I'm not proud of it. As you've probably guessed, Hawk isn't his real name. It's actually Reginald Wentworth; he's been living in a bubble for as long as I've known him. My husband introduced him as a college chum; he was, indeed, overly chummy. You might have noticed that he thinks he's the star of the movie. Of course, Terry's the same." Gina paused for a moment and waited for Tioga to say something, anything. When she didn't speak, she went on. "Sometimes the Valley strikes me as a refuge for scoundrels, pirates, outlaws, and criminals, though I know there are wonderful people too, like Louis and Isabel Marchetti."

Waiting appeared to make Gina uncomfortable. Silence seemed to unnerve her. Tioga played with the letter opener on the desk and resisted the impulse to scratch the spider bite. Then she wet her lips with the tip of her tongue and smiled. She was surprised how happy she was to learn that Hawk and McCoy had been college chums. "I see," she said, remembering that she had used the same two words in conversation with Hawk. She was making a habit of them. "I see," she repeated and added, "That's an awful lot of information about Mr. Reginald Wentworth to spring on me all at once. It will take me a fortnight to digest it."

She paused a moment and looked at the photograph on the wall of a man with whiskers and a stiff collar who had to be a prominent Victorian, though she didn't know precisely which one. "And you say you want me to know this because you can't bear to live with a lie. That's very good of you."

She tried to sound sincere, but she saw from the way Gina winced that she wasn't convinced. Tioga moved her body from side to side until she found a more comfortable position. Sitting had been a challenge all day. Standing had not been much better. What about prone, she wondered? That remained to be seen. Hopefully, she and Storm would lie down in one another's arms in the delicious darkness of their bedroom. "I'm sorry if I sound sarcastic. My nerves are shot, and the day isn't over yet. I do appreciate the information about Hawk. I won't broadcast it."

She meant it too, though she didn't promise Gina not to share the name Reginald Wentworth with Camilla and with Buddy Moscosco, who loved Tioga when she threw him a bone. The best bones were always the latest gossip about the Mar Monte, its crew and guests. "So Reginald and Terry were tight in college?" Tioga asked.

Gina peered over the top of her granny glasses, which sat on the bridge of her nose. "Reggie and Terry played rugby together, took up surfing on the Big Island with your ex and then pretended to be smugglers. Nothing serious, mind you. They had a small sailboat. It was just boy hijinks. Fortunately they outgrew them. Wentworth's father, who was Irish, and whose mother was Jamaican, put them to work in their hotel in Ocho Rios. I know they smoked *ganja*—all the tourists did. Terry was wild about Mrs. Wentworth, a Caribbean beauty." She peered down at the ledger and then asked, without making eye contact with Tioga, "Have you heard from your ex?" She seemed to be on a fishing expedition.

Tioga again stared at the photo of the Victorian gentleman. "Who's the fuddy-duddy?"

Gina glanced over her shoulder. "Oh, that's Gladstone, Queen Victoria's prime minister. He keeps me honest. Without him, I'd be lost in the unruly sea that threatens the Valley."

Tioga tried and couldn't stop herself from scratching her spider bite. "My ex was a real pick. He still is. He blabbed to Hawk about my private life. Hawk threw it in my face when he came to my office and wanted to hire me."

Gina twirled a pencil between thumb and index finger. "So you're working for Reginald!" she said and sounded genuinely surprised.

Tioga looked at Gladstone and smiled. "No, I'm not working for Hawk. He promptly fired me soon after he hired me." Then she leaned forward and asked, "Have you heard from my ex?"

Gina placed her palm on the ledger, as if about to swear on the family Bible. "Why would I hear from him?" she asked and sounded incredulous. Then she added, "It's Terry I'm worried about. He's drinking and smoking again; he doesn't shave, wears rumpled shirts, and, when I complain about his appearance, he tells me I'm not his mother. The only person he cares about is Lawrence."

Now Gina looked up, leaned forward, reached across her desk and with her fingertips touched Tioga's knee. "We're having a little dinner party tonight. I know this is so last minute, but I'd be thrilled if you and Storm would join Terry and me and a few of our closest friends. I mentioned the party to Storm earlier, and she wasn't against the idea. You know, she loves Jonny's cooking as much as I do."

Tioga looked surprised. Ever since her phone conversation with Storm, she had assumed that they would enjoy a quiet meal together: cucumbers with Japanese vinegar; tomatoes, burrata and basil, olive oil and salt; and then watermelon. It sounded more appealing than a dinner party.

Gina winked slyly. "Louis and Isabel Marchetti have accepted my invite. Matt Chehab will be there, of course, along with a gentleman from Sacramento named Robert Cohen, whom you'll adore. Sean Dyce will be making his signature cocktails. It'll be an intimate group."

Tioga didn't say yes or no or shake or nod her head, but Gina clapped her hands anyway. "Then it's settled," she gushed. "Jonny is making a special dinner with local vegetables. He was hoping to serve the roast boar that Terry bagged the other day when he and Matt went hunting. But it was such a hot item that we're already out." She paused a moment and looked at the shop girl Stephanie, who stood in the doorway and waited for Gina to notice her. "Yes. What can we do for you, my dear?"

Stephanie stood as straight as she could, her eyes bulging. "There's a woman who wants to buy the photo of Lewis Carroll kissing Alice Liddell, but she wants to know if it's the original and not a copy. What do I tell her?" Gina opened the ledger, turned the pages, stopped and ran her index finger from line to line. "Tell her it's a genuine copy, and she can have it for 10% off if she pays in cash today."

Stephanie curtseyed. "That's brilliant," she said, then backed away slowly as if she was at court.

Gina picked up her landline, called the Mar Monte and asked the receptionist to put her through to the penthouse.

"Storm, Tioga's here right now; she wants to come to the party … Yes, yes … of course you can … That's wonderful!"

In no time at all, Gina had settled the matter. "So there," she said, after she ended the call. "It's win-win for everyone, and you won't have to be on your best behavior." Gina walked Tioga through the shop, opened the front door, and stepped onto the sidewalk. "Your ex knew weirdos in the Valley," she said as if baiting a hook with a fat, wiggly worm.

Tioga took the bait. "What do you mean?"

Gina smiled a crooked smile. "I can't put my finger on it exactly. They seemed cultish. Sluts and pimps. Your ex apparently encouraged them." A warm breeze buffeted Gina and Tioga; a stream of bicyclers came so close they were nearly knocked down. "You don't happen to have anything to smoke, do you?" Gina asked. "I mean one of those vape pens everyone is using. I suppose I could tap my husband, but I'd prefer not to. He has a double standard."

Tioga repeated the line that she had rehearsed for moments like this one. "Why would you think I'd have anything to do with something like that?" she asked and did her best to sound like Mr. Gladstone, or at least what she imagined he sounded like in 1851.

Gina window-shopped at the window for her own shop. "Sorry. I hope I didn't rub you the wrong way."

Tioga looked at the time on her cell and then at the little shop girl waiting to be told what to do. "Not a problem. You might ask at the hotel. Someone there will know where you can find product to smoke." She looked at the line of traffic that stretched all the way back to the plaza. "You know, don't you, that Queen Victoria used it? Her Irish doctor, William Brooke O'Shaughnessy, prescribed it for menstrual cramps. Apparently it worked wonders. Maybe it will help you. Cheerio. Ta-ta."

Easy Come, Easy Go, Daddy-O

Tioga turned away, crossed the street, wandered across the plaza and found herself feeling that Gina had cajoled her and hijacked her, though she knew that she was too curious to turn down an invitation to a dinner party at the Mar Monte, even if the room would be packed with strangers. Jonny Field was a magnet. Indeed, he was combining ingredients that no one in the Valley had ever combined before: morels and cheddar cheese; risotto with pomegranate, arugula and pork, including the skin; and for dessert, blackberries, ginger, Balsamic vinegar and licorice root.

Once Tioga sat next to Jonny and invited him to divulge kitchen confidentialities: "How much cheddar cheese do you add to the morels, and how many morels do you use?"

Jonny shrugged his shoulders. "I don't weigh and I don't measure. It's all about the feeling, like jazz and like sex, you know what I mean."

Now in the Underground again, Tioga sat down at the bar, asked for a shot of Bushmills and knocked it back.

Sean Dyce leaned over, whispering, "It's crazy, but guests are staying here longer than anticipated just to eat one or two or three more meals prepared by the great Jonny Field."

Tioga spun the tumbler on the bar. "See you at Gina's party."

She scampered across the lobby and aimed for the elevator, then changed her mind. There was no point returning to the penthouse to change her attire. So what if she was wearing the same kaftan? Who was going to squawk? Nobody! If anyone did, McCoy would crack the whip.

Tioga walked to the Sebastiani, bounded upstairs, unlocked the door to her office, sat down at her desk, booted up her computer and typed up a report about the house at forty-nine, and her quirky conversation with Travis Syrah, whom, she wrote, "knows more than he admits, afraid, no doubt, that he'll cast suspicion on himself." She checked her email; Mitzi reminded her "to steer clear of my dad." Her own father, Philippe Vignetta, wrote to "beg a visit, see my new work and dine at Craig Stoll's new restaurant." She emailed back, "Soon, Dad." Then she looked at the time, called Analytics and asked for the results for the blood work they were to run. What she heard bowled her over. "Really? How could that be? ... You've never made a mistake like that before ... I don't understand ... How could you get them mixed up ... No, I don't want a refund ..."

She sat there and stewed longer than she wanted to sit and tried to wrap her head around the nasty little fact that there would be no report on the blood that she and Camilla had gathered along the creek and from the house on Avenida de la Virgen. She shut down the computer, turned off the lights and locked the door. On the way across the plaza, she checked her cell. Maggie Brazil had sent a text with one word: "Urgent."

Tioga was in no mood to jump. "Urgent" made her want to be delinquent. Doctor Finkelstein might have been right when he explained that she had something called "Oppositional Defiant Disorder." "So?" she had replied. "Everyone has a disorder." That had been a long time ago. She had just graduated from the Badminton School for Girls and had embarked on a quest that took her nowhere.

Now in the plaza, she lingered under a pine tree, its cones on the ground. She removed a cigarette from the pack that lived in her purse, then looked up and saw the "No Smoking" sign and another that read "Drug Free Zone" and its companion in Spanish: *Zona libre de drogas.*"

Oh, dear, she had forgotten the rules once again. She tossed the pathetic cigarette into the recycling bin and cut a path through the crowd that stood around and watched as four women strutted and preened on a makeshift stage in front of City Hall. On the kettle drum at the back of the stage, she saw the name of the band, "The Valley Virgins."

Reluctantly she punched in Maggie's number. "I'm so glad you called back right away," Maggie said. "I want to retain your services."

Tioga sat down on a bench in front of the duck pond and read the sign that said, "No Playing in the Pond." Then she admired a boy and a girl who frolicked in the water without any clothes. Apparently they could break the rules.

She pictured Maggie under the photo of Cantinflas at El Buen Comer. "What exactly do you want me to do? I'm not sure that I can help, though I know I offered. After all, you've been investigating on your own, and you haven't turned up a thing. Nor have the police. What makes you think I'll have better luck?"

Maggie's answered swiftly. "You'll know where to look, who to question, when to play rough and when to play nice. I get too emotional about the whole thing and can't think straight. Come on, Tioga, you're the pro. I'm an amateur."

Tioga murmured, "Easy come, easy go."

"What's that?" Maggie asked.

Tioga shot back, "Oh, nothing, just talking to myself." She stood up and took one last look at the naked boy and the naked girl. "Okay, you sold me. I'm on it. I don't believe the thieves were arrested and turned over to ICE. That's bullshit. Ambrose and his deputy don't have a clue and won't admit it."

Maggie cleared her throat. "I want the satisfaction of knowing who broke in. Meanwhile I'll mail you a check."

Tioga walked to the curb, and then peeped at the sign in the window of Louise's Lingerie Plus that read, "Hurray! Fall Bras Have Already Arrived." "Make it for a round thousand. That'll get me going."

"Cool," Maggie said.

"Bye, bye," Tioga chirped.

"Bye, bye," Maggie echoed.

Tioga retraced her steps, returned to her office, drew up a contract with Maggie, attached it to her email and fired it off. Then she remembered that she had forgotten to type up Gina's story about Wentworth's connections to Terry McCoy, going back to their college days together and jumping to *ganja* and surfing in Hawaii. "What the hell brought them together and then pulled them apart?" she wondered. "Have they been druggies all along?"

She closed the Wentworth file and created another that she called "Dorothy Baynes," though she wasn't sure what to enter, except a question mark. She printed both documents and placed them on top of the file labeled "Divorce."

The landline pulled her away from memories of Tomás. On the fifth ring, she answered. "Hi, Dad. Can't talk now. Gotta run. Later. Love you."

Her father growled, roared and barked. His voice was all over the place. "I want my paintings back," he screeched and sounded like a kid having a tantrum. "My New York agent has a buyer in Zurich. They're willing to pay the price I'm asking. You'll get a cut."

Tioga lifted her eyes from her desk, scanned the paintings on the wall and stuck out her tongue. "I don't think so, Dad. In fact, I want to put all of them in storage where no one can ever see them again. Goodbye, Dad."

Part IV
Party Time

Gina's Little Party

By the time Tioga arrived at Gina McCoy's not-so-intimate dinner party, the guests were no longer clean and sober. In fact, they struck her as loosey-goosey and ready for anything and everything that might come their way. Sean Dyce, on loan from the Underground, stood at the improvised bar and cranked out cocktails. Tioga watched him make a concoction with rye, gin, vodka and rum. He didn't stint on the booze.

Tioga offered him the wine bottle that Travis had given her as a kind of going-away present. "Open this and let it breathe. It's at least eighty-five years old. Tell me what you think."

Dyce placed the bottle behind his makeshift bar. "You look beat."

"Thanks," Tioga replied. "You look great too."

Dyce poured a martini, extra dry, and offered it to Gina. "I'm still looking for a vape pen or even a righteous ounce," she announced as if she hoped someone might hear her and offer her a sample. Then she winked at Tioga and added, "You can't have a real party these days without dope."

Tioga surveyed the crowd, then turned away and faced Dyce, who didn't ask her what she wanted but instead mixed a mojito and topped it off with mint leaves that smelled freshly picked.

"You're right at home here," Tioga told Dyce, "though you have no wine, no beer, no bitters, no ports and no liqueurs."

He handed Tioga the mojito and wiped the perspiration from his upper lip. "It's hot as Havana! Only not as humid and not as exciting either. Why the hell can't we have Latin bands and live sex acts? That's what I'd like to see: a bit of old Havana, Hemingway Havana, Meyer Lansky Havana. Fuck the guerrillas and the revolution. Give me the sleaze."

Tioga leaned forward so she could hear Sean over the din in the room, which boasted a high ceiling and a burnished wood floor. The picture windows overlooking the plaza had been festooned with sunflowers with bright yellow petals and dark brown centers. "I disapprove of live sex acts," Tioga said. "But think about it, Sean, Terry's a budding Meyer Lansky and if you hunger for salsa and rhumba go to Esperanza, Esperanza. The Mapaches de Zacatecas play every night. Granted it's not Hemingway Havana, but it's as close as you can get to Cuba before the revolution." Then she saw the boy she had first seen in the elevator. This time he wore a jacket that matched his trousers; his hair was neatly combed and parted on one side. He struck Tioga as a proper young Edwardian gentleman.

Gina patted him on his head. Then she bent down, whispered in his ear and urged him to move closer to the bar. "I'll have a Pimm's," he said, sounding as if he was entitled to an adult drink.

Dyce leaned over the bar, looked down at the boy and laughed. "Calvin Klein suit not withstanding, you're under age," he said. He filled a glass with fizzy water, added a maraschino cherry, walked around the bar and offered it to the boy, who had taken out his slingshot and fired off a marble.

Tioga watched him make mischief. "Do you know who that brat is?"

Dyce wiped his hands on his apron. "He goes by the name Lawrence, and he's been here for a month. Most of the time, he's away at school. I suppose he'll inherit the Mar Monte. Terry is grooming him. Gina is his surrogate mom."

Dyce reached behind the bar and retrieved the wine bottle, now uncorked, that Tioga gave him when she arrived for the fête. "It tastes like vinegar."

Tioga nodded. "Dump it."

She turned away and counted the number of plates on the table and the number of bottles of red, white and rosé. The reds had been uncorked and were breathing. Also there were bottles of water, still and sparkling, and two bouquets of long-stemmed roses that added color to the room, which had been overheated by the rays of the sun. Tioga kept her eyes on Gina, who wore a dress that had to be mock Victorian and who moved around the room as if skating on ice. Near the head of the table, she stopped and conferred with a young woman wearing black trousers and a black blouse. Tioga remembered meeting the woman at the Mar Monte swimming pool where she had introduced herself as Aden. Like Flor, Aden was too beautiful, Tioga decided. She had perfect red hair and a perfect nose. Unlike Flor, she acted stuck-up.

Tioga couldn't hear what Gina said, but she followed her eyes and her index finger as she pointed here and pointed there. Her drink finished, she held onto the glass and stepped away from the makeshift bar where she heard Gina say, "Everything has to be perfect. If it isn't, there'll be hell to pay."

Gina walked around the table and straightened the silverware. Aden made sure the linen napkins were folded perfectly. When they weren't to her liking, she took them apart and refolded them until they were perfect. Tioga moved closer to hear what they were saying. "Mr. McCoy is harder on you than anyone else at the Mar Monte," Aden grumbled. "It's not fair."

Gina's Victorian bosom rose and fell. "Well, yes. He's the king. I'm just his consort."

Buddy Moscosco, in a wrinkled suit and scuffed loafers, carried a bottle of Rogue River IPA. He nodded to Gina and cut across the room and stopped when he arrived at Tioga's side. "Sometimes you see a couple and realize you don't know anything about them," he said as he studied Terry and Gina, who now stood near the foot of the table.

Moscosco sipped his IPA. Tioga clinked her empty glass with his half-full bottle. "Where'd you find the IPA, Buddy?"

Moscosco looked like a delinquent teenager. "Smuggled it in. I knew there wouldn't be anything for me to drink up here in this rarefied atmosphere." He paused and added, "I'm not staying for dinner. Wasn't invited. Besides I gotta keep my eyes on a couple of Indians who just checked in and don't look kosher to me."

Tioga raised her eyebrows. "Yaqui Indians?"

Moscosco shrugged his shoulders. "Indians is all I know. Or should I say Native Americans. They didn't wear labels to identify their tribe."

Tioga removed the lint on Moscosco's tie. "About marriages, Buddy. Sometimes when you're on the inside you don't know what's going on, anymore than someone on the outside. Trust me, I know. My ex pulled the wool over my eyes for years. Maybe I let him."

Moscosco handed his now empty beer bottle to the waiter. "Your ex sounds like a wolf in sheep's clothing."

Tioga sighed, scanned the room, then zeroed in on Matt Chehab, who wore an ascot, a white jacket and matching white trousers and who licked his lips as if he was eager to pounce on someone half his age. "He's a survivor," Tioga observed. "I'll say that much for him."

Moscosco walked his eyes around the room and chuckled. "Chehab has outlasted all his wives. One was a Muslim, another a Cairo Copt and the last babe an orthodox Jew. Maybe next time, she'll be an agnostic."

Tioga watched the tête-à-tête unfolding between McCoy and Chehab who stood jowl-to-jowl in the furthest corner of the room with drinks in hand, oblivious of everyone else. Suddenly Terry's face went dark. What happened? It must have been something Chehab said. But no, that wasn't it. Terry's eyes were fixed, not on Chehab, but on a couple Tioga didn't immediately recognize: a disheveled man and an equally disheveled woman who stood in the shadows, near the entrance to the dining room, and looked like they wanted someone, anyone, to throw them a life preserver. They were out of place, indeed, in a crowd of guests who had dressed up rather than dressed down. When they moved out of the shadows, she saw them clearly. Camilla's hand was still bandaged, her hair bedraggled and her attire the same old same old that she had worn all day. Jeremiah Langley wore baggy trousers and a wrinkled shirt and looked like someone had roughed him up while gathering info for a story he was writing about gangbangers.

Gina conferred with Aden who added two more settings and two more chairs to the table, which brought the total number of people who would sit down to eleven.

Buddy Moscosco wandered from corner to corner, looking for trouble, and when he didn't find any he threw up his hands as if in despair. "There are less of us than there were at the Last Supper. But when there's a party this big, there's bound to be bad blood. I'm just saying."

Tioga leaned against Moscosco. "What do you know about the history between Terry and Jeremiah?"

Moscosco seemed to be shaken by Tioga's question; for a moment or two he wobbled. Then he raised his arms, took a deep breath and regained his balance. "I suppose there's no harm telling. McCoy invited Langley back as the editor at *The Gazette*. These people hate each other one minute and then love each other the next. They're crazy." Moscosco played with the hair behind his ears. Under his breath he added, "Chehab blabbed the news about Jeremiah and McCoy the other day at the Underground."

Tioga watched Langley put his arm around Camilla's waist and gently pull her toward him, seemingly without any resistance on her part. "I know what you mean about the love-hate thing," she said. "I can't stand George Ambrose, but I can't seem to live without him. Ditto for me and my father."

Moscosco folded his hands in front of his belly. "This ain't my idea of fun! I'd rather be in the lobby keeping a lookout for creeps. If I see Hawk again, I'll kick his ass all the way to Napa."

He chuckled to himself and drew Tioga's attention to Gina as she herded Lawrence out of the room, though he clearly didn't want to go. When Aaron arrived and took his hand, he had no choice. He bowed his head, then raised his eyes, stared at the adults and looked like he was going to cry.

"Poor dear," Tioga said, "I know the feeling."

At the far end of the room, where the sunlight was brightest, Langley bellied up to the bar, nodded to Dyce and waited while he opened a bottle of Pellegrino, added ice cubes to a tall glass and then poured. Camilla came straight at Tioga, eyes bulging and now apparently happy to be free from Langley's hand, his gaze, his everything. "I'm sorry. He invited me to come with him, though I didn't realize until just now that he didn't have an invitation."

Tioga kept a close eye on McCoy and on Chehab, both of whom had drifted close to the table. She turned away from them, put her arm around Camilla's waist and noticed that she liked the feeling. "McCoy looks royally pissed. Gina told me he hates people who crash his parties. I hope Buddy Moscosco doesn't get the signal to toss you and Langley out on your ears." She glanced at her empty cocktail glass and then turned it upside down.

Camilla fidgeted. "Are you angry with me?" she asked in a loud voice that attracted more attention than she intended. Then quietly, she added, "I know I fucked up by coming with Langley, but I hate it when you don't say what you're thinking."

Camilla waited for a long time before Tioga spoke. "I'm royally pissed, but not at you. Analytics mixed up our samples with someone else's."

Camilla shook her head. "That's not right about Analytics!" she exclaimed. Then she went on rather methodically. "I saw Mrs. Baynes. She wants to talk to you in person. Somebody called and left a threatening message on her machine. I guess someone doesn't want her to talk." She paused and then added, "Oh yeah, there's one more thing. Matthew Chehab has the title to the house at forty-nine. He bought the place from the Syrah family for a song and a dance. Travis could have been rich."

Tioga handed her cocktail glass to the waiter in black. "Refill please." Then she sniffed and jerked her head back. "I could use a shower. I'm sure you could too."

She lifted the kaftan and scratched the spider bite. "Relax. You're not in trouble, Camilla. Besides Langley's a big boy and can take care of himself. Get a drink and go and talk to Louis and Isabel. He has the white beard and the dumb hat. She's the redhead in the gorgeous gown and looks like she's had a boob job. Tell Louis you love his rosé, and he'll be your friend for life."

Tioga raised her chin and pointed it in the direction of Louis and Isabel Marchetti, who stood together near the center of the room and who appeared to be waiting for something momentous to happen.

Camilla gave Tioga a guilty look and then streaked across the room. Tioga couldn't see the expression on her face, but she noticed the smiles that radiated from Louis and Isabel and concluded that she had said something endearing.

Camilla was a fast learner, sometimes.

Tioga Loses Her Virginity

Tioga snagged a canapé from a silver tray floating by, scarfed it and then turned her head toward Jeremiah Langley, who now looked down at her from a height she thought of as Olympian. At six feet six inches and two hundred fifty pounds, give or take an inch and a pound either way, and biceps to spare, Langley could be as intimidating and as alluring as Tioga's ex and his surfer buddies who preened on the beach with their long boards, their sculpted pecs and their high-test testosterone.

Ever since they first met, when Tioga was investigating an unsavory case in the Valley, Langley had worked hard to give her the impression that he knew more than she did. Indeed, during his initial tenure as *The Gazette's* editor-in-chief, he had published a list of the names of the women who had been sexually assaulted in the Valley, as if to show that he was an expert on the subject. McCoy had hired him and fired him and hired him again; they'd been around the track several times already.

Tioga felt especially wolfish, indeed more wolfish than she had felt for days. She sniffed the air and studied Langley, from the brown and white Spectators on his two left feet to the hair on the top of his head, which he parted down the middle in the manner of H. L. Mencken, his alter ego. Many times over the years, Tioga had read the quotation from Mencken that Langley had taped to the wall above his desk at *The Gazette*: "Puritanism: The haunting fear that someone, somewhere, may be happy." It struck Tioga now that Langley was as puritanical as anyone else in the

Valley. He was drinking fizzy water, and he turned up his nose at the canapés that came within arm's reach, including crab with avocado. At the same time, there was also something comical about his big beefy hands, which didn't look like they were meant to hold a pen or a pencil and edit copy. Tioga laughed. Langley waited for her laughter to die a natural death.

"I suppose you haven't heard," he began as if to taunt her. "News travels at a snail's pace in the Valley." Tioga took the bait.

That had been her MO all afternoon. "Unless your news is about Reginald Wentworth, aka Hawk, I'm probably unaware of what you have in mind, sir, so lay it on me please, sir."

Langley looked untroubled by Tioga's repetition of the word "sir," which would have been more appropriate at Fort Benning—where he had trained—before he received a dishonorable discharge from the military for insubordination. They had that in common: a disinclination to follow the commands of men and women in uniform. From his Olympian heights Jeremiah stared at Louis and Isabel, a petite woman who seemed to be distinctly Gallic, or so Tioga thought.

When Jeremiah was certain that she had fixed her eyes on Mr. and Mrs. Marchetti, he told her in his big booming voice: "McCoy made an offer on their spread. He wants to turn it into a destination for the wine and weed crowd and cut out the competition. I think it's a brilliant move. It's the shot in the arm we need right now."

With Langley, Tioga found it nearly impossible to distinguish his unabashed self-promotion from his devotion to an unwritten moral code that he adhered to when it suited him. When it didn't suit him, he ignored it. "What about your hero, H. L. Mencken? Isn't he turning over in his grave knowing you've become a flack for Terry McCoy?"

Langley opened his mouth and then uttered just three words, "About Mencken, I ... ," before he was interrupted by Gina who stood at the head of the table, rang a cowbell and summoned the guests. "No one's allowed to monopolize anyone else. Except for Terry and me, of course."

Tioga laughed and so did Jeremiah. "I bet we're in store for a spat. Bet the happy couple has rehearsed."

Tioga looked up at Langley, who peered down at her. "You know, of course, that Terry also made Reggie Wentworth an offer for his share in the hotel and that he couldn't refuse. Now he owns it all, though Chehab wants to buy a piece. He has the cash from his rental income."

McCoy stood next to Gina and stroked his beard as if lost in thought. Tioga scratched her invisible itch. "That's a very interesting tidbit about the hotel," she said. She added provocatively, "Maybe you'll explain why you and Roxanne Jacobs were slinking around town today." She added parenthetically, "I've heard about Gina's parties. But this is my first time."

Langley whispered, "Congratulations, my dear. You're about to lose your virginity." He laughed, paused and added, "Everything that happens here stays here. That applies to you as well as to me."

Tioga looked at a card with her name and another with Langley's name. "Gee, Gina seated us together. That suits me." Then she read the handwritten menu on parchment paper. "Oh, Lord, six courses and a different wine with each one. This is going to an endurance test. I'd better pace myself."

Langley smiled generously, moved Tioga's chair away from the table and, once she was seated, brought it close to the setting reserved for her. With great fanfare he took his own seat, leaned toward Tioga and said, "About Roxanne Jacobs, she's a private person, and it's not just because she's Old World and old school. You'll understand when you meet her."

Tioga wondered what Langley might mean and what she might say to him now. She had long operated under the assumption that to get information she had to give information. "Hawk hired me to find Roxanne and then told me abruptly that he no longer needed me." She squinted her eyes and focused on a painting on the far wall that she had not previously noticed, perhaps because she was stoned. It was one of her father's portraits in which she had served as model and as muse. "What the fuck!" she said aloud, though no one seemed to have heard her or noticed the likeness between the face of the girl in a painting and the face of the woman sitting at the table. "How the hell did Terry get that painting?"

Tioga unfurled her white linen napkin, draped it across her lap and looked at McCoy who fumbled with his belt and then sat down.

She soon realized that there were two dinner parties: one revolving around McCoy at the head of the table, the other revolving around Robert Cohen at the foot of the table. Tioga, who was closer to Cohen than to McCoy, didn't want to be a satellite of either one. She drifted in and out of both orbits and tracked the conversations on both ends of the table. Surprisingly they both veered toward agricultural matters, both legal and illegal, or rather "extralegal," as Cohen called them.

"Well, ag is all illegal in one way or the other," McCoy said. "Either the crop is illegal or the field workers are illegal or the farmers are using pesticides that are outlawed in California."

Cohen bristled when he heard McCoy's remark. "You seem to forget that we're aiming for total compliance, though you wouldn't know much about that. We'll catch up with you and make you pay."

Cohen wore a white jacket and a black bow tie. His bald-head looked like polished marble. "I'm Robert Cohen," he said to Tioga when they were seated. "But call me Bobby." In a gravelly tone of voice he added, "I'm a lawyer slash lobbyist in Sacramento. Surely Terry has told you about me." He seemed to want his legend to precede him.

Tioga shook her head. "Sorry. You are an unknown entity to me."

Cohen shrugged his shoulders. "I thank you very much," he said, though it wasn't clear to Tioga why he was eager to offer his thanks. Perhaps that was the way of Sacramento lawyers and lobbyists.

Tioga kept an eye on Camilla, who moved closer to Cohen and who seemed to be as charmed by his manners as she had been appalled by Hawk's. Cohen told old Sacramento stories, though they weren't the kind of stories that Tioga wanted and needed to hear, not then and there. She had not accepted Gina's dinner invitation to be talked at by a Sacramento lawyer slash lobbyist, but rather to see and be seen, and to eavesdrop too, an occupational obligation she accepted without resentment.

Cohen fussed with his tie and then straightened the collar on his white jacket. "I have worked one-on-one with Terry, though he's become impossible of late. These days I'm rarely in court. But I'm all over the state house and behind the scenes, of course."

He puffed himself up. Tioga imagined that he would explode and his body parts would be scattered around the room, but he seemed to know when to slow down, take a breath and decompress. "I have the governor's ear on vital matters. I've told him marijuana ought to be legalized, regulated and taxed, and I've advised him on the efficacy of the twin-tunnels in the delta that will bring water to the parched southland."

Like the bicycle guy, Travis Syrah, Robert Cohen sounded like a bullshitter, though a bullshitter who used big words like "efficacy," which Tioga immediately googled on her cell. "Must be related to bribery and trickery," she told herself.

Storm sat between Buddy Moscosco—"the house dick," as Gina introduced him, and who had joined the party under protest—and Louis Marchetti who watched Aden, the gorgeous red-headed sommelier, open a bottle of the Metafor Winery chardonnay bearing a label with the image of a wolf baying at the moon. Storm turned her head from Moscosco to Marchetti; she looked like a martyr stranded between a sinner and a saint. She didn't know what to say to either of them.

Tioga had grown weary of rescuing her at Valley functions. She watched Storm sip the chardonnay. When she finished the third glass, she stood up and grabbed her handbag. "Excuse me, my dears. Don't drink all the wine while I take a powder."

When she returned after a few minutes, Tioga smelled skunkweed in Storm's hair and clothes. Poor, stoned Storm languished in that cocoon where Terry McCoy had something urgent to say at every turn.

Cohen filled Tioga's glass with a 2016 chardonnay and waited for her to sip and pass judgment. "Is it too dry or too sweet?"

Tioga swirled the wine and tasted. "It's not bad. But I prefer French blends to California varietals." She paused a moment and added, "Frankly I'm far more curious about your life in the fast lane than in Louis's chardonnay." Tioga emptied her glass in a vase that held two enormous sun-flowers and then helped herself to the cab that looked more robust and inviting than the white. Then she reached across the table and touched Cohen's hand. "A lobbyist, Bobby?" she asked, batting her eyelashes in the manner she had learned along with her classmates at the Badminton School for Girls.

Cohen put down his knife and fork and peered into Tioga's eyes as if gazing at the sky overhead. "Lobbying is very rewarding in more ways than one. I wouldn't give it up for Hollywood, though I adore my friends in the movie colony."

He sipped the cab, rolled it in his mouth and swallowed.

"California is where it's at. In fact, right now, Bakersfield is where it's at. I've just returned from a fact-finding trip and met the nicest folks. You know we're the fourth largest economy in the world, and we're growing at an unprecedented rate. Before long we'll be exporting cannabis around the world, and we'll show the Canadians we can beat them hands down."

Tioga rolled her eyes. So did Langley. "Bobby boy, are we supposed to be impressed by a fact that California is boom-country USA? We've known that forever!"

Cohen stood up, banged his fork against a wine glass and addressed the whole table. "I think we should sing, 'I love you, California.'" No one except Moscosco joined him, though he offered a lovely rendition of the song he obviously knew by heart, beginning with the line, "I love you California, you're the greatest state of all."

Marchetti had been the last of the guests to join the table. He was the outlier in the party. Aden and the maître d', Paul Lipski, who was known as "Lip," helped him find his seat between Camilla and Storm. For what seemed to Tioga like an awfully long time, Louis wore an expression of sadness, as if he was going away on a long journey and did not know when he would see his beloved vineyard again.

Poor Mr. Marchetti. Beyond the boundaries of Metafor, he seemed lost, though when Tioga took pity on him and asked about his cab, he regaled her with tales about dry farming, biodynamic marijuana, organic grapes and "regenerative ag," as he called it, which he regarded as something magical. He stood and raised his glass. "To Dionysus," he said, sipped the cab and added, "Nobody makes better cab than me." He made it sound like a fact and not an idle boast.

Tioga offered Louis a seductive smile that produced a blush on his face and turned Robert Cohen green with envy. "Haven't you observed that farmers rarely have manners?"

At the head of the table, McCoy flirted with Isabel Marchetti, who, like Storm, had had too much to drink and was now slurring her words.

Tioga heard her say, "affair." She leaned as far toward Isabel as she could and listened as she said to McCoy, "I had a thing with Louis's ex-partner, who now manages a restaurant in San Francisco that made the Michelin Guide three straight years. But I have never thought of leaving my husband. No one else would put up with me."

McCoy could be as charming and as seductive as Isabel, especially when he looked at her adoringly, touched her chin and lifted it slightly. Tioga wasn't bored. There was something to entertain her every direction she looked. Now she eavesdropped on Marchetti who was talking to Moscosco about hotels.

"They're in my blood," Moscosco insisted.

"Oh, no," Marchetti said. "You won't find them in the state of nature."

Maybe Cohen was right about farmers. Marchetti tucked his napkin inside his shirt and used it as a bib. "Marchetti is graceful in a clumsy sort of way," Tioga said to Cohen.

Marchetti clearly heard her but seemed to pretend that he didn't. Tioga noticed how well he concealed his thoughts and feelings when he wanted to. "I love cold soup in summer and hot soup in winter. We always eat seasonally at the farm, and we love to cook for ourselves."

So Louis loved something besides his wine and his wife. That was good to know. Tioga begged Aden for water. "I can't hydrate fast enough. Probably because of the weed." Once again she smiled at Louis. "I've read that wolves killed sheep on your ranch."

Now Marchetti's lower lip trembled. Tioga thought that his lip trembled a tad too much. Either he was a timid fellow who was afraid of his own shadow or a good actor who had practiced the art of trembling. "I've lost a few sheep, though the story in *The Gazette* blew it up. The police told me wolves are not their problem. I got the same song and dance from Fish and Wildlife."

Cohen's jaw dropped in slow motion. Then he reared back, also in slow motion. "Excuse me. There are no wolves in Sonoma. Someone must be pulling your leg, or what's between your legs. You must mean coyotes."

Marchetti frowned. Then he placed his knife and fork across the citrus salad that he had not yet touched. "No, no, no. I've lived here long enough to know the difference between wolf scat and coyote scat. You don't understand. I'm only half an hour from here, but it's another world out there."

Cohen smiled, smirked and guffawed until he realized that Marchetti didn't mean to be funny. He seemed to have more to say, but he paused for a moment, formed his right hand in the shape of a gun and with his thumb as the hammer and his index finger as the barrel pointed it at the ceiling and shouted, "Bang! Bang! That's the only language people understand."

Tioga wanted to like Marchetti. Now she wasn't sure that she could even be civil to him, though she wasn't ready to let go of him either. He seemed worth cultivating. "If you talk about killing a single wolf, Louis, you'll have no end of trouble from the Save the Wolves Foundation. Wolves only take what they need to survive. If you slaughter them, you upset the whole balance of nature."

Tioga made her face look wolf-like. She had had lots of practice. "How's that for a wolf?" she asked and waited for Marchetti to laugh or cry. When he did neither, she lifted her head and produced a long, slow howl that woke Storm from her nap. Tioga blew her a kiss and then turned her attention again to Marchetti who leaned back in his chair and folded his arms across his chest. "Go on. I'm waiting for you to enlighten me about wolves."

Tioga didn't need encouragement. "I tracked them and lived with them at the Wilderness School for Women. I saw wolves put the brakes on out-of-control deer populations, and I saw that wolves brought back trees, shrubs, birds and beavers. They ate coyotes, which was a godsend. Bears and raptors returned big time."

Marchetti shook his head. "Oh, so wolves are natural-born environmentalists, is that it? You don't know the first thing about *Canine lupus*."

Tioga reared back and snarled, "The Latin is *Canis lupus*, sir, not *Canine lupus*."

Marchetti held his left flank with his right hand as if he'd been injured. But he replied gently, "You'll have to come to Metafor Winery and see our vines and how we're diversifying. Diversity is the name of the game. We have wine and weed weekends. We're a model for the whole Valley."

He turned toward to his wife, who smirked and quipped, "Yes, dear." Then she faced Tioga and explained, "We have wolves who have mated with dogs and dogs who have mated with wolves. Like me, they're mongrels."

Isabel's comment surprised Tioga, who had taken her for a trophy wife. In fact, she could put together a coherent sentence and sound intelligent. "Wolfdogs," Tioga quipped. "The puppies are adorable."

Isabel nodded. "Yes, they are. Don't believe everything Louis tells you. He doesn't believe half of it himself."

Robert Cohen had been scribbling on the back of his menu. He put on his glasses and read what he'd written. "First of all, taxonomically speaking, the ordinary wolfdog pup is categorized by scientists as a subspecies of *Canis lupus*. I know because I had to testify at a trial in Alturas last month when the so-called experts failed to distinguish wolves from dogs and both of them from wolfdogs. There's no way to resolve the issue. That's the beauty of it."

Cohen glared at Tioga and at Louis and added, "I think you're both barking up the wrong tree."

The laughter woke Storm briefly. Then she went back to sleep. Aden and Lip—who bowed and scraped as if serving royalty—cleared the soup bowls and soup spoons, lined up the silverware, picked up the napkins that had fallen to the floor and issued new ones and placed the second course in front of the guests.

"What the hell is it?" Tioga asked. "Animal, vegetable, mineral?"

Lip grinned as if he was privy to classified information. "Rabbit terrine with shelled pistachios, crushed hemp seeds, garlic and shallots. Jonny made it from scratch. It's sensational."

Tioga watched Louis devour the dish and decided to abandon all caution. In fact, the marijuana made up her mind for her. Ravenously hungry, she polished off the rabbit and immediately savaged the next course: day-boat scallops seared in olive oil with garlic and chili peppers.

Louis ate more slowly than anyone else at the table. "The Sustainable Valley thing is bullshit. Regenerative ag is where it's at. My sheep move and mow and poop and don't pollute. It's not about science. It's magic, and I'm ready to plant hemp."

Tioga heard Bobby Cohen's stomach growl and wondered how he could still be hungry. But he was. Moreover, he had the gumption to ask for butter, which he smeared on a thick slice of bread baked, the menu said, in the Mar Monte brick oven.

Tioga glanced at Jeremiah, who ignored her. Then she remembered her last civil conversation with McCoy on the subject of *The Gazette*. "I'm not going to go back on the promise I made to readers to boot Jeremiah when he crossed the line," he said. "If I didn't, nobody would trust me."

Tioga had looked at her reflection in the mirror. "What makes you think you're trusted now?" she asked.

Sean Dyce winced. "Oooh, hitting below the belt."

Now at Gina's party, Tioga poked her elbow into Langley's rib cage. "Where the fuck did Terry get the money to buy out Hawk, and how the hell is he going to come up with the cash to snap up Marchetti's vineyard and winery?"

Langley leaned back in his chair. "A big chunk comes from investors back east, but I don't know who's behind all of it. The Chinese are hot for California real estate and the California cannabis industry. There's a worldwide market."

Tioga hiccupped once, hiccupped again and held her breath. The hiccups went away. "By the way, congratulations on your reappointment. McCoy always liked the stories you made up, albeit for his own obscure reasons."

Langley's face melted. His whole frame seemed to collapse too, though he didn't fall apart. Aden made her way around the table, poured wine and made small talk in a way that didn't seem to bother anyone. "Enjoying the meal so far?" "Shall I pour more red?" "Would you like a new napkin?" When she arrived at Langley's side, she filled his glass halfway. He looked up at her and scolded. "I'm a full glass kind of guy."

Aden refilled his glass and patted him on the head. "Good boy." She might have used the same tone of voice with Gina's lapdog.

Tioga held her glass up to the light, took in the psychedelic colors—violet, red and black—finished the wine and signaled for Aden who came round and poured again. "After this, I'm not giving you another drop. You probably can't see straight anymore, and you don't even know it."

Tioga dismissed Aden with a wave of her left hand. "Whatever." Then she closed her eyes and listened as Chehab asked Camilla, "What have you been doing all summer, my dear?" as if he was a beloved uncle. Before Camilla could say a word, he told her, "I've bought an olive orchard and an olive press. You ought to join me on a jaunt. We'll have fun."

Camilla listened politely. "Thank you so much. That's very kind of your, sir. I'm sure we can schedule a time." Then she reared back and said, "You do own a lot in the Valley, don't you, sir, like that lovely old house on Avenida de La Virgen."

Chehab added smugly, "I like to keep my hand in the game."

Camilla's retort, "Apparently a lot of games," stuck Tioga as a barb that might have hit home, but Chehab didn't seem to mind.

Tioga did her best to ignore McCoy, but he wanted her attention. Tioga could feel his eyes on her even when she didn't look at him. When she did look she saw that he ate with his mouth open, wiped his hands on the sleeve of his jacket and speared food from Isabel's plate.

"Facts are facts!" he bellowed. "There's no getting around them, though we're drowning in lies—about the Mar Monte, especially." He paused for a moment, blew his nose loudly, gathered his thoughts again and went on oblivious of everyone else. "Ladies and gentlemen. Let's be friends, play nice and forget about the little things that keep us apart."

Moscosco laughed. He was the only person at the table who wasn't shitfaced, as Tioga thought of it. Chehab shushed Moscosco.

Then Louis screamed at Chehab. "Don't shush!"

Though Langley had advised Tioga to treat everything at the dinner as confidential, he was now taking notes, compulsively it seemed, in a little green book that he had removed from his pocket and placed on the table in front of him where everyone could see it.

Cohen lifted his glass and tossed water in Langley's face. "Everything's off the record here. Put down your pen."

Langley replied, "Fuck you, asshole."

McCoy pounded both fists on the table. "Shut up, everyone. Calm down and get ready for Jonny's *pièce de résistance*: roast duck breast stuffed with pine nuts, currants and shitake mushrooms."

Gina rang the cowbell. The double doors to the kitchen opened.

Gorgeous, poised Aden and equally poised Lip balanced eleven plates between them. The arrival of the entrée generated "Oohs" and "Ahs." For a nanosecond, no one spoke; the duck looked too tasty for talk. With knife and fork, Tioga cut a sliver from the breast and stared at it as if transfixed. "This is something else," she swooned and then paused and added, under her breath, "What the fuck is happening here?" She had forgotten that she was stoned. Her taste buds, which had gone electric, reminded her that the weed was still at work.

She ate slowly and didn't say a word. No one else at the table spoke. The only sounds in the room were the sounds from the street that poured through the open window where Langley now stood and looked down.

"I'm not going to mess with it this time," Tioga said, though she wasn't sure whether she had actually spoken the words aloud or merely heard them in her head, which seemed to have expanded. And what might she have meant by "it," she didn't know.

Chehab and Cohen both looked at her queerly. Then Gina broke the silence that spanned the room. "You'll never guess what happened the other day at the shop. Greg Allman's ex bought an English croquet set. Of course, I had to ask about her husband when I saw her name on the American Express card." 'Oh, yes, that,' the ex said. 'I started as a groupie and after my marriage tanked ended as a groupie.' I carried the croquet set myself and placed it in the back seat of the biggest Mercedes I've ever seen. Way bigger than yours, Matt."

Bobby Cohen peered at Tioga and asked, "Who the fuck is Greg Allman?"

Before Tioga could reply, Gina said, "You know, Bobby, the blind Allman Brothers from Alabama. They had a slew of hits and performed for Obama in the White House."

Tioga thought Gina was joking and laughed. McCoy knew better and scowled.

"Faux pas," Isabel murmured.

For a moment, it seemed that McCoy would let Gina's comment pass, but then his upper lip curled, and Tioga knew he couldn't resist the urge to have a word or two. "First, the Allman Brothers aren't from Alabama. Didn't you ever hear *Georgia Peach*? Second, they're not blind. Third, they never performed for Barack. They were too white for him. They played for the peanut farmer." He glared at Gina and added, "Better to remain silent and be thought a fool than to speak and to remove all doubt."

Bobby Cohen nodded. "Touché, Mr. Lincoln!" Chehab knocked over his glass and stained the tablecloth. Aden mopped up the spill. Isabel glanced at the portrait on the wall and then at Tioga and nodded knowingly. Gina hid her face in her napkin. Terry picked up his knife and fork and cut the duck breast into bite-sized pieces, minced the Swiss chard and mashed the roasted potatoes. Then he stacked small amounts of each on the end of his fork. "Eating is an art form that requires discipline. Like sex you can't rush it."

Tioga watched McCoy eat methodically. Then she aimed her gaze at Gina who waved her napkin as if to clear the air. "There is nothing sexy about the way you eat. In fact, it's a turnoff."

Gina took out her cell and texted. Across the table, Chehab put down his knife and fork, picked up his phone, read the text, smirked and then dropped the phone into the pocket of his jacket.

Tioga thought that he looked pleased with himself. Gina glared at Terry. "I hope you're happy. I hope I haven't spoiled your dinner."

Tioga turned up her nose at the remains of the duck, pushed her plate away and reached for a bottle of red wine that seemed to wait for her. She put both hands around the bottle, lifted it above her head, put her lips around the mouth and poured Marchetti's 2016 cab down her throat. Yes, yes, it was very good cab. Maybe the best cab she had ever had. There was no such thing as too much of Marchetti's cab. Life in the Valley was good. It was robust, and it was intoxicating.

Taking Aim

The room grew smaller and darker, and the noises from the street grew louder. Tioga turned her head and saw Matt Chehab stagger toward McCoy. He had a bottle in his hand. Isabel propped him up. "You're a pig and a bore. Apologize," Chehab said.

McCoy stood up, kicked his chair back, reached down, picked up the duck leg from his plate and hurled it at Chehab. He struck him on the chin. Then he rushed Chehab and tried to wrest the bottle from his hand. When that failed, he circled Chehab's waist with his arms and squeezed. Chehab kicked and screamed and tried to strike McCoy, but he missed again and again. He couldn't control or coordinate his limbs, which flayed about. He collapsed on the floor, the bottle fell from his hand, smashed into pieces and scattered.

Langley tried to pry McCoy and Chehab apart. "Cut it out, boys, before someone gets hurt."

Chehab twisted and turned like a wild man unwilling to be tamed. Finally he broke free, got to his feet, reached for a knife, held it above his head and laughed like a ghoul. McCoy held the broken wine bottle by the neck and crouched close to the floor. Except for Tioga, the guests formed a circle around Chehab and McCoy, who swiped at Chehab's nose with the jagged edge of the bottle. Blood spurted, then trickled down and around the corners of his mouth and formed a puddle on his double chin. Blood dripped on the floor. It coated Chehab's hand. "Oh, shit. Call the doctor."

Tioga reached inside her jacket and moved her hand toward the snub nose that felt hot to the touch and heavier than ever before. The gun came to life. Tioga cleared the fog in her head. McCoy spat at Chehab, who gave him the finger—a bloody finger at that. Tioga wrapped her hand around the snub nose, glanced at the ceiling and then focused on her father's portrait. She lifted her arm, raised her hand, put her finger on the trigger, and took aim at the little girl in a red cape and with a toothy wolf at her side. She fired a single shot, heard the bullet shatter the glass and rip into the face of "Little Red Riding Hood."

McCoy and Chehab looked equally stunned. Then they backed away from one another. Tioga wrapped the snub nose in a napkin and handed the package to Aden who tucked it under her arm. "Stash it please, sweetie. In the pantry with the pasta so I can find it."

Aden seemed oddly, yet remarkably, calm as if she was accustomed to hiding weapons in the pantry. "Nobody saw you, save for me. They were fixed on the main event."

Aden dashed down the passageway. When she came back, she removed the shattered painting from the wall and stashed it behind the makeshift bar.

Tioga admired her alacrity. Then she searched anxiously for Storm, whom she did not want to abandon and whose head still rested on the table, even after the gunshot. The room went silent again, though the racket from the street grew louder. McCoy's face had frozen with a grotesque expression. Chehab reached up and caught the napkin that Moscosco tossed toward him. "Take off your shirt. Clean up fast, big boy."

Aden attended to Chehab's bloody nose, which had finally stopped hemorrhaging, thanks to an ice pack that Lip applied. Moscosco picked up the wine bottle with its jagged edge, placed it in his jacket and then gathered

Chehab's bloody shirt and squeezed it into a tight ball and tossed it to Aden.

Then Moscosco put his hands on McCoy's shoulders. "Sit down, Mr. McCoy, and make yourself presentable. I'm going downstairs to make sure nobody does anything stupid."

McCoy wiped his face with a moist napkin that he had dipped in his water glass. "Aye, aye, Buddy, sir." With his right hand, he smoothed his hair.

Gina removed bits of duck embedded in his tangled beard. "You look more or less presentable. Try not to treat what just happened as a joke for your own amusement."

Lip came out of the kitchen at a gallop and offered Chehab a white shirt, a black leather tie, a pair of jeans, and a belt. He helped him get undressed and then dressed again, while the guests turned away to respect his privacy. "Good as new," Lip said and handed Chehab over to Aden who squeezed antibiotic on his nose and added a butterfly bandage.

Storm raised her head once more and glanced from side to side. "Did I miss something?" Then she laid her head down and moaned.

Tioga went to the largest of the windows and peered down at the street where a crowd had gathered near the entrance to the hotel, kept at bay by Aaron with his big body and booming voice. Tioga heard reggae that rose from the plaza; it sounded like the Wailers', "Get up, Stand up." She wanted to join the crowd, but then she heard a siren in the distance that came closer and closer. A police vehicle arrived in front of the hotel. The flashing red and blue lights looked psychedelic.

After a minute that seemed to drag on and on, Moscosco entered the room with Chief Ambrose and his deputy, both of them nipping at his heels. Aaron followed a few steps behind in a cap and brocade coat that looked more impressive than the police uniforms.

Ambrose looked from wall to wall and from ceiling to floor, as if hoping to detect the signs of a crime or at least a misdemeanor. When he noticed Chehab in a white shirt that looked spotless and newly ironed he raised his eyebrows. "I've never seen you so spiffy, Matt."

Chehab looked like a kid at his own birthday party. "I like white. I look good in white."

Ambrose sat down in the chair that Moscosco had vacated and glanced at McCoy. "What the hell is going on here, Terry?" McCoy stared into space. Ambrose looked right through Tioga, or so it felt. "A hotel guest called and reported the sound of a handgun. He knows what gunshots sound like. Said he did a tour of duty in Iraq." Ambrose took in the spotless tablecloth and the pristine floor. "You people look awful tidy after a dinner party." Then he added cheerfully, "We don't mean to break up the fun and the games. Just doing our duty. Had to see for ourselves."

McCoy leaned back and watched Ambrose and Clark, who stood behind the chief like a footman ready to run an errand. "Dessert, guys?" McCoy asked. "Anything you want, anything!" Then he laughed and added, "No guns have been fired here, George. The guy who did the tour of duty must have thought the popping of champagne sounded like a weapon. Maybe he's suffering from PTSD." He looked around the table and from face to face. "Right? No guns here."

Marchetti was the first to reply. "Righto." Chehab added, "That's correct." Isabel nodded her head. Langley gave Ambrose two thumbs up, and Camilla smiled without parting her lips. Storm raised her head and said, "I was passed out. Didn't see nothing!"

Ambrose nodded his head and with his big brown eyes threw darts at Tioga. "And you, Ms. Op? What can you tell me?"

Tioga put down her spoon, which she had balanced on the end of her pinky. "Just a little celebration. Nothing drug related, sir. Gotta cut loose now and then."

She watched Clark as he eyed a serving of panna cotta sitting all by itself as if begging to be claimed and eaten. He wet his lips and with his index finger pointed right at it. "I'd like that." Saliva gathered at the corners of his mouth.

Ambrose turned around and gave Clark a look that he habitually reserved for rookies who didn't defer to him. "Wipe the drool off your face. We're on duty. It's their party, not ours." Then he made for the exit. Clark followed him. "Sorry folks," he said. "Have a nice evening."

Tioga sighed. Then she turned to Aaron. "Take Storm upstairs and put her to bed, please. I think she can get into her PJs by herself. Tell her not to wait up for me, though given her condition she'll probably sleep like a rock."

Aaron gathered Storm in his arms. "Goodnight all."

Storm kicked her feet and squawked. "Put me down." She beat Aaron's chest with her fists. "I want dessert."

Aaron put her down gently. "When you want me, whistle."

Jonny Field came out of the kitchen, placed his hands on his hips, counted the number of guests still at the table and retreated slowly. Lip reappeared and helped Aden add new wine glasses at each setting. "Let's start all over again," she said. "Pretend nothing happened."

Tioga fidgeted in her seat, stood up, roamed around the room, and then plopped down in the chair that Marchetti had occupied. Isabel traded places with Camilla while Langley leaned against the wall and observed the festivities.

Marchetti stood at the window and enjoyed the breeze, all by himself. Tioga felt sorry for him and joined him.

"Musical chairs," she said aloud. Marchetti chimed in with, "Better than pin the tail on the donkey."

Tioga sniffed the air from the plaza. "Smells like weed down there. There's no escaping it."

Marchetti peered at the crowd. "A fellow is selling joints. He was there when we arrived and he's still there. The runt of the litter."

Tioga leaned out the window and scanned a crowd that looked as motley as any she had ever seen. "Which one is he? Can you point him out?"

Marchetti learned so far out that Tioga thought he might fall. "Careful now," she said.

Marchetti realized the danger and brought himself back. "Over there." He pointed to a runt of a man who ducked in and out of the crowd, his head bobbling up and down and his hands moving frantically. By the time Tioga fixed her eyes where Marchetti had invited her to look, the runt of the litter was gone. "Missed him. He vanished awfully fast."

She turned away from the window and watched Aden as she disappeared behind the kitchen doors, reappeared a few moments later and placed three bottles of Marchetti's 2015 gewürztraminer on the table, spaced equally apart.

Tioga read the label on the tall slender bottle that said "Gold Medal winner" and turned her attention to Marchetti, who cradled a bottle of the same gewürztraminer in his arms. "This is my baby. I grew the grapes on a parcel that juts into San Pablo Bay where it's cooler than here. The brix was zero point nine when we harvested. Fermentation lasted two weeks."

Somebody—Tioga didn't see who—began to applaud and then everyone at the table clapped. She applauded too, though she wasn't sure what or whom she was applauding. Was it the gewürztraminer or was it Louis, or perhaps the man and the wine indivisible?

Jonny Field, in his chef's hat and white apron, burst through the kitchen doors, balanced a large tray above his head, circled the table and, with a flourish, served the panna cotta in small ceramic bowls, one for each person. The dessert was over the top, but no one complained, not even Storm who picked up a spoon and began to eat as if she had worked up an appetite while she had slept.

McCoy put his hand on the back of Storm's neck and rubbed it gently. "It's been a grand party. Thanks, my dear."

Storm stood and kissed McCoy on the lips. Then he kissed Storm and laughed as if to make light of kissing her. "You never missed a party when you were little and your mother—may she rest in peace—invited her friends, served spiked punch, cucumber sandwiches, played bridge soused and made you come down and sing."

Storm looked shaken. "I've tried to forget. It's not good to remember those days."

Tioga checked her cell. It was only 9:29, much earlier than she thought it was. Then she noticed the empty chair at the foot of the table. "Where's Bobby?"

Langley put his arm around Tioga. "Didn't you see? Cohen fled. Too bad. I was beginning to like him. Oddly enough, he gave Marchetti his card, and Marchetti gave him a bottle of his cab. And at the start of the evening they were nipping at one another."

Louis and Isabel said their goodbyes together. Gina kissed them on both cheeks, first Louis and then Isabel. "You must visit my shop," she said to Isabel. "I have pretty things. I can see you have good taste."

Isabel took Gina's hand and kissed it. "Thank you. I'll come. We'll chat."

Aaron arrived on the landing, went for Storm and lifted her in his arms. "Night all," Storm said sweetly. "It has been a lovely evening." She rested her head on Aaron's shoulder.

"Carry me away, dear man." Aaron took a deep breath and mounted the stairs.

Langley and Chehab vanished without a handshake, a kiss, a thank you or a good night.

Tioga wanted go, but she caught sight of Camilla, who sat alone at the table, her eyes downcast. She knew she couldn't leave without a word. Camilla stood up and shook her head. "You are insane. I can't believe what you did. You only got away with it because ... oh, I don't know why."

She kissed Tioga on the lips. "That was not a goodnight kiss." She joined her lips to go to Tioga's once again. They kissed longer this time and then pulled away and gasped.

"I don't want this to end," Camilla said. They held hands and drifted toward Gina, who floated as if on air. In the spot where McCoy had nicked Chehab's nose and blood had flowed, they formed a circle, put their arms around one another and nuzzled.

Then Gina broke away and said, "I have to find my husband. Did either of you see where he went? He's always running away."

Tioga shook her head. She went behind the makeshift bar, looked at her father's painting which she had damaged, grabbed the last wine bottle and hurled it at her likeness. "Fuck you, Dad."

Then she reached out and touched Gina. "You're too good for Terry."

Camilla added, "You husband's a slob. I don't see how you can live with him.

Gina dimmed the lights and stood in the shadows at the edge of the room. "I'll let you in on a secret. My husband and I don't get along. We never have. The marriage was rotten from the start. But we all make compromises." She walked across the dining room, cut through the shadows and burst through the kitchen doors.

Tioga and Camilla sat down at Sean Dyce's makeshift bar and watched him pack up the bottles of rye, gin, vodka, and rum that he'd used to make cocktails. He seemed weary, more so than anyone else who had lingered, including Aden and Lip who gathered dishes, wine glasses, empty bottles and silverwear.

"I'm no coward as you know," Dyce began. "But as soon as I see a fight brewing I make myself scarce. I've cracked too many skulls in my day. No more." He sat down and added, "I don't like duck and haven't had anything to eat since breakfast, except for one of Jonny's marijuana cookies, which wasted me."

He rubbed his belly as if to quell the rumblings and grumblings. "Funny thing, Louis Marchetti asked me, before he went off with his drop-dead gorgeous wife, if I thought marijuana was like a martini or like heroin. I told him, 'Hey, try it, man. Maybe you'll like.' 'I have tried it,' he said. 'I like it. I like it a lot. I just wanted to hear what you thought.' Then he wanted to know if Terry smoked dope. 'Is the Dalai Lama a Buddhist?'" I fired back.

Tioga kicked off her shoes and stretched her legs. "So, Sean, tell me what's up with Mr. and Mrs. McCoy. They were in rare form tonight." She opened her purse and took out the nearly empty pack of American Spirit. "Go ahead; have one. Camilla and I will join you. We'll burn in hell together."

With the BIC lighter she had purchased at the dispensary, Tioga fired up a cigarette, inhaled and passed it to Camilla who blew smoke rings. Dyce watched them rise toward the ceiling. "Terry and Gina are a pain. All fuckin' week Gina has been crying on my shoulder."

Tioga looked startled. "She didn't look like a crybaby tonight, but she's awfully dumb sometimes."

Dyce puffed on his cigarette and grinned. "I guess you haven't heard. Of all the people in the Valley, I thought you'd know."

Tioga flicked the ash from her cigarette and handed it to Camilla. "Don't stuff it, man. Spit it out."

Dyce added the last bottle to the case and closed it. "Terry has been having an affair. Gina just found out. It'll probably torpedo their marriage, though Terry doesn't see why. He'd like nothing better than to have a wife and a mistress. The more the merrier."

Tioga purred like a big cat. "A mistress? I don't hear that word much anymore. Is it somebody I know? Like Langley's ex? Terry had an eye for her, and she was hot for him, though I don't know why."

Dyce put his arms around both Tioga and Camilla and held them close. "I don't know the name of the woman. But I do know this: the kid, Lawrence, who lives in the hotel when he's not away at school, is Terry's son. Gina isn't his mom."

Tioga pulled back from Dyce's embrace. "How do you know that?"

Dyce offered a boyish grin. "I don't know it for a fact. But Terry opened a bank account for the kid in the name Lawrence McCoy. Moscosco told me and swore me to secrecy."

Tioga nodded her head. "Very interesting." She put her arms around Camilla and kissed her. Then she found the photo that Hawk had given her and handed it to Dyce. "Recognize her? She calls herself Roxanne Jacobs."

Dyce smiled in a wistful sort of way. "Yeah. I'd know those cheekbones and blemishes anywhere. I met her once in the Underground. She was with Terry; they had an awful row. You wouldn't know it to look at her. Little Miss Dutch Girl, all milk and honey, has the biggest balls of any woman I've ever met, present company excluded." He laughed nervously and went on haltingly, as if it was hard for him to comb his memory. "You know, she faked her own death in the port at Amsterdam," he whispered, as if talking might land him in trouble. "Real name was Geertje van der Beek. I saw it in the obits in the Dutch papers and have never forgotten it."

He closed his eyes and looked as if his memory was working overtime. "The Amsterdam harbormaster concluded that it was arson. The Dutch cops couldn't find a body, but a witness came forward and swore she'd seen Geertje run through the flames, dive into the water and not come up. The cops found her stuff floating in the harbor. The insurance company paid up. Randy Scheck could fill you in on the details. He was her lawyer."

Tioga blinked her eyes. Then with the tip of her index finger she wiped away a fat teardrop that had landed on Dyce's check. "I'm really sorry."

Dyce looked embarrassed. "I didn't think I'd get choked up like this. Roxanne and I only had a very brief thing, but I still remember her. She was good to me." He shuttered his eyes, kept them shuttered for a long time, and then opened them slowly, looking from Tioga to Camilla and back to Camilla. "What about the two of you?" he asked with a mix of curiosity and sadness, or so it seemed to Tioga. "How do you two connect to Roxanne?"

Tioga put her hands around Camilla's hips "You go. You're not stoned like me."

Camilla shook her head. "No, you. I wouldn't know where to begin. There are too many pieces going around in my head like a clock out of whack—though it's true, I'm not stoned. At least I don't think so."

Tioga placed her hands on her forehead and squeezed gently, as if she might force her mind to open and reveal what was inside. "Okay, I'll go. Reginald Wentworth, aka Reggie, aka Hawk, paid me cash to find Roxanne Jacobs, said he was worried about her and didn't mean her any harm. Camilla went to the address where Hawk thought she lived, or had lived, and then …"

Tioga stopped, glanced at Camilla and then at Dyce who said, "Yeah, I'm good. I get it. Don't stop now."

Tioga cleared her throat. "Two Yaquis and a couple of loopy women got Camilla fucked up on hash and kicked her out of the house. I had to rescue her. By the time we went back, the Yaquis and the women had cleared out. I saw a bloodstain on the floor in the living room. The basement had been used to warehouse weed, which might explain the blood and the disappearance of the people who lived there."

Tioga reached for a glass of water and sipped slowly. Then she went on. "Soon after that, Hawk sent me a text that said 'terminating our deal.' I don't think the cops know about the blood on the floor or the Yaquis and the women. If they did, they'd have brought us in for questioning, though we bumped into Ambrose and Clark on Avenida de la Virgen where Camilla got fucked up."

Tioga lit another cigarette, puffed without inhaling and disappeared in a cloud of smoke. "It might be coincidental, though I'm not sure. Chehab owns the house where the women and the Yaquis lived. Also, two days ago Ambrose showed up at my office and laid out a dozen photos of a woman named Dorothy Baynes whose body was found on the highway across from Metafor Winery. She was raped and murdered. Her body looked like it had been dragged a distance, though whoever did the dragging tried to make it look like she'd been tossed on the side of the road."

Dyce had finished packing the empty bottles. He closed the box and taped it shut. "I ought to be able to listen and not freak. I'm not a kid. But I can't take it anymore, not rape and murder and bodies dragged or dumped and bloodstains in a house in The Springs."

He picked up the box and held it both hands. "I'm taking this to the back of the hotel for recycling. Tomorrow is another day."

Tioga kissed Dyce. Then Camilla kissed him. Dyce walked bowlegged toward the neon exit sign that sputtered in the darkness.

Tioga and Camilla headed for the larder behind the kitchen, next to Buddy Moscosco's dark cubbyhole, where the door was wide open and the radio crackled. Moscosco was not napping in his leather chair.

"Funny," Tioga said. "He usually locks his door when he's not in."

Camilla stepped into the larder and then moved her hand in the darkness until she found the dangling string. She yanked and the light bulb came to life.

"That's too bright," Tioga gasped. Camilla pulled the string again, and the larder went dark, though there was enough light from the hallway to see the shelves, cans, boxes and jars, everything neatly arranged from "A" for anise and arrowroot to "Z" for za'atar with lots of garlic and ginger and a few varieties of saffron in between.

"There's enough food here to feed a village for a year," Camilla said, looking as if she could see villagers lined up with soup bowls and spoons in their outstretched hands.

Tioga scanned the shelf with pasta, noticed the bulging box that said "Penne," dipped her hand inside and came out with her snub nose. Then she sniffed the barrel. "This baby has been fired recently. Better clean her up before somebody gets wind of what happened, starts asking questions and pointing fingers." She placed the snub nose in the holster and hung the holster on the hook at the back of the door. Then the smell of strawberries washed over her. "Preserves. The best of summer."

She felt Camilla's fingers on her mouth. "Yes, yes, I want you." She removed her shirt and her trousers. When she reached her boxer shorts, she paused. "Cross-dressing," Camilla quipped. "I like it. Kind of like a chastity belt."

Tioga laughed, wriggled the shorts down to her ankles and then kicked them into the air. Camilla undressed swiftly, starting with her beret and working her way down her body. She dropped to her knees, pulled Tioga toward her, licked her belly and her belly button, roamed across her thighs, found her clitoris, kissed it, licked it and sucked it. Slowly she rose to her feet, caressed Tioga's breasts, licked her neck, and inserted her finger inside. She kept it there and moved it slowly while Tioga stood on her tiptoes and sighed.

Camilla smeared more jam on Tioga's lips. "Strawberry," Tioga said. "I love strawberry." Tioga licked her lips and let the jam dissolve in her mouth. She felt Camilla's soft, silky skin against her own skin, and wondered, for a moment, why this, why now, why here, and then accepted it for what it was, something new and strange and wonderful. She kissed Camilla's fingers, pressed her nose into Camilla's radiant hair and breathed deeply. Then she leaned against the door that had closed without a sound. Camilla, on her knees once again, kissed the spider bite on the inside of Tioga's thigh. "I want all of you. I have wanted you for a long time."

Tioga spread her legs and cupped her hands behind her head. "You have me. You have all of me."

Camilla held Tioga's hips and kissed her mons. She slipped her index finger inside Tioga again, made her wetter, stickier and more supple. "Sugar. You are all sugar."

Tioga licked her lips and wondered when she might forget the weight that she had carried for as long as she could remember. The weight fell from her back and disappeared down, down, down, into the darkness. She sprawled on the floor, wrapped her arms around Camilla and inhaled the aroma of the spices and the jams.

Tomorrow or the next day, or the day after that, she knew that she would take her mind back to this larder where she and Camilla made love. Strawberry love, she called it now. She closed her eyes and saw a list of the bad words that she had learned at the Badminton School for Girls. In the larder, those words vanished. The door opened, a piercing light blinded her, and a moan-like groan broke the silence. "Oh, it's you," the voice said. Tioga blinked and then glimpsed the fingers around the flashlight, the muzzle of the gun aimed at her, and the eyes of the house dick that wandered obscenely.

Moscosco holstered his .357 and switched off the light. For a moment, Tioga saw the portrait her father had painted of her "in the nude"—as he called it. "No. Stop."

Buddy Moscosco froze in his tracks. "I think you both better get dressed and come out of there before someone sees you." He turned away. Modesty had gotten the better of him. "There's a vacancy on the first floor. Folks never cancelled the reservation and never showed up. It's all yours. Compliments of the house."

Camilla and Tioga slipped hurriedly into their clothes. "You're too kind, Buddy. You know, sometimes I get carried away."

Buddy stepped into the hallway. "Don't I know it! Don't we all."

At the front desk, Tioga collected the key from the night clerk. In the room, she and Camilla undressed again, showered and shampooed. Tioga sat down on the toilet with the bathroom door open, her cell in her right hand and checked her messages. "Nothing urgent. Just something from one of the Yaqui brothers. They can wait."

She sprawled across the queen-sized bed with the fluffy pillows and coddled and kissed and watched the play of light and dark behind the curtains. There was more sex, slower and more tender this time, and less pungent than sex in the larder. But it, too, was good.

Tioga smoked a cigarette, though the sign on the door read "No Smoking." Then she looked at the spider bite. "It's getting better. Sex is the antidote." She laughed and so did Camilla, who bounded out of bed, opened the sliding glass door, stepped onto the enclosed patio and looked up at the night sky.

Tioga watched her and wondered what stars she saw. "Come back to bed," she said, reaching out with both arms.

In the room again, Camilla leapt into bed and bounced up and down, though she hit her head, accidentally, on the ceiling and let out a yelp. "I get carried away sometimes." Then she settled down and arranged two pillows behind her head. "I'm going to accept Chehab's offer to escort me around the Valley."

Tioga extinguished the cigarette, pulled her knees up to her chin and wrapped her forearms around them. "Oh, that feels so good. My back has been killing me." After a pause she added, "You could ask Roly-Poly Chehab to show you the house on Avenida de la Virgen. I can't be there with you. I'll be hunkered down with Mrs. Baynes."

Camilla turned off the lamp on the night table. Then she wrapped her arms around Tioga who had turned away and faced the painting on the wall that depicted a young girl in a white tutu, her arms spread as if in flight, her lips a bright red, her eyes dark slits. "I guess I'm not the only girl who has posed for an artist." Camilla kicked her feet and then spread her legs. "If you don't mind my asking, did you buy your boxer shorts online or at the mall?"

Tioga planted a wet kiss on Camilla's mouth. "Are you looking to buy for yourself? Sometimes boxer shorts fit my mood perfectly. Sometimes they don't."

Camilla laughed. Tioga put both hands around Camilla's waist. "The boxer shorts have reminded me not to fuck with men. Now I won't need to be reminded again."

Camilla rubbed her nose against Tioga's neck. "What was it like with your ex? I mean … " Her sentence trailed off in the darkness.

Tioga sighed. "You don't want to know, and I'd rather not remember. I've let go of so much weight that I was carrying for so long."

Camilla replied, "It can't have been that bad." She had taken her voice up an octave and it cracked.

Tioga rolled onto her back, stared at the ceiling and sighed once more. "Well, here goes. You might be sorry you asked. Tomás was all about his dick. He wanted me to jerk him off, suck him, tie him up and tie him down. He had to be in control. If I didn't go along with his agenda, he'd sulk and rage and call me hateful names I won't repeat." She clapped her hands as if to banish them.

Camilla rolled onto her back, stared at the ceiling and took Tioga's hand in hers. "I don't understand why you stayed with him so long."

Tioga closed her eyes, then opened them slowly and scanned the room as if hunting for something she had lost and wanted desperately to find. "Oh, shit, where did I put my cell? I keep misplacing it."

Camilla laughed and then cupped her right hand over her mouth. "I'm sorry. I didn't mean to make fun of you, but you sound like a husband. You had your cell in your hand when you sat down to pee."

Tioga wrapped herself in a white hotel bathrobe. "You'd make a good husband," she quipped. "Husbands expect their wives to keep track of everything, especially their dicks." In the white bathroom, Tioga found her cell next to the bar of Ivory soap. In the bedroom, again, she removed the robe, draped it over the TV, tossed her cell onto the night table and watched it clatter to the floor. "Have I told you? Tomás and my mother conspired to control my life. The wilderness saved me. The white she-wolf saved me."

Camilla's cell rang. She opened her purse, accepted the call and stood at the curtains that stretched in front of the sliding glass door.

"*Hola. Sí, mama. No tengo problemas. Es cierto. I'm in the Mar Monte ... Entiendo ... Sí, es terrible. Sé cómo te sientes... Hablaremos más tarde. Adiós, mama.*"

Back in bed, she said, "My mom just heard about Dorothy Baynes's murder. Maggie Brazil told her and now she's worried that ... " Clearly she didn't want to finish her thought.

Tioga tried but could not think of anything to say, except, "We're all moving targets now."

By the time they fell asleep, on opposite sides of the queen-size bed, it was dawn. A few hours later, Tioga woke and saw the note that Camilla had left on the bed table. "Gone home. Talk soon, Love, Big C."

Tioga wrapped herself in the hotel robe, grabbed her stuff and took the elevator upstairs. In the penthouse, she peered down at Storm, still asleep, a pillow over her head.

Tioga showered and shampooed, put on a pair of silk underwear from Louise's Lingerie, and added grey slacks, a white Oxford shirt and a maroon tie. She cleaned her snub nose with a rag, put the gun in its holster, strapped the holster over her left shoulder and added a lightweight grey jacket. At the mirror in the bathroom, she applied eye shadow and lip gloss and then wiggled her toes and inserted her feet into a pair of flats.

Storm stirred in bed. "Why do I have a terrible hangover?"

Tioga brought her a glass of water and a bottle that said "Vitamin C, 1000 mg." "Take these. Drink plenty of liquids and go back to sleep and then get exercise. Force yourself. I'll see you at the movie."

Storm was already asleep again and snoring.

Tioga rode the elevator down to the first floor where she glanced at the front page of *The Gazette* that featured a photo of Langley and a caption that read, "Editor returns to old post." Above the fold, under his byline, a headline screamed, "Langley Promises New Era."

At Aaron's mobile coffee cart, Tioga watched him make a cappuccino to go. "What a fuckin' miserable night," he moaned. "A man beat your Latina friend in the plaza and nobody did anything to stop him. I called the cops but by the time they arrived, the man was gone and so was she. Probably crawled into an alley."

Tioga munched on a croissant. "Why didn't that beating make it into the paper?"

Aaron wiped the steam wand on his beloved machine. "Must have been too late for the morning edition."

Part V
The Bust

The Drive By

Tioga sipped the cappuccino, closed the container with a lid, set it down on the edge of Aaron's cart and grabbed hold of the lapels on his jacket. "I'm gonna visit Dorothy Baynes's monster-of-a-mother. If you don't hear from me by noon, Aaron, get on your Harley and rescue me. I'll be at 1148 Mazatlan. It's in the Sunset Mobile Home Park. Or call on my cell." Then she sang, "I'm lonely and I'm blue … come on and rescue me."

On her way out of the Mar Monte, she noticed the long line at the registration desk—guests checking in and checking out. She stopped at the entrance to the dining room where two waiters in black jackets and black trousers hustled and bustled and nearly collided with one another.

On the chalkboard she read:

Specials today:
Hearty Vegetarian Hash
Superlative Sonoma Duck Confit
Luxurious A.M. Mimosas

The plaza was nearly empty, except for a family of quail, scurrying toward the underbrush, and a homeless woman, her bare feet dark and dusty, holding a coffee container from the Mar Monte.

Aaron must have been kind to her. Outside the movie theater, she glanced at the marquee that read Bogart and Astor on one line and on another *The Maltese Falcon*.

On the road to the Sunset Mobile Home Park, eucalyptus trees provided a canopy. Then came a stretch of ugly cedars, the branches knotted and tangled. Along the highway, she replayed the opening scene of the movie. She passed through two flanking stone columns, parked her car, crossed the pavement and knocked on the door. At the entrance to Mrs. Baynes's home, a magenta crepe myrtle bloomed.

When no one answered, she stepped inside. "Knock, knock. Anyone home?"

A large, muscular man came toward her. "Can I help you?" he asked, though he didn't sound like he meant to be helpful. He had dark skin, black eyes and long black hair and might have been one of the suspects in the robbery at El Buen Comer.

Tioga extended her right hand. "I'm an op, a private detective, investigating the murder of Dorothy. Mrs. Baynes called and left a message.

The man looked at Tioga's hand. "Excuse me. I don't mean to be impolite, but I've been sponge-bathing Dorothy's mother, and my hands are wet and soapy." Then he added, "I'm Pablo. Come in. I'll be with you in a sec. I know who you are."

Tioga saw the residue of soapy water on Pablo's big and very brown hands. The low ceiling weighed down on her head. Her heart beat faster, then skipped a beat and beat faster again. Pablo disappeared down the hallway. Tioga heard the sound of gurgling water. She took two baby steps toward the center of the room and then two more baby steps, looked at the bric-a-brac that crowded every available surface and the faded photos of Dorothy on the wall:

Dorothy at six, Dorothy at eight, Dorothy at twelve. Her whole life had been documented on film. Tioga half-expected her to appear suddenly and break out into song as if she was in a musical with an unhappy ending.

Tioga turned her head and saw Mrs. Edna Baynes in a robe decorated with a fire-breathing dragon. She slid her feet along the carpet and propelled herself down the hallway with her hand. Pablo followed behind, ready to assist. "She had a ministroke. She's on meds, and you might not understand her. Sometimes I don't know what she's trying to say."

Pablo helped Mrs. Baynes settle in an armchair with an antimacassar. Then he knelt down. "What do you want, *mi amor?*" Mrs. Baynes pointed to a bottle of rye that sat on the table next to the TV. "Thaaattt."

Pablo shook his head. "Oh, no. Doctor say no booze."

Mrs. Baynes lowered her head and folded her hands. "Shhheet."

Pablo glared at Tioga. "You don't need no translation for that."

Tioga circled Pablo and crouched down at his side. "Do you know where I can find Roxanne Jacobs?"

Pablo snorted horse-like. "Fuck, no. Roxanne's dead."

Tioga moved closer to Pablo. "How do you know Mrs. Baynes?"

Pablo went on holding her hand. "I ran with Dorothy. I might get in trouble for this. But sometimes you have to take care of somebody else."

Tioga looked at Pablo once again, only more carefully this time. "You're Yaqui, aren't you?" she asked though she thought she already knew the answer to her question.

With his big thumb Pablo pointed to his chest. "Me?" he asked defiantly. "You want my story, where I come from, where I'm going and what my rap sheet looks like?" He seemed eager to confess, or at least to tell his story. "All right, lady. My mother pure Yaqui. My father some kind of mongrel." Now he was warmed up and ready to roll. "The police arrest me first time in Sonora; say I steal a Coca-Cola from the *tienda*. The second time narcs bust me in Santa Monica for growing weed in Woodlawn Cemetery, and then the third time …"

Pablo wasn't ha-ha funny, but ha-ha strange, the way he seemed unable to stop himself from talking. Tioga didn't want him to stop, but there was something she had to tell him before it ate away at her. "Camilla Sanchez, who works with me, rubbed shoulders with you and your friends on Avenida de la Virgen. That wasn't nice of you to get her fucked up."

Pablo wiped his hands on his jeans. Then he reached out and took Tioga's hand and held it affectionately. "You wanna get high? I have dried flower from this year's not yet totally cured but still good holy herb. Twenty-percent THC and five-percent CBD. It will kick your ass."

Tioga smiled smugly. "Sure, though I didn't come here to get my ass kicked. I came to talk to Mrs. Baynes about the murder of her daughter." She looked at Mrs. Baynes who had nodded off. "She won't mind if we smoke?"

Pablo shook his head slightly, removed a pre-rolled joint, a fatty, from behind his ear, produced a lighter from the pocket of his jeans, fired it up, inhaled and blew a thick column of smoke at Tioga. "Hey, you can get a contact high just sitting next to me." He had turned into a living, breathing dragon.

Tioga waited until the smoke rose and the air cleared a bit before she spoke. "I'll take a hit." She brought the fatty to her lips and inhaled. "Oh, man, this tastes super." She heard her voice and laughed. She sounded like a novice getting stoned for the first time.

Mrs. Baynes woke with a start and made eye contact with Tioga, though she gave no sign that she recognized her. Tioga moved closer. She knew that she had to seize the moment or else it would fade away. "Thank you for seeing me. I'm sorry …" The smoke swallowed her words.

Mrs. Baynes nodded and then drooled. "Dddoohry."

Pablo wiped away the spittle from her lips. "Yes, Dorothy. She's in heaven now."

Tioga leaned forward, peered into Mrs. Baynes's cloudy eyes and spoke slowly and deliberately. "You've had anonymous phone calls, haven't you? I'm sorry. You didn't need them after all you've been through."

Mrs. Baynes nodded again and turned to Pablo. It seemed to be too difficult to speak and too frustrating to make herself understood. Pablo took the conversation into his own hands. "*Si*, I mean yes. There were calls. I answered once. Mrs. Baynes the other times."

Tioga noticed the white princess phone that sat on a round table with carved elephant feet. "Tell me about the voice. Maybe we can identify the caller."

Pablo nodded. Then he shook his head, as if he couldn't make up his mind how to answer Tioga's question, or even if he should answer at all. "Yes, I think I know the voice and then I change my mind and decide not. It was a man or maybe a woman trying to sound like a man. The person was disguising the voice."

Mrs. Baynes had been listening; she wasn't totally out of it. Then in a crazy, desperate kind of way she pulled out a patch of white hair on the top of her head and flung it into the air.

Tioga watched it flutter to the floor. "It's hard to know the good guys from the bad guys. Nobody's wearing a white hat or a black hat."

Pablo relit the joint that had gone out on its own and puffed until his head vanished behind yet another cloud of smoke. "It isn't Dorothy's ex-boyfriend who's been calling. I know that. He's stupid, but he's not evil like some people I know."

Tioga raised her hand and rested it on Pablo's shoulder. "You mean the horse trainer? Or the man who came back with her and her baby?"

Pablo peered into Tioga's blue eyes. He looked as if he had been insulted. "You know nothing. They're the same man."

Tioga took the slow burning joint from Pablo's fingertips and inhaled. "If it's not the ex-boyfriend making the calls, who is it?"

Pablo rubbed Mrs. Baynes's hand. "I can't …" he said and then didn't finish his thought.

Tioga wanted answers, and now all she could do was sigh.

Pablo cocked his ear. "I don't like the sound of that. Did you hear?"

Tioga looked toward the largest of the front windows, and then into the street as far as her eyes would take her. "Tires on the pavement. A vehicle moving slowly. Maybe a lowrider. Could be a drive-by."

Pablo lifted Mrs. Baynes, carried her across the room and set her down on the floor behind the green sofa. He reached underneath the sofa and pulled out a sawed-off shotgun. "Scoot over here," he whispered.

Tioga crouched down, scooted across the floor and joined Pablo and Mrs. Baynes behind the sofa. Then she opened her jacket and revealed her snub nose. "Better not fire unless we have to. Not this time."

Mrs. Baynes moaned. Pablo cocked his right ear once again. "But maybe there's no next time." He cradled the shotgun. "For now, chill, baby." He bent down and kissed the muzzle.

Tioga heard the purr of an engine and the squeal of tires on the pavement. Then came a rapid series of pips— Pip! Pip! Pip!—followed by an explosion and the clatter of breaking glass, first at one window, then the next and the one after that. Bullets nicked the top of the sofa, pierced the wall and shattered the glass cabinet with its bric-a-brac. The whole thing crashed. Stuffing poured out of the sofa. The wall groaned, split down the middle and revealed the insulation.

Then, except for Mrs. Baynes's wheezing, the house went suddenly silent. Tioga held Mrs. Baynes's hand and took her pulse. "She's off the chart and needs to lie down and rest. Otherwise it might be quits."

Pablo lifted Mrs. Baynes, carried her to a room with wall-to-wall carpeting and a double bed and laid her head down on a pillow, while Tioga propped up her knees with a bolster. With a thin blanket, Pablo covered Mrs. Baynes's body, which seemed to suddenly shrink. "I can't hang. You gotta call 911 and make up a story."

Tioga sat down on the edge of the bed. She opened her purse and handed Pablo one of her cards, though he shook his head. "I know where to find you." Then he bent down and kissed Mrs. Baynes on her forehead. "When your daughter dies before you, it's a killer." He removed the ring on Mrs. Baynes's finger and held it up to the light. "Dorothy never knew when to stop. The wrong guys came along at the right time and in the right place, and she was gone." Pablo put the ring back on Mrs. Baynes's finger.

Tioga stood up, opened the rear window in the bedroom and felt the clean, cool air on her face. Then she followed Pablo into the front room with its bullet holes, broken bric-a-brac and the sofa that looked like it had been slaughtered.

Pablo ducked into the kitchen. In a few moments he came out again holding a Hersey bar and a Coca-Cola in one hand and the shotgun in the other. The gun seemed like an extension of his body. "I hope the police get to the killers before they get to you and the girls on Avenida de la Virgen."

Tioga bore down on Pablo. "How do you know Roxanne Jacobs is dead?" Pablo did a double take; his neck sounded like it had snapped. "You gotta be fuckin' kidding. I read the newspapers from over there. Roxanne Jacobs ain't comin' back in this lifetime." He turned and dashed down the hallway. "*Adios.*" He let himself out the door at the back of the house.

Tioga sat down on the sofa, dialed 911 and asked for an ambulance to be sent to one one four eight Mazatlan. Then she called the police and talked to the sergeant who answered. "Tioga Vignetta. There's been a drive-by shooting. You'd better tell Ambrose to get out to the mobile home park on Mazatlan. He can't miss it. The windows are gone." She went to the back of the house and opened the screen door just in time to see Pablo disappear around the corner with the shotgun at his side.

Randy Scheck Prevaricates

Tioga sat down in a corner of the front room and punched in Randy Scheck's number. When he answered, she purred, as if purring would help her get what she wanted. "So Randy, my dear, let's dispense with the chit-chat and cut to the chase. What can you tell me about Roxanne Jacobs?"

Randy cleared his throat and coughed. "Now's not a good time to talk."

Tioga stood up, walked along the hallway and peered into the bedroom where Mrs. Baynes's hands were folded as if in prayer. "But you do know who I'm talking about, don't you?"

There was a long pause. For a moment or two, Tioga thought that she had lost Randy, but he came back. "It's a very sad story, sad, very sad," he said, sounding instantly morose. "Her houseboat went up in flames; the fire fighters couldn't save it, nor could she. It was hideous."

Tioga entered the bedroom and looked at Mrs. Baynes. She was still breathing, just barely. "I'm sorry to hear that. I'm sorry I never did get to meet her, and I'm sorry you never introduced me to her and her to me."

An eerie silence came from Scheck's end of the call. Tioga listened and waited for a response. When it didn't come, she asked, "How often was Roxanne in the Valley?"

Scheck cleared his throat once again. "Not often." Then after another silence, he added, "KLM has an inexpensive, non-stop flight to Amsterdam. In the old days, when I knew the Provos, I'd fly from SFO, arrive for breakfast, take a nap, hang out with Roel van Duijn and Rob Stolk, then hit the cafes and maybe catch a museum or two."

When it seemed that he would go on, Tioga broke through his monologue. "The Provos must have been before my time. I suppose Roxanne was a Provo too."

Scheck didn't seem to hear her comment. "If you haven't been to Amsterdam, I highly recommend that you go, and don't wait until you retire," He said, sounding like a travel agent selling a package deal. "Dutch art is great and not just the old stuff. Dutch cheese is fantastic and the Dutch coffee shops are sensational. You can even sample weed from the Valley."

Tioga listened impatiently. "Why do I think you're giving me the runaround? You haven't provided me with any information that I couldn't find in the Lonely Planet's guidebook to Holland, except about the Provos, whoever they might be. That really was before my time." Then in frustration she added, "What's the deal, Randy? I've never known you to be this weird."

Once again near silence radiated from Randy's end of the call, though Tioga could hear his breathing. "Are you okay? Do you want me to call another day?"

This time Randy answered promptly, though oddly, weirdly Tioga thought. "You haven't remembered the rules."

Now Randy Scheck was Mr. Rebuke. She rubbed the back of her knotted neck. "I'm sorry. I forgot about that, but with Roxanne gone what difference does it make?"

Randy perked up. "I'm due to return to the Valley. I miss the wine, and I miss you and Camilla." Suddenly he was gone. He had not given Tioga the chance to tell him, "We love you."

Billy Bones's Aliases

The EMT boys arrived, made their way through the broken glass and bric-a-brac, and around the battered sofa. They carried Mrs. Baynes from the bedroom to the ambulance and strapped her down so she wouldn't bounce around on the journey to Mercy.

"Does she still have vital signs?" The ambulance driver nodded as he climbed behind the wheel, turned on the siren and sped away. Next-door neighbors leaned over the fence and gaped. George Ambrose emerged from an unmarked black police vehicle as the ambulance took a left at the end of the street. He lumbered up the steps, burst through the open door and stepped into the living room where Tioga waited, arms folded and brow knit. "No Clark this time?"

"No Clark this time," Ambrose replied, sounding like he was on automatic pilot. A man with a real camera followed in his footsteps.

When he aimed at Tioga, she shouted, "Don't take my picture, please. I'm shy."

He aimed the camera at the sofa and then at the punctured wall. "Okay, lady. Whatever you want."

Tioga followed Ambrose as he wandered from room to room. "I didn't get a look at the vehicle or the license plate or see anyone inside. I think it was a random drive-by."

Ambrose sneezed, took out his handkerchief and sneezed again. "Maybe the bullet was meant for you. Ever think of that?"

In the bedroom, the outline of Mrs. Baynes's body was now barely visible. Ambrose sat down and peered into the

249

corners of the room. "I heard the stroke slurred the old battle-axe's speech, and no one could understand a word she spoke." In the living room again, he stopped abruptly, pivoted on his heels and ran his eyes from Tioga's head to her feet. "You don't have a scratch on you. But you must be rattled, no?" He pulled on his suspenders, held them away from his body and released them. "Smells like dope in here."

Tioga sniffed the air. "It could be Mrs. Baynes was using weed for her stroke."

Ambrose guffawed. "Bullshit." He learned against the wall. "You'd better hear this now, before I forget. Mitzi told me about Dorothy's ex, Billy Bones. We sent out an APB, along with a description, his former known addresses, and a list of aliases—Guillermo Schmidt and William Thompson and, get this one, Vladimir Kopalov. Billy boy is a born loser." Ambrose removed a flask from his jacket, took a swig and returned it to its home. "Mitzi visited the other day. She found her high school yearbook and showed me a photo of Dorothy—Dot she was called—in a cheer-leader's outfit, though she looked like a hellion."

Tioga's face darkened. "Mitzi didn't tell me she was going to visit. I wish she had."

Ambrose moved away from the pockmarked wall and placed his hands on his hips. "Don't take it personally. It was a quick visit. She stayed long enough to tell me that she went to a sip and see for Dorothy's baby. The boyfriend showed up, gave Dorothy a black eye and tried to take the kid. Mitzi drove Dorothy to the shelter. The guy stalked Dorothy and threatened a lawsuit."

George took another swig and offered the flask to Tioga. "No thanks. I'm on the wagon."

Ambrose chuckled. "That's a good one." Then he raced ahead like a man late for his own wedding ceremony.

"Unfortunately no one saw Bones batter Dorothy. When she gave up the baby for adoption, he went berserk and knocked out a couple of her teeth. No one saw that either. Mitzi feels guilty. Of course, you know all about guilt."

Tioga had learned not to take Ambrose's remarks personally. Mitzi was right. Her father aimed to keep everyone off balance. The trick was not to fall for his traps. Tioga counted to ten. "What about the place in The Springs?"

Ambrose snapped his suspenders again. "No go. Mitzi went to Avenida de la Virgen where I bumped into you. The girls weren't around, and that idiot Travis knows nothing." Ambrose took out his pocket-sized notebook and scribbled madly. "You didn't fire a shot! Good thinking. You kept your cool."

This Case Feels Like Stuffing

George Ambrose picked up a handful of the stuffing that had poured out of the sofa, held it in his hand, squeezed it into a tight ball and then let it drop to the floor. "This case feels like stuffing. It all falls apart."

The photographer hovered nearby, invited Ambrose to please smile and then snapped his picture half a dozen times. Ambrose obliged though he looked bored. "If you don't mind, Tioga, I'd like to see your gun. Just covering the bases."

Tioga opened her jacket, took out the snub nose and handed it to Ambrose. "What was it you said about Clark?"

Ambrose moved his jaw up and down. "Clark is on administrative leave. Maybe he'll shape up. If not, he'll ship out. The Valley isn't meant for the incompetent." Ambrose gave Tioga a look that made her want to turn away, though she didn't give in to the urge.

Ambrose brought the snub nose to his nose and sniffed. "This baby has been recently cleaned." He gave the snub nose back to Tioga.

She held it in the palm of her hand and felt the heft of it before she returned it to the holster. "Cleanliness is next to godliness." She buttoned her jacket and lowered her shoulders. The spider bite had flared up again, but she resisted the urge to scratch it.

Ambrose scribbled in his notebook. "Something anchors Dorothy's ex here. Probably the hope that he'll take his kid back and settle a few scores." Ambrose descended the front steps, looked at the black unmarked police car in the street and turned toward Tioga. "I know you're a big girl and can handle yourself. But you might want to sit down about now."

Tioga looked at the baby-faced detective who unraveled a yellow plastic strip that said "Police Line Do Not Cross." "Naw, I can take it standing up, no matter what. Shoot, George."

That was all the encouragement Ambrose needed. "Two kids found a dead body in a field in Kenwood. Murder for sure and drug related. I'm going there now. You ought to join me." Ambrose scratched his chin. "Think about cooperating, Tioga. It could work for you."

Tioga picked up a shard of glass and tossed it onto the porch. "It's a two-way street, George. Think about cooperating with me."

George smiled. "I already have. I didn't have to share the information Mitzi dropped in my lap."

Tioga walked down the front steps and crossed the street. "Thanks, pal."

The Dead Body, the Pot and the Pigs

The St. Mary's Lane sign was so bent out of shape that it was unreadable. A skunk lay on the side of the road, picked apart and devoured by the turkey vulture circling overhead. Under a willow tree, a girl with a lollypop frowned like an eighty-year-old.

The marijuana field, or rather what was left of it, looked like a Christmas tree farm that had been decimated by a squad of mad lumberjacks armed with chainsaws. Surrounded by two tall fences, one wood and the other wire, it was set back a hundred yards or so from St. Mary's Lane. Tioga followed Ambrose through an iron gate, headed for the space between two eucalyptus trees and then parked in the shade. It was hot and dusty. The air was close. Brittle leaves cracked under her shoes. "I was here the other day—close-by anyway. I didn't suspect pot in this neighborhood."

Tioga counted the rows and the number of stumps in each row; it added up to 1,008 plants. "There must have been a million dollars worth of weed here."

The drip irrigation system was still intact, though the emitters had been crushed. The wire cages that had supported the branches of the trees were scattered about. Here and there a stray marijuana tree remained. "This is the new normal," Ambrose said, sounding as if he was resigned to fields of marijuana in the Valley. He cast his eyes at the horizon and added, "I've seen bigger and I've seen smaller; this is about average. You gotta grow big if you wanna make money today. No more mom-and-pop operations."

One plant that had survived the assault towered above Tioga; it had to be eight feet tall. Yet another was easily ten feet. A dozen or so plants had apparently been trampled in the rush to harvest and get out fast; under the hot sun and without water they would not last much longer. Nothing left was worth saving, commercially speaking, though a desperate pothead would have grabbed every branch and every flower and walked away in ecstasy. The butchered field disoriented cop and op.

Ambrose wore his wraparound Ray-Bans. Tioga wore her new Smoke X Mirrors. They might have passed for two hipster dealers who had just had their big crop taken out from under them and refused to believe what they saw with their own eyes. The wind blew dust in Tioga's face. The leaves on the eucalyptus trees snapped and crackled and fell to the ground. Otherwise, it was too quiet, though a small plane came out of nowhere and circled the field, once quickly and again more slowly, before it climbed higher in the sky.

Ambrose trudged along and headed for a building that looked like a packing shed at the far end of the property. Tioga went ahead of him, pried open the door, stepped inside the cool darkness and removed her sunglasses. The air inside smelled deadly. With the light on her cell, she illuminated the walls, the drying racks, the fans and a dozen or so plastic containers. She opened one of them and found it empty. She opened another and found it packed with branches full of ripe flowers. "They must have been in a panic to get out. Maybe something spooked them. Maybe there's an eyewitness."

Ambrose removed his Ray-Bans, opened the nearest container and peered inside. The aroma knocked him back. "There's a shitload in here. It must have taken a platoon to run this sucker." He scoured the rafters and counted the plants that were still hanging upside down. "What the hell am I going to do with all this weed? I can't burn it because that would pollute the air, and I can't bury it. That would contaminate the ground. I can't sell it; that would be illegal, and I can't give it away either. What do you call this? An albatross." Then he paused for what seemed like a long time before he added, "It's no wonder that on the black market, the price has gone down like a torpedoed battleship."

Tioga fanned her face with her hand. Ambrose picked up a large box that read "Rat Poison" and then handled another that displayed a skull and crossbones and said "Danger." Beneath that line another read "Caution: Do Not Breathe Fumes."

Tioga gagged and covered her mouth with the back of her hand. "Fuckin' toxic dump," she gasped as if sinking beneath the surface of a dark lake. "It's too hot and too claustrophobic. I'm getting out before I have a panic attack."

She stepped in the sunlight, wrapped her glasses around her face, cleared her throat and blew her nose. In the distance, she saw a tall, lanky stick-figure. As it moved closer, she recognized Jeremiah Langley with a pencil behind his ear. A camera dangled from his neck. She dashed toward him as if he might provide her with a sense of order in a field of chaos. When she got close enough to touch him, she noticed a bright green, bushy marijuana plant at his feet, the leaves covered with dark splotches. On her first foray, she had missed it. Perhaps Ambrose had not wanted to spring it on her.

Langley toed the pot plant with his shoe. "Look at the blood. Katrina Hawley was cut down with a machete along with everything else that lived here. I've asked around about her. She's not local, but she worked in the industry. They removed her body, and they're waiting now for a coroner from Sacramento to examine it. This case is too big for our own man to handle."

Huffing and puffing, Ambrose pulled alongside Langley and Tioga. "I didn't want to shock you. Funny thing, we found Katrina's wallet. She had Randy Scheck's business card and, on the back, your name and phone number in pencil, Tioga."

Tioga had kept her cool all day. Not now. "So! Plenty of people have Randy's card. Anyone in the pot biz would have known about him. But I'll tell you, George, I have never met anyone named Katrina Hawley. It doesn't mean shit that she had Randy's card."

Ambrose looked amused. "Nobody is accusing you of anything. I don't suspect you of any wrongdoing. But I wonder what are you hiding?"

Tioga peered down at the ground and kicked a pebble with the tip of her shoe. Langley snapped Tioga's photo and took a few shots of Ambrose with the bloody marijuana plant and the spot where Katrina Hawley's body, sliced in half, had baked in the sun.

Tioga noticed another stick-figure moving toward them. From a distance, she did not recognize anything about the person—although if Camilla had asked, she would have said, "He walks like a man." When he got close, she recognized him from the Mar Monte. He was the runt who had eluded her for days, and now he stood before her as if he had nothing to hide and had done nothing wrong. "Name's Billy Bones. I'm a neighbor. Came over to see what the fuss was about." He wore jeans, work boots, and a sleeveless white T-shirt. On his neck he had a tattoo of a flower, and on his right shoulder a tattoo of a guitar.

Ambrose approached him, Tioga thought, as if closing in for a kill, or at least a bust. "I think you murdered Dorothy Baynes out of jealousy and in a rage. We've had an APB out for your arrest. It's mighty white of you to turn yourself in."

Bones extended his arms, though they didn't extend very far. "Go ahead, cuff me, you racist dog."

Ambrose studied Bones, shook his head and backed off. Bones reached down, picked up a brittle marijuana leaf and twirled it between thumb and index finger. "If I done something, arrest me. But I'll tell you this, you ain't going to find anyone who will testify against me in a court of law. There are no witnesses and you won't find any prints anywhere, except on my own beautiful fingers."

He raised his hands and looked at Tioga imploringly. "Hey, you wanna tell the chief to book me? If you do, I'll hire your buddy, Randy Scheck. A whole lot of shit about the two of you will come out in *The Gazette*."

Ambrose turned white. His face looked as if it had been suddenly bleached by the sun; he backed into the shade. Tioga came forward. "Just what do you do around here, Mr. Bones?" she asked in a Mr. Rogers tone of voice.

Bones borrowed the Mr. Rogers voice for himself. "We raise pigs. And not just any kind. Ours are a cross between Gloucestershire Old Spots and Large Blacks. We like them a lot, and we think they like us. Pigs are much more intelligent than humans think. We also have a table-to-farm collective and bring tourists out to smell the manure. It's a tonic we're happy to share."

Langley snapped a photo of Bones's profile and several of his tattoos too, though Bones did not seem to enjoy having his photograph taken.

"We?" Tioga asked. "Who is we?"

Bones gave her a puzzled look. "Sorry, I missed that." He seemed to be distracted by the sun or the wind, or the dust that swirled around and mixed with Katrina Hawley's blood.

"You used the word 'we,'" Langley said. "Tioga wondered who you were referring to."

Bones chuckled, seemingly as much to himself as to anyone else. "Oh, that. I sometimes forget myself. It's the royal we, if you know what I mean. I'm a lone pig farmer and proud to be one, too, though just about everyone else in this neck of the woods knows me. I'm famous, or maybe infamous. It depends on who you talk to."

He seemed to thrive in front of the op, the reporter and the chief of police. He would bowl them over all at once. "To be perfectly honest, I have grown weed. But I don't see the point anymore what with the permits that are required. This time of year the odor is horrific. If you ask me, the growers are getting away with murder."

Tioga looked at the dark red marijuana leaves. "Are you local?"

Bones chuckled again. "I suppose I am. My roots go deep."

Ambrose wiped the perspiration from his brow and from his neck. "Might we see some identification, son?"

Bones placed his right hand on his hip and wore an expression that struck Tioga as oddly poisonous. "I didn't bring my wallet. Didn't think I'd need it. I'm just across the lane by the red barn." He turned, squinted his eyes, peered into the near distance and pointed with his chin. "That's my place. I can run over, fetch my wallet and bring it back, lickety-split."

Beads of perspiration trickled down Ambrose's face. He seemed to have developed an instant allergic reaction to something in the air. "That's okay, son. We'll walk over with you and see your heritage pigs. I was 4-H as a boy."

Ambrose stood on one side of Bones, Tioga and Langley on the other. Not surprisingly, Bones seemed to feel that he was suddenly out-flanked. He took a step back and gazed toward the eucalyptus trees, Tioga thought, as if they might provide a place to hide.

"It's a bit of a hike," Bones said with a smirk. "I meant to save you the effort, chief."

Ambrose began to walk toward the gate. Langley joined him and so did Tioga. Bones brought up the rear. "You're okay for an old man."

His tone of voice irked Tioga. "What did you hear the day of the rip-off and the murder of Katrina Hawley?"

Bones turned his head and looked back at the marijuana field. "Didn't hear nothing. I'm a sound sleeper. When I put my head down, I'm dead to the world. It's a blessing."

Bones took the lead now and passed through the gate. Ambrose went next, followed by Tioga and finally Langley, who stopped every so often to shoot. "Can you please stand still for a sec so I can photograph you properly?"

Bones obliged. He folded his arms across his chest and smiled for the camera. "You're Jeremiah Langley. You're pretty good for a small-town photographer, but your reporting is for shit. You let the big boys off the hook."

He leaped over the fence and darted across a field with thistles. Langley straggled behind. When he finally caught up to Tioga, she tugged at his shirttails that flapped in the wind. "Email me a couple of your best shots." Under her breath she asked, "What do you make of Bones?"

Langley shrugged his shoulders. "I dunno. Pig farmer. Rural idiot. First class asshole. He doesn't seem a killer. I think he called Ambrose's bluff."

Tioga laughed. As she crossed St. Mary's Lane, she trudged along the shoulder, her eyes pinned to the ground and her back to the wind that had kicked up and blew the dust around and around in a whirlwind. A red pickup truck with a mesh wire cage in the bed sat in the driveway. Tioga wrapped her fingers around the wire. "Smells like shit in there."

Bones stood next to her and sniffed. "Pig shit." Then he rattled the cage. "I use this rig to transport my pigs when they're ready to be butchered. I'll have to give you some of the bacon."

Bones raced for the cabin. Tioga gazed at the open field that she and Camilla had crossed after they came up from the creek. "I was almost right here at this spot. The blood from Dorothy's body led down to the creek and then up on this side."

She pointed into the distance. "The blood started over there, near the tractor." Outside the cabin, Tioga admired the naked ladies in bloom. Then she peered into the pigpen. "The sow is eating pot."

Ambrose leaned against the fence enclosing the pen. "Pigs eat most anything. They even eat human flesh and bones."

Langley stood on the lowest railing of the fence, balanced himself and snapped still more photos of Ambrose, the Gloucestershire Old Spots and the Large Blacks. Tioga ambled across the front yard littered with overripe pears that had fallen from a gangly tree and attracted swarms of bees.

Bones came out of the cabin smiling and waving a wallet above his head. "Found it," he chirped and handed Ambrose a driver's license that said "California" in large blue letters. Tioga looked over Ambrose's shoulder at the snapshot and the text: 135 pounds, 5 feet 6 inches, slate gray eyes. PO Box 1198, Boyes Hot Springs.

Tioga googled "Billy Bones." A Facebook page showed a Billy Bones in the Valley, identified him as "a pig farmer" and "a member of the Grange." He had 1,209 "friends."

With his cell, Ambrose took a photo of Bones's license and emailed it to himself. Then he returned it. "You'll have to come down to the station and give us a full statement."

Bones stuffed the license into the front pocket of his jeans. "Can't we get it over with here and now? That would save all of us a lot of trouble over nothing."

Ambrose followed a flock of migrating birds in the sky. "I'd like to oblige. But it goes against regulations. One of my detectives will be waiting for you."

Tioga offered Bones her card. He took it and read it slowly, his lips moving line by line. "So you have an office on the plaza. You're lucky to be there. You know, that place is magical."

Ambrose walked away from the pen, then pivoted and walked back the way he had come. "Don't your pigs get stoned on the weed you feed them?"

Bones stopped and looked over his shoulder at the sow and her piglets. "Oh, no. The pigs eat the pot and poop and the soil is much better. It's a win-win."

Ambrose placed his hands on the fence. "Katrina Hawley, did she donate weed for your pigs?"

Bones gazed at the tin roof of his cabin and scratched his head. "Maybe she did, and maybe she didn't. I don't keep records." He backed away from Ambrose, looking as if regret had grabbed him by the throat. "It's been a pleasure, sirs and ma'am. I gotta get back to work."

Bones wandered through the field of thistles. Ambrose crossed the lane and headed for the shade of the eucalyptus trees where he had parked his car. Tioga lingered with Langley hoping he would open up to her. "Bones is something else!" she exclaimed. "I'd call him a dyed-in-the-wool sociopath. I'm not sure it was wise of Ambrose to let him walk."

Langley wore a glum expression on his sunburned face. "Maybe. I'm no psychiatrist, and neither are you. Bones is definitely weird, but not crazy. Ambrose will give him enough rope for him to hang himself."

Tioga crossed the lane and passed through the gate that brought her back to the decimated pot patch, which had been roped off. A squad car with its rear doors open sat under the sun. Two highway patrol officers stood guard. For the first time, Langley looked worried. "I was hoping we could get together later and talk about some personal stuff."

Tioga unlocked her car. "Okay," she said, though she didn't sound okay. "You wanna give me a time and place?"

Langley squinted his eyes and gazed at the sun as it went down in slow motion behind the trees, then oddly enough bounced up again when it hit the horizon. "I'll call you," he said, sounding unwilling to commit himself to anything definite. He put on his sunglasses, climbed into his car and drove off, kicking up dust all the way to the pavement.

Behind the wheel of her Mini Cooper, Tioga took out her phone, clutched it, then juggled it and fumbled it. Before she could catch it, it disappeared in the space between parking brake and her bucket seat. "Oh fuck. Jittery me." Slowly she fished out the phone with her fingers. When she had it in her hands again, she stared at it scornfully, then retrieved the photos she had taken of Bones and sent them to Mitzi with a text, "Do you recognize this man?" She sent the same photos to Camilla and added, "See what you can find on Bones."

For a minute or two, she sat as motionless as she could, counting from one to ten, once and then again, breathing in and breathing out and letting her thoughts race across the screen in her head without following them, at least not very far or for very long. She wanted to heave a sigh of relief, but she choked up. She wiggled in her seat, nestled and got cozy, turned on the radio and listened to Howlin' Wolf belt out "Shake It for Me." The song made her long for something—Wolf's songs did that—though now she didn't know what she longed for. Perhaps to hear the sound of falling rain again, to smell the rain as it came down from the sky and washed away the bitter dust that she could taste on her lips and her tongue.

She was still stoned. The weed had not worn off. How many hours had it been? Time had lost track of her, and she of it. She slowed down along the blind curve, signaled with the directional, crossed the double yellow line and pulled into the dusty driveway that took her past the sign that read "Metafor Winery" and along the fruit trees in the orchard. She stopped, put the car in neutral and turned off the ignition. Then she walked through the orchard, stopping here and there to touch and to squeeze one pear after another until she found one that she liked.

The ripeness swept over her. She wiped away the layer of dust on the fruit, admired the golden brown skin and took a bite. The juice ran down the sides of her mouth, and she licked it away. She picked another pear and ate it too, only more slowly than the first one, letting the fruit dissolve in her mouth before she swallowed. She wandered along a gravel path that brought her to a patio where men in shorts and T-shirts and women in frocks sat under umbrellas and sipped wine—a most civilized rite, she decided. A garden with flowers and vegetables caught her eye. She opened the gate, went inside and admired the pumpkins, the acorn squash and the last-of-the-season sunflowers bursting with seeds.

She heard the sound of footsteps on the gravel pathway followed by a voice that said, "Can I help you?" followed by "We don't have tours this week. You'll have to come back another time."

When she turned and looked, she saw a large man wearing sandals and a sunhat that made it impossible to see his eyes. "I'm sorry," she said and realized that she didn't feel sorry for anything she had said or done, certainly not for picking and eating two pears and also not for entering the garden to admire the vegetables. Immediately, she knew that the fellow before her was Yaqui and probably Pablo's brother. Indeed, they might have been twins. "I'm a friend of Louis's," she said, though that wasn't true. "I'd like to talk to him. I'm a private eye investigating the murder of the woman whose body was found along the side of the road across from here. Another woman was just found murdered on St. Mary's Lane."

She paused for a few moments, enjoyed the warm breeze on her face and then added, "You must be Pablo's brother. I see the similarity."

The man placed his Felco clippers in the leather holster attached to his belt and gazed at Tioga with an expression on his face, as if trying to remember if he had met her on another occasion. "Louis isn't here. He's in Sacramento, and he's not coming back until late tomorrow."

Tioga frowned, turned around and followed the gravel path leading beyond the fence and the lush garden. "That's too bad Louis isn't here. But maybe you can help." She extended her hand and added, "I'm Tioga Vignetta, and to whom am I speaking?"

The man opened his mouth and laughed. "To whom are you speaking!" he replied as if he might have belonged to the grammar police. With his arms at his side, he added, "I've never heard that expression before, though I know who or whom you are. I saw you a day or so ago with another woman when Clark wrote a ticket. I could have warned you. Now you're on your own."

Tioga began to walk, or rather to saunter. It felt more like sauntering than walking. She wasn't sure where she was going on foot or with the conversation, which seemed to have come to a dead end before it had really begun. At first, the man in the sunhat tried to mimic Tioga's gait. After a bit he kept to his own pace. Her legs, though long, were shorter than his, and her body, while muscular, didn't have his sheer mass. He slowed down and walked slightly behind her, which made her uncomfortable. She felt his eye staring at the back of her head. "You can assist me," she said, sounding genuinely in need of a helping hand.

She listened to the crunch of the gravel under her shoes and said, "Like, for example, did you notice a car slow down early on Friday morning, stop and then drive off, after leaving a body along the side of the road opposite the entrance to Metafor?"

The man pulled at his earlobe. He deliberated. Then he gazed at a red-tailed hawk perched near the top of a tall Douglas fir tree that cast much of the ground in shadow and provided relief from the heat. "No," he said firmly. "No," he repeated and sat down on the bench beneath the arbor. He added, "I didn't see what you described. I would have because I was on the John Deere that day. In the flatland it's all about elevation."

Tioga sat down on the bench and gazed at the vineyard where a crew picked grapes and a tractor with a gondola moved slowly between two rows. "Why aren't you out there?"

The man stretched his legs and placed his hands behind his head. "I'm supervising from here. I can see every cluster the crew has missed. Besides I have other business on my mind." When Tioga looked surprised, he added, "Wine and weed. That's the way to go. Terry McCoy and Matt Chehab aren't the only ones who can play that game."

Tioga opened her purse, removed a joint, fired it up, inhaled and handed it to the man in the sunhat who scoffed at her offering, then removed his sunhat, took a bodacious blunt from the lining, fired it up and offered it to Tioga. "Try this. It's 20:1, heavy on the THC, light on the CBD."

Tioga inhaled, held the smoke in her lungs and then exhaled slowly through her nostrils.

The man returned the sunhat to his head. "You're bad," he said. "Has anyone ever told you that before?"

Tioga shrugged her shoulders as if to say that his comment and his question were both equally irrelevant. "You wouldn't happen to know who adopted Dorothy Baynes's baby, do you? I figure the child has to be five or six years old now."

The man removed his hat again and pushed his slender brown fingers through the dark brown hair on the top of his head. "You working for Bones? Is that the deal?"

Once again, Tioga was taken by surprise. "Bones?" she asked and sounded as if she meant to stand her ground and defend her honor.

The man scowled. "Don't play games with me. You know who I mean."

Tioga gave the man a look of innocence. "Billy Bones. Do you know for sure that he's the father of Dorothy's baby?"

The man looked dumbfounded. "Duh," he said in a gruff tone of voice. "I thought you were smart. That's what it says about you in the magazine."

Then he began to undress her with his eyes. "You look better in person than you do in the photo in the magazine."

Tioga stood up, gazed down at the gravel path at the purple peonies that formed a border and had wilted in the heat. "I like you," she said, feeling like she was walking on a narrow plank that crossed a deep chasm. She would seduce him into submission if she had to. "Could we please walk and talk at the same time? Someplace where it's not so hot."

The man stood up and took the lead. He still had not volunteered his name and didn't seem inclined to do so. Tioga followed him across the pear orchard, then around the open space in front of yet another outdoor tasting room where more couples with wine glasses sat at round tables and sipped. Together she and the man entered a large red barn, the doors wide open. Hanging upside-down to dry from the rafters at the front of the building were rows and rows of garlic.

"The stinking rose," she said and followed her guide to the back of the barn where huge fans circulated the air. Marijuana hung, also upside-down, from the rafters. The smell of the stinking rose gave way to the stinky marijuana.

The man put his hands on his hips. "We're one of the few places in the Valley that hasn't been hit by thieves. He laughed and added, "Maybe it's the wolves that have kept them at bay." He pointed to the upside-down marijuana plants above his head. "It's all about the terpenes and the genotypes and phenotypes."

Tioga walked between the rows of marijuana, smelled the pungent flowers and touched the branches with her fingertips until they were sticky. "Any idea who's behind the rip-offs?"

The man pulled a yellow leaf from a branch. "Yeah. It's the biggest gang in California. Who else would have Black Hawk choppers?" He vanished behind a row of marijuana that stretched from one side of the barn to the other. Tioga couldn't see him, but she heard him. "It's not one or two or three bad cops. It's a battalion of them and they're all over the state. They've banded together to eradicate weed. Ambrose is one of them."

Tioga rubbed her fingers along the trunk of one of the largest of the marijuana plants. "And these cops haven't hit you yet because they're afraid of the wolves around here, is that it?"

The man walked toward a large, high table, reached for something in the dark and came out with a sawed-off shotgun in his hands. "Anyone who tries to steal this holy herb is gonna have their fuckin' heads blown off. It's not just me. It's all those guys in the vineyard. Any weird shit starts to go down, they'll be here in a sec with automatic weapons."

Tioga looked toward the dappled light that spread across the ground outside the barn. "Why are you telling me this? You don't really know me."

The man coughed once, cleared his throat and covered his mouth with his hand. "I'm telling you this because when the shit hits the fan, I want you to be in my corner. Me and the guys in the field are gonna need all the help we can get."

Tioga walked toward the light. It was too close and too stinky in the barn. Outside again she looked for the hawk at the top of the Doug fir. He was gone. The blue sky was gone. Clouds had moved in from the coast and blanketed the Valley. It felt like the end of the long green growing season and the beginning of harvest time. "I suppose that Louis doesn't know any of this. I suppose he's in the dark."

The man took Tioga by the arm and walked her toward her car. "I hope to see you again," he said. Then when they reached the parking lot, he pulled her close and kissed her on the lips. She pressed her lips against his. Then she drew back, surprised by herself. What was happening? She didn't know.

The man put his arms around Tioga's waist and gave her a beatific smile. "Louis is taking care of stuff in Sacramento. He's good with regulations. I'm good in the field."

Tioga nodded her head. "Oh, yeah, Louis is tight with Bobby Cohen."

The man handed Tioga the last of the blunt. "A going-away present," he said sweetly. Then his sweetness vanished. "I'm not my brother's keeper, and he's not mine. Pablo isn't evil, but he's gone over to the dark side. Hawk keeps him in line."

Art Theft

The door to the office was ajar, but it was dark and quiet inside. Tioga put away her key and pushed the door open with her right shoe. "Camilla? Are you here?" Tioga closed the door and examined the lock. "Jimmied." She flicked the switch for the overhead lights. Papers were scattered on the floor, and the door that separated the outer from the inner office was wide open. "Camilla? Are you here?"

The room hummed with the sound of machines. Tioga stared at the screen of Camilla's computer, switched it off and then shut down the printer. Now it was too quiet. She picked up the papers scattered on the floor and arranged them on Camilla's desk, then entered her own dark office where she knew instantly that something was very wrong. The walls were bare, and the paintings were gone. "Oh, fuck! Who the hell did this?"

She called Camilla and when she didn't answer left a message: "Somebody broke into the office." Then she walked along the wall where the paintings had hung. Her heart skipped a beat and then again and yet again. "Atrial fibrillation." A crazy heart was not a good thing to have, not for anyone—and especially not for a private investigator, who had to be cool, calm and collected, except on those occasions when cool, calm and collected were out of place. One size definitely did not fit all situations.

Tioga placed her right hand over her heart, held it there, circled the room, circled her desk and then looked down at the stack of files. Her heart had gone back to a regular rhythm. The file on top of the stack read "Divorce." But the two files that she had added to the pile—and that were labeled "Baynes" and "Wentworth"—were not there, not anywhere on the desk, and not anywhere in the file cabinet either, though she hunted for them.

Had her father broken into her office and stolen the paintings, she wondered, or had Hawk picked the lock and removed the file about him and about Dorothy? It wasn't fair. It wasn't nice. The spider bite itched all over again. Then the phone rang.

"What's up?" Camilla asked in a cheerful tone of voice.

Tioga winced. "Skip the good cheer." Then in a mournful tone of voice, "You didn't happen to leave the office unlocked, did you?"

Camilla gasped. "No, I did not. I turned off the lights and locked the door.

Tioga walked to the picture window, gazed at the tops of the trees in the plaza and listened to the mockingbirds mimicking the sounds they had recorded and now played back.

"My dad's paintings are gone and so are the files I created on Hawk and Dorothy."

Camilla blew air through her nose. "Maybe Hawk took the files and stole the paintings to make it seem like they were the main thing."

Tioga turned away from the window and stared at the photos of the suspects that she had tacked to the wall: Billy Bones, Travis Syrah, Bobby Cohen and Reginald Wentworth. "It's a mixed blessing not to have the paintings. I was sick of them, sick of looking at nubile me, as my father called it." She walked to her desk, sat down and stared at the hefty stack of files. "Learn anything when you were with Chehab?"

Camilla took a deep breath. "Yeah, sorta. He drives a Jaguar. The car broke down on the road. He called Lyft, and we cruised around the Valley, visited an olive orchard, an olive press, and a winery that he said he owns with McCoy. When I asked if they owned other properties, he hemmed and hawed."

Tioga opened the file marked "Divorce" and flipped through the pages. Camilla raised her voice an octave. "Are you listening or are you multitasking? I hear you doing something."

Tioga closed the file and leaned back in her chair. "I am listening."

Camilla took another deep breath. "Pay attention, please. When I told Chehab that I knew he owned the house at 49 Avenida de la Virgen, he didn't flinch, though he called it an 'albatross' and said the former tenants had moved out and had stiffed him on the rent. He insisted on going there. I didn't have to beg him." With a number two pencil, Tioga beat a crazy rhythm on the top of her desk.

Camilla cleared her throat. "We ran into Travis. Pablo was there too. I'm not sure he remembered me. If so, he didn't let on. I asked why he was hanging out. He said Travis was repairing the gears on his bike. I asked him if he knew a woman named Roxanne Jacobs. I swear he jumped out of his skin. I told him Reginald Wentworth aka Hawk had hired you to find her and threw a whole bunch of money at us. 'How do you know Hawk?' I asked. Chehab pulled me away from Pablo before he could answer. Then he took me inside the house, offered to pay the utilities if I signed a year's lease. Oh, and there's no blood on the floor, not even a faint stain. The floor has been sanded, waxed and buffed."

Tioga reached for a sheet of paper and a pen, made a sketch of a portly Matt Chehab with his pants around his ankles, signed it and tacked it to the wall next to the photos of the suspects. She heard something that sounded as if Camilla was sucking liquid through a straw. "Having a soda?"

The sucking sound stopped. "No, it's a smoothie. But get this, Tioga, the biggest thing I learned is that Hawk showed up yesterday on Avenida de la Virgen. He went inside. Travis heard him. Then he turned up the volume on the drumming and snuck around the back where he could see inside the house, but Hawk couldn't see him. After awhile someone else arrived. Travis didn't see who, though he's sure it was another man. They had a conversation about storing shit in the basement. Then they talked about guns and ammunition. The man who arrived after Hawk wanted to take his with him. Hawk didn't like the idea, so they agreed to disagree. Very civilized of them. Travis said he heard Hawk say, 'I'm gonna stash my ...' But he didn't catch the rest of it."

Tioga was eager to end the conversation and move on, go elsewhere, somewhere, anywhere away from her desk and away from the office. "Nice talking to you. Catch you later, thanks."

Camilla screeched. "Wait, I'm not finished; my mother wants us to come over and talk about the robbery at El Buen Comer."

Tioga smiled. Oddly enough, Camilla sensed it, knew it instinctively. "I can tell you're smiling." Tioga blushed again for the second time that day. "No, I'm not smiling. But thanks for the thought." She added, "What if you go back to number forty-nine and see when you can see?"

She heard the sound of Camilla sucking on the straw. "There, all done with my smoothie. Yeah, I'll hit the house. I'm kinda lonesome for it. Ha, ha, ha."

Half a minute later, Tioga punched in the number for her dad and let the phone ring, ring, ring. If he were in his studio, it would take him time to reach the landline in the kitchen.

"Hello." Philippe Vignetta sounded genuinely irritated. "Whoever this is, don't you know I paint this time of day? You're breaking my routine."

Philippe Vignetta was more predictable, Tioga knew, than the N-Judah streetcar that rattled and clanged outside his house on Carl Street in San Francisco near Golden Gate Park where he walked every evening after he finished painting a canvas. "It's me, Dad. Sorry to disturb you, but it's real important."

Philippe chewed his gums. "Really? What could be more important than painting?"

Her father had always been a hopeless case. There was no point engaging him in small talk. "Someone broke into my office and stole your paintings." There it was, out in the open, what she had been afraid to say. Still she was unprepared for his response.

"You always hated my beautiful paintings," Philippe said. "You're probably ecstatic that you don't have to see them anymore. They won't hurt your precious eyes."

Her heart beat against her rib cage. She took a deep breath and then another. "Well," she began but wasn't certain where to go next. Better to say something than to say nothing at all. If she said something hurtful, she could take it back and apologize. "Well, you never did ask me if I wanted you to paint me in the nude."

Philippe Vignetta chortled and then blasted away. "You were twelve-years old, Ti. You didn't know your own mind or your own body. Someone had to capture your beauty. Better me than anyone else."

Tioga sat down in the chair behind her desk and stared at the wall. "That's it. I was twelve. You were an adult. I have never trusted you ever since then. You were a bad dad." She would have gone on, but Philippe slammed down the phone so hard it hurt Tioga's eardrum. "Fuck you."

The room went silent except for the dialogue from *The Maltese Falcon* rising from the movie theater and seeping through the floorboards. "You know whether you do or not," Miss Wonderly aka Brigid O'Shaughnessy said. "I don't," Spade replied. "It's easy enough to be nuts about you."

There was more dialogue, but Tioga didn't hear any of it, not from O'Shaughnessy, Spade, Lieutenant Dundy or Detective Tom Polhaus. Instead she heard her own sobs, which took her by surprise. Tears streamed down her cheeks. The white spaces where her father's pictures once hung were now just a blur. "That's enough," she told herself. "Don't feel sorry, baby, or you'll be dead before you know it."

It felt good to climb the steps of the hotel and to be greeted by Aaron Holmes who looked snazzy in his new uniform, though it was now days old. "Have you seen Reggie Wentworth?" Tioga looked down at the red carpet, which began at the curb and ran to the big doors at the front of the hotel.

"Not yet, but we're getting closer. Any day now."

She raised her head, peered into Aaron's big round eyes and watched his smile vanish. "Have you been crying?"

Tioga lifted her chin and slowly tilted her face and stared at Aaron without blinking. "Allergies. They always hit me hard this time of year."

Aaron reached into the pocket of his jacket, removed a perfect joint—pre-rolled, by the look of it—and handed it to Tioga, discreetly, of course. "The first of this year's crop. The terpenes are great." Then he placed his right hand on

Tioga's left cheek as if he might smooth the wrinkles that seemed to have come out of nowhere. "Your Latina friend came by earlier. I was ready to chase her to kingdom come, but she had a black eye and bruises. She doesn't have a cell anymore, and her son ran away. I told her you had an office in the Sebastiani Building. I pointed to the window up on the third floor."

Tioga looked across the plaza. "I haven't seen Flor. But someone broke into my office and stole stuff."

Aaron eyed the window of Tioga's office. "Maybe Flor ripped you off."

Tioga darted into the hotel, made for the ladies, looked at her reflection in the mirror and applied mascara, eyeliner and lipstick. Her face was ready for Sean Dyce. On her way across the lobby, she snagged a copy of *The Gazette* with a headline that read, "Wolves Terrorize Valley," which made her laugh. She claimed her habitual place at the bar and waited until Dyce saw that she had entered the Underground's sacred space. He moseyed along as if nothing troubled him, not the bottom line nor the drunks who argued with the barflies, who were just one rung above the alcoholics in the pecking order.

Two men traded comments. "Alison Krauss has nicer tits that Taylor Swift," one of them said. The other added, "I guess you're not counting Dolly Parton."

Dyce grinned. "What'll it be, honeybee?" he warbled.

Tioga gazed at her reflection in the mirror behind the bar, looked for signs of tears, and when she didn't see any beamed brightly. "Nothing just yet. I'm feeling my way along. Don't know yet what I want to put into my body."

Dyce looked impressed. "That's cool you're getting ahold of yourself," he said as if he was Tioga's life coach and aimed to provide her with positive reinforcement. He added, "That's a first step. I congratulate you."

Tioga offered a smirk. "Don't jump the gun. It's too soon to pat me on the back for something I might not ever do."

She felt something or someone coming toward her and destined to strike. By the time she turned around, he was almost on top of her, out of breath and looking rather shabby, his gut hanging over his belt. "Jeez, George. Slow down before you give yourself a heart attack."

Ambrose stood with his feet wide apart, his arms folded across his chest, and looked as if he might have been a bouncer at a nightclub, sworn to keep out the rabble. "Don't joke, Tioga, Billy Bones is on the loose. He has a gun. A neighbor called and reported that he let his pigs go and cleared out of his cabin. I'm worried sick that he's going to come after you. The neighbor found a note that read 'Get the bitch,' with your phone number and then half-a-dozen exclamation marks."

Tioga didn't appear to be ruffled. Hawk frightened her, but not Bones. "I'd like to see the note, George," she said. "I'd like to see the handwriting."

Ambrose wiped his brow with his handkerchief. "No go right now. I left it at the evidence locker. Could be handy when we pick him up and charge him."

Tioga gazed at Dyce and signaled for the Bushmills. Then she turned back to Ambrose. "Pick him up for what? Feeding pot to pigs? Threatening me? Beating the crap out of Dorothy Baynes because she wouldn't allow him to have his own baby? None of that is going to bring her back to life." She paused, letting her words sink into Ambrose's fortress-like skull, and then added, "I don't like Bones any-more than you do. But we don't really have a case against him."

Ambrose sat down on the bar stool next to Tioga and pointed at the tumbler that Tioga held in her hand. "I'll have one of those."

Tioga lifted her glass and sipped. Ambrose knocked his whiskey back and wiped his lips on his sleeve.

He looked as if he might have been a gunfighter itching for a showdown at high noon.

Suddenly Tioga felt sick to her stomach. She placed one hand over her mouth and another on her belly, which swelled up. Dyce reached under the bar and came up with a plastic bucket that he handed to Tioga just in time for her to puke. When she lifted her head, Dyce handed her a dish towel. "Wipe yourself. Go ahead. I won't look."

Tioga cleaned her face and then her hands, walked behind the bar and tossed the dish towel in the stainless-steel sink. Then she gathered the bucket and walked toward the darkness at the back of the bar. "Going to the ladies. Be back in a jiffy. Don't either of you abandon me." When she returned to the bar—though not in a jiffy as she promised—her face was well scrubbed. George Ambrose was gone, and Sean Dyce was making enough margaritas to fill the hotel swimming pool. He paused, retrieved a bottle of Pepto-Bismol from a cabinet labeled with a red cross and handed it to Tioga, who ripped off the cap and glugged the pink liquid. "I feel better already."

Dyce went back to the cocktails he was making and looked more than ever like a mad chemist concocting the ultimate alcoholic drink. "Ambrose went to hunt down Billy Bones. He'll shoot him on sight."

Tioga handed Dyce the glass with the Bushmills, which was still half-full. "I hate to waste good whiskey. But my stomach won't take any more abuse. I've got to have a level head when I talk to Storm. It's been a long time coming."

She blew Dyce a kiss, aimed for the curtain, which she parted, took the corridor to the lobby and dashed for the elevator. Just before the door closed, she waved to Buddy Moscosco who shouted, "Keep a stiff upper lip."

One Last Time

Tioga pushed the elevator button and rode to the end of the line. The door to the penthouse was locked, and when she couldn't find her key, she knocked on the door. "Let me in. I have to pee really bad."

The door opened. Storm moved away from the entrance and gave Tioga room to enter. The front room was a mess, except for the solitary suitcase sitting in the same place she had left it and reminding her of how much she had wanted to go away fast. She ran to the bathroom and sat down on the toilet. "I almost wet myself. This feels so good."

Everything in the apartment was topsy-turvy. On the floor, in the middle of the bedroom, the sheets—that had been stripped from the bed along with the pillowcases—lay in a pile that looked like a rat's nest. In the living room—once a paradigm of order—there were two open suitcases, one of them piled high with panties, bras, camisoles, leggings and socks. The other bulged with blouses, skirts, jeans and sweaters. Jewelry was spread out on the counter that separated the living room from the kitchen.

Tioga fixed her eyes on the rings, necklaces, bracelets and brooches that glittered in the light. "I see you're packing the loot you inherited from your mother."

Storm wore panties that no longer fit; her socks hugged her ankles. Her breasts never seemed fuller or firmer. Her nipples never perkier, and her ass never more rounded. If she had deliberately wanted to tantalize Tioga, she could not have done a better job. A cigarette dangled from her lips; the smoke curled up toward the ceiling. From the loudspeaker came the voice of a woman singing "Put Me Down Easy." It had to be Catherine Russell, Storm's idol. "I'm taking everything that's *mine*, and I'm getting out of Dodge. The Valley has been killing my soul and killing my music."

Tioga borrowed Storm's cigarette, flicked the ash on the floor and inhaled. "This feels sudden," she said tentatively. Then with more confidence she added, "I had no idea. But tell me, where will you go, my dear?"

Storm gathered the linens and pressed them down in a wicker basket that was already full. "The hotel will wash everything and clean up my mess. I'm not saddling you with anything onerous." Then she gazed at the mountains on the horizon. "It's not that sudden. I've been thinking of going away for a long time and didn't know how to tell you. I thought you'd feel abandoned. Now I know you'll be happy with Camilla. The other day I looked at your suitcase. It looked back at me and told me I had to go, that I never have had a real career in this shithole Valley and never could express myself. Nobody ever really wanted to hear me sing the blues, though my friends and admirers liked everything I did just because it was Storm, the little orphan girl making a fool of herself on stage and didn't know it."

Storm turned away from the mountains and looked at the jewelry on the counter. "Terry knows people in L.A. I know I'll have to suck up. But I've done that before. There's nowhere for me to go but up."

She retrieved the cigarette from Tioga's lips, puffed and puffed, and then extinguished it in the ashtray on the countertop. She took Tioga by the hand and led her to the bed where she lifted her in her arms and placed her gently on the mattress. Then without taking her eyes from Tioga, she slowly removed her own socks and the panties, undressed

Tioga, spread her legs, licked her thighs, and went down on her with a delicate fury that gave Tioga chills. Lying on her back, with Storm astride her, her mind went blank.

Nothing was sweeter than Storm's lips, nothing was juicer than her body, the body that she had grown to love and that would leave her, perhaps forever, never to return, never to yield up its pleasures again, Storm's glorious body. It felt like a miracle, this last sacred time, and took her out of herself and into the void beyond the void, beyond knowing. It seemed like it would last forever. But then there was Storm lying on her back gazing up at the ceiling and looking blissed out. And there she was too.

Tioga saw herself from above, looking down, even as she knew she was inside her own body—lying on her back, breathless, broken, quivering and redeemed, with only the spider bite on her thigh to remind her of bitterness and hurt. She felt Storm's kisses on her lips, her eyes and her ears until it was quiet again. Then she heard Storm ask, "Will you stay here after I go?"

Tioga rolled onto her side, curled up in a fetal position and stared at the bare wall. "I won't stay for long. Terry won't let me go on living here, not with you outside this cage of ours. You're the only reason he let us stay here for so long, though I never could really understand why. I still don't, though I always felt that you had something on him. Do you? Will you tell me now that you're going?"

Storm got to her feet, straddled Tioga triumphantly and said, "Terry and me. I guess that's another mystery you'll have to solve."

Tioga stood up, walked to the bathroom, turned on the hot water, then showered, shampooed, brushed her teeth and her hair. She put on jeans, a sweater and stiletto heels that made her feel much taller than her actual height. In the living room again, where Storm wore a bathrobe and slippers, she felt a sense of inner calm. "I'm going with Camilla to see *The Maltese Falcon*. You're welcome to join us."

Storm picked out a necklace, held it up to the light and then offered it to Tioga. "Take it. You'll make it look better than it ever looked on anyone, including my mother."

Tioga glanced from the necklace to Storm and then back to the necklace that still glittered in the light. "Are you sure you want to let it go?"

Storm took the necklace from Tioga's hand, walked behind her, arranged it around her neck and closed the clasp. "Go ahead. Have it and wear it, before I change my mind." Then she kissed the back of Tioga's neck and added, "I guess that both of us wanted one last time together."

Tioga looked at herself and at the necklace in the mirror. "I guess so." Then she turned away from the mirror and took in Storm's gaze. "I'm glad we're not fighting about who gets what."

She looked at the time on her cell. "Gotta run. Love you."

The Maltese Falcon

Along line snaked outside the Sebastiani, but Camilla had staked out a spot close to the box office. Tioga spied her in an incandescent blue beret. Camilla extended her arms above her head and waved. Tioga picked her way through the crowd and inserted herself in the line. Camilla put her arms around her and held her close. With her credit card, she bought a ticket for herself and another for Tioga. "Where do you want to sit?"

Tioga looked around at the rows that were filling up fast. "You decide. I can't do much of anything right now."

Camilla pointed to two empty seats in a row midway between the front and the back of the theater. She went down the aisle. Tioga followed her. "Look, over there," she said and pointed to the front of the theatre, half-a-dozen rows from the screen. "It's Gina and Jonny. I guess they're a couple. I guess they want everyone to know."

Camilla couldn't stop herself from looking. "Seeing is believing. Now I'm a true believer. I wonder if Jonny's cooking won her over?"

She squeezed Tioga's hand. "My mother is expecting us after the movie. She's making tamales."

The theater darkened, the screen came alive, the soundtrack unwound, and the credits rolled. It was time for movie magic. "*The Maltese Falcon*," Tioga said aloud. Reading the names of the actors she was shushed into silence. "Assholes." She felt her old self again. Camilla squeezed her hand and then held it tenderly. "Chill, why don't you?"

Tioga had seen the film more times than she cared to remember. She knew, or thought that she knew, what to expect, though she also wanted to see something she had never seen before. She wanted to be surprised and at the same time, she didn't want to ruin the film for Camilla who was feasting her eyes, for the first time, on the likes of Bogart, Astor, Peter Lorre, Sydney Greenstreet, and Elisha Cook, Jr., Tioga's favorite character, the gunsel who wasn't as bad as he thought he was.

Now in the Sebastiani, which passed for a genuine old-time theater, she didn't reveal the plot to Camilla, though she played a game with herself. Before a scene unfolded, she remembered as fast as she could the dialogue that would unfold between Sam Spade and Miss Wonderly aka Brigid O'Shaughnessy, whom she had always disliked from the moment she appears on screen. "What crap? No detective in her right mind would believe anyone who calls herself Miss Wonderly." After Spade's partner, Miles Archer, is shot and killed and Joel Cairo and the Fat Man talk about "the black bird," Tioga couldn't hold back. "This is the best film noir ever, and O'Shaughnessy, whom I have always loved to hate, is the best femme fatale ever …"

She would have gone on, but Camilla interrupted her. "I'm not that dumb. I know a femme fatale when I see one on the screen—and in real life too."

A man sitting behind them begged them to be silent, and for a while they watched without comment. Then Tioga leaned against Camilla and whispered in her ear. "Life imitates art more often than art imitates life."

Camilla's fixed her eyes on the screen. "We all have parts to play." When Spade catches Captain Jacoby as he falls down, along with the parcel he has carried, Camilla gasped. "Oh, no, he's been shot." Then she calmed down and whispered in Tioga's ear: "Somebody's always chasing somebody else, somebody's always running, someone always has a gun."

Tioga watched the screen with one eye and Camilla's face with the other. She saw her choke up when Spade says to O'Shaughnessy "Don't be too sure I'm as crooked as I'm supposed to be." When O'Shaughnessy goes down in the elevator, Tioga felt tears on her face.

In the lobby, Camilla stopped and admired the old movie poster for *The Maltese Falcon* that showed Spade with a fedora on his head and a gun in his hand. "I'm going to ditch my beret. My mother has a fedora she's kept for years."

Gina, who had been standing behind Camilla, giggled. "You'll look great in a fedora," she said and sounded like Brigid O'Shaughnessy. "Really, I mean it," she added and giggled again before she whispered, "You and Tioga are made for one another. I mean that too."

Jonny Field put his arm around Tioga and Gina and Camilla. "My three favorite women in all the world." Tioga blushed yet again. It was a big day for blushing. Then Jonny added, "Gina and I are going for tacos and beer at El Buen Comer. We'd love you to join us, right, dear?"

Gina nodded her head. Tioga pulled her eyes away from the poster on the wall. "Thanks. That's kind of you. But we have a date with Camilla's mother, Victoria. Another time, I hope."

Field put his long arm around Gina. She put her arm around him. Side by side, in the lobby of the theater, they looked like an odd couple, indeed. He was thinner than the proverbial string bean. She was as plump as a Victorian matron. But there they were, together, seemingly in love and oblivious, Tioga thought, of fat men like Kasper Gutman, femmes fatales like Brigid, gunsels who kill the very men they're paid to protect and the kind of cops that Sam Spade outwits.

Tioga faced Field and asked, "So Jonny, are you going to go on cooking at the Mar Monte?"

Field gave her a quizzical look as if to say he couldn't or didn't fathom her question. "Why would I not go on? I'm the executive chef. Nobody's pushing me out."

Tioga shrugged her shoulders. "Oh, I don't know why not. People change their minds. Sam Spade changed his."

Field laughed heartily and looked like a man at home in his own body. "I've never met a perfect man or made a perfect meal in a perfect kitchen. Anyone who thinks she doesn't change her mind, and anyone who believes there really is a falcon, has her head in a very dark place."

The sidewalk outside the Sebastiani was wet, slick and slippery. The black pavement glistened, and the windshields on the parked cars were dotted with tiny raindrops that had splattered and cascaded. It was only a drizzle, but it had already cut through the dust that had built up for months and that had blanketed the Valley. Still Tioga knew that the dust was invincible. It would come back again and again, even after rain, wind, fire and flood. That thought made her feel sad.

Tioga peered into the moist darkness overhead. "Why don't we take two separate cars? You'll be at home, and I'll go off on my own."

Camilla winced. "I don't like the sound of that. Where will you go? Not back to the Mar Monte, I hope."

Tamales

Victoria Sanchez's house on Siesta Way looked like it was sinking into the ground, though the stairs that led to the front door felt sturdy enough, and the floor in the living room had not yet begun to sag. Camilla took Tioga from the front to the back of the house. "This is where my parents slept when my dad was alive. This is the bathroom that he tiled right before he died. This is where I slept." She stopped at the entrance to a tiny room with a single bed, a crucifix on the wall, a small writing desk, posters—including one of Troy Donahue—and an assortment of stuffed animals, including wombats of different sizes and colors.

"Don't tell me," Tioga said, wearing a big smile. "You were a fan of Donahue on *Hawaiian Eye*. You must have watched the reruns."

Camilla sat down on the bed and looked across the room at the poster on the wall. "I ought to take the Donahue poster down. It's not me, not anymore, but somehow or other I'm attached to it."

From the front of the house came Victoria's high-pitched voice, "*Ven a comer.*"

Camilla's mother had prepared tamales—more than enough to feed the cast of *The Maltese Falcon* or the staff at the Mar Monte—plus rice, black beans, *pico de gallo* and fried plantains. Tioga filled her plate, took a linen napkin and silverware, sat down in a brown armchair and balanced the plate in her lap. Camilla filled her plate and sat across from Tioga. Victoria stood next to the table, her arms folded as if it was her job to guard the food. From the kitchen came the sound of a banda hit with Giselle Vergna, the vocalist, and João Carllos on guitar, which Tioga had heard on the bilingual station KBFB, which broadcast from The Springs.

Tioga cut into a steaming tamale and looked at the insides. "I want to hear what you have to say about El Buen Comer. Anything and everything."

Victoria looked down at the table. "You know the dishes on the menu at the restaurant are from Oaxaca, from my own family's recipes. It's not a big deal, but the señora takes the credit for herself. That's why I'm leaving. I'll have my own food truck, Victoria's Antojitos, parked across the street."

Tioga blotted her lips. She felt unsure what to say or how to say it. Victoria Sanchez looked like a reluctant source. It struck Tioga that it was easier for her to provide food than information. "I'm sorry to hear about Maggie and El Buen Comer. I'm happy you'll have your own food truck."

Tioga rose from her seat, returned to the table and helped herself to the *pico de gallo* and yet another tamale. "I love your cooking, Victoria. It's the best." She sat down again and balanced her plate in her lap. "Tell us what you remember, *por favor.*"

Victoria covered the tamales with a napkin. Then she walked across the room and stared at the drizzle in the darkness. "It's my fault. I guilty."

Camilla smiled. "My mother always feels guilty. Father Innocente Clemente at Holy Name has made her feel like a sinner."

Tioga laid her fork across her plate. "Guilty of what?"

Victoria sat down, crossed her ankles and looked as if she'd broken not only a law but a commandment. "I knew about the money. I saw it living there everyday for weeks.

I told the señora, 'Put it in the bank.' Then at the fiesta I told everyone that the señora was too lazy or too busy or something to take it to the bank. I wanted to shame her. Shame on me."

Tioga leaned forward and placed her head in her hands. "Who heard you?"

Victoria leaned back in her seat. "I don't know. I was thinking about myself and the good that I was doing. I didn't think of the others."

Tioga took out her phone and opened the file with the photos of the suspects who might have robbed the restaurant. It made for a long list: Hawk aka Reginald Wentworth; Billy Bones; the Yaqui brothers, Pablo and No Name; Travis Syrah; the two women that Camilla had met at number forty-nine, Maya and Katrina; Matt Chehab and Maggie Brazil herself. For the hell of it, Tioga had added a picture of Terry McCoy.

Mrs. Sanchez looked at the photos and gasped. "All these people were there. And others, too, who are not in your phone. There were two guests from the hotel." Victoria pointed to the picture of portly Chehab and said, "He's taking tourists around the Valley. He had a driver and a stretch limo that blocked the street. A busybody called the police. The kid detective came and blew his whistle and said, 'If you don't stop the racket, I'm going to arrest all of you, take you down to the station and book you, so play nice. Okay.' After that everyone was quiet. I forgot about the money and danced with Maya and Katrina. Travis played drums and Pablo's brother who never gives his name to anyone took up the accordion."

Tioga glowed, beamed and even rejoiced, though she could hear the dark rain as it fell from the night sky. Not everyone steals, she told herself, and not everyone thinks about stealing. Victoria Sanchez tried to do the right thing and still felt guilt. Tioga bore down on Camilla, who was so caught up in her mother's story that she hadn't touched the food on her plate. The tamales still beckoned, and so did the beans and the rice.

Tioga stood up, grabbed a folding chair from the table, placed it in front of Camilla and straddled the seat. "I want you to talk to everyone you can find who was at the party. I don't care how long it takes, but get it done ASAP. We'll eliminate the suspects one by one. Don't rule anyone out." She emailed Camilla copies of the photos in her phone, along with a list of the suspects. Camilla looked helpless. Tioga was ready to throttle her. "What are you waiting for? Get out there, beat the bushes and text me when you have something."

Camilla grabbed her backpack, opened the closet in the hallway, disappeared behind the jackets, coats and trousers and came out with a fedora on her head and a lightweight raincoat over her arm. "My mother's brother's hat. He was in the Mexican mafia. Right, Mom?"

Mrs. Sanchez shook her head. "Why does she have to tell family secrets? I know why—to make me look bad."

Exit Camilla, Enter Randy

Tioga walked Camilla to the front door. "Don't worry, I'll get back to my car." Camilla descended the stairs, walked down the street in the drizzle, started her car and drove off.

From the opposite direction, Tioga heard a car door open and close and then the clatter of shoes on the pavement. A figure emerged from the darkness. A shapeless shape moved toward her and gradually came into focus. Then Randy Scheck stood at the bottom of the steps that led to the front porch of Mrs. Sanchez's house, which seemed to sag even more. Scheck wore jeans, loafers, a blue and yellow sweatshirt that said "Cal," and around his neck a red scarf that Tioga pulled playfully.

"You just missed Camilla. Too bad."

Randy Scheck peered into the darkness. "I saw her leave. I couldn't take the two of you at the same time. Too much beauty all at once. Besides I wanted you to come with me. Langley was going to fetch you, but he has a deadline. Apparently, McCoy is cashing out. The hotel is going on the market. It's a big story. Langley will be along in no time."

He reached up, took Tioga's hand and helped her down the stairs, though she stopped midway and looked back. "I have to say goodbye to Mrs. Sanchez. I don't want to be impolite."

Randy closed his eyes, gave Tioga a peck on the lips and opened his eyes again. "We don't have time for that. We're late already."

Tioga backed away from Randy. "I need my purse."

Randy pulled her closer. "No you don't. You have your cell. That's all you need. Come with me now. You can swing by later for your purse and make amends with the old lady." He turned and walked uphill.

Tioga followed him and grumbled. "Where are you taking me?" she asked, sounding, she thought, like a child waylaid by a parent, her father.

Scheck unlocked the doors to a silver Porsche with New York plates and sat behind the steeling wheel. Tioga fastened her seat belt. Scheck fastened his and gunned the car. Tioga braced herself. "Turn on the headlights." The high beams illuminated a sign that read "Slow Children at Play." Scheck did not slow down. He did not stop at the stop sign either, but ploughed right through it without looking in either direction. "We're not in New York, Toto. Slow down."

Scheck barreled along as if he was on I-5. "Relax. I know what I'm doing."

Tioga gripped the overhead strap and swayed back and forth and up and down as the car bounced on the rough pavement.

In The Springs, a block or so before the white buildings of Soulful Spa—which glimmered in the night—Scheck took a sharp left on Diego, parked and killed the lights and the engine. "We walk from here." He took Tioga down an alley lined with red brick walls and then down another alley with stonewalls so high she could not see over them.

In a few minutes, they entered a lot clearly marked "No Parking," though cars were parked every which way. There was no moon and no stars, but a single streetlight overhead made walking less difficult than it might have been in the darkness and wet blanket of mist. Randy crept along the side of a two-story stucco building painted red, green and white. Tioga recognized it. All was well. She was on familiar territory. She followed Randy's shadow and stopped at the rear entrance to El Buen Comer where a hand painted sign read, "Deliveries."

"I know where we are," she said proudly, standing under the light perched above the doorway. She shook her head and added, "I don't get the hocus-pocus if we're just going into El Buen Comer."

Randy stood in the shadow and, with his handkerchief, wiped the moisture from the hair on the top of his head. "We're not going into the restaurant, dummy," he said, sounding like Mr. Know-it-all. "We're going upstairs. If I'm not mistaken, you've never been there before. Maggie has kindly provided the space for our confab. She owes us all big time."

Roxanne Jacobs Back from Depths of Amsterdam

Randy opened the door, ushered Tioga inside, and then with his back leaned against the door until it closed. Tioga blinked her eyes and waited until they became accustomed to the dim light. "What do you mean owes us?"

Scheck grabbed hold of the banister. "She fucked up big time. I mean the way she faked the whole thing. I don't mind telling you that was reprehensible."

He propelled himself up the long carpeted flight of stairs that muffled his footsteps and Tioga's, too, until she stopped midway and looked up at Randy. "What do you mean?"

At the landing, Scheck took a deep breath, filled his lungs with air and coughed. "She took the money and invested it—nearly a quarter of a million—into a big grow. Thieves ripped off the whole crop. She lost everything. Serves her right."

Tioga peered down the flight of stairs she had just climbed. "I get it. She couldn't take money out of the bank or get a loan."

Randy leaned against the wall and gazed down at Tioga. "Duh." He knocked on the door that said "Private" and then went right in. That was his way. Tioga could not remember a time when he waited for an invitation.

The private space proved to be much larger than she had imagined it would be. The wail of a saxophone washed over her, and she swooned. "Lester Young." A CD sat on the bookcase. No, it was not Lester but Zoot Sims. Oh well. Close enough. Zoot was also cool when he was hot. Curtains covered a window facing the street, and that made the room feel claustrophobic. From the first floor came the smells from the kitchen below—oil, tomatoes, garlic, onions, corn and jalapeños—all mixed together in a hypnotic stew.

Jeremiah Langley sat in a wicker chair behind a card table and with a pen in hand marked up the front page of *The Gazette*. The headline read, "Mar Monte on the Chopping Block." A joint dangled from his lips. "Too many typos, and I still have to find out the asking price." He shook his head and looked up at Tioga. "You wanna job as a copy editor?"

Tioga waved her hand. Langley nodded ever so slightly, puffed and puffed and then placed the joint in an ashtray that already held several roaches. Langley was a cool hipster albeit without a hipster brother to dig Zoot Sims. A cloud of smoke engulfed the head of the woman who sat opposite Langley and reshuffled the deck of cards.

Scheck opened the window a tad, unfolded a chair, dragged it to the table and offered it to Tioga. Then he leaned against the wall and turned down the volume on Zoot.

Tioga sat down and just let the sax take her into her head. "Hey, Jeremiah, I was beginning to wonder when I'd bump into you so I could tell you that your editorials have been shit. You haven't changed one bit."

Langley gave her a goofy look as if to say that he didn't care whether he had changed or not and whether she liked his editorials. "It's all good," he said in a world-weary tone of voice. "Read or don't read, it's all the same."

Tioga beat a rhythm on the table. "Is it true about McCoy cashing out?"

Langley lifted the newspaper and folded it in half. "Read it in tomorrow's edition and weep with joy."

Tioga sat down and stared impolitely at the woman who was playing cards; solitaire from the look of the game. The smoke cleared. Tioga recognized the face and knew her name, though she would not say it now. Nor would she say her own name. Names would come in time—or not. The card player had short brown hair dyed blond. Tioga saw the roots. She wore orange sneakers, black sweat pants and a matching hoodie. Her face was round rather than oval; her chin was prominent and her eyes were blue. She had high cheekbones and a long, thin nose. The photo that Hawk had given Tioga was a good likeness indeed. Tioga looked pleased and relieved. So Roxanne Jacobs had big balls after all, just as Sean Dyce had told her.

"It's all good," Tioga said sarcastically. "It's been a great day for me. I haven't been shot, raped, robbed or brutally beaten." Her phone pinged: a text from Buddy Moscosco read, "Man with gun in the MM. Took off half-an-hour ago with Lawrence. Gina's freaked. McCoy called the cops."

Tioga let out a long, slow hissing sound. The woman swayed back and forth in her seat. "Bad news?"

Tioga looked at her and then at Scheck and Langley. "Yeah, a ruckus at the hotel. Stay tuned."

The woman turned her cards over slowly. "The Mar Monte seems so uncivilized, though it tries to be something else entirely."

Tioga watched her shuffle the deck and start a new game. "McCoy does a good job hiding shit when he needs to."

The woman laid out her cards. "Don't knock him. Terry isn't flawless, but he has his virtues, least of which is loyalty. He hasn't ever betrayed me."

She turned over her cards rapidly and took the game as far as she could take it. Then she hit a dead end. She collected the cards and dropped the whole deck on the table. She then raised her hands and opened her palms.

"I give up. It's your turn. Maybe you'll have better luck, Jeremiah. You always win no matter what. I hate to lose. It feels so shitty." She turned away from Langley and gazed at Tioga. "You understand, don't you? I have to take precautions. The Russians put a price on my head. No doubt the money is still on the table, so to speak, though for now I'm out of reach. I've heard they still believe I went up in flames in Amsterdam."

Tioga took the deck from Langley and laid out the cards. "How do you figure in all this, Jeremiah?"

Langley looked impassive. "Just following a lead. Besides I love Roxanne's company. Get her to tell you stories about the Russians. They'll blow your mind."

Roxanne smirked. "Jeremiah is shameless. He thinks flattery will help him. He's dead wrong, of course. I don't want him to write my story. I'm the only one who can do it justice."

Tioga nodded her head, then looked down at the cards on the table. She placed a Jack of Hearts on a Queen of Spades and a seven of clubs on an eight of diamonds. "So Randy," she began slowly and then with a sense of urgency added, "when you told me you were going back east for your mother's sake, that was a lie, wasn't it?"

Randy looked his cherubic self, even though Tioga had accused him of trying to deceive her. "No, not a lie," he said, loosening the red scarf around his neck. "Just a convenient fiction. One of Roxanne's former confederates was on trial in Brooklyn. I sat in the courtroom and listened to the testimony. The confederate didn't mention Roxanne by name, except to say that she was burned to a crisp on her houseboat in Amsterdam, along with a ton of Moroccan hashish."

Langley fired up the joint, which had gone out on its own. He admired the red glow at the tip, inhaled and passed the joint to Roxanne. She held it briefly between her fingers and passed it to Scheck. He grasped it greedily and couldn't inhale soon enough. "You can't get weed like this in Brooklyn. This stuff is fuckin' dynamite."

With her right hand, Roxanne cleared the smoke in the air. "You always were a pig when it came to pot." Then she smiled at Tioga and touched her face with the tips of her fingers. "You have lovely skin. I suppose you inherited it from your mother, a socialite, if I'm not mistaken."

Tioga reached out and touched Roxanne. "You are not mistaken, and for a Dutch girl you don't seem to burn under our sun."

Roxanne withdrew her hand. "But I did burn myself in Amsterdam." She turned her wrist and revealed a scar that had taken the shape of a flower. "A sail on fire crashed to the deck, and an ember burned me. I stayed to the end to make it look good."

Tioga winced. "Scars make a body beautiful."

Roxanne pulled at a large hoop earring that dangled from her earlobe. "I should tell you that I caught on to your little Latina friend who followed me around for a day. I made her an offer she couldn't refuse. She's followed you ever since. You get around quite a lot, I must say, though Flor isn't going to be trying to keep up with you anymore."

"No!" Tioga said and sounded shocked.

"No," Roxanne said. "ICE picked her up, but they didn't get her kid." Roxanne looked at the curtain once again. "I admire your taste in women, though Storm is definitely a handful."

Tioga didn't blink and, while she felt under attack and wanted to strike back, she restrained herself. "You have to meet Storm to appreciate her. The long-distance thing doesn't work."

Roxanne took out her cell, opened her photo album and showed Tioga the screen. "This pic was taken two days ago in the plaza. I bet your ex didn't tell you he was in the Valley. Sneaky fuck, isn't he?"

Tioga looked at the photo of Tomás and then let loose with a howl. "Are you trying to get me riled up? If so, you're doing a very nice job. I'd like to see Tomás rot to death."

Roxanne slipped the phone into the pocket of her hoodie.

Tioga reached for the remains of the joint that had gone out, relit it, brought it to her lips and inhaled. "So where the hell is all the weed that's been ripped off?"

Roxanne went to the window parted the curtains and peered down at the street. "I don't like the looks of it. Something's fucked up. Go down, Jeremiah, and check it out."

Then she turned to Tioga. "I'm gonna split, but don't worry. I'll hook you up with Maya. She lived on Avenida de la Virgen and knows the story better than I. Right now, she's terrified and with good reason. Hawk and Tomás would like nothing better than to snuff her out. And to think they were once such nice boys."

In a flash, Langley returned from the street with a grimace on his face. "You're right. Something's definitely weird down there. A guy behind the wheel of a Honda Civic, with the motor running, has a gun in his hand. He has a kid with him. You and me better split."

Roxanne covered her head with her hoodie, gathered the Zoot Sims CD and smiled at Tioga. "Look for a package from Dyce, and ask Randy to fill you in on all the details I haven't had time to share." She walked toward the door, opened it, paused and looked back at Tioga. In the next second, she and Langley were gone.

Time suddenly felt like it was going faster and faster. Tioga took the snub nose from the shoulder holster and held it in the palm of her hand. She walked to the window, parted the curtain and looked down at the Honda Civic and at the man with the gun and the boy at his side.

A radio blasted the Stones' "Gimme Shelter." Headlights poked holes in the night. On the sidewalk, a girl played with a dog and a boy in shorts kicked a ball against a wall. Tioga glared at Randy Scheck. who had retreated to a corner of the room. "It's Billy Bones. I'm going down and take his gun away from him before he hurts himself."

She cocked her ear and kept her eyes on Bones, who had rolled down his window and was talking gibberish: *wopadokit ii ojup qty*. And there was more: *qoonopp lpyeeqr*. He had finally flipped. A car door closed, gears engaged and tires squealed on the pavement. Was that Jeremiah and Roxanne? No, it was too soon for them to make their getaway. Tioga took out her phone and sent Ambrose a text: "Bones outside El Buen Comer w/the kid, armed. Going to take him down."

In the near distance two car doors closed quietly. An engine turned over. Headlights illuminated the billboard that read *"Beba más leche. Te hará un hombre."* "Yes, of course," Tioga said to herself. "Drink more milk. It will make you a man." That's exactly what the world needed now: real men. She turned her head, cocked her ear and added, "That must be Jeremiah and Roxanne getting away." She gritted her teeth.

Scheck nodded knowingly. "I'll stay here and keep an eye on the street while you deal with Bones. But don't do anything dumb."

A siren screeched. Mick Jagger wanted someone to give him shelter. Tioga peered down at Bones who now stood in the middle of the street. In one hand he waved a gun above his head. In the other he clutched Lawrence who was barefoot and wrapped in a blanket that read "Mar Monte." Cars swerved around them. Horns honked.

Drivers hurled obscenities. Bones fired a shot into the air. The blackbirds on the telephone wire took wing. Then Bones dashed toward the restaurant. Tioga had steeled her nerves. "I'm going now." She bounded out of the room, flew down the stairs, hit the street, gun in hand, and saw herself in a black-and-white movie hurtling along toward some dark finale.

Two cars pulled into the parking lot at the front of the restaurant. Ambrose struggled to get out of an unmarked police vehicle. Clark propelled himself from a second vehicle that said "Valley Police." They were together once again: a cop team.

Tioga saw the action unfold as if in slow motion. Clark held his service revolver at his side and crept toward the door. Ambrose crouched down and duck-walked until his knees gave way. He stood up slowly and leaned against the wall. From inside the restaurant, a gun went off. Something cracked, something crashed. A boy wailed.

Clark reached the front door and went down as close to the ground as he could. Ambrose joined him and cupped his hands around his mouth. "Put your gun down, son, and come out with your hands above your head. The place is surrounded. There's no escaping alive."

The window above Ambrose's head shattered, and shards of glass landed on his uniform. "Fucking bastard," he said, and then to Clark he added, "Go around the back and make sure he can't get out that way. Shoot, if you have to. But watch out you don't shoot the kid."

Clark slinked away. Tioga took the place he had occupied. "Bones, it's me, Tioga Vignetta. I want to help you and Lawrence. It's not too late. We know you didn't kill

Dorothy or Katrina. Do as Chief Ambrose says. Toss your weapon, let the boy go and come out with your hands raised. I'm on your side."

Bones fired another shot; the bullet grazed Tioga's head. "Fuck you, bitch. Come and get me." He exceeded her expectations—and fulfilled them too.

Tioga tapped Ambrose on the shoulder. "I'm going in. Bones knows me. He won't shoot."

Ambrose grimaced. "Not on your life. He'd just as soon kill you as slaughter one of his pigs."

Tioga listened to the sounds from inside El Buen Comer, as if from a madhouse. There was more babble: *pljtok mkqrtz.*

Ambrose held his index finger on the trigger of his service revolver. He crouched down and with his shoulder leaned into the screen door, forcing it open just enough for him to squeeze through. The spring brought the door back.

Tioga craned her neck for a glimpse of Bones. She couldn't see him, but she heard the shot that he fired. It ricocheted off the floor in front of her. Lawrence shrieked. Bones's next bullet shattered the front window with the sign that read "El Buen Comer: Authentic Mexican."

A Valley fire truck arrived. Fire fighters in uniforms and fire hats poured out of the hook and ladder and milled about in front of the restaurant eager for action. Cop cars from Santa Rosa arrived, and deputies gathered for an assault. Tioga eyed the fire chief who had white hair, a red nose and a short stocky body to go with his big square head. When he got off his cell she approached him. "What can you tell me?" she asked.

"A man inside has a gun and a boy he mistakenly thinks is his own son," the fire chief said. "He's nutso. The kid belongs to Mr. McCoy."

Tioga nodded. "Yeah, his ex gave their kid up for adoption, and there's no way to get him back." Then she looked toward the restaurant and added, "I reckon that George went inside sixty seconds ago. If he doesn't come out in the next sixty, I'm going in. I'll grab the kid and get him out of there fast." She counted backwards from sixty. When she hit zero, she went down on her haunches and entered the restaurant low to the floor covered with shards of glass, silverware and bits of food. She scanned the wall for the photo of Cantinflas and didn't see it. The overhead fan revolved. The door to the stainless steel refrigerator reflected Bones' silhouette and the outline of the boy.

Suddenly there was a burst of gunfire that sounded like two different weapons had been fired from opposite directions and just a split second apart. Then from deep inside the restaurant came an animal cry and a stream of obscenities. Bones had been caught in the crossfire. At least one bullet had to have found the target. Someone was hurt. Someone was bleeding. It wasn't Tioga or Ambrose or Clark, who held his gun in his hand and smiled like a kid.

"You got him, chief. Nice shot."

Then from Bones came a howl that echoed inside the restaurant. Tioga darted around the counter. Ambrose holstered his gun and wiped the perspiration from his brow. Bones was sprawled on the floor, face down, legs spread apart, his body swimming in a pool of blood that oozed from his chest and his head. Ambrose bent down, put two fingers on Bones's neck, near his windpipe, and held them there. "There's no pulse. Can you believe it? The crazy son-of-a-bitch came back to steal again. Now we won't have to go through a trial."

Lawrence cowered in a corner and cried out, "Come get me. There's blood everywhere."

Tioga stepped over Bones's body, put her arms around Lawrence, held him close and shielded his eyes from the blood, the money and the gun. He had already seen more than enough for a lifetime. "It's all right," Tioga said, walking backward a step at a time. "You did good, Lawrence."

Ambrose peeked at the boy whose teeth chattered and who nestled as close to Tioga as he could get. Then the chief rested his right hand on Tioga's shoulder. "No one but Bones would do something this stupid. He'll be front-page news. It's what he always wanted."

Clark listened without comment. Now that he was on the chief's good side again, he waited to be told what to do. All at once and in a roar, the fire fighters entered the restaurant with Gina in tow. "Where's my boy? I want my boy."

Tioga surrendered Lawrence and sauntered into a night that looked as dark as any that she had ever seen. Gina placed the boy in the back seat of a Porsche parked on the sidewalk, the motor running. Maggie Brazil arrived in a robe, inspected the damage, corralled Ambrose and peppered him with a string of who, what, when, why, and how questions. He waved her aside and motioned for the EMT boys to carry Bones's body to the ambulance. They strapped him down and slammed the rear door.

When Maggie got nowhere with Ambrose, she pounced on Tioga. "Did you see what happened?" Tioga had wandered into the restaurant again as if in a movie that had gone wild. "George," she murmured. "Don't tell me to leave the scene. I've been with this case from day one. And don't tell Maggie to leave either. It's her place."

George scowled. "It's highly irregular," he said. "I'll get in trouble, but go ahead and don't touch nothing."

Tioga peered at the cash register and at the receipts scattered on the counter and on the floor. She bore down on Maggie and said, "When I was up above I saw Bones in the street, waving a gun and carrying Lawrence. I didn't see George pull the trigger, but I heard the shots, five of them, maybe six. Bones fired a couple of times, for sure. It was either him or George."

Maggie gazed at the bullet holes on the wall. "What was he thinking? Take the money and run until he had to rob again?"

With a towel that she moistened at the sink, Tioga wiped her shoes that had been stained by the blood that had leaked out of Bones' body and gathered in a pool on the floor.

Maggie walked to the cash register and peered inside with anxiety written all over her face. "What happens to my money?"

Tioga gave her a piercing look. "Don't worry, you'll get your money, and Bones won't trouble you ever again." Tioga picked her way through the crowd and stood alone in the street where Bones had stood. She turned her head and watched the ambulance make its way slowly through the curious onlookers.

Randy Scheck appeared, as if out of nowhere and with the air of an official meant to supervise the scene. "You got your man," he said to Ambrose. "Nice work."

Tioga stared at the chief, who was now all puffed up and clearly proud of himself, though he also appeared to be near the end of his tether. "Someone give me something to drink. My throat is on fire."

Scheck turned to Clark. "Get George a glass of water before he croaks." He took Tioga by the arm and led her to the parking lot at the back of the restaurant where his car waited under the branches of an oak. "I'm feeling a bit woozy myself," he said, gazing at the blue-black sky. "Give me a second to clear my head. It's been a shock to my system."

The rain came down, and the darkness gathered around him. He fumbled with the keys and then, reluctantly, it seemed, unlocked the car. Tioga opened the door on the passenger side, climbed inside, rolled down the window and felt the moisture on her face.

Scheck went on standing in the rain. Finally he sat down in the driver's seat, gripped the steering wheel and stared at the brick wall in front of him. Tioga smoked a cigarette. "Take your sweet time. I don't have to be anywhere soon, though I'd like to retrieve my purse, and I'd like you to come clean with me, Randy, if you want to remain friends."

Randy took out a handkerchief, dabbed his eyes and blew his nose. Tioga removed the snub nose from the holster and held it in the palm of her hand. "Have you every felt the weight of this baby?" With a sad voice she added, "I came close to firing a shot. I might have killed Bones."

Scheck looked at the gun without blinking. "Well, you didn't fire it, and you didn't kill Bones. Maybe you won't ever have to kill anyone. Maybe people like George Ambrose will do the killing for us." He revved the engine and turned on the radio. Van Morrison's voice filled the car. Scheck joined the chorus and sang, "oh oh Domino/Roll me over Romeo."

Tioga looked at her reflection in the mirror behind the visor and closed her eyes, as if she had seen something that she didn't want to see. "Take me back to Camilla's mother and then to the plaza."

For a change, Scheck followed orders, albeit in his own way and at his own speed. He weaved in and out of traffic, passed cars on the right and on the left, and honked the horn when the spirit moved him, which was every few seconds. "Where do you want me to begin the story?" he asked sheepishly. Tioga leaned back in her seat and braced herself for what felt like an inevitable crash, unless she could persuade Scheck to drive more cautiously. "Slow down before you kill the two of us." Then she put her left hand on the back of Randy's neck and played with his curls until he began to relax and to slow down. "Start at the beginning, unless you want to start at the end and go backward. Just don't start in the middle. That doesn't work for me."

Scheck eased up on the accelerator, turned on the wipers and squirted liquid on the windshield. With a few wipes, the visibility improved, though the rain began to come down heavier than before and made it harder to see the blacktop. "Very good, Randy. You can unlearn New York driving after all."

Indeed, Scheck paid closer attention to the curves in the road and to the traffic while Tioga went on playing with the curls on the back of his head. "The beginning. That's going back a-ways," he said. "But if you insist. I'll give it a whirl. You can't repeat it to anymore—and certainly not to Langley, who has his heart set on writing a book about Roxy. That's why he hangs out with her and why she uses him. Do we have a deal, Tioga?"

"Deal. Cross my heart and hope to die." She crossed her heart, and also crossed her fingers as her schoolmates had taught her. Scheck turned away from the road and stared at Tioga. "I'm sharing because we have a history together. Also I have to tell or I'll implode."

Scheck kept his eyes on the traffic ahead. "Back in the day, as they say, Terry, Matt, Roxy and Hawk were buddies. She had product that she distributed in Europe with help from the Russians. The guys wanted to bring it to the states and cut out the comrades in Kiev. They saw easy money, which they wanted so that they could renovate the old hotel on the plaza.

"They had a deal. It was all set, but then Hawk and your ex ripped Roxy off, which landed her in trouble with the

Russians who were pressuring her from the east. That's when her houseboat caught fire. At first I thought the Russian were behind it. Not so. When Terry heard Roxy was alive, he sent your ex as an envoy and invited her to come west. The Valley, he told her, was a good place to hide and to make money fast."

Scheck pulled over to the side of the road and put the car in neutral. He was all choked up. For fresh air, he rolled down his window and took a deep breath. Then he went on. "Terry gave Tomás a suitcase with cash that he delivered to Roxy. Given all the shit that went down, I advised her against a deal with the guys. She ignored me. I attribute that to her innately reckless nature. In that respect you and she are twins."

Randy turned on the directional and pulled onto the road again. Tioga lowered her shoulders that had hunched up around her neck. "The crop that Roxanne wants back badly, is it really hers?"

Scheck bit his lower lip. "It's not clear who owns what, though it's clear that someone—or someones —ripped off the weed on St. Mary's Lane where they found the body of Katrina, who had worked for Roxanne. That's why Katrina had my business card. I had written your name on the back."

He pulled off the highway and parked in front of Mrs. Sanchez's house, which looked as if the rain had helped it sink a little bit further into the ground. "I'll be right back." She kept her word and returned with her purse and with a package wrapped in foil. "Tamales. A midnight snack." She placed the package on the back seat and lowered the volume on the radio, now playing Marvin Gaye singing "I Heard It Through the Grapevine." "What about Bones? How does he figure in all this?"

Scheck squirmed in his seat, shifted into reverse, backed up and made a U-turn. He took Big Ranch Road and traveled on Juniper Boulevard, which ran along the creek and, with the rain, threatened to overflow its banks. "Bones did odd jobs and hustled weed. He was the lowest of the low on the totem poll, and he resented it."

Tioga leaned her head against Randy's shoulder. "Yeah, I get it, but to go back for a moment. It gave me a fright when George told me that they found your card with my name on Hawley's body. I thought someone was setting me up. After that, at night when I went to sleep I saw a bullet coming at me. It was still there in the morning. The same bullet."

Randy reached Broadway, stopped at the intersection, took a right, circled the plaza and looked for a place to park. "Katrina acted as Roxanne's go-between. She took messages back and forth when I was helping Roxanne get settled here, anonymously, of course. Katrina ought to have memorized your name and destroyed the card, as I told her to do. It's the little things that fuck you up."

Tioga pointed to a parking space opposite the Sebastiani. "Over there. Get it before someone else does. It's shark city here. No one wants to walk, not even half a block."

Randy parked, rolled down his window and let the car idle. "I'm not going to come up to your office. Another time. Meanwhile, sit tight. Someone will contact you very soon with a package from Neiman Marcus."

Tioga reached for the tamales, opened the door, extended one leg, placed her right shoe on the pavement and then turned and glared at Randy. "Do I understand you? I'm supposed to help Roxanne find a crop that might or might not belong to her and in return she'll help me nab Dorothy Baynes's killer?"

Scheck held Tioga's chin and then kissed her on the lips. "I wouldn't put it that way. You're coming to the aid of a friend."

Tioga stood on the sidewalk and looked inside the Porsche. "I see. It's all about friendship."

Scheck revved the engine. "Now you've got it. Now you can keep it, for future reference."

A Friendly Drink

In the lobby of the Mar Monte, Tioga received a text from Langley who seemed to speak the same language that Randy Scheck spoke. "Meet me for a friendly drink." Tioga didn't want to make nice or be friends with the editor of *The Gazette*, but when she thought about it she realized that he could take her places she couldn't go on her own. She texted, "Thanx. You're on."

She walked to the ladies, studied herself in the mirror, fussed with her hair and applied lipstick. She crossed the lobby and read the menu outside A Chez Nous, then opened the curtain that separated the long dark corridor from the Underground. In the dim light, with George Shearing in the background, she sat down at the bar and placed her cell and her purse in plain view.

Langley had already staked out his own territory and had engaged Dyce in what Tioga called man-talk. That meant that they were talking about cars, horsepower, speed and the latest Tesla, which the editor wanted to buy and had even taken for a test drive in Marin. "I like it, I like it a lot."

Dyce reached for a bottle on the shelf behind him. "You're talking about a lot of dough."

The furrows in Langley's brow deepened. "But there's great resale value."

Dyce read the label that said Stolichnaya, opened the bottle, added ice cubes to a glass and drowned them. "I'm weaning myself from tequila and switching to vodka. It's the new thing. Everyone wants Comrade Stoli. Forget about Señor Cuervo."

Tioga wore a look of boredom, but she cleared her throat and then dropped her cell on the floor. Langley turned, looked down, picked up the phone and handed it to Tioga. "I didn't hear you come in. You must have walked on cat's paws."

Tioga took the phone and added it to her purse. "I'm all stealth these days. Not hard to do around men. You're all into your own heads. Couldn't solve a crime if you tried."

Langley lifted the Stoli that Dyce had poured. He sipped. "Oh, I like it. It's very smooth and very citrusy. Hit me again." Then he turned to his laptop, which sat on the bar next to a basket of pretzels. "I knocked off a draft and showed it to Terry, as a courtesy. He read it a couple of times and said that he didn't think it struck the right note. So I'm reworking it, giving more credit to the firemen and the police. What I'd like to know, Tioga, is did you actually see Ambrose shoot Bones?"

He turned the computer so that Tioga could see the whole screen. She read the headline, "Valley Drug Dealer Dies in Hail of Bullets." She smiled. "I wonder what a hail of bullets really looks and sounds like."

Langley laughed. His whole face relaxed, and he looked as if he was suddenly as happy as could be. "Gee, I hadn't thought of it like that. Thanks. I'll have to rethink the headline."

Tioga elbowed the computer back to Langley. "I love the alliteration in the title, Jeremiah. You do have a way with words."

All this time Randy Scheck had sat quietly off to one side, kept his own council and nursed a drink. He raised his glass and looked sheepishly at Tioga. "Can I buy you a cranberry vodka cocktail? That's what I'm having. It's what Sean is making for the party squeezed into the last booth."

Tioga drilled her eyes into the back of the room, but it was too dark for her recognize a single face. "Tourists?"

Langley lifted his fingers from the keyboard. "Out-of-towners on a package tour. They're hoping to hunt wild boar. I touted them on Terry."

Tioga turned her back on the out-of-towners and made eye contact with Langley. "To come back to your question, Jeremiah, I did not see George shoot Billy Bones." She spoke in an even-handed tone of voice, hoping not to provoke Langley. "I only heard shots. The last one came, oh, maybe ten or fifteen seconds after the first one. I think there were six or seven shots all together from George and from Clark, though I don't know for sure which ones were from George and which ones were from Clark. Plus, Bones managed to get off a few shots, though in his state of mind, it's a wonder he could fire at all. Bullets from his gun have to be embedded in the wall at the front of the restaurant. It might make for an interesting installation and bring in out-of-towers who want to soak up some local color."

Langley's index fingers moved up and down the keyboard and from side to side. Tioga watched his hunt-and-peck method and marveled at his speed. "Are you getting all this down, Jeremiah?"

Langley stopped typing and rested his elbows on the bar. "So when did you first see Bones? I mean from inside the restaurant, not from the second floor."

Tioga kicked her right leg back and forth in a kind of nervous gesture as if to release some kind of pent-up emotion. "Bones was on the floor, bleeding like a stuck pig—if you'll pardon the expression—from his head and his chest. He had a gun in one hand and cash in the other: tens, fives and singles. I looked. Maybe he had one thousand dollars total. Nothing to write home about."

Now Langley typed furiously and without looking up from the keyboard. "So was George's final shot really necessary? Or was he just getting off his jollies when he stood over Bones's body?"

Tioga wanted to laugh, though there wasn't anything funny about Langley's question. When she did laugh, it was out of nervousness, as much as anything else. "It's hard to know and hard to say, Jeremiah. I didn't see the last shot; my vision might have been impaired. The coroner ought to be able to provide you with a better answer than I."

Langley lifted his finger from the keyboard and sipped his Stoli cocktail. "What about this: do you think Bones was the person who had previously robbed the cash register at El Buen Comer? And if so, what did he do with the money?"

Tioga signaled Dyce that she wanted a Pellegrino. "That could be, but a dozen or so people knew that a ton of cash was lying around. It seems like an inside job, but how far and how deep inside, I'm not prepared to say for sure. Maybe it was Maggie herself. Maybe it was someone who worked in the kitchen or the zoot-suit waiter. Take your pick. What matters is that it's gone."

Langley expelled the air in his lungs and shook his hands, which seemed to have cramped. "Thanks, great quote. I assume everything you've said is on the record."

Tioga lifted her glass and looked at the bubbles that rose to the surface. "No. It's off the record. You can't use any of it. Sorry, but that's the way it is. Confidentiality!"

Langley slapped the computer with the back of his hand. "Fuck you. I'll return the favor." He got up, folded his computer, placed it under his arm and walked out seemingly in a kind of silent rage.

Tioga reached inside her jacket and pulled out her snub nose. "Right now I'd like to blow his head off."

Randy Scheck moved to the seat that Langley had just vacated. He unwrapped his paisley scarf and placed it around Tioga's neck. "It would be less messy to take Jeremiah to court for invasion of privacy and more than to shoot him. But by tomorrow everyone in the Valley will have read his story. They'll see your words in quotation marks, and they won't think whether or not you were on or off the record. Nobody cares about that stuff anymore." He stood up, opened his wallet, lifted a twenty and placed it on the bar. "Thanks, Sean."

Tioga got to her feet. "Where are you going?"

Scheck stuffed his hands in his pockets. "I have a date with Roxy. Gotta take care of unfinished business."

Tioga raised her eyebrows. "Where is she? I won't tell."

Scheck removed the scarf from around Tioga's neck and held it in his hand. "Hiding in plain sight. She has a suite on the second floor overlooking the pool. This is the last place Hawk and your ex would think to look for her."

Tioga finished her Pellegrino. "I ought to go back to my office and catch up on paperwork."

Scheck wrapped the scarf around his neck and sauntered toward the exit. "No rest for the working girl. I hope you're getting paid well." He laughed and vanished behind the curtain.

Tioga grabbed her cell and her purse and took a step toward the exit, but Dyce reached across the bar and tapped her on the shoulder. "Wait. Take this!" He extended his arm and handed her a shopping bag labeled "Neiman Marcus."

Tioga turned around and looked at Dyce. Then she took the bag and placed it on the bar stool next to her. "Okay. Now what?"

Dyce rubbed his right hand across his face as if he wanted new features. "Don't rush me, dear. Go to the ladies, get into a stall, close the door, change into the stuff that's in here and leave your own stuff in the bathroom cabinet. Take the rear exit, walk to the end of the alley and take a right. Go to the end of that alley and duck into Toys for Toddlers on the corner. Got it?"

Tioga lifted the bag by the handles. "Everyone wants to hijack me."

In the ladies, she removed the clothes she had worn all day and slipped into a polka dot skirt, a red blouse and flats. She stood in front of the mirror and adjusted a wig that turned her into a blond with curly hair. "I hardly recognize me." She stuffed her clothes into the Neiman Marcus bag and stowed it in the wicker cabinet next to the sink. Before she left the ladies, she added the pink flamingo sunglasses and peered at her reflection in the mirror. "I know who you are. I just figured it out."

She followed Dyce's instructions: out the back, down the alley, where the kids on bikes gave her dirty looks, then down the next alley with "I love the Valley" graffiti scrawled on the wall. The whole way she hummed the Beatles' "Nowhere Man," which she heard her first year at the Badminton School.

Behind the counter at Toys for Toddlers, a young, perky saleswoman was trying her best to please a woman who wore a veil, white gloves and a tailored suit and who looked as if she had stepped out of the glossy pages of *Harpers Bazaar*. The one and only Mrs. Vignetta, Tioga's mother, perused the magazine on the divan in the California room where she demanded that her daughter learn to say, "*tout va bien*," "*merci beaucoup*," "*les enfants de la patrie*," and other expressions that sounded useless to her when she was a teen.

Now at the front of the store a doll with braids and overalls called to Tioga. She looked at the price and tossed it aside. Then a stuffed wombat caught her eye, and she placed it under her arm. When she looked behind her, she saw the Yaqui with no name, or rather the Yaqui whose name she did not know. Pablo's brother.

He wore a fedora with a brightly colored cloth around the brim, frayed corduroy trousers, a silver belt buckle, cowboy boots and a cowboy necktie. "Hey, Don Juan." Pablo's brother was not amused.

"Spare me. I have way better stories than Don Juan and Carlos Castaneda, the fucking fake professor."

The saleswoman must have heard the world "fucking." In no time at all, she dashed across the room. "I'm sorry but I am going to have to ask you both to leave. We have young children and mothers in the store."

Tioga tossed the stuffed wombat on the counter and lowered her pink flamingo sunglasses. "We're just leaving. Thanks."

The Yaqui stepped forward and said, "We're trying to avoid her crazed husband! Is there a back exit?"

The saleswoman frowned, but she pointed to the rear of the store. "That way. If you don't mind dumpsters."

Tioga lowered her sunglasses. "We love dumpsters."

They found their way over boxes and around dumpsters and crossed an unpaved parking lot. No Name aimed for a white Ford pick-up truck with four doors sitting alone in the far corner under a billboard that read "Stover Cream: It Makes a Body Healthy" with an image of a cartoon cow with a large udder.

Tioga adjusted her wig, which had slipped from the top of her head. "Are you going to blindfold me?"

No Name did not slow down, though he turned his head and glanced over his shoulder. "I'll ask you to lie face up in the back seat of the cab. It's unnecessary for you to know precisely where we're going, but I'll tell you it's not far."

Tioga shrugged her shoulders and stumbled along. No Name helped her into the truck. Tioga peered under the seat and saw a rifle that she recognized as an assault weapon of the sort that she thought had been outlawed in California. "What's this for?"

No Name reached for the assault rifle and cradled it in his arms. "It's my AR-15 with a bump stock. I'm going hunting. You can come with."

She reached inside her jacket and removed her snub nose. "Thanks, but I have my own." She kissed the barrel and returned the gun to the holster.

No Name laughed and reached under the front seat and came out with another assault weapon. "You could use the AK-47. I think you'd like it better than the AR-15."

Tioga lay down on the back seat of the cab and closed her eyes. "Let's get this over with. I don't like traveling to unknown destinations horizontally." The air conditioning came to life and cooled down the cab. Tioga opened her eyes and let her mind wander, though it didn't wander very far. It kept coming back to the AR-15 and the AK-47.

No Name drove slowly. She didn't have to look at the speedometer. She could feel it in her bones. No Name spoke slowly, which acted like a tonic on Tioga's nerves, and didn't seem to have anything in particular he wanted to say. "On the subject of peyote, I rarely talk. That would be disrespectful to a sacred plant. But if you're curious, in my opinion, it's nothing like LSD. And if you want, I will take you to the Mojave and introduce you to friends. It's best if you are pure of heart for the ceremony."

Tioga listened to the hum of the tires on the pavement, the honking of the horns and the wail of a siren. "That's kind of you to offer. Maybe if we both come out of this alive." She paused, wet her dry lips and added, "I had a bad acid trip one Christmas and vowed not to do it again, though I did mushrooms at Easter when I went back to the wilderness in Washington. My ex and I snorted more cocaine than I care to remember."

No Name cleared his throat. "Ditto on coke. Same for speed." He paused and added, "We're almost at the end of the trip."

The truck stopped and the engine idled. Tioga heard what sounded like a gate opening. The truck moved forward again over what had to be cobblestones. Then it came to a complete stop and the engine went silent. "Time to get up and see the world."

Tioga rolled to one side, pushed herself up and lowered her legs. She gazed out the window and saw a grove of olive trees, a series of raised beds with flowers and a small house with a tin roof and wind chimes dangling from a beam that extended over a patio. No Name approached a weathered door that looked like it had been assembled from barn wood. He knocked, took two paces back and, when the door opened, took two more paces back. "I'll leave the two of you to go at it. I'll be at the front gate to make sure no one shows up unexpectedly. If you want me, my cell is 831. 777. 0041."

A young woman with a face the color of chocolate stood in the doorway, her eyes downcast. "Come in," she said, though she did not move and neither did Tioga. The woman was barefoot. She had tattoos of snakes and frogs around her ankles. She wore turquoise bracelets on both wrists, a wrap-around yellow skirt and a black haltertop. While she appeared to be timid, she spoke ferociously. "I knew you were coming. I worried what I would say. I thought I had it figured out. Now I don't know, except that when I try to remember what happened, it makes me feel like I'm watching a movie that has gone haywire." She turned away from Tioga, as if she wanted to hide her face.

But she went on talking. "I kept coming back to one word, like it was my mantra. I said it over and over again until I nearly lost my mind."

Tioga looked into the distance. The white pickup truck waited next to a pile of rocks in the shape of a pyramid. "What was your mantra?"

The woman jangled her turquoise bracelets. "Disappear. Sometimes you don't know a person has been there until they've disappeared, and after they've disappeared they're more present than ever before." The Turquoise Woman braced herself against the wind from the coast, which blew away the hot, heavy air that had accumulated under the eaves like layers of snow. "The Valley is my home, though I'm not from here. I don't want to leave, and I don't want to die, not now."

Tioga waited for a space where she could insert a word or two, though the woman seemed disinclined to offer her an inch. "I feel like I have lost my nerve," Tioga told herself. "But don't worry. It will change. It always does."

The Turquoise Woman smiled. She offered Tioga a welcoming gesture of sorts with her hands, though she did not move from the spot where she had planted her feet.

Tioga gazed at the brown field beyond a barbed wire fence too high to scale. A kite circled the field as if preparing for a kill. A herd of goats grazed lazily beneath the open sky. The woman raised her right hand and jangled her bracelets again. "The Zombie Devils fed me and gave me a place to sleep. I thought they loved me, and I thought I loved them, but they are loveless creatures."

Tioga watched the kite go round and round in smaller and smaller circles. "Them? What Zombie Devils?"

The woman had a crazed look in her eyes. "I have cursed them. To mention their real names would break the spell. They are the Zombie Devils. That's part of the curse. For a long time, I did everything they wanted me to do, even after the police came to the warehouse, and we weren't arrested."

The kite swooped down, captured a snake in its claws and soared high above the field. Tioga enjoyed the spectacle in the sky. "You mean Ambrose and Clark?"

A rooster crowed, and a coyote yipped. "No. These men were not from the Valley. They had a car with no license plates. They wore suits and ties and carried attaché cases. I never see police like that before."

Tioga's eyes rested on the dry grass in the field. "How do you know they were police? Maybe they were gang members."

The Turquoise Woman went inside the cabin. Tioga followed her. On the wall she recognized a Mayan figure from the Dresden Codex that her Ojai uncle had described as the Moon Goddess.

The Turquoise Woman wouldn't allow herself to be distracted by Tioga. "I smelled them when I served rum and Coca-Cola, and they talked about Rico. I know cop smell. They could not have bleached it away." Tioga waited for a long time before she spoke. Finally she couldn't wait any longer. "Maybe Rico wasn't a man but a thing. The Feds have something they call RICO when you do an illegal activity again and again."

The Turquoise Woman wanted nothing of Tioga's explanation. "Whatever. After Rico, everything went crazy, like the Zombie Devils thought they had a pass from hell to do everything they wanted to do." The woman sniffed the air again. "You are not a cop. I can tell. If they find you, they will make you talk. But you will have nothing to say, except you met a little woman with turquoise in a small house with scratches on the wall."

Tioga looked at the figure of the Moon Goddess, reached inside her jacket and touched her snub nose. "I know it will probably sound silly to you, but I won't go down without a fight.

The woman went to the tie-dyed curtain, parted it and stepped behind it. When she came back moments later, she said, "I'll make mint tea." She moved her eyes from bare corner to bare corner and added, "I know there's nowhere to sit except on the floor, but the floor is a good place to be."

Tioga sat down, crossed her legs and assumed the lotus pose that she remembered from Yoga 101. "Who dragged Dorothy across the creek and made it look like she was dumped on the side of the road?"

The kettle whistled. The woman went behind the curtain again and reappeared with a tray that held a teapot and two small Japanese-style teacups. She placed the tray on the floor, sat opposite Tioga and assumed the same yoga pose that Tioga had adopted. "I'll get to that. But first I need to tell you that the Zombie Devil men gave Dot heroin, then they raped her and killed her. I thought they were going to rape me and kill me."

Tioga shuddered. She turned her head one way and the other and heard her neck snap. "Why? What did Dorothy ever do to them?"

The Turquoise Woman poured two cups of tea, handed one to Tioga and placed the other at her side. "Dot threatened to go to police for the Valley. Besides they hated her because she loved Billy Bones and not them."

Tioga knit her brow. "I thought Bones beat her."

"He was not as terrible as the Zombie Devil men. The tall thin one gave Dot the needle; the other one, with the yin yang, made her do terrible things and pushed the other to do more things." The Turquoise Woman put her head in her hands. Then slowly she lifted her head and looked at

Tioga. "When Dot scream, they laugh and tape her mouth shut and tie her hands so she can't move."

The Turquoise Woman reached out and touched her toes. "I see this from the balcony. The yin-yang man, he shot Dot one way and the tall thin one shot her the other way. 'Let's dump the bitch in The Springs,' one says. Then the other, 'Let's spread the bitch's blood and really fuck with their heads.' Then the first one: 'Brilliant. You're a fucking genius.'"

Turquoise Woman took a deep breath. "I trip and make a noise. They know someone is on the balcony. I jump through the window and run. I call Katrina and tell her to go fast. When the Zombie Devil men show up with masks, she doesn't have a chance. "Billy cross over, hide behind the shed, take photos, email to me. I send to Roxanne. The Zombie Devil men throw Katrina's body in the field, take the crop and swear they'll kill the girls if they try to escape. They take Dot to The Springs in a silver body bag. Travis sees them arrive in the Tesla, open the trunk and carry the bag into forty-nine. By then I feel like I operate a switch-board and run a network. I tell Travis run, hide, but he want his hands on the weed so he stick around. He lucky he alive."

She paused, lifted the cup, held it in both hands and sipped slowly. "Bones call me again, say Dot's body in the pig pen. Tell him, 'Go to the cops.' He say, 'No one will …'"

Tioga interrupted her. "You're telling me these guys, who you call the Zombie Devil men, drove from the bunker to The Springs and then to Bones's place with Dot's body and left a trail of blood everywhere they went?"

The woman nodded. "What they didn't count on was Bones dragging Dot across the field over the creek to the highway. He thought he was safe because no one saw him, except he leave a trail of blood. I try to clean up his mess.

That's when I see your friend. She found Dot's things before I could get to them." She paused for a moment, learned forward and listened to the sound of the wind chimes that came through the window. "I thought I heard something from the gate."

Tioga listened. "No, I didn't." The wind whipped up the dust and swirled it around. Tioga could hear it and taste it though she couldn't see it. She sipped the tea, then unfolded her legs and stretched them across the floor. "If you don't mind, I'd like to see the photos you have."

The Turquoise Woman reached into her wrap-around skirt and pulled out a smart phone.

Tioga reached out with her hand. "You'll have to testify if you want them to go to jail."

The woman nodded her head. "I understand. I have to be not afraid."

Tioga held the smart phone in her hand, walked to the window, stood on her tiptoes and peered outside. "The Yaqui who brought me here ... I don't know what to call him other than, 'No Name.'"

The woman gathered the teacups and the teapot and balanced them in her outstretched hands. "I can't help with that, but I can tell you the place where you have to go now, the place across from the empty lot at Hidalgo and Perez. You park behind the tattoo parlor, cross the stream and go into Zombie Devil land through the doggie door that goes to the basement. The watchdog won't bark. They make him stupid, and you won't set off the alarm. It doesn't work; never did. You climb stairs to the balcony."

Tioga hugged the woman gently. "Thank you. I love you." She opened the door, stood under the eaves, listened to the wind chimes and sent a text to No Name, "Ready to rock 'n' roll." She walked across an open field toward the white pickup truck and heard the rustling of the wind in a dusty cornfield, the ears of corn all picked, the stalks leaning to the side and ready to be cut down. In the distance she saw the Mayacamas and knew that she was somewhere in the Valley, somewhere not far from the Plaza, the Mar Monte and her own office.

No Name looked happy to see her. Tioga rested her arm on his shoulder. "Do I have to lie down again in the truck?"

No Name opened the rear door. "I told you, it's for your own good."

Tioga looked at the AR-15. This time she noticed a canvas bag packed with ammunition. "Can you head for the tattoo parlor in The Springs? I have to take care of unfinished business with the Zombie Devil men. Maybe you'll come with me."

No Name turned the key in the ignition. "*Por supuesto.*" The truck rumbled across the cobblestones, the gate squeaked, the tires hit the pavement and the radio broadcast a *corredo*. No Name sang along with the singer. "Valentín Elizalde. Bet you never heard of him. Bet you didn't know he was gunned down in Tamaulipas at the age of twenty-seven, just two years younger than me." He found Valentín's picture on his phone and passed it to Tioga.

"He must be a *mal hombre*," she said. "He's wearing a black hat." She listed to Valentín, then reached up with her arm and gave the phone back to No Name. "Maybe I should call you, '*El Lobo*,' or something like that."

Valentín's voice faded, and the DJ came on the air. No Name turned down the volume. "That's okay. I'm the man who doesn't have a name. It's better that way."

Tioga squirmed, then turned on her side, squirmed some more and placed her hands under her head, prayer-like. "I'm going inside the building next to Mono's Tattoo Parlor. Dorothy Baynes was raped and murdered there. The weed is there, and your brother might be too."

No Name pumped the air with his fist. "You don't mind if I take my AR-15 with me for company, do you?"

Tioga raised herself and peered out the window. "*Por supuesto.* I suppose it's okay now if I see where we're going."

From the front of the cab came two words, "*Por supuesto.*"

Zombie Devils

No Name drove the speed limit along the highway, turned on the directional, stopped in the middle lane and pulled into the parking lot for Mono's Tattoo Parlor, where he killed the engine and removed the key from the ignition. Under the blue sky, he locked the car and with Tioga close behind him walked under the neon sign, around the back of the building and into the thicket, where he stopped, picked a berry and ate it.

Tioga found a footbridge where they crossed the stream. No Name crouched down, danced across the bridge and walked along a deer path leading behind the bunker that had no windows on the ground floor and looked like it might survive, Tioga thought, an assault by Navy Seals. Mounds of dried dog shit littered the yard. Tioga knelt down, squeezed through the doggy door and then turned her head around and grabbed hold of the AR-15 that No Name handed her. He had a tougher time than she crawling through the door; his shirt ripped and he cut his ear. "Ah fuck," he whispered.

Once inside, he wanted to be Mr. Tough Guy. "Not too worry," he said, leaving Tioga to carry the canvas bag with the ammo while he toted the AR-15. They entered a storage room with a rusted washing machine and a dryer that had been cannibalized for parts and climbed a stairway that took them to a balcony.

On the wall Tioga saw three faded words that spelled "Genoa Sausage Works" with an image of a string of sausages followed by a phone number and an address. She remembered the key with the letters "GSW" from Dorothy's autopsy. "GSW: Genoa Sausage Works." Dorothy had sent a message the only way she knew how.

The smell of marijuana assaulted Tioga. It made her want to sneeze, and she didn't think she could prevent herself from sneezing. No Name shook his head and placed two fingers across his lips. On hands and knees, an inch at a time, first No Name and then Tioga crawled along the carpet until they reached the edge of the balcony. It was a long way down to the ground floor below. No Name lay down on his belly with the AR-15 at his side. Tioga peaked over the edge and saw a sea of marijuana plants hanging from the rafters. Fans whirled. Vents expelled the fumes that made her eyes sting.

Hawk stood in the far corner of the room with a cell phone in one hand and a clipboard in another. He wore his Borsalino and his yin-yang pendant, and he broke into a rendition of Kid Rock's "Early Mornin' Stoned Pimp." When he finished his performance, he grunted and moaned as if he was in pain, though he did not appear to be hurt or injured. Pablo emerged from the upside down marijuana forest and applauded. "You da best. You da boss."

Hawk smacked a woman with dreadlocks. "Move, bitch."

Four women, all bare-breasted and barefoot and in cut-off jeans, moved between a row of upside-down plants and pulled dead leaves from the stems. The floor was littered with them.

Hawk cracked a whip. "Hustle. We're running out of time." He walked across the length of the room, then stopped in the space directly under the balcony, where he began a conversation with someone whose voice Tioga could hear but whose face she could not see.

A German shepherd tugged on its chain, barked and lunged toward the woman with the dreadlocks. Tioga felt an instant loathing for the dog. "I'll shoot him if I have to," she whispered.

A black spider crawled across No Name's arm. Tioga watched the beast move one way and then the other, as if searching for a passageway to safety. With thumb and middle finger, she flicked it into the air and saw it land upside down, then right itself and vanish in the carpet.

Hawk was still talking to the invisible presence. "We fronted the dude thirty pounds," he was saying. It was the same voice she had heard the day he threw money at her, as if money grew on a tree. Apparently it did, at least for him. The man under the balcony, whom she couldn't see, uttered a stream of words that didn't sound like English and might have been Russian. She had Russian on her mind.

Hawk went on with his story. "The asshole rolls the truck, which is packed with weed. He steals a truck from a faggot in the woods, picks up his load which has tumbled down the ravine and gets out of there like a bat out of hell."

Then came another break in Hawk's story while he listened to the man under the balcony, his words still unintelligible to Tioga.

After an interval, Hawk picked up the thread of the story he had been telling. "In the Valley, the dude goes one way and the *chingada* cop goes the other way. The guy gets away! Isn't that the dope! That's us, bro! We're getting away without a scratch."

Hawk laughed, and the man under the balcony laughed with him. A slim taut body emerged from the shadows. The man stood in the light and removed a mask that had turned him into a wolf with a long snout and dark eyes. "Bitches," the man shouted, then placed the wolf mask over his face again and howled wolf-like. He knew what he was doing. He had practiced, or maybe howling was innate, or maybe he was the Wolf Man. He wore no shirt and no socks or shoes. He had the body of a surfer. A pair of faded jeans hung from his hips, along with a holster that carried two guns. His body was covered with sweat; bright green marijuana leaves stuck to his arms, shoulders, chest and belly.

Tioga's head pounded, and her stomach heaved. She was going to puke. She felt like a little bird condemned to hover forever, never able to land on a branch or to nest in a tree. She looked down at the sea of green. The woman with dreadlocks stopped in the middle of a row of marijuana and put on a T-shirt that read "Guadalajara."

Hawk stormed across the room and slapped her breasts. She screamed, and he slapped her again. "You're not getting paid to cover your tits, bitch." Hawk turned to the man with the surfer body who stood behind him. "Isn't that right, Tomás!"

Tioga wanted to scream.

No Name held the AR-15 in his hands, finger on the trigger.

"No, don't," Tioga whispered. "I don't know and you don't know what the Zombie Devil men might do." She looked at the watchdog and the woman with the dreadlocks. "I'm going to backtrack and call the police. I need you to come with me and not do anything crazy."

No Name's nostrils flared. His face caught fire. "I don't want to, but I will." He turned around and crawled across the floor on his belly, with the AR-15 in his hand and ready to come alive with a touch. They went down the stairs, first Tioga, then No Name, out the doggy door and through the dried turds in the yard behind the bunker that felt like a minefield.

In the thicket along the stream, Tioga stopped, picked a ripe blackberry and placed it on the tip of her tongue. It was as sweet as any jam she had ever tasted. Then she and

No Name followed the path that brought them back to the neon sign outside Mono's Tattoo Parlor. Tioga looked back at the bunker. "That was my ex with the mask. That was him howling. He stole that from me and perverted it."

No Name snickered. "Too late now for me to blow him away, though I wish I had."

Tioga looked back at the bunker and wanted to howl. She opened her mouth wide and couldn't bring herself to do it. Beneath Mono's neon sign flashing on and off, she sent Ambrose a text: "Killers holed up in the old sausage factory in The Springs next to the tattoo place. There's a shitload of weed. It's the jackpot. But you gotta move fast and bring all the fire power you've got."

No Name stowed his AR-15 under the front seat of his white pickup truck. "If the cops are coming, I got to go."

The neon sign flashed on and off. "I heard the same thing from your brother after the drive-by at Mrs. Baynes's. It was sad to see her so far gone, but I'll say this for Pablo, he treated her like a queen."

No Name sat behind the wheel and turned the key in the ignition. Tioga took out her cell, checked her messages and shook her head. "Nothing for me."

In the distance, a siren wailed. Ambrose and Clark would arrive with plenty of backup. Hawk and her ex would go down for the count and the women in the bunker would be set free.

No Name fastened his seat belt. "Are you coming with me, or are you staying?"

Tioga walked toward the thicket. "I don't know." Then she raised her head, opened her mouth and howled. "Wait! I'm coming with you, No Name! Ambrose doesn't need me. My ex will get everything that's coming to him."

What Matters Is

Tioga ordered a Kir Royale. Dyce made it new school style with champagne instead of white wine. She took a cigarette from her purse, lit it and inhaled. "I feel bruised on the outside and bruised on the inside. I need a smoke and a drink."

Dyce put the Kir Royale on a coaster and smiled the sweetest of smiles. Nothing seemed to put a dent into his cheerfulness, not a wildfire or a flood or the Valley bleeding from inside out. "I never liked your ex, even when you were married. I'm not sorry he's gone for good. Ditto for Hawk." Then he gave Tioga a disapproving look. "You can't smoke in here!"

Tioga wore a sweater, slacks and sturdy shoes. She peered into the mirror and turned her head from side-to-side. "Wait a minute. People get drunk in here every night of the week, and nobody squawks. Tourists get high on weed, but I can't smoke a lousy cigarette. Something's wrong with this picture."

Dyce wore his cute little boy face, which he could put on and take off whenever he wanted. "Oh come on now. That is so such bullshit, and you know it! You just don't like anyone telling you what to do."

Tioga sipped the Kir Royale. "Who leaned on you to lean on me?"

Dyce filled a glass with water from the tap and offered it to Langley, who had taken a seat at the bar and unfolded *The Gazette*. "Nobody leaned on me. Nobody leans on anybody around here. No smoking, get it? That's the policy. I don't like it any more than you do, but people pay a mint to stay here because they can drink as much as they want and not have to breathe cigarette smoke."

Tioga listened politely. She ought not to have complained. The Kir Royale was very, very good. Indeed, it never tasted better. She ought to have been grateful for Sean Dyce's Kir Royale and not whimpered. She tossed her unlit cigarette in the stainless steel sink. "I'm quitting for good this time, starting tomorrow."

She turned to Langley who wore a bemused expression on his face, a face that now seemed longer than she remembered. "Don't look so smug. Your fucking story got it all wrong. Mr. H. L. Mencken must be rolling in his grave."

The unreconstructed editor smiled benevolently. "I love you, Tioga. But you stick to your job and let me stick to mine. I know how to write. You know how to pry secrets from stones. Maybe we should work together."

Tioga poked Langley in the ribs. "You missed all the little details. There *really* was a ton of marijuana at the old Genoa Sausage Works. I didn't hallucinate. The Zombie Devils crashed and burned in Hawk's Tesla on the way to Avenida de la Virgen, not on the way to the Mar Monte, and Pablo is still at large here in the Valley."

Langley shrugged his big broad shoulders. "You're quibbling. What matters is that the Zombie Devils, as you call them, are dead. The feds seized and destroyed the weed from the bunker, and now finally Terry's selling the hotel. Sorry to burst your bubble, Tioga, but I got all the important stuff right." Langley stood up, placed a $20 bill on the bar, saluted Dyce and blew Tioga a kiss. "Got a meeting with Terry in the penthouse. We're expanding the paper and creating thevalley.com. Mitzi Ambrose is coming back to live and sell ads. That should make you very happy."

Tioga grimaced. "I wonder why it doesn't."

Langley smacked her on the rear with a rolled-up copy of *The Gazette*. "Try not to be stoned twenty-four, seven."

Tioga glared. "Watch it! You're asking for trouble."

Langley laughed. "You know, don't you, that Gina took Lawrence back east to boarding school?"

Tioga had already tuned him out and was listening to Aretha on the loudspeakers above the bar. Dyce listened too and served a lager and an IPA to an elderly couple who sat at the end of the bar and munched on popcorn. Then he mixed a martini for a woman with long, shapely legs. She wore gloves and a hat with a veil as if she was trying to pass for the Underground's very own femme fatale. Tioga had learned to steered clear of her, and so had Dyce. They knew how to tell a genuine femme fatale from a fake. Also, now that Storm was gone, the hotel had lost much of its luster.

Dyce wiped the lipstick stains from a wine glass. "You should have been here when the shit went down. About five a.m. a Ryder truck pulls in. The kid deputy, Clark, is in the street blowing a whistle and directing traffic around the police barricade. A wild-looking Indian and some of his tribe, all of them wearing fedoras, jump out of the truck, unload a zillion yellow and brown containers, lug them into the hotel and down to the basement. Jonny Field is making breakfast for a horde of real estate agents holding their annual get-together. Gina is running in circles. Bobby Cohen is arguing with Chehab, and Terry is threatening to fire everyone who doesn't shape up."

Tioga sipped her drink and toyed with the swizzle stick. "Sorry I missed the action. I'm always too late for all the good stuff. I wasn't around when my father's pictures were ripped off and shipped to a dealer in Zurich who sold them for a cool million." She reached for her wallet, opened it and placed a $100 bill under the coaster. Then she slipped her fingers inside her jacket, as she had done so many times, and reached for her snub nose. When she couldn't find it she looked glum. "I forget. I left it in the office. I'm turning over a new leaf, so it speak."

She gazed at the lines in the palm of her right hand as if she could read her own future. Then she looked at Dyce imploringly. "Won't you please take me down to the basement?" she asked seductively. "I wanna see for myself. You must have the keys."

Dyce smacked his lips. Then he made a call on his cell. Aden showed up with her red hair in pigtails. "I've got you covered. Take your sweet time."

Dyce led Tioga down to the basement where he unlocked a steel door and walked her through a cold room with sacks of potatoes, carrots, cabbages and apples. They passed into and out of the wine cellar with reds on one side and whites on the other.

He unlocked a second steel door that brought him and Tioga into a room with a cement floor, a low ceiling and no windows. Tables and chairs were stacked against one wall. There were a couple of dehumidifiers, a few boxes of latex gloves and half-dozen jars with clipping scissors turned upside down and sitting in a solvent. Dyce surveyed the scene. "Believe it or not, there was a shitload of weed here. Maybe you knew and looked the other way and maybe you were in the dark and didn't know. It doesn't really matter to me. You don't have to tell."

Tioga wandered from the front to the back of the room where she noticed a dry marijuana leaf on the floor. She bent down, picked it up, crunched it in the palm of her hand and scattered the pieces. "I wonder whose weed it really was?" She opened her purse, removed a cigarette and placed it between her lips. Dyce flicked his lighter inscribed with "Mar Monte" and an image of a woman in a beret and a cigarette holder. She looked a lot like Camilla.

Tioga inhaled and then blew smoke rings toward the ceiling. "It's funny the way things and people disappear in the Valley, isn't it? The photo of Cantinflas has never turned up, and the guys who bashed Camilla's car have never been identified."

Tioga paused a moment. "I believe you, Sean. I'm sure there was a shit load of weed here." She ambled toward the steel door. "Funny, too, that neither Roxanne nor Randy told me they were going back east to be with his mother. If I were them, I would have said something. I guess I don't count. Maybe I've outlived my usefulness."

Tioga stood under the neon sign that read Exit. Something itched. Oh, yes, the damned bite. It had come back. Or maybe it had never really gone away. If she ignored it, it would vanish on its own.

She looked at the exit sign. "There's so much I wanted to do," she said. "Now I can't undo any of the things that I did, and I can't undo the things that didn't turn out the way I wanted them to. I'll never see Flor or her boy again. I might never visit my own father either, not that it will make any difference to him, now that some idiot art lover in Switzerland has the nudes of me, Tioga Vignetta. That's how I'll be remembered. Tioga Vignetta, daughter and muse of Philippe Vignetta."

Dyce removed the key ring from his pocket, locked the lock, and turned the knob to make sure it was secure. Tioga's heels echoed in the cold room. "Camilla and I are using the money that Hawk paid us to rent a duplex together." She stopped and looked down at the potatoes, carrots, cabbages and apples. She helped herself to a bright red apple. "Nobody blames apples for rapes and murders."

Dyce reached for a carrot, bit off one end and chewed loudly. "No, not any more. Now marijuana is the monster. But I'm not sure if we created it or it created us."

Tioga tossed the apple in the air, caught it in the palm of her hand, polished it and took a small bite. "Camilla and I are forming an LLC: Sanchez and Vignetta, Ops."

Dyce led the way up the stairs and into the cold, dark corridor where Buddy Moscosco stood with his hands on his hips, chewing on an unlit cigar. "Bobby Cohen has been hunting all over for you, Tioga," he yelled. "You can't just run off. He has an appointment with you."

Tioga extinguished her cigarette in the bucket of sand next to the door leading to the parking lot. In the corridor, she looked at herself in the full-length mirror.

"Yes, Buddy" she said and shivered. "Send him over to my office."